"Fun, fascinating and amusing Wo... spirit of *THE DIRTY DOZEN* and K...

> — **JOHN E. NEVOLA,** Award-winning author of *THE LAST JUMP – A NOVEL OF WORLD WAR II*

ISLAND OF THE PHOENIX strikes an extraordinary balance between the inhumanity of war, and the very real humanity of the men and women who must fight it. Vic Mills is one of those rare authors who can weave action, adventure, and romance into a single seamless tapestry. This book is destined to become a modern classic.

> — **JEFF EDWARDS,** Award-winning author of *SEA OF SHADOWS* and *THE SEVENTH ANGEL*

Part *MCHALE'S NAVY*, part *BAA-BAA BLACK SHEEP*... A view of the Pacific that will capture the imagination and bring it home. I recognized more than one former shipmate and battle-buddy! Oddly enough, or maybe not so surprisingly, the American Spirit transcends generations, and can be found in the damnedest places!

> — **BRAD McGUIRE,** LCDR, USN (Retired)

What Readers are saying about *ISLAND OF THE PHOENIX*...

... the author made the story come to life, by blending key figures and historical facts about the WW II Pacific Theater.

... entertaining

... very realistic

... loved the story!

... a fun read

... captivating

... takes the reader through the full range of emotions—courage, fear, desperation, love ...

... hated having to put it down.

... intrigue, humor, passion, and a story line to keep me reading.

ISLAND OF THE PHOENIX

ISLAND OF THE PHOENIX

Vic Mills

ISLAND OF THE PHOENIX

Text Copyright © 2012 by Vic Mills

Cover Copyright © 2012 by Navigator Books, LLC

Edited and prepared for publication by Navigator Books, LLC

ISBN-13: 978-1483947730

Printed in the United States of America

I dedicate *Island of the Phoenix* to the brave men and women of World War II, and to all those who wear the uniform of our nation's military. To those who have served on the front lines, and the many who have worked so hard behind the scenes here at home.

May their labors and their sacrifices never be forgotten.

God Bless Them All!

— Vic Mills

In memory of Roger Howe, a steadfast friend of many years.

Acknowledgements

My heartfelt thanks to Wilbur Johnson, retired Master Sergeant USAF (1946 to 1966), mechanic, flight engineer and instructor, for sharing his profound knowledge of aircraft, and especially of World War II fighter-aircraft engines. Early in his 20-year stint in the Air Force, Wilbur participated in the Berlin Airlift. After retiring, he served as a flight engineer and instructor for the Boeing Company, working with crews from all over the world.

Glenn Davis spent 30 years in the U.S. Navy, and retired as a Chief Warrant Officer. Glenn provided much-needed assistance in sorting out naval ranks and terminology.

A good friend, Robert A. Strong, United States Coast Guard (retired), spent some time in the waters off Vietnam. His encouragement and editing suggestions were instrumental in bringing *Island of the Phoenix* to life. Thanks Bob!

World War II veteran, John McDougall, was one of my earliest readers. He entered the war as it was drawing to a close, but his personal experiences in that era of human history were invaluable to this book. His strong support and enthusiasm for my work has kept me pushing to continually improve my writing.

To long time friends, Marci Williams, and Gloria and Larry Campbell: if not for their years of ongoing encouragement, I would have never written a single sentence. Mrs. Campbell teaches writing classes in college, and counsels new as well as experienced authors. Her husband, Larry—also a writer and editor—is a World War II Veteran.

PROLOGUE

By March of 1943, the war in North Africa had finally taken an encouraging and decisive turn for the Allies. The Axis forces in North Africa—which were primarily German, Italian, and Vichy French—had suffered high casualties. A few months after Rommel was relieved of his command, his tank corps was soundly defeated by the combined efforts of General Montgomery of the British Army and General Patton of the American Army. The remainder of the Axis troops had either retreated en masse or been captured. By April, many units of the U.S. Army Air Corps and mechanized units were slated to move to the European theater, some bound for England, and others headed for newly-formed bases in Italy.

CHAPTER 1

Nearly the Beginning

---

22 October 1942

Dear Mom, Dad, and Stevie,

> *Well, here it is, nearly the end of October already. As I've mentioned in other letters, the summer was really hot and prone to sandstorms. It's been cooling off a little and no one here has been complaining about that.*
>
> *For the nearly four months we've been stationed in Morocco, we haven't seen any air combat. We've been flying mostly ground support runs, knocking out power stations, oil refineries, and attacking the occasional German tank convoy—nothing too serious.*
>
> *I've seen a few German planes some distance away, mostly Me-109s. They are similar to our P-40 Warhawk, which is certainly a wonderful aircraft. The 109s sport an inline-V liquid-cooled engine, similar to my fighter.*
>
> *Our mess hall is okay. The chow is pretty good, but not as good as your cooking, Mom. No one can top your mess hall. Oh, thanks for the cookies. I shared them with a few of the fellows.*
>
> *I'm sorry for such a short letter, but I have to get ready for an early morning patrol flight. Also, the mail plane is here, and I want to get this in the outgoing mail pouch.*

I miss you all very much.

Love, Michael

First Lieutenant Michael Hollands wasn't happy about the lack of total honesty in his letters home, but he didn't like to worry his family any more than he had to. Actually, the Army Air Corps and the Royal Air Force encountered Axis air power on a regular basis, but that was beginning to taper off. As 1942 wore on, enemy incursions were becoming less frequent and less determined. The enemy's airfields were well out of the range of fighter aircraft, and the Allied pilots seldom encountered a Messerschmitt.

Hollands folded the letter, and slipped it into the envelope. The last words he had written were still in his mind. He really *did* miss his family deeply. He wondered if he would ever see them again.

8 NOVEMBER 1942:

Lieutenant Hollands keyed his radio. "Shotgun One, calling Buckshot Base. Over."

The receiver in his Warhawk was quiet.

He tried again. "Shotgun One, calling Buckshot Base. Over."

The only reply was static.

Hollands had taken off at 0530 for an air reconnaissance mission—the target area about two hundred miles north by northeast of his base. He had completed the run without incident, and now he was on the return leg. He was about ready to start his final approach, if he could only get the tower to roger up to his radio call.

He keyed the mike again. "Shotgun One, calling Buckshot Base. Over."

The radio rumbled with a reply. "This is Buckshot Base. Go ahead with your message, Shotgun."

"This is Shotgun. Mission accomplished. Returning to base. ETA fifteen minutes. Over."

"Roger, Shotgun. Your ETA is one-five minutes. Buckshot out."

Most reconnaissance flights consisted of two or three planes, but yesterday's sandstorm had damaged several planes, leaving the squadron temporarily short on aircraft. Hollands understood how critical it was for his commanders to keep track of what the Krauts were up to, so he had volunteered to fly the one-plane assignment.

Hollands made an easy turn to the southwest to line up on the compass heading from the tower, and brought his fighter down to fifteen thousand feet. When his altitude was low enough, he peeled off his oxygen mask with his customary sigh of relief, glad to have that uncomfortable monstrosity off of his face.

He felt the simple satisfaction of a job well done. Except for the throaty purring of his engine, everything seemed quiet. This mission was in the bag.

Suddenly his headphones blasted with a painfully loud message. Someone was shouting into the radio, the voice completely unintelligible.

In reflex, Hollands momentarily let go of the stick, pulled off his headphones and vigorously rubbed his ears with both hands. Then he quickly donned the headphones again.

He keyed his mike. "Christ, Lewis, you damn near busted my eardrums. Now, knock off the yelling, and try it again. *Over.*"

"Definite two bandits on radar. Your position. Above you, at angels thirty. Speed, two-seven-five. Coming from the west. They're nearly on top of you, Lieutenant!"

Sweeping his eyes across the clear blue sky overhead, Hollands quickly spotted the enemy planes. There were three, not two. And to make matters worse, his lone P-40 had been spotted.

Two of his three adversaries rolled over and started down to intercept him.

Most of the pilots in the squadron respected the P-40 as a tough, reliable old bird, but they knew it was outdated, and no match for the German fighters. Their CO had made it clear that his pilots were to avoid dogfights if at all possible.

Hollands pushed his stick forward and nosed his aircraft into a dive. The Germans probably thought the lone American airplane would be easy pickings.

At five thousand feet, Hollands leveled off. He momentarily lost visual with the two enemy aircraft, but the dozen or so tracers that flew past his canopy gave him a pretty good idea where the two enemy planes were. Not all of the rounds were misses. He could hear and feel some of them slam into his fuselage.

The throttle was shoved forward to its full position, and—although the dive had momentarily taken his airspeed to over four hundred miles per hour—the P-40 settled back to its top speed of three hundred-fifty in level flight.

Distracted by the need to get clear of the tracers, Hollands pulled back hard on the stick and banked left, to gain altitude for maneuverability and to get out of the enemies' gun sights. But the sudden G-force momentarily starved the engine of fuel, slowing his airspeed dramatically for several seconds before engine power was restored.

The two Krauts had been gaining, but surprised by these tactics, they peeled off, one to the left and the other to the right to avoid colliding with the Yank.

Hollands rapidly regained some lost altitude.

"Shotgun to base. Shotgun to base. Over."

"This is Buckshot. Go ahead Shotgun. Over."

"Got two 109s on my tail, and a third hanging back at altitude. Any help available?"

Lewis' voice crackled in Hollands' earphones. "Negative, Lieutenant. Nothing on radar. What is your location? Over."

"About eighty miles northeast of base, passing over the old British outpost."

Another burst of tracers screamed past his canopy, and Hollands decided that it was time to try something different and dangerous. Pulling on his oxygen mask, he took a deep breath, hauled his throttle back to half, and lowered his flaps. Then he pushed the stick all the way forward and held it there as his aircraft slowly flipped upside down, heading the opposite direction.

Righting his ship, he saw his two adversaries, still in their turns with nearly two miles separating them. Hollands opened the throttle wide, brought up the flaps, and banked to his right to pursue the nearer German, who was a thousand feet above. It would take only a few seconds for the other enemy pilot to close on the Warhawk.

The German appeared to be unaware that he had become the pursued. He had turned hard to port, which temporarily obscured Hollands' location. But by the time the 109 turned back to starboard, Hollands was only a couple of hundred feet below and a half a mile away, coming head on.

With the nose of the P-40 up, Hollands fired a long burst from the six .50 caliber machine guns, hitting the enemy fighter in the front fuselage and engine. Immediately the 109 began to spew black smoke, and it wobbled noticeably as the two fighters whizzed past each other.

Then Hollands banked to port, to search for the second 109. The German was gaining altitude and racing to join up with the third plane some distance away—headed for home, perhaps unaware of his comrade's predicament.

Hollands looked behind him for the wounded German plane, and was surprised to find a trail of blue-gray smoke coming from his own bird. As he completed his turn, he saw the smoking German fighter wandering aimlessly across the sky in the distance. He spotted a parachute.

A few seconds later, the crippled 109 exploded in mid-air.

Hollands turned his attention back to his own plane. The earlier maneuver had cost him a lot of altitude. The Warhawk's engine was now overheating and losing power. The cockpit had begun to fill with smoke.

He looked at his altimeter, and saw that he was too low to bail out.

He grabbed for the radio mike. "Mayday, mayday! This is Shotgun. I'm going down near old British outpost. Mayday, mayday!"

"Roger, Shotgun. We copy! Sending help."

The terrain was rough and rocky except for one short stretch of what looked like a dirt road. Hollands lowered his flaps and landing gear, and headed for the makeshift landing strip. He hauled open the cockpit canopy, right as the motor sputtered its last gasp of life.

The ground was coming up quickly, but he caught a good enough look to realize that the 'road' was actually soft, deep sand. He quickly retracted the wheels to keep from flipping tail-section over propeller.

The plane hit hard on its belly, and the jarring force of the impact resonated upward through his ribcage. Then he was careening across the sand, the underside of the Warhawk's fuselage grinding against the dry earth with a rumbling hiss that threatened to stun his eardrums.

Trailing an enormous dust cloud, the plane slid for seventy or eighty yards before it ground to a stop. The air was heavy with the scorched flint smell of overheated sand, and the sweet chemical odor of fuel.

Hollands grabbed his water and survival kit, and scrambled out onto the port wing. He saw a lot of smoke coming from the engine.

He jumped off the wing and ran from the aircraft, not wanting to be anywhere near the thing if the fuel caught fire.

Shaking with adrenaline, Hollands took a hasty look around, and spotted the German pilot lying motionless on the ground a hundred yards away. Drawing his sidearm, a Colt 45 semi-automatic pistol, he cautiously walked towards the man.

As he approached the downed enemy flier, he thought back to something his father had told him years before. "There are few times in life when you will know the exact right thing to do, son. Sometimes the wrong thing will be easier to recognize. Trust in God and your natural instincts, and never be afraid to act accordingly."

The German was lying on his back. Hollands cocked his pistol. The pilot was young—perhaps nineteen or twenty. Hollands was only twenty-two. As the American stood there, he observed that a small trickle of blood was coming from the injured man's mouth, and that his breathing was labored.

"Treat all men as brothers, regardless of the outcome of your actions," his father had advised. "The true enemy is a government; soldiers are merely pawns. Death is never a celebration."

Hollands knelt down next to the man, and relieved him of his sidearm.

The German opened his eyes, and—in halting English—said, "We have been told that your P-40 aircraft is inferior. Not good fighter. They say it cannot maneuver as you did."

Hollands simply asked, "Can you drink some water?"

"Yes, that would be good."

Hollands took out his handkerchief, dampened it with a few drops of water, and gently wiped the blood from the young pilot's face and mouth. Cradling the man's head in his arm, he placed the canteen of water to the pilot's mouth.

The German took two swallows and said simply, *"Danke, danke!"* Then, he passed out.

During the next two hours, as the German drifted in and out of consciousness, Hollands made him as comfortable as possible. The crash-landing had been at 0837. At 1040 hours Hollands heard a truck approaching.

He crouched behind a sand dune. He doubted a German patrol could be anywhere near, but there was no point in taking unnecessary chances.

When the vehicle rolled into view, he breathed a sigh of relief. A British flag hung from the short flag staff.

Help had arrived.

10 MARCH 1943:

Four months later, the clerk of the 122nd Fighter Squadron, Corporal James Rodriguez, entered the officers' barracks. Their quarters consisted of three tents laced together, and looked like an elongated Quonset hut.

With a small stack of transfer orders in hand, Corporal Rodriguez announced, "Gentlemen, sirs! I'm sorry to disturb you so early, but I have orders for some of you. Please grunt or groan if your name is called."

He glanced at the top sheet of paper. "Lieutenants Bishop and Hitchcock?"

From the far end of the tent's darkened interior came soft, sleepy groans. "Over here, James. We're over here."

After handing out the new orders, James asked, "Is Captain Hollands in here?"

Silence.

"Captain Hollands, are you in here, sir?"

Again, silence.

The missing Captain Michael Hollands had recently been promoted and placed third in command of the squadron. The lanky six-footer had been in North Africa for nine months and flown many missions.

Back in the States, he had graduated from the University of Washington in the spring of 1942, with a major in aeronautical engineering and a minor in English. Throughout college, he had been active in the ROTC program. At the end of his sophomore year, he had enlisted in the U.S. Army Air Corps Reserves.

As Rodriguez left the tent he bumped into Hollands who was just entering. "Oh, sorry sir. I didn't see you."

"Of course not, Corporal, it's scarcely dawn," Hollands said. "I didn't see you either. What's up?"

"*You're* up, sir," the corporal said. "You're being transferred."

Hollands raised an eyebrow. "I wasn't aware that the squadron was moving."

"They're not, sir. The squadron is staying put. It's just you and two others," the clerk explained. As he thumbed back through the sheets of paper, he added, "Hitchcock and Bishop are headed back to the States for reassignment."

Hollands grinned and leaned against the wooden doorjamb. "Hot damn, I'm going to England! I can finally get out of this sandbox."

Rodriguez looked up apologetically. "Well, sir, not quite. You're getting out of Morocco, but you're not going to England. You're being sent to another sandbox... The South Pacific."

The smile on Hollands' face was quickly replaced by disappointment, and he muttered an expletive under his breath. "South Pacific? Why am I going to the South Pacific?"

"I don't know, sir. But you've been requested by name. Some Navy commander wants you in the Solomons. The Army has ordered you to proceed by air transport to Pateroa Island Naval Air Station."

Hollands shook his head in disbelief and glowered at the ground. "I don't know any naval officers."

"Neither do I, sir," the corporal said. "But that's what it says on your orders. Your transportation will be here about noon today. From here you fly to England, then on to the States. The Army has given you ten-day travel orders. Sorry about that, Captain!"

"That's all right, James," Hollands said with a sigh. "Maybe I'll take you along with me."

"That'd be okay by me, sir," the clerk answered with a smile. "Maybe I better go pack my duffle bag right now!"

Both men chuckled.

Dawn had nearly given way to daylight. Hollands took a deep breath and with a long drawn-out sigh, said, "Look, I've been up all night at Operations. I've gotta get a few hours sleep before I pack up to leave."

He handed the clerk a sheet of paper. "Here are today's flight orders. Briefing is set for ten hundred hours. Post that on the ready board."

He glanced at his wristwatch. "Wake the rest of these bums up in about four hours, in time for their briefing. Oh, and give me a shake at eleven thirty, unless the transport's late."

"Yes, sir. I'll take care of it all."

Pausing, Hollands added, "I wish the CO were here. I'd like to say goodbye; but he's not due back from Command for two more days."

He turned to enter the tent. "Thanks, James. See you in a few winks."

Everyone on base, including James, liked Captain Hollands. It wasn't exactly a secret that Hollands had done some quiet wrangling to get corporal-stripes for Rodriguez. And even though the invisible abyss of rank separated them, Rodriquez and the others always knew that Hollands respected them as fellow soldiers.

Hollands was travel weary after the long flights from Africa to England, and England to the U.S. It was 7:30 in the evening on March 13 when his flight finally left New York for California. The big, four-engine Skymaster settled down on the Moffett Field runway some thirty miles east of San Francisco at 0650 Pacific Time the next morning.

Stepping onto the tarmac, Hollands was happy simply to be on the ground again. He chatted briefly with the crewmembers, shaking hands with them.

"Captain Hollands?" a voice called out. "Is there a Captain Hollands here?"

Hollands saw an Army major approaching the group. He came to attention and saluted. "Good morning, Major. I'm Captain Hollands."

Returning the salute, the major said, "Good morning, Captain. You look tired."

"Thirty-six hours in the air in a transport can do that to a fellow."

"I suppose you're right," the major said. "Anyway, welcome to NAS Moffett Field."

Hollands looked at him. "NAS?"

"Naval Air Station," the major said. "But this base was under the command of the Army Air Corps until a few months ago, and there are still a few of us Army types lurking in the shadows."

He glanced at the green canvas bag slung over the captain's shoulder. "Do you have all your gear?"

"Just my duffle," Holland said. "My foot locker is somewhere between here and England. At least I *think* it is."

"I'll keep my eyes open for it," the major said. "My name is Coffman. Dan Coffman. You can call me Dan. Okay if I call you Mike?"

Hollands nodded. "That would be fine... *Dan*."

Coffman looked around. "My clerk will see to it that all of the other passengers get wherever they're going. Strictly as a courtesy. They're not Air Corps, so they're not really my problem. You, on the other hand, are an Army flier. I'm the liaison officer for the Army Air Corps, so that makes you my responsibility. What do you say we start by getting you some breakfast?"

"Absolutely!" Holland said. "My duffle bag was beginning to look appetizing."

"When did you eat last?"

Hollands made a face. "I chewed the ends off of my bootlaces somewhere over the Great Lakes. But I can't remember the last time I actually saw *food*."

"Say no more, Mike," Coffman said with a chuckle. "This will not be from a mess hall. Hope you won't mind coming to the house. I live nearby, and you get to sample my wife's good cooking."

"This is certainly an unexpected pleasure, Dan, but I wouldn't want to put your wife or you to any inconvenience. Besides, I'm not exactly presentable."

"You look fine. We're happy to do this."

"Well," Hollands said with a big smile, "I hope it's a *big* sample then, because England was a long, looooooooong ways back."

Laughing, Coffman said, "My car's parked over this way. Get your ID out for the MP at the gate."

When they finished breakfast, Mrs. Coffman smiled and asked, "Captain, would you like to use our telephone to call your family before you go?"

Hollands broke into a grin, "That would be wonderful, Mrs. Coffman. Thank you."

The five-minute conversation with his parents left Hollands in high spirits as he rode with Coffman back to the base for further processing.

"We'll stop by my office for a moment to pick up your updated travel orders," Coffman said.

As the two waited for the orders to be processed by a clerk, Coffman asked, "How is it that you got pulled out of North Africa for the South Pacific?"

Hollands shrugged. "Frankly, I was hoping *you* would know. I was wanting to go to England, and I don't mean for a midnight fuel stop."

"It sure seems—well, like the military," Coffman said with a grin.

"Here are your orders, Captain," the clerk said. "Good luck to you, sir."

Hollands nodded. "Thank you."

He wasn't scheduled to leave Moffett Field for a few days, so Coffman drove him to a single-level barracks.

Entering, Hollands dropped his duffle bag at the front door and took a tour. There were a few small rooms, each with a real bed.

"We like to refer to this as the 'VIP Bungalow,'" Coffman explained.

At the far end was the shower area near an open area Coffman referred to as the living room.

"Do you treat all of your, ah *'guests'* like this, Major?"

"Usually the bungalow is reserved for the brass as they come through," replied Coffman. "So far, we've managed to hang on to the bungalow for Army use, but the Navy will be getting their hands on it before long. They're using Moffett as a base for their dirigible, and we're moving out as they move in.

"Most of the Army Air Corps personnel are already gone. The rest of us are based on this side of the field. We'll be transferring to Travis and Hamilton Airbases sometime in the near future. But there's no brass scheduled to be here for several weeks, so there's no reason for you not to be comfortable while you're here."

Coffman pointed to one of the bedrooms. "This is the best bed. You'll sleep well in this bunk."

Hollands retrieved his duffle bag and tossed it on the bed.

"Gee, this is really terrific, Dan. I truly appreciate it."

The two men shook hands.

As Coffman drove away, Hollands checked out the living room. Next to the phone was a sheet of paper with base phone numbers.

"Hey, there's the laundry number," he said. He dialed it and made arrangements to have his dirty uniforms picked up and washed.

His body clock was so many time zones behind that he'd lost count. He needed sleep.

At 1600 hours he stripped to his skivvies and t-shirt and gratefully stretched out on the bed. "Wow! Dan was right, this bed is delicious!"

He pulled a blanket over himself as his head settled onto the pillow.

At 0630, he woke up. Feeling a bit stiff, Hollands reached into his duffle bag and pulled out his Army PT shorts and sweatshirt. A hint of sunlight was beginning to stream through the windows. He dressed quickly, unlocked the front door, and headed outside. As he loosened up his muscles with some bends and stretches, he looked around for a route he could run.

Deciding on one that looked promising, he took off at a brisk pace. It felt good to be working out the kinks. Part of the run took him north, past the main gate where he waved to the MP on duty, and then continued parallel to the perimeter fence.

He had run a mile when he intersected a path that led toward three hangars another half-mile away. He turned onto it. But a hundred yards short of his target, he was abruptly forced to stop.

Major Coffman was driving his jeep to the bungalow to see Hollands when two MPs stopped him and told him to report to the MP station and Provost Marshal's office.

When Coffman entered the office, he saw Captain Michael Hollands sitting on a hard wooden bench, handcuffed and glowering. Hollands looked up, frowned, and slowly got to his feet.

Coffman's face reddened as he glared at the desk sergeant. "Who authorized the handcuffing of this officer?" he demanded.

"I did, Major," stated the desk sergeant. "I don't know that he is an officer. He failed to stop and identify himself when ordered. He kept right on running, and when he headed for Hangar Building T-663, my MPs stopped him. He had no ID on him, so they brought him here."

Hearing the heated debate, the provost marshal, a lieutenant colonel, stepped out of his office. "What the hell's going on out here? Dan, what are you doing here, and who is this man?"

Coffman whipped off a salute and said, "Good morning, Colonel Dickinson. Begging the Colonel's pardon, but Captain Hollands is an air-combat veteran who has been unjustly detained, apparently for taking a run without his ID. But how often do we carry *our* ID while doing PT? Where the hell would we *put* it?"

He glanced back at Hollands. "But it looks to me like he's wearing his dog tags!"

Coffman turned his attention back to the desk sergeant. "Did anyone even think to *look* at his dog tags, Sergeant? And by the way, what's so special about Building T-663? It's been empty for nearly five years."

"May I say something?" asked Hollands.

"Of course, Captain," said the colonel.

Hollands nodded. "Yesterday morning, I completed a thirty-six hour air transit from North Africa. This morning, I simply wanted to go for a run. When I ran past the gate guard, we waved at each other."

He pointed toward the MPs. "*No one* asked me to stop until I met these four men."

The colonel walked over to the desk sergeant's phone and dialed the guard station. "Corporal, this is Colonel Dickinson. About thirty minutes ago, you had a lone runner go past your gate. Did you challenge him or in any way ask him to stop? I see. Thank you. No, you did right, son."

Putting the phone down, he turned to the desk sergeant. "Tell me, Sergeant... Where did you get the idea that the captain had refused to stop?"

"Well, sir, the gate guards call in every twenty minutes, and when that guard checked in, he told me that a man had come running past him a few seconds earlier. I *assumed...*"

Dickinson cleared his throat. "The corporal informed me that he saluted Captain Hollands, because he recognized the captain from yesterday morning when he accompanied Major Coffman off post."

He shifted his gaze to Hollands. "Does that sound about right to you, Captain?"

"Profoundly, sir."

"Get these cuffs off this man," the provost ordered. "And, tear up that paperwork. This incident never happened. Do you get my meaning, Sergeant?"

The desk sergeant nodded vigorously. "Yes, sir!"

With relief, Hollands and Coffman rode quietly back to the bungalow. As the jeep came to a stop, Coffman said, "I'm really sorry about this, Mike."

"Not your fault," answered Hollands. "There's been no damage, sir."

"Let's step inside," Coffman suggested. "I have an idea that may help smooth things out for you."

"Okay, Major. I'll listen."

As they approached the entrance to the bungalow, Hollands saw his bag of clean laundry sitting at the door. Picking up the bundle he walked inside, the major close behind.

Coffman commented wryly, "I'm glad you didn't have to do all that laundry yourself."

Hollands chuckled. "Me too. Is the mess hall still open? I'm hungry, and I could sure use a cup of coffee."

"I'm hungry, too. Look, you grab a shower and we'll walk to the mess hall."

Ten minutes later, Hollands, showered, shaved, and in a clean uniform, came back. "That feels better. I was getting cold."

The two men entered the mess hall and helped themselves to food. As they sat down to eat, Coffman asked, "How would you like to have a full three days at home with your folks?"

"This is a joke, right?"

"Nope! I've got a problem... a Warhawk that was supposed to be at Boeing Field last week. You fly it up there and you can have three, maybe four days in Seattle with your family. Then you can head to Hawaii from there."

"When can I leave?" asked Hollands.

"Well, let me put it this way. I can phone over to the flight line, and in five minutes I'll have your flight plan filed and the plane gassed and warming up. So, what say you?"

"Make that call, Dan!" Hollands said with a big grin.

"Oh, by the way, your foot locker arrived earlier this morning. I'll send it on to Hickham Field for you."

The flight from Seattle to Hickham Field, the U.S. Army Air Corps Base on Oahu, was smooth and uneventful. Hollands' mind was filled with fresh memories of his family, friends, and home. The four-day leave had gone by in a flash. Now, he was back to duty.

He had been scheduled to fly out the next day to the Solomon Islands, but, because of service delays on the Army's C-54 transport plane, his departure was postponed.

Late in the afternoon of his second day in the paradise called Hawaii, Hollands visited an off-base officer's club to have dinner. While he was eating, he overheard a Marine Corps pilot talking about how he and his two buddies were hitching a ride to the Solomons on an R5D Navy transport.

Walking over to the Marine, Hollands could see a first lieutenant's bar on the man's collar. "Excuse me, Lieutenant. But did I hear you correctly? You have a flight out to the Solomons?"

"Sure enough, Captain! Pateroa, I think it's called. Do you need a ride, too?"

"Yeah, I sure do. When are you leaving?" Hollands asked.

"I was told zero-five-thirty."

"I'll be there! And I have a jeep. Do you and your buddies need a ride in the morning?"

"Sure thing, Army! Thanks. We'll meet you at our main gate."

Many hours and time zones later, the flight finally touched down at what was going to be Hollands' home for the foreseeable future.

When they stepped off the plane, Hollands and the three Marine fighter pilots saw no fighter planes.

The Marine lieutenant raised an eyebrow. "Hey, Army, where do you think all of the fighters are?"

Aside from twenty B-17 bombers parked on the ground near the three maintenance hangars, Pateroa appeared deserted. Those bombers wouldn't mean a thing when it came to air combat—they would only be additional targets.

Hollands glanced around and shrugged. "Your guess is as good as mine."

Off-loading footlockers and duffel bags, the four pilots thanked the transport crew for the ride. Hollands shook hands with the three Marines. "You guys take care. It's been good flying with you."

The Navy had sent a jeep for the Marines. The kid driving pointed to the far end of the field where he thought the fighter squadron might be located. It looked to be about a two-mile hike.

Hollands waved to his comrades, and as they rode away, he could hear one of them griping. "I wish I had remembered my earplugs. Someone answer that damn phone. It won't stop ringing."

Hollands had stuffed a wad of cotton into each ear during the flight, which had helped. And although he didn't have a headache and ringing in his ears, he was worn-out from the trip.

Shouldering his duffel bag with one hand and dragging his footlocker with the other, he groaned inwardly about the walk, the load, the heat, and the lateness of the hour. "Those damn planes might as well be on the far side of the moon," he sighed.

The Japanese had been chased out of this part of the Solomons only a few months earlier, with the U.S. Navy and Marines doing most of the chasing. The Army Air Corps' bold raid on Japan the previous spring, courtesy of Colonel Jimmy Doolittle, had done much to bolster morale—not only throughout all branches of the military—but also for everyone back home in the U.S.

The American message was loud and clear. "Hold on to your Kimono, Tojo! We're coming to get you!"

Along part of the base perimeter, Hollands could see damaged American and Japanese aircraft. But with no fighters on the ground or in the air, there was a cold eeriness about the base.

As he trudged along, he surveyed his new neighborhood. The South Pacific seemed excessive in both heat and humidity. A lot of palm trees adjacent to the runways had been taken down. The sandy ground was a bright, bleach-white, and the glare was hard on the eyes.

Hollands stopped for a moment and donned his dark pilot's glasses. "Much more of this toughening-up, and I'll be too pooped to move the stick or the rudder."

He had hiked about a quarter of a mile when he heard a small engine behind him. Looking back he saw a yellow service tractor approaching from where the Navy transport plane was still sitting. These tractors were used for towing aircraft.

Hollands mentally rehearsed his military growl, a technique he'd never been particularly good at in the past. He reminded himself that rank does have its benefits, at times, and maybe never more than right now!

As the vehicle approached, the young soldier at the wheel offered a nod, intending to drive on by. When driver and machine came even with Hollands' left side, he shouted, "*Halt!*" His tone would have made his drill sergeants in basic training proud.

With a few short scraping sounds from the hard rubber tires, the tractor squeaked to a stop. The driver jumped off the yellow vehicle right in front of Hollands, came to attention, and saluted. "Good afternoon, sir!"

The young soldier was shirtless, and was perhaps all of eighteen or nineteen years old.

"At ease," Hollands ordered. "What's your name and rank, soldier?"

"Sir, Private First Class Lynch."

"Are you on a dangerous mission, Private Lynch?"

"Oh, no, sir. When we're not busy, I try to be somewhere else. It's best to look busy and stay out of my sergeant's hollering range, since we don't have anything to work on."

Hollands was puzzled. "You don't have any *what*, Private?"

"Airplanes, sir!" the private said. "I'm an aircraft mechanic."

"Where *are* the aircraft, Private? I understood this to be an airbase with fighters."

Private Lynch nodded. "Yes, sir, it was that all right. But except for the transports and medical planes—oh, and those B-17s that came in a few hours ago—we haven't had any planes here in weeks. All air groups have been transferred out, sir."

He glanced back toward the hangars. "But the ground crew will have those bombers and that R5D gassed up and ready to go right soon, sir."

"Well then," Hollands said, "since you're not engaged in some vital mission, give me a hand with my gear. I need a short ride."

"Yes, sir. I thought you were looking a little hot and uncomfortable."

Hollands nodded. "That I *am*, Private."

"Yes, sir. Where to, Captain?"

When the duffle bag and footlocker were secured, Hollands said, "You can ease up some, kid. I'm just another Army grunt myself."

"Thank you, sir," Private Lynch responded. "Hey, Captain, want a cold drink?"

Reaching inside a canvas water bag, the kid pulled out an icy cold bottle of Royal Crown Cola. He handed the bottle to Hollands along with a bottle opener from the toolbox.

"Is this the only one you have, Lynch?"

"Oh no, sir. I've got lots back at the barracks, and a couple more here in the bag. We're not supposed to drink these on duty, but I don't much like the water here. I have to force myself to drink a little water every day. But you really look like you could use a cold drink, sir."

"Private, you must be a gift from the war gods," Hollands said. He took his first swallow. It was cold all the way down.

"Man, that hits the spot!" he said softly.

"Where to, sir?" asked the private, with a big smile on his face.

"Just keep heading for those buildings at the end of the base."

As the tractor began to move, Lynch asked, "Are you looking for the 9th Fighter Squadron?"

"That's right."

"Gee, I haven't seen any of their new Thunderbolts flying around here for several days now, sir. They must've pulled out, too. A month ago, they had P-40s. Haven't seen them either."

A few minutes later, after swerving around hangars and Quonset huts, Lynch parked at the door of what had been the squadron's company headquarters and orderly room.

"Here you are, sir."

As he lifted Hollands' gear to the ground, Lynch added, "Well, they've gone alright. You sure you got the right outfit, sir? Maybe you should come up to my company area. There's lots of room. Or I could drive you over to the base HQ."

"No, it's getting late," Hollands said. "I'll be fine, Private. But thank you for the ride, and the cold drink. You've been a lifesaver."

Hollands smiled at the younger man. "Will your sergeant chew you out for being gone so long?"

"Hell no, sir." Lynch chuckled. "But it's getting close to chow time, and I should get back to check in. Nice meetin' ya, Captain."

The young soldier saluted, and climbed back onto the tractor. With a momentary grinding of the gears, he was gone.

Hollands dropped his gear at the door and began his first look around. Lynch had been correct. No one was home, and it was obvious they weren't coming back anytime soon.

He took a depressing, thirty-minute tour of the facility. A door to the only hangar was partially open, so he walked the few short yards to look inside.

"Empty," he sighed. Then to the west of the hangar, a hundred yards away, he spotted one lone aircraft.

"Hmmm... Looks like a Thunderbolt," he said to himself. Momentarily forgetting his exhaustion, he hurried over to see the plane.

This was Hollands' first look at the newly-designed aircraft, reportedly the largest single-engine fighter made. It was sure a lot bigger than his old P-40.

He climbed up onto the wing to inspect the craft more closely. "Wow! You're a beaut," he whispered. "But what are you doing here all alone, sweetheart?"

He shook his head and slid off the wing. The top of the engine cowling, he guessed, was nearly fifteen feet off the ground. As he walked back toward the deserted HQ, he took one last admiring glance at the big fighter.

His tour of the facilities finished, Hollands headed for his gear. He took the duffel bag and the footlocker on into the building. Now what? He needed to report to someone. That was one of those peculiarities the military was a stickler for.

It had been quite late in the afternoon when his flight landed, and now it was well into early evening. He found that the orderly room had working lights. Adjacent to it he discovered a smaller room equipped with a desk, an Army cot, a rolled up mattress, and a blanket. Probably the CO's room.

Although he was hungry, Hollands decided that sleep should be his first priority. He unrolled the mattress and stepped outside to shake out the lone blanket. Then he watched quietly for a few moments as twilight took over from sundown, and rapidly moved towards night.

It wasn't quite dark when he turned out the overhead light at about 1900 hours. Stripping to his skivvies and T-shirt, he promised himself that he'd get everything straightened out in the morning.

He had been asleep for about two hours, blissfully trading growls of hunger with light, contented snores, when he was awakened by the sound of the squeaky front door opening.

Darkness had been in full sway outside for some time, and several things went through his mind. He was now in the South Pacific, and Pateroa Island happened to be in an active war zone. Where was his pistol?

A vaguely familiar voice called out, "Hey, Army! You in here?"

A second voice asked, "Captain? Where are you, sir? Look, Lieutenant, here's some of his gear; he must be here."

But Hollands—still more asleep than awake—couldn't quite identify the voices. He had been a long way down the dark, deep well of exhaustion, and he was slow to emerge.

Struggling to make sense out of what he was hearing, Hollands called out, "Who's there?"

"Oh, there you are," a voice said.

Someone switched on the light, and Hollands slapped his hand over his eyes to protect them from the sudden glare.

The door was partially ajar, so the young Marine pilot pushed it the rest of the way open. "Nice place you got here!" he declared. "Must be the maid's year off, right?"

Carrying a mess hall tray, he said, "Hey, sorry to wake you, Army. But I hope you like Marine chow."

Dumbfounded, Hollands rubbed the sleep from his eyes as they readjusted to the light. "What are you doing here? How'd you find me?"

Then, he spotted Private Lynch in the doorway behind the Marine lieutenant.

The Marine set down the food tray, moved to the lone window, and slid the blackout curtain over the glass. "I brought ya some chow and a beer," he said. "Hope you like steak and potatoes. That's all I could find on short notice. Not too many good restaurants on this rock."

"Boy, am I glad to see you," Hollands said. "I'm starved! But how'd you know?"

The lieutenant handed the tray of food to Hollands. "Well, shortly after me and my buddies checked in, I found out that your outfit had moved to some other island." He lit a smoke. "Don't tell anyone about this. I mean about the food I commandeered, 'cause Marines don't fraternize much with the Army, ya know."

He laughed. "It might make me look bad. Anyway, I got to thinking... You're kinda stuck, at least for a day or so."

He pulled up the lone wooden chair and sat backwards on it, facing

Hollands. "I mean, no company mess hall or anything. So, I was walking around trying to guess which way you'd gone. Then, as luck would have it, I ran into your taxi driver. And with a borrowed jeep and a trip to the mess... Well, here we are. By the way, how's the steak?"

The Marine glanced at the nearly-empty tray. "Damn! You didn't eat it. You inhaled it!" He chuckled. "Hell, you might not have survived till morning."

Hollands grinned. He was beginning to feel human again. "Hey, I really appreciate this, fellas," he mumbled as he continued to stuff food into his mouth.

Finally, he washed down the last bites with a swallow of beer, put the tray aside, stood up, and pulled on his pants. "You know, Lieutenant, we must have breached some military etiquette somewhere along the way. I don't know your name, or you mine."

He wiped his hands on his shirttail and extended his right hand to clasp the Marine's. "Mike Hollands. And I am *very* glad to meet you, Lieutenant."

"Bruce Buckner," the Marine said. "It's a pleasure. I've never liked anyone in the Army before now."

He paused. "But I've never known anyone in the Army, either. Shit, this may ruin the whole damn war for me." He laughed again.

"You know, Buckner, you may have been right," Hollands said.

The Marine raised an eyebrow. "Right about *what*?"

"I might not have survived till morning," Hollands said with a chuckle.

After Hollands tied his shoes, the three men went outside. Few clouds and a half moon allowed plenty of light to define the outline of an airplane sitting on the grassy area. The two aviators began talking about flying. Private Lynch started back to the jeep to wait.

"Hey, where are you going, Private?" Buckner asked.

Then Hollands suggested, "C'mon Lynch, let's take a look at that bird."

The young mechanic looked pleased and flattered to find both officers insisting that he join them. "Yes, sirs. I'm right with ya!"

As the two fliers talked, Lynch took a flashlight from his pocket and hurried ahead to the lone aircraft.

Buckner looked at Hollands. "Have you had a chance to look around yet?"

Hollands pointed to the shadowy form of the abandoned plane. "Other than the dirt, that's all they've left behind. I figure it must not be a flier."

He scratched his head. "It's strange, though. The P-47s are brand new; they've just been placed into service. So why did they leave a perfectly good airplane behind?"

Buckner was quiet for a few moments, then asked, "Tell me, Hollands, have you flown in combat yet?"

The Marine's tone caught Hollands' attention. "Sure. I flew P-40s for nine months with the 122nd Pursuit Squadron, in North Africa."

Trying to avoid bragging, Hollands added in a matter-of-fact tone, "I was credited with taking out a 109 and a 190, along with a lot of ground action. Trains, power stations, fuel depots, and convoys. Stuff like that."

He shook his head. "Those 190s are tough birds to score on, if you're flying a P-40. We had just been assigned an even-dozen of the new Mustangs before I left. I haven't flown one yet, but I'd sure like to."

He looked toward the Marine. "How about you?"

Buckner took the last drag of his cigarette, then field stripped it. "Hell, other than having my orders lost in the States for five months, me and my two buddies are fresh out of flight school."

Hollands handed the last of his beer to his new friend. "What's your assignment? What outfit are you going to be flying with?"

"The VMF-214," Buckner said. "Out of Villa something-or-other. The CO is a Major Boyington."

Buckner downed the last swallow of beer, and tipped the empty bottle toward Hollands. "They're flying Corsairs. Or at least that's what I've heard."

"Sounds good to me," Hollands said. "The Corsairs have been out for a few months, and between them and the new Hellcats, the Navy has been kicking the hell out of the Japs."

Pausing, Hollands asked, "When are you supposed to report?"

"That's the sixty-four dollar question. There are no transports available, and my packet's lost again. It's probably somewhere between San Diego and Tokyo. The staff here isn't even sure I exist."

Continuing their slow walk, Hollands said, "Boyington... Oh yeah... Greg Boyington. Now I remember him. I think he grew up near Seattle, went to the University of Washington like I did. That's where I'm from. He was nine or ten years ahead of me, though."

"I heard he flew with AVG in China," Buckner interjected. "An outfit called the Flying Tigers."

"Well, he was knocking down Nips the hard way, using the P-40," Hollands said. "Sounds pretty gutsy to me."

Hollands gave the Marine a thoughtful nod. "Ya know, Buckner, if a guy like that can knock Zekes out of the sky with a P-40, just think what he, well—what *you*—can do with a stronger, faster plane like the Corsair."

Buckner smiled slightly, somewhat relieved at that idea. Then the two pilots caught up with Lynch, who had been looking over the aircraft.

Motioning toward the plane, Hollands said, "Is she ready for the bone yard, Mr. Lynch?"

Both pilots were surprised at the answer. "No, sir!" the private responded emphatically. "She's practically brand new. Without running her and checking her over in the shop, I can't say for sure, but from what I can see here everything checks out fine, sir. The batteries are dead. That's all that I can see wrong right now."

Private Lynch was sounding a lot like a mechanic, and not at all like the young kid Hollands had met driving the tractor earlier that afternoon. Both officers were impressed.

Scratching his head, Lynch suggested, "Ya know, sir, maybe I could kinda sneak down here after chow in the morning with some tools. It'd be swell to actually get to work on a bird again."

"*Swell* idea!" Hollands chuckled. "Well, you're the grease monkey, so have at it."

"Captain," Lynch said more seriously, "I haven't really worked on a plane since I got out of aircraft mechanics training in Texas. That was seven months ago. Oh, I've changed the oil and sparkplugs on a few, ya know. The ones just passing through. But no real repairs."

"What the hell you been doing since you arrived here?" asked Buckner.

"Mostly policing the area, sir, like back in basic. Picking up butts, moving a rock from there to here, and the next day moving it back. And picking up more butts. Months before any Army planes came, the Navy had two squadrons of Wildcats here. But the most excitement I've had in a long time was watching those bombers land today, and giving the captain a ride. Oh, and going AWOL, sorta, this evening, sir."

Hollands asked quietly, "How did you do in Texas?"

Even in the moonlight, Holland could see a proud grin on the kid's face as he said, "Out of my battalion, sir, I was number three."

Buckner declared, "Hell, kid, I don't care if you *are* Army, you can throw a wrench at my bird anytime. As soon as I get one, that is."

"Same here!" Hollands affirmed, making it unanimous.

As Lynch walked toward the jeep, Hollands quietly said to Buckner, "A mechanic like that, and they have him picking up butts. There's something seriously wrong with this Army."

The two officers turned to follow Lynch, who was now several yards ahead. Hollands heard Buckner mutter under his breath, "It ain't just in the Army."

The next morning, Hollands found out just how bright, warm, and humid a South Pacific morning can be. Glancing at his watch, he saw that it was nearly 0630. He took a quick look through the window, and saw the tractor parked out near the plane.

As he hurriedly dressed, he sniffed the air. "I smell bacon," he said. "Boy, I've gotta see the flight surgeon and get my nose checked."

When he entered the outer office, he was surprised to find a still-warm tray of bacon and eggs, along with a large cup of coffee.

Looking out the door toward the plane, Hollands saw the engine cowling lying on the ground and two men on top of the engine working. He knew that one of the men was sure to be Lynch. He assumed the second man was another Army mechanic.

Hollands attacked the tray of food before heading out. Then he eagerly approached the aircraft as the two men continued to work on it. When he got closer, he was surprised to see that the second man was Lieutenant Buckner, complete with grease and oil up the arms of his overalls and on his face.

Now he could clearly hear the two men talking. It wasn't anything like the exchange Hollands usually expected to hear between a low-ranking enlisted man and an officer. They sounded more like two kids working on an old car in the back yard on some sunny afternoon back home.

From a short distance away, Hollands called, "Hi fellas! Is she ready for inspection?"

The two men had been so engrossed in what they were doing that neither had noticed Hollands' approach. He was amazed and entertained at how much they were enjoying the work they were doing together.

"Oh, good morning, Captain. Did you know that Buckner, eh... sorry, sir," corrected the private, looking at the Marine officer. "I mean *Lieutenant* Buckner was a mechanic back home? He worked in a filling station!"

"No, I didn't," answered Hollands. "Is he any good?"

"He's damn good, sir."

"Well said, Private Lynch," joked Buckner. "And don't you forget it!"

Looking down from the top of the engine, he said, "Hey, Hollands, give me a hand down; I've got a leg cramp and I think my toes have fallen off."

As he helped Buckner down, Hollands said, "Thanks for the chow. Was it Army or Marine?"

"Army, sir," answered Lynch with a grin. "I hope you like your coffee black."

"Lynch, I'll drink it any way I can get it," Hollands answered.

"Amen to that!" Buckner said with a chuckle.

"Sir, with your permission," said Lynch, "I'd like to kick her over, and see what we've got. She seems to have plenty of fuel."

He pointed to the large battery carrier he had stowed on top of the tractor. "I've brought our hot box along, sir. We can plug into the plane's electrical system."

The captain looked at Buckner and asked, "What do you think, Lieutenant?"

"Hollands, the kid's got real brass," exclaimed the young Marine officer as he wiped oil and grease from his hands and face. "I've never met anyone who knows engines better than this man. I'd trust him!"

"All right, Lieutenant." Pausing, Hollands turned to Lynch and said, "Well, Private Lynch..." Hollands stopped abruptly and asked, "Lynch, what is your first name?"

"Osborn, sir," the private said, wincing. "But back home all of my friends and family call me Skip."

"Okay, Skip it is!" Hollands said. "It's your bird, Skip. Do it!"

Enthusiastically, *Skip* replied, "Yes, sir! Could I ask you two officers to pull the prop two full revolutions to clear out any oil that's drained into the lower cylinders?"

Both men stepped up to the huge propeller, and each grabbed a blade. "Hey, I remember this from one of the first lessons at flight school," said Buckner. "I didn't like doing it then either."

Skip jumped to the ground, and hurriedly connected two cables from the battery box to the plane's electrical system. As he climbed back onto the wing, he asked, "Sirs, when the engine catches and is running, could one of you pull the cables and the other switch off the battery?"

The two officers had completed their first full turn of the propeller, and Hollands answered, "Will do, Skip."

Skip climbed into the cockpit. "How's it going, sirs?" he called out. "Is the engine turning smoothly?"

"It feels fine, Skip," said Buckner. A few seconds later, he called out, "Okay, Skip. We're done!"

Lynch leaned his head out of the cockpit and said, "Well, Captain... Lieutenant... She'll either start up, or blow up! Clear the prop!"

"Prop clear!" both officers called in unison.

Hollands grabbed the fire extinguisher from off the tractor as he and Buckner moved several yards in front of the aircraft.

Then Skip engaged the starter. An unmistakable whine came from the engine as the plane's large, four-bladed propeller began to turn slowly. After several rotations, the whine ceased and the propeller came to a stop.

Skip called out, "Now we'll go for real."

The young mechanic flipped on the engine's magnetos, cracked the throttle an inch, primed the engine, and then hollered, "CLEAR!"

The grinding whine of the starter once more filled everyone's ears as the huge propeller began to turn. The engine immediately showed signs of life as belches of blue smoke exploded from the two exhaust ports. A thick, bluish haze obscured the aircraft momentarily.

Beneath the haze, the ground started vibrating and the whole front portion of the plane shook violently. It was as if life was once more being born in each of those 18 cylinders. Sputtering and coughing at first, the giant radial engine steadily increased speed, turning faster and faster, and, within moments, it smoothed out.

Hollands ran over to the battery and switched it off while Buckner— carefully avoiding the spinning propeller—disconnected the cables. Then the two officers returned to their places thirty feet in front of the aircraft.

Skip ran the engine at a relatively low RPM for a few minutes, adjusting the fuel mixture before finally shutting it down, and the huge fighter once more rested in silence.

He climbed out of the cockpit and slid down the backside of the starboard wing. Wearing a grin that could have put the Cheshire Cat to shame, the mechanic joined Hollands and Buckner.

With real enthusiasm Hollands said, "Excellent job, fellas."

Wiping oil from his hands and face, Lynch said, "I can't do any more out here in the field, sir. I'd like to get her inside the hangar, give her a tune-up, fresh oil, purge the fuel tanks, and check over the fuselage and the cables."

Then he said, "Captain, I don't think there's a whole lot wrong with this ship. I bet it got left here 'cause they didn't have a pilot, or because of a lazy mechanic."

He pointed to the wings. "I even took a peek at the machine guns. Other than needing a good cleaning, sir, they seem fine, too. But our ordinance men will have to check 'em to be sure."

"Ya know, Hollands," Buckner interjected, "The kid could be right. I mean about being short a pilot."

"Perhaps," Hollands acknowledged. "But it sure seems strange they couldn't have found someone somewhere to at least ferry her over to their new base."

"Well, Captain," the Marine said as he chuckled, eyeing the Thunderbolt, "you've got a plane, but no army. I have an army, but no plane. The classic military snafu, am I right?"

Hollands smiled and answered, "I'd have to agree. Let's get cleaned up. I really need to get over to base headquarters. Maybe I could fly this bird to whatever island the 9th was sent to."

Skip got busy hooking up the tractor to the plane's tail wheel, while Hollands and Buckner headed back to the company buildings to look for some clean water to wash up.

Hollands wanted a shave and Buckner needed to wash the oil off. Fifteen minutes later, the yellow tractor—with aircraft in tow—chugged up to where the two officers were waiting. They clambered on board the tractor and Skip slowly started off.

As they rode along, Hollands asked curiously, "Skip, who's your CO?"

"Captain Murray, sir."

"When we get the American Girl to your area, I'll check with your CO."

He paused. "Also, paint that name, '*American Girl*,' on both sides of the engine housing."

"Yes, sir, Captain. Can do."

CHAPTER 2

The "American Girl's" Revenge

Private Lynch was a member of the Army's Delta Company, Aircraft Maintenance. The Army Air Corps only had a few operational squadrons and maintenance facilities in the South Pacific and were still stretched thin.

Most of the Navy and Marine air and ground forces had been reassigned to Henderson Field on Guadalcanal and islands nearer to the 'Slot,' a deep ocean trough running through a narrow channel about ten miles wide.

But Navy, Marine and Army fighter squadrons slated for the South Pacific region, had been delayed due to logistics and a shortage of planes, pilots, and ground crews. The Navy brass had developed plans for ground bases using some carrier aircraft, which allowed for stronger (albeit temporary) air and ground support for the 'mud' Marines, and for the few Army ground units. It was a good idea that was slow to be implemented.

Right from the beginning, the U.S. focus was concentrated on Europe, so most of the men and materiel were being sent to England, to save her if possible.

With the early U.S. war production thus diverted, resources for the South Pacific arena were stretched to their limits. Had the Japanese realized how ill prepared and vulnerable the Allies were in the Pacific, the war there might have had a much different outcome. Short on supplies in every category, U.S. forces in the South Pacific took heavy losses, but the sheer guts and determination of the U.S. Marines and Navy kept the enemy off balance long enough for production to begin catching up to the demands.

As Hollands, Buckner, and Lynch rode on the tractor hauling the Thunderbolt, Hollands asked their young driver, "What about the Japanese? How often do they attack?"

While Lynch thought about the question, Buckner interjected, "The Marine's commanding officer says the Japs fly a few medium bombers in. Bettys, mostly. Once a week or so. Drop a few eggs, make some new craters, and leave. They know there's no air defense here, so they rarely send a fighter escort. Either they don't realize how vulnerable this island is, or they're stretched pretty thin themselves and are unable to retake it."

"What about the Army's 9th? Didn't they help?" asked Hollands.

Lynch replied, "Don't know, sir. I only know that every time the Nips came, the fighters were gone, and that's when they still had the P-40s too. Six or seven months ago this base was owned by the Japanese. My CO thinks these attacks are from a small airbase about 400 miles southeast of here, but he says that the Nips are building a larger one due east, only seventy-five to a hundred miles away. That could be a problem."

"Four hundred miles is definitely within the round-trip range of a Betty," mused Hollands. "That'd be eight hundred miles here and back."

Skip brought the tractor to a stop and turned to reassure his two passengers. "I don't think there's anything wrong, sirs. Just need to double check the hook-up to the plane."

Two minutes later, they were on the way again.

As they approached the two maintenance hangars, Hollands observed an officer coming out of the door between the two buildings. "Who's that officer, Skip?"

"Oh, that's Captain Murray, my CO, sir," Skip responded. "There must be a briefing next door. He seems to be in a hurry."

The Maintenance Company CO appeared to be preoccupied, and unaware of the noisy tractor and the aircraft towing behind it. He hurriedly headed between the two hangars and toward the outside stairs of the adjacent building.

Hollands jumped down from the tractor, and called out, "Captain Murray! Excuse me!" He ran to catch up.

Murray stopped and turned. "Yes? What can I do for you, Captain?"

Hollands extended his right hand. "Hi, Captain. My name's Hollands. I'm a pilot, supposed to be assigned to the 9th. I arrived here yesterday."

Murray shook the offered hand. "I'm Ben Murray. Glad to meet ya... uh... Did you say *pilot?*"

"That's correct. Fighters. I've just been transferred here from North Africa."

"North Africa? I thought most of you guys moved on to Europe. So, what can I do for you, Captain?"

"With the 9th gone, I'm kind of looking for a home," Hollands said. "I'm on my way to headquarters to check in with the base commander, but I wanted you to know that I had borrowed one of your mechanics. Private Lynch."

Murray nodded. "Meeting the base commander is easy; he's over here for a briefing. In fact, he's upstairs right now. I'll introduce you to him myself. But what's this about Private Lynch?"

"Well," Hollands explained, "the 9th left one of their fighters behind. A Thunderbolt. Lynch has been working on it this morning, and he was able to get it running. I know borrowing your man without permission isn't exactly by the book, so I wanted to let you know that Lynch's absence from his normal duties was *my* doing."

"Mine too, Captain," Buckner said, as he trotted up behind Hollands.

Hollands turned slightly as his Marine friend came to a stop. "Oh, sorry, Buckner. I didn't see you."

"I can't let you have all the blame for the fun we've been having!"

Hollands turned to the CO and said with a grin, "Captain Murray, this is Lieutenant Buckner. We arrived on the same transport late yesterday afternoon."

Buckner saluted Murray, who returned it. The two shook hands.

"It's nice to meet you Gentlemen," Murray said. "But I've got to get to the briefing."

His eyes widened as he looked beyond them to see the rear of the parked tractor, and tail of the Thunderbolt. He shook his head and called out, "Private Lynch! Front and center! On the double, soldier!"

Skip secured the tractor and ran the few yards to his CO. He stopped and came to attention, snapping a salute, "Yes, sir!"

"Well, Skip, looks like you finally found some work. Think you and a couple of the boys can get that bird checked out, and have her ready to fly in an hour or so?"

"Yes, sir!"

Murray smiled, pleased with the young mechanic's enthusiasm. "Carry on."

With a quick salute, Skip raced back to the tractor, hollering out to three or four fellow mechanics who were within earshot.

Captain Murray turned back to Hollands and Buckner, "Our Aussie coast watchers have sighted five Bettys heading this way."

"How do you know we're their target?" asked Hollands.

"Because the Japs practically own all the other rocks in this sector. If we're not their target—and that's a pretty small 'if'—we'll know within 90 minutes or so. But I'm sure we're it. We'll be going on full alert soon..."

Interrupted by the wail of the siren, the captain added dryly, "Or perhaps right now!"

"If the Japs are headed this way," Buckner interjected, "I should check in with my guys and help out with ground defenses."

"How well do you remember your boot camp, Lieutenant? Your rifle training will come in handy. A few rifles and one .30 caliber machine gun are all the fire power we have available."

"Aren't there any anti-aircraft batteries?" Hollands asked.

Murray's answer was grim. "No! Nor are there any ground troops to speak of. Nothing but mechanics, cooks, and clerks. Nearly every other warm body has been sent up north to reinforce Guadalcanal. No, Gentlemen, we're well beyond short-handed."

"Hell of a way to fight a war," snapped Buckner. With that, the Marine saluted Captain Murray and excused himself to join his unit.

"Come on, Hollands, I'll introduce you to the base commander," Murray said.

As they walked, Murray continued to paint a rather bleak picture of the situation. "The Nips usually stay just out of range. However, a Thunderbolt could really give them something they wouldn't be expecting. Without fighter protection, Hollands, the Nips' bombers would be easy prey."

Pausing for a moment, he asked, "You can fly a Thunderbolt, can't you?"

Hollands nodded. "I've never flown a P-47, but I'm a fast learner, Ben."

He followed Murray up the stairs to a small office area.

Coming out of the bright sun, both men took a few seconds to adjust to the dimly-lit room. Two junior naval officers sat at a small rectangular table listening to the base commander, a short, stocky gentleman with graying hair who stood reading a report. The two Army captains approached the group as the briefing was breaking up.

"Commander Sessions, this is Captain Michael Hollands, Army Air Corps."

As the commander turned to meet them, Hollands came to attention and saluted. "Good morning, sir. Captain Hollands reporting for duty. My orders, sir." He handed a large envelope to Sessions.

Commander Sessions returned the salute. As the two men shook hands, he said, "You, Captain, are a mistake!"

"I beg your pardon, sir?"

"Oh, I don't mean you personally," Session said. "The Army was supposed to send a Captain *Mitchell* Hollings, but for several days they couldn't locate him. I guess your name was close enough for some clerk. You see, Mitch was my nephew..."

"*Was* Sir? I don't understand."

"We were related by marriage," explained the commander. "My sister's daughter's husband. Unfortunately, I was told just this morning that his transport was shot down over three weeks ago—by friendly fire of all things. A nasty accident! Nice young man, too."

Hollands slowly shook his head. "My condolences to you and your family, sir. I think that would be just about the worst way to..."

"Thank you, Captain. I'm sure you know by now that your unit has moved on, although it was never really here all that much. Right now, however, we need to brace ourselves for a short but noisy visit from the Japs. We have no guns and no fighters, but at least those B-17s won't be here as targets."

"Right, sir," Captain Murray acknowledged. "All but one of them. It had engine trouble. But we may have a little surprise for our visitors, sir."

"What in blazes are you talking about, Ben?"

"The 9th left one of their fighters behind, a nearly new Thunderbolt. My mechanics are looking her over right now. We might have her operational and in the air, sir, before the Japs attack."

"Excellent, excellent! I like surprises like that," the commander exclaimed, almost jubilant. "Let's get her in the air, Ben."

He turned to Hollands. "You gonna take her up, son?"

"Yes, sir!"

"Good. I'll take your orders with me to HQ. We'll talk more later. Good luck. And get a couple for me!"

"Yes, sir. I'll give it my best."

As the two captains were preparing to leave, a yeoman came up to the commander and handed him a slip of paper.

After scanning the message, Sessions said, "Damn! Gentlemen, this is a follow-up message from the coast watchers. It looks like there'll be two separate Nip groups, roughly 15 minutes apart. Ten bombers, about five planes per group. And it looks like there's a five-fighter escort! That's the first escort we've seen in weeks."

The three men stood quietly for a moment, and then Commander Sessions said to Hollands softly, "I can't ask any pilot to go up against those kinds of odds. You better grab a bomb shelter with us, son. Sit this one out."

"Thank you, sir," Hollands said. "But it's a beautiful day for flying. If you'll excuse me, I have some work to do, sir."

Hollands saluted the Navy commander, but Sessions stuck out his right hand and the two men shook again.

"Godspeed, Captain."

Hollands exited the building, almost running down the stairs with

Captain Murray right behind trying to keep up.

"Hey, Hollands, slow down a bit."

The pace slowed and Murray commented, "I've known you for less than fifteen minutes, but you've got something cooking, haven't you? Come on, tell me. What gives?"

"You said one of the B-17s was still here."

"That's right. Why?"

"Is it armed?" Hollands asked.

"Of course it is," answered Murray, sounding slightly annoyed.

"Pull the waist guns and ammo, Ben!"

"Huh?"

The two captains stopped, and Hollands looked at Ben and repeated, "Pull the waist guns and haul out any of the others that you can grab quickly. That's four, maybe six—or even *ten*—.50 caliber machine guns and ammo."

Murray grinned. "Excellent idea!"

"If the Japs are sending a fighter escort, they're going to bomb for effect. This isn't going to be another practice run. And I'll bet most of their aircraft will be well under 5,000 feet. That's shootin' distance, Ben! Now, let's find Corporal Lynch."

"Yeah. Yeah! You're right, that *is* shootin' distance! Hey, what do you mean, 'corporal?' Lynch is a private."

Hollands grinned. "Let's see what he's accomplished."

The two men rounded the corner into the open hangar. Inside were close to thirty men busily getting ready for the enemy's attack. Five Army mechanics, plus one Marine lieutenant were swarming over the Thunderbolt.

"Hi, Buckner," Hollands called out. "I thought you were heading to your unit."

"What the hell for? There's nothing to fly, nothing to shoot. Maybe I can help throw rocks. Besides, they're about finished here, I think."

Captain Murray called out, "Private Lynch, where are you?"

A head popped up out of the cockpit. "Oh, Captain. We're nearly finished with the tune-up. Changed the oil. And we have seven of the eight machine guns working. They've been cleaned and loaded. We've taken the other one to our armory to be repaired. We need about an hour, sir, to complete everything and to reinstall the eighth gun."

"Lynch," Murray interjected, "this plane has to be in the air in thirty minutes or less. The Japs are sending ten bombers, and this time there's a fighter escort."

Hollands added soberly, "I need to hit them while they're out over the water."

Climbing out of the cockpit, Skip sat atop the windscreen. He looked around the plane, clearly going through a mental checklist, and then stepped down to the wing and jumped to the concrete floor. There he stopped momentarily, bending to inspect the belly of the plane, all the while mumbling to himself.

Standing up, he turned to quietly confer with a couple of the other men. Then addressing Murray and Hollands, he announced, "Captains—twenty minutes on the taxi lane!"

Hollands and Ben nodded, and Skip went back to work, quietly taking command of the crew.

Turning to Buckner, Hollands asked, "Do you think a U.S. Marine would mind firing a U.S. Army .50 caliber machine gun?"

A little surprised at his question, Buckner said, "It's the same damn weapon in the Marines! Hell, I'd shoot Tojo's weapon if I had it. But Captain Murray here just told us..."

Hollands held up his right hand. "Forget that and listen. The one bomber that was left here was grounded due to engine trouble."

Buckner straightened up. "Say no more, Army. Captain Murray, where is she?"

"Next hangar."

Murray saw his crew chief and called to him, "Sergeant Browne, drop everything. Get eight or ten men with toolboxes, and follow us over to the B-17. Right now, on the double! We're going to pull some of its machine guns."

He raised his voice. "Everyone, listen up. We're going to have a surprise for the Japs this time, men. We'll have a fighter in the air and we'll have some fight here on the ground. We're gonna sting 'em a little."

Everyone let out a cheer and hurried back to work.

Buckner proceeded to enlist the help of his Marine pilots and in a few minutes several of the big bomber's guns had been removed. They were hastily set up outside in strategic positions.

A few minutes later, Skip ran to the next hangar where the parked bomber was located. "Captains, she's ready and eager, sirs! We test-ran the engine. She's gassed up and rarin' for a fight."

Then he hurried back to the hangar.

Murray stuck out his hand to Hollands and said, "Good flying! I hope you know what you're doing."

"Thanks, Ben. So do I! Since I haven't been checked out in the T-Bolts, what can you tell me about them?"

"Well, if you and the plane come back in one piece, we'll call it your check ride," Murray said with a chuckle.

He handed Hollands a stick of chewing gum and a wad of cotton. "The P-47 is a tail-wheel plane," he said. "When you're on the ground, the nose is going to be in the air, right in the middle of your forward field of vision. You're gonna have to do a series of S-turns as you taxi, to give you glimpses of the runway. When you're lined up, don't forget to lock the tail wheel in position. Otherwise, it's going to try to wander on you during takeoff."

"That's good to know," Hollands said. "Anything else?"

Murray nodded. "Remember, that engine has eighteen cylinders and close to 2800 hundred horse power. Don't jam the throttle on full from a standstill."

"Thanks, Ben, I'll try to remember that."

Hollands began to work on the gum as he stuck some of the cotton in his ears. Walking out of the hangar with Murray, Hollands nodded towards Lynch. "*Corporal?*"

Murray nodded back and said, "Maybe!"

The crew had pushed the Thunderbolt out of the hangar. A near miracle had been performed under Skip's supervision. Using a few shortcuts, they had done to that plane in 45 minutes what should have taken hours.

Skip handed Hollands a flight suit, parachute, headgear, and a torn scrap of paper with the word "Sheriff" scrawled in pencil on it.

"Sir, your call sign is 'Sheriff.' The tower is 'Pateroa Control.'"

Hollands smiled as he was helped into the flight suit and parachute. "Damned appropriate, Skip. I feel like the *Lone Ranger* right about now."

"Since you're one gun short, sir, I stuck a camera in that empty hole. Good luck, sir."

"Thanks, Skip. You did a swell job. Tell the others too."

"Yes, sir. I'll tell 'em."

"Don't worry, I'll be back," Holland said. "I like it here. And I'll bring your plane back, just so you'll have something to do."

As Hollands was about to climb up onto the wing, Captain Murray hurried over with a message. "The Japs have been fighting a head wind, Hollands. They're running a little late. By the way, do you play poker?"

"Yeah, a little. Why? Wanna lose some money, Ben?"

With a serious look on his face, Ben answered, "I'd like nothin' better. How about tonight?"

"Sounds good to me!"

This was a different way to wish someone 'good luck,' but that was clearly what Murray was saying. By all rights this could be a short, one-way flight. Hollands probably knew that better than anyone.

Hollands eased into the pilot's seat, and one of the ground crew helped him with the harness. Sitting in the cockpit of the largest single-engine fighter ever made, he took a deep breath. His palms felt sweaty. His mouth and nose were dry. It was the same before each mission he had ever flown. For a split second, he wondered what Seattle's weather was like right then; "*Probably raining,*" he smiled.

The crewman kissed the cross he wore and said, "I'll pray for you—for your safe return, sir."

"Thank you," Hollands acknowledged with a nod.

"Yeah, prayer's good," he said to himself. "I should do more of it. Hope it's not too late."

"Clear!" he hollered.

Skip, who was standing on the ground next to Sergeant Browne, answered back, "Clear, Captain!"

The grounds crew moved off to the side.

Apart from a one-plane recon flight, Hollands had not flown a single-plane mission prior to this. He tested the yoke and pedals, then hit the fuel primer once. Switching on the two magnetos, he quickly ran his eyes over the gauges. Everything checked out okay.

He engaged the starter. The propeller made half a revolution and the huge radial instantly came to life. He looked down at Skip and gave him two thumbs up.

"Pateroa Tower, this is Sheriff. Ready to taxi!"

"Sheriff, this is the tower. You're cleared to takeoff right from your taxi lane. Bogies, fifty miles out, south by southeast. Over."

"Roger and rolling. Sheriff out."

Hollands knew that timing and surprise were essential. He thought, *I know I can take a few of the enemy bombers out before they can...* His mind wouldn't finish the thought.

He released the brakes and slowly moved the throttle forward. The Pratt and Whitney, Double Wasp eighteen-cylinder radial engine took over from there. Within a few yards, the tail came up. Watching and rechecking the gauges while concentrating on the taxiway in front of him, he saw the speed clicking off: 100... 125...

Hollands ran the throttle up to full. The engine responded as expected, and the 'American Girl' seemed to leap off the ground. The lone fighter was airborne.

The tower continued to update the headings and speed of three groups of enemy planes. As Hollands had guessed, the enemy bombers had dropped well below their normal altitude, and according to the radar reports from the tower, they were approaching at three thousand feet.

Bringing up the landing gear, Hollands slowly worked on the flaps and trim. Because the P-47s were new, he wanted to make the most of his first flight. He was truly impressed as he noted how sweetly the plane handled compared to the slower, lighter weight P-40 Warhawk he had been flying. Skip was truly a magician.

"Pateroa, this is Sheriff; climbing to angels-six. Over."

"Roger, Sheriff. Angels-six. Bogies should be in view in two minutes."

"Roger. Sheriff out."

Hollands put his ship into a steep climb and leveled off just short of 6,000 feet. The tower continued to read off headings of the inbound enemy planes. "This is Pateroa; fighters are on our screen. Angels-eight, five miles back of first bomb group."

Following the compass heading from the tower, Hollands hoped to intercept the Japanese bombers long before they crossed the coastline. Then he'd climb higher and hit the fighters.

He spotted two groups of enemy bombers, five aircraft in each group, approaching from five degrees off his port side. They were four miles to the southeast and closing fast.

Hollands radioed his findings and position. He was nearly 3,000 feet above the enemy bombers.

Meanwhile, the men on the ground were readying a surprise of their own. There had been only time enough to remove eight of the machine guns from the grounded B-17 Fortress.

Crude, makeshift tripods to hold the machine guns were quickly fashioned. Four of the emplacements would each have two of these machine-guns, along with four men, an officer or sergeant. All men would trade off firing. In addition, the one .30 caliber machine gun would be set up in a fifth site with two men.

Buckner carried two of the makeshift tripods to his emplacement near the base's southern perimeter several yards southeast of the hangars where sandbags were still stacked in place. His four men stood waiting there with their two assigned machine guns.

"Okay men," Buckner began, "I'm new here, and want your help. So if you know anything about previous attacks—like the direction the enemy is likely to come from—sing out."

Pausing for a moment he asked, "Do we have enough ammo? Do you know how to fire these weapons?"

One of the young men meekly held up a right hand to speak.

"You don't have to do that, Private," Buckner said with a slight smile.

"Besides, I doubt we have much time, so speak up quickly."

"Well, sir," the young man began, "we have plenty of ammo. About five hundred rounds for each weapon. But these guns are different from our basic infantry training, and we ain't never fired anything like this before, sir."

Another soldier piped up, "And Lieutenant, the Japs usually attack from the south, over those huge palm trees."

"Thank you, men. That is the direction we'll watch then," Buckner said. "Quick—let's get these guns set up and stack some sandbags around the legs of the tripods. We'll need those to kneel on."

Then in a deliberate fashion he showed the four men how to load their weapons and where to locate the safety switch. "All right, now; let's make sure these weapons will fire."

Pointing the weapons high over the palms, Buckner ordered, "We'll test fire on 'three.' One... two... three!"

Their weapons simultaneously belched out ten rounds. The four GI's jumped to their feet and cheered.

"Good job, men! Now everyone split up and double time over to the three other gun emplacements and assist as needed. Have the men at the sites test fire a short burst with each weapon. If anyone questions you, tell him it's on my orders. Understood?"

"Yes, sir!" came a chorus of voices.

"Okay; get going, and hurry your butts back here. You've got five minutes."

Closing in fast on the enemy, Hollands flipped off the safety on his seven, working machine guns. At less than a mile from the first group, he rolled his bird over on her back and began his descent in a continuous slow spiral, firing long bursts from his plane's .50s, concentrating on the three lead aircraft. The American Girl shuddered from the vibrations as tracer-rounds found their marks.

Immediately, two bombers started going down, one bursting into flames. The port engine of the third began smoking, then blew apart. The bomber spiraled out of control following its comrades down to the sea.

Hollands had really surprised them. There were no enemy tracers coming toward him. The two remaining Bettys began a 180-degree turn.

Hollands had flown over and beyond the first group, and overshot the second group of bombers. They were now two or three miles behind him.

He needed to angle in on that second group. Putting the American Girl on her back again, Hollands pulled the yoke toward him, making a half-loop to reverse his direction. As the G-force pressed on him, he struggled to remain conscious and focused.

The maneuver worked. At nearly four-hundred-twenty miles per hour, he quickly gained on his quarry's tail feathers. In a slow continuous roll, he began his next attack and unleashed his guns once more as he closed in.

Two ships in the middle of the pack exploded in flaming debris, which, in turn, seriously damaged a third. Engines on two other bombers streamed black smoke as the pilots struggled to turn around.

"Pateroa Control, this is Sheriff, going to angels-ten. Over," Hollands radioed.

"Roger, Sheriff," acknowledged the tower. "Angels-ten. Adjust heading fifteen degrees east. Bogies at five miles."

Banking hard to port, Hollands headed for the fighters.

"There they are," Hollands said to his plane. "They're Tonys. No match for you, sweetheart."

Circling down behind them, Hollands closed to within five hundred yards, but they spotted him and broke formation. Kicking his rudder pedals left and right to cause his aircraft to yaw back and forth, he put his first burst into two of the enemy fighters as they made a starboard turn.

One went down in flames and another turned away, smoking badly. Hollands watched as the two pilots bailed out of their crippled birds. A third fighter dove for the watery deck, executing a turn to retreat south.

Hollands surveyed the sky for other enemy aircraft and saw the two remaining fighters coming in on his right two miles away. Moving the throttle to full, he brought his fighter's nose up sharply. The two enemy planes passed beneath and made a sharp turn south.

Hollands pursued them for a few miles, and he fired a couple of short bursts at them to make sure they kept going. He was surprised when he observed one of the Tonys emitting irregular puffs of black smoke. He hadn't realized that he'd gotten a hit.

"Pateroa Tower, this is Sheriff. Over."

"This is the tower, Sheriff. Go ahead. Over."

"What is the status on the ground? Over."

"Two bombers got through," began the tower, "but were shot down by our ground fire and crashed on the runway. No bombs loosed. Well done, Sheriff. Well done. Bring your bird back to the nest."

As Hollands flew over Pateroa base, he could see the wreckage of the two downed enemy bombers strewn over part of the airfield, but—as the tower had reported—there was no damage to the runways.

Making a wide turn, Hollands lowered the wheels and safely touched down. It had definitely been a successful morning!

The men were jubilant and cheered as Hollands taxied the fighter over to the hangar area and parked. The engine fell silent.

Buckner was the first one over to him, asking, "Hollands, are you all right?"

Hollands jumped to the ground and said, "Yeah, I'm fine." Assessing the plane, he said softly to himself, "*Nice going, Lady. Nice going.*"

"This is one sweet bird," he said to Buckner. "You oughta get one of these for yourself."

He rubbed his ears and smiled. "Sure glad I had the chewing gum, and the cotton. By the way, it looks like everyone was busy here on the ground!"

"I guess you could say that," agreed Buckner, looking around at the debris on the field. "But I'd much rather have been up in the sky with you."

Two grounds crewmen placed chocks at the Thunderbolt's wheels and then stood up, looking at Hollands with respect. One gestured to the burning enemy wreckage, "Those are the best Japs, sir. Dead ones!" His friend grinned in agreement.

Moving between the two, Hollands placed an arm around each one. Taking a deep breath, he solemnly said to the two young soldiers, "There are parents, wives, and children who will cry and mourn their loss. I went to college to learn engineering, but also to teach—perhaps high school. And those men lying in the wreckage out there, a few years ago, may have been students, artists, or teachers. Who knows? But *they're* not the true enemy. They're only instruments of their government—just as we are."

Both men stood quietly, their smiles gone.

Then Hollands gently added, "We are in a war neither you nor I wanted, or started. It is right for us to defend ourselves, our way of life, and our country the best we can."

"Thank you, Captain," one of the young men said softly. "One of my high school buddies back home is Japanese. Think I'll write him and his family a letter."

As the two young soldiers slowly walked away, Buckner and Hollands moved in the direction of the hangar. "I never thought of that before," Buckner said thoughtfully as he helped relieve Hollands of his parachute.

"What's that?" Hollands asked.

"What you told those two," Buckner said. "It's the governments who are at war. We're just the chess pieces, aren't we?"

A large group of military personnel accompanied Commander Sessions and Captain Murray as they hurried out to meet Hollands. Sessions and Murray shook hands with the airman, congratulating him for an extraordinary job. The commander then whispered something to Murray. Captain Murray quickly called out, "Everyone, quiet please. Fall in at-ease."

Sessions took a couple of steps forward and said, "I have something to say and I want you all to hear it. Captain Michael Hollands' travel orders were in error. He arrived here yesterday by mistake, and I thank God he's here. And I hope to keep him around for a while. Because of his leadership and fortitude we have finally put up a fight." Sessions shook Hollands' hand and said warmly, "The men on this base thank you. Great flying! Great shooting!"

The commander stood and faced the formation. "The Japanese will not soon forget this day. We have given them a poke in the eye and bloody nose. They *will* be back, and in force—tomorrow, next week, or next month—we don't know. But we have put them on notice that the military establishment of the United States of America—the Navy, the Marines, the Army, and the Coast Guard, all working together as one—will not go down, will not give up. The enemy is in for a fight! So, let's be ready to welcome them again in the same manner. That's all for now; let's get back to work."

A loud cheer erupted from all as the group dispersed.

CHAPTER 3

Counter Punch

"Captain Hollands, Captain Hollands. Sir, you're wanted in the officers' mess, on the double."

Shortly after the successful repulse of the Japanese attack on Pateroa, Commander Sessions had instructed the clerk to move Captain Hollands' gear into the naval officers' quarters which were situated on a slight ridge behind base headquarters. One lone taxi-lane led up to the front of HQ. The main airfield and maintenance hangars were directly south, a half a mile away.

Bedded down in his new location, Hollands peeked out from under his pillow to see a seaman third class standing near the bunk. "I'm Pruitt, sir, headquarters clerk. We met yesterday."

Rubbing his eyes, Hollands struggled to sit up and then asked, "What time is it, Seaman?"

"Zero six-thirty, sir."

"My compliments to Commander Sessions. Please inform him I'll be there in fifteen minutes."

"Aye, aye, sir."

Hollands couldn't remember the last time he had slept so soundly. As he sat on the edge of his bunk for a moment he grumbled, *"How can anyone be that energetic so early in the morning?"*

Hollands groggily gathered up his uniform and toiletries and headed for the showers.

Sixteen minutes later, Hollands entered the officers' mess. Buckner left his seat and hurried over to meet his new comrade, blurting out excitedly, "You won't believe what's been reported over the Nips' radio this morning."

Hollands addressed the commander. "Good morning, sir. Sorry to be late. May I ask what's going on?"

"CinCPac is livid. Pleased and confused, but livid," gloated Commander Sessions. He and Murray were seated at the table.

Across from the CO were two additional naval officers, an ensign, and a lieutenant junior grade. Except for this group, the mess hall was nearly empty.

Sessions introduced the two Navy officers to the rest of the group. After basic greetings were exchanged, the commander, who was about to burst with excitement, said to the ensign, "Tell them what Tokyo Rose had to say about yesterday's actions, and what's being reported via Japanese military radio."

The ensign took a sheet of paper from a file folder, saying "Thank you, sir." He glanced first toward Hollands, and then around the table. "Captain Hollands, this isn't exactly verbatim, but it's close. According to 'Rosie,' here are the results of your skirmish late yesterday morning. Their Zeros shot down eight of our fifteen fighters, while their own losses were three fighters and one bomber. She says that—because the Americans were overwhelmed by the large number of superior aircraft from the Imperial Japanese Navy—the Americans wisely retreated. Oh! And apparently, Pateroa base was destroyed, and several hundred ground troops were killed."

As the ensign was ending his report, the steward served Hollands some coffee, a plate of something resembling ham, and slightly green scrambled eggs. Hollands nodded his thanks to the steward and quickly reached for the coffee.

Sessions, still grinning, asked the lieutenant about the communiqués he had received late into the night and early morning from CinCPac.

"Well, sir..." The naval officer paused for a moment, trying to figure out which of the two reports he should read first.

"It's all so... unbelievable," he said looking at Hollands. "Oh hell, sir, I'll read this one first. It's from Army Air Corps Major Franks, CO of the 9th Fighter Squadron stationed on the Russells. He wants to know where we came up with fifteen of anything resembling airplanes, let alone fighters. Then he states, 'I hope no one tried to fly the one we left behind!' Evidently, their crew chief had reported that the engine was bad, and beyond repair."

Pausing to take a sip of his coffee, the lieutenant referred to the second paper. "This is a personal note from Admiral Walker, CinCPac, Pearl. It reads in part, 'To Commander Sessions:' etcetera, etcetera. 'Congratulations to you and your men for the good work in repulsing the enemy attack. Please forward to my office the squadron designation. Sorry for the damages. We'll try to get help to you soon. P.S. When and where did you get fifteen fighters and the several hundred ground troops?'"

Amidst low laughter, Commander Sessions slowly rose from his chair. "That will be all, Lieutenant. Thank you."

Relighting his cigar, the commander said reflectively, "There's more, but in my twenty-five combined years in the active Navy and the reserves, I have never been so profoundly proud of so few. I sound a little like Churchill, I guess. However, other than telling the Navy brass this morning that we are really okay, I haven't figured out what in blazes I am going to put in my report to Pearl. What happened yesterday was the result of one man—an Army Air Corps pilot—Captain Michael Hollands. He had the foresight to determine what *should* be done; the initiative to do with courage what *could* be done, and the true American spirit to say, 'screw all the military manuals' to do what *must* be done. He did the impossible, and caught the enemy flat-footed."

Hollands was stunned and red-faced as Sessions concluded his remarks with, "God bless you, Captain Hollands, for what you did, not only in breaking up the Jap attack, but also in helping all here to achieve a measure of pride in ourselves. You gave us a much needed boost in morale. You planted a good right cross on the chin of the enemy. You've also put me between a rock and hard place with about a half-dozen admirals—for which, I must admit, I'm most grateful."

Sessions was quiet for a moment before he continued. "It would be easy to glory in this one achievement, and to say that the Japanese are not very smart. Well, we'd better not underestimate them, because they're an intelligent and aggressive foe. We all know that from their attack on Pearl Harbor nearly sixteen months ago. We have a long way to go before this war is resolved."

Still standing, the commander prepared to leave and motioned for the two naval officers to join him. Hollands, Murray, and Buckner stood up until the commander was some distance from the table, then sat back down.

Somewhat stunned, Hollands said softly, "We were all a little busy yesterday."

Buckner raised his coffee cup in a salute to Hollands as he answered, "That's right, but it was you, Army, that got everyone here out from hiding. It was you and your quick thinking." Then with a smirk, he suggested, "Of course, those of us who really know you will realize it was just a bit of luck, but your secret's safe with us."

Hollands refilled the mugs from the coffee urn on the table and said quietly, "Fifteen fighters, eh? Amazing!"

Murray, who had been rather quiet through all this, stroked his chin, adding, "You know, Hollands, after I heard the message from Franks about the condition of your airplane, I had a little talk—no, I had a *long, serious* talk, with Corporal Lynch and Sergeant Browne as to what the mechanics had done to get that plane ready and in such short time."

Taking a big swig of warmed-up coffee, Murray continued, "Lynch was emphatic, as was Browne. At first, no one could find the log. But after wheeling the plane inside the hangar, one of the other mechanics found the log stuffed under and behind the seat. Lynch and Browne showed it to me. The clipboard was missing and since the sheets of paper were wrinkled and oil-smudged, it was pretty hard to read. There were only three entries! The plane was nearly new; it had flown only a few hours, and it showed *no* shop time. All that Lynch and the crew did was to pull a basic service and tune-up. Oh, and they replaced a short piece of damaged control cable."

Murray slowly shook his head. "We didn't have much contact with the 9th because they had their own mechanics, but this is damn serious. I need to send a copy of my report to Major Franks. Someone's head is going to roll."

Later as the three officers exited the building, Hollands asked, "Ben, did I hear you say 'Corporal Lynch?'"

The two men smiled at each other. Captain Murray offered, "Want a ride over to the hangar? We may have the film from your flight ready soon."

"Thanks, Ben, but I need to stop in and see the CO again. I'll come by later."

As Murray and Buckner drove off in the jeep, Hollands headed next door to Sessions' office. The clerk was sitting at his desk near the main entrance. The XO's office was first on the right and Sessions' office was straight back. Hollands had not met the executive officer because the man had become ill and had been flown to Pearl for medical treatment.

"Good morning again, Captain," the clerk said. "I'll tell the commander you're here, sir."

"Thank you, Seaman."

A few seconds later, Sessions hollered out, "Hollands! Glad you stopped by. Come on in."

"Sir, sorry to barge in like this, but I'm a little confused as to my status here."

"Don't blame you for wondering. Unfortunately—or fortunately for *me*—Major Franks says he has all the pilots and planes he needs right now. And because of the number of Japanese planes in the air in his sector, I can't risk a transport flight to deliver your friend Lieutenant Buckner and his Marines buddies to their respective duty stations."

"Is there any air support or recon I could fly, sir?"

"No, not at this time."

"There must be something I can do, sir. I can't just sit around."

"Hollands, I know how you must feel. But I don't have an answer."

Hollands paced in front of the Navy commander's desk, first staring at the floor and then at the ceiling. Then an idea popped into Hollands' head.

"Sir, counting myself and the Marines, you have at least four, maybe five fighter pilots on your hands, but no aircraft. And there probably won't be any in the foreseeable future."

Looking up at Hollands, Sessions nodded and asked, "What's on your mind, son?"

"Well, sir, I was thinking. Our one plane could pull double or triple duty. This may sound really crazy, but *what if*," Captain Hollands explained, "the Thunderbolt could first, and most important, give the other pilots some much needed flight time? *What if* we could fool the Japanese into believing that there really are several planes here?"

"Well, you've got the '*what ifs*' working for you," Sessions reasoned. "Go ahead, I'm listening."

"By changing the insignias from Army to Navy to Marines, and even to the Coast Guard for each flight, the Nips would be more than confused. At least for a while."

Hollands paused to think. "Each of us could fly a regular one or two hour patrol close in, then land, refuel, change pilots and markings, and take to the sky again. Granted, sir, most Nip pilots are probably as familiar with our various aircraft as we are with theirs, but since the T-bolts are new, sir, the Japanese aren't going to know if they're common in all four services. The enemy will just see four different planes. Perhaps they'll believe some of their own propaganda."

Sessions was now rubbing his chin, "Not bad, not bad. It could keep them from getting in too close, even if only for a few days. What about their own recon flights? The Jap pilots are going to take photos of an empty air field."

Hollands chuckled as a large grin appeared on his face.

"What do you find that's so amusing, Captain?"

"Well, sir," Hollands explained, trying to contain his laughter. "Picture, if you will, our U.S. Army Air Corps plane being spotted and photographed a hundred fifty miles south of here, and two or three hours later the same Nip recon flight spots another Thunderbolt sporting the Coast Guard markings two hundred miles northwest of Pateroa. Other Nip flights could report similar aircraft from our Navy and Marines."

"It would probably drive em a bit daft," Sessions agreed.

"Now, sir, about the enemy's recon flights over *this* base. I've given that some thought as well. When the transport I was on the day before yesterday approached your airfield, sir, I could see old wreckage of planes—ours and theirs—scattered around the base-perimeter. If we could stand them up in a line near the taxiway of the field and throw some canvas over 'em... Hell, from twenty-five thousand feet, we'd look damn busy. The Germans and Italians sometimes painted pictures of planes on their runways and did mock-ups of planes and buildings. It fooled us a few times. But this ploy might buy us—buy *you*, sir, more time in which to get a squadron of Hellcats or Corsairs in here."

Right then, the clerk entered the open office doorway, "Excuse me, Commander; Captain Murray's on the phone."

Sessions nodded to his clerk, and, as he picked up the receiver, said to Hollands, "Excuse me, Captain... Commander Sessions here. Yes, he's here, too. Good idea, Ben. Thanks, we'll be right over."

Hanging up the phone, Sessions looked over at Hollands who had just taken a seat, "Well, Captain, let's go to the movies."

"Movies, sir?"

"Captain Murray said the film of your flight is ready. Let's go see just what kind of a pilot you really are. You drive."

"Yes, sir."

Skip was waiting in front of the hangar when Sessions and Holland drove up. Saluting, he offered, "Good morning, sirs. We have the projector set up in the office. Follow me please."

"Thank you, Corporal. Lead the way," the commander nodded.

As the three started their walk across the floor of the hangar, Sessions said, "Hey, congratulations! When did you get that second stripe, son?"

"Thank you, sir. Captain Murray promoted me yesterday just after the raid—I think with the help of Captain Hollands. I'm only an *acting* corporal until brigade approves it."

Hollands had a slight smile on his face as he said, "Skip, you only got what you deserve, and you can take that any way you want. But it was you who put that plane in the air yesterday. I just held on for dear life."

As Sessions entered the room, someone called, "*Atten-hut!*" and everyone stood up.

Sessions calmly responded, "As you were!"

Hollands looked quickly around the room and spotted Buckner, the other marine pilots, and their CO, Major Jeff Hanks.

As they waited for the film to be threaded, the Commander re-lit his well-chewed, soggy stogie.

Sergeant Browne was doing the honors of running the projector. "Sorry, gents," Browne joked. "There will be no cartoons or popcorn. Lights, please."

Except for a few thin shafts of sunlight coming through the window coverings, the room fell dark. Little blurry numbers running backwards lit up the screen as Browne brought the picture into focus.

"The camera installed in Hollands' plane, sir," began the sergeant, "had been set up to run continuously as soon as the engine was started. So the first few moments you will see the taxiway and takeoff. We've edited out a lot of blue sky."

Hollands found it strange to review the beginning of his flight in this detached setting. With a few slight turns of the plane, the enemy bombers came into sight. Then the view inverted as the fighter rolled onto its back, entering into a slow corkscrew and dropping down to engage the enemy. The picture blurred from the reverberations of the machine guns. It was an excellent view of the fight. The plane did two or three continuous slow rolls while all the guns fired their long bursts, sending tracers toward their targets.

"Sergeant, stop the film for a moment," ordered Sessions. "Good Lord, that makes me dizzy!"

He turned to Hollands. "I'm not a pilot, but where in the world did you learn such a maneuver, Captain?"

"Well, sir, I was thinking as I was climbing to altitude how to multiply one plane's fire-power, especially since I was one gun short."

Hollands paused, and scratched his head. "The two outside guns are nearly thirty feet apart. In doing a slow roll, I figured to increase my field of fire by creating a circle of fire thirty feet around. It probably made me a harder target for the enemy to sight in on too. In truth, sir, I just made it up."

"I'm going to forward a copy of this film to the Navy and to the Army Air."

"Thank you, sir."

As the film rolled on, Sessions was able to ascertain that Hollands had shot down six enemy planes for sure and damaged three or four others.

"It'll be hard without a squadron designation," Sessions said. "But I'll confirm those kills for you, Hollands. There's no doubt in my mind."

When the lights came on again, Sessions walked over to the lone window at the rear of the little room. Opening the gunnysack curtain he saw two old hulks of what were once proud P-40s. "Captain Murray," Sessions called out.

"Yes, Commander."

"I want every available man on this rock to turn-to, and collect all the wrecked planes possible from along the base perimeter. From twenty to thirty thousand feet I want them to appear as clean and air-worthy as possible."

He puffed on his cigar for a moment. "That B-17 in the hangar... Is there anyone on base qualified to fly it?"

"Yes, sir, I am," answered Murray.

"Good. Is she ready to fly?"

"I plan on flight-testing her early tomorrow morning, sir."

"Excellent! Tell the Army that their bomber won't be ready for a week or two. I think there is a parts shortage. Hollands will fly escort on your test flight. He'll explain the rest of his—ah, *our* plan."

"Hollands, I'll drive myself back. If you guys need anything, you let me know. I'll borrow it, buy it, or you guys can steal it."

"Yes, sir!"

"And Gentlemen, I want those old planes sitting on the line by tomorrow noon." As he walked out of the office, Sessions added, "Work all night if necessary."

"Yes, sir," responded both officers.

Murray turned to Hollands. "What the hell's going on? What's got into the ol' man's shorts?"

"Ben, you said you like to play poker. Well, we're simply going to deal the Japs in. But we'll need the best poker faces we can muster."

"You mean all that old junk?"

"Absolutely! Hell, it'll look awfully impressive from five miles up."

"Now I get it!" Ben said enthusiastically.

He turned to Sergeant Browne and Skip. "Move out, men. Take the deuce-and-a-half around the island. Pick up every available man."

Within an hour, Skip returned with a work force of twenty men. They quickly got busy with picks and shovels, digging out old planes long embedded in the sandy clay of the island. They used the winch from the deuce-and-a-half to haul out the downed war birds and drag them to the grassy median that paralleled the runways a few yards in front of the hangars. Many of the planes had been stripped and cannibalized and most didn't have much of an undercarriage left, so the men rested them on blocks or sawhorses before covering them with tarpaulins.

The next morning at 0800, Hollands sat in the cockpit of the Thunderbolt, warming up the engine and testing the controls. Two runways over, with a three-man crew, Ben was in the pilot's seat of the big bomber checking out her four engines. Buckner was in the co-pilot's seat, and Sergeant Browne was sitting at the navigator's table. Generally a repaired engine was simply tested on the ground, but Ben, a former bomber pilot, loved to fly. Although at thirty-two he was considered too old, now he got to play in the clouds and to thumb his nose at the brass at the same time.

Ben took off first and Hollands followed three minutes later. Once airborne, Hollands radioed in. "Tower Control, this is escort Papa Four Seven. Over."

"Papa Four Seven, this is Tower Control. Over."

"Control, Papa Four Seven. Group climbing to angels two-zero. Over."

"Roger, Papa Four Seven. Angels two-zero."

Hollands and Ben rendezvoused about ten miles south of the field. It was a clear, warm morning.

"How's she running, Ben?" Hollands radioed.

"She's doin' just fine, Hollands. It's sure nice to be up here."

"I know that feeling too. Hardly seems to be a war going on."

After a few minutes of pleasure flying, Hollands got a call from the tower, "Papa Four Seven, this is Tower Control. Single bogie, twenty miles southeast, your position. Speed 200 at angels two-five. Over."

"Roger, Tower."

Taking a quick look over his shoulder at the large Fortress, Hollands called, "Ben, did you copy?"

"Roger, Hollands. I'm heading for the barn."

"Negative. Climb to angels three-zero. Let this clown see us."

"Hollands, I'll be a sittin' duck up here. We haven't reinstalled the machine guns."

"Trust me, Ben. He's out sightseeing with his new Kodak. Let him take our pictures. After that, he'll turn tail. Besides, I'm curious what their radio report will be later on today. Pretend you are part of a bomber command on the radio. I'll do the same as fighter command. Tower Control, did you copy?"

"Roger, we copy."

"What's an open frequency that the bogie might hear us on?" Hollands requested.

"Papa Four Seven, you are Blue Leader; Bravo-one-seven, you are Red Rover. Change radio to niner-zero point seven. Over."

Hollands and Ben acknowledged the tower as they climbed to their newly assigned altitude. The two pilots engaged in some creative radio chatter as they continued to fly southeast to intercept the Japanese aircraft. Hollands switched his radio back to its original setting for a brief moment, "Tower control, Papa Four Seven. Any change in bogie status? Over."

"Captain Hollands, you're right on top of him."

Hollands switched the radio back, "Blue Leader to Red Rover. We have a streak just below us. Over.

"Roger Blue Leader. I see him. Over."

There it was, a bright shiny Zero. The pilot had seen the bomber all right. Hollands rolled his plane over on its back, and started his shallow dive. The enemy pilot was so engrossed in watching the Fortress he had failed to see Hollands' Thunderbolt. Hollands buzzed the Zeke close and fast, blindsiding the pilot, just yards away from the enemy plane's open canopy. The startled Japanese pilot quickly went into a dive and reversed his direction.

Hollands switched his radio back to the normal channel. "Pateroa Tower, I think the bogie thought he had seen the boogieman. He sure high-tailed it out of here."

"Red Rover, this is Pateroa Tower. Your bogie's gone home. There's no other traffic. You are cleared for a straight-in approach at your convenience, runway two. Over."

"This is Red Rover. Roger Tower. Runway two. On my way down. Over."

This little game paid off. By four that afternoon Japanese intercepts were stating that the Pateroa base had twenty B-17s, and as many fighters. The Japanese put a lid on the pot with an early morning recon two days later when they took photos of the mock-ups; their communiqués demonstrated their conviction that a sizable force was now operating from the island.

Over the next ten days, Hollands and the Marine pilots took turns putting up the Thunderbolt, a plane better known as the Jug, due to its milk-bottle shape. Ben got to play with the bomber a few more times as well.

On a gray morning around 0500, Hollands was jolted from sleep by the unmistakable sound of radial engines. "Aircraft coming in low and slow over HQ," he whispered.

Although only half awake, Hollands' first thought was, "Could it be a Japanese raid?" But there was no siren alerting the base and he dashed to his window. From the early dawn light he counted five aircraft passing overhead, preparing to land.

Perhaps the Navy was stopping to refuel. No. It was too early for that.

Shortly after the initial five aircraft passed over, he heard the sound of a twin-engine airplane, motors running at almost idle, as it passed overhead at rooftop level. He wondered if it might be a transport.

It was a little past dawn now and Hollands could clearly make out the twin-engine plane as it touched down. "A PBY," he muttered to himself. Then looking up the taxiway, he saw something that every little boy wishes for.

"Judas Priest," he shouted. "Look at those Corsairs—sonofabitch—five beautiful Corsairs!"

Hollands was now definitely awake. He found his clothes and dressed hurriedly. Dashing outside, shirttail flapping in the breeze, he ran down the hill to meet the pilots and to find out what they were doing there. He had hopes. Oh, did he have hopes! Might these planes be staying?

Halfway across the open grassy field, a jeep pulled up next to him, "Jump in, Captain."

It was Commander Sessions dressed only in his skivvies and a bathrobe. The clerk who was driving had managed to pull on trousers and a T-shirt. But this could be an important event, and there was little time for formality.

By the time the reception committee arrived, all the aircraft including the huge floatplane, or PBY, were parked in a neat row in front of the hangar, engines at rest. A Marine lieutenant colonel exited the passenger compartment of the PBY and began to assemble his pilots and collect their logbooks.

The jeep halted in front of the officer of the newly arrived group. Grinning from ear to ear, Sessions slowly climbed out and said, "Colonel, I'm Commander Sessions, commanding officer. What is all this?"

"Good morning, Commander," began the Marine officer. "I'm Lieutenant Colonel Miller. Someone in Halsey's command sent a message to me last evening that I was to ferry five F4Us to this base."

He glanced around at the mock-ups and standing junk. "These are to help replace the planes you lost a few days back."

He shook his head. "Sure looks like you can use them, Commander."

Like a child with a new toy, or a soldier suddenly given a weapon and some hope, Sessions turned and slowly walked down the line of the five, almost-new war birds.

Spotting pilot wings on Hollands' shirt, the colonel said, "Hi, Captain, I'm Joe Miller, Flight Officer for Halsey. What's your name, and what the hell's been going on here?"

Hollands saluted and then stuck out his hand. "Captain Hollands, Colonel, and we have been playing one huge bluff. Come on, sir, I'll show you."

The two officers walked a few yards to the first hangar, and Hollands slid the door open partway. Pointing into the cavernous darkness to the two shadowy figures of the B-17 and the P-47 parked within, Hollands explained, "This has been our only air defense since I arrived here two weeks ago—these two and the junk we've assembled on the ground."

"You've been flying just one fighter? Can't be!"

"That's correct, just one," Hollands explained. "The last ten days or so, four of us have been taking turns with this one fighter, changing colors and service designations, with an occasional appearance of our one-and-only 'Fortress Bomber Group.' The only reason we've gotten away with it so far is that we've surprised the Japs. In the past, their bombing runs against this island have gone unopposed."

Grimacing slightly, the colonel said, "I know the Japs exaggerate. Hell, we do too. We heard about your little skirmish via enemy intercepts. That was just short of a miracle. You all may be up for sainthood."

"Well, maybe not sainthood, Colonel, but I'd sure settle for these five planes you brought us. Now perhaps we can fly real patrols. And with these Corsairs and my Thunderbolt we could take a little of the fight to the enemy, and help to keep them away from this base."

"Well, you'll also have an extra pilot," Miller said. "Second Lieutenant Tony Pagnaro will be TDY for a while. He is fresh out of flight school and he *knows* Corsairs."

"We can sure use him. Some of the boys haven't flown a Corsair yet, or even seen one. He'll be a big help."

"But, Captain, you can't go out on your own and attack the Japanese! You don't have any authorization or even a squadron designation."

"Colonel, we don't even exist, except in the fertile minds of the Japanese—and now CinCPac."

"Point well made, Captain; point well made."

The Colonel's eyes scanned the hangar. "Well, I'm not going to say anything about this operation. Who are your other pilots?"

"Four marines who, like me, are stuck here because of some paperwork snafu."

"Sweet heavens! Talk about inter-service foul-ups. Don't worry, Hollands, your secret is safe with me. Damn! No one back at command would believe such a report anyway."

Then Hollands asked, "Do you and your men want to stay for chow, Colonel?"

"Yeah! Think we will. Thanks. And call me Joe."

The colonel sighed. "Even though I'm seeing this, I don't believe it!"

Hollands and the colonel continued to chat as they walked back toward the rest of the group. Skip had shown up with Lieutenant Buckner in a second jeep. Everyone piled into the two jeeps and while names were being exchanged, headed for the Navy's mess. The mood on the field had improved noticeably.

At 0700 Hollands, Buckner, and Skip stood and watched as the PBY slowly lifted off into the rising sun.

"If those birds are ready for it, Skip," began Hollands, "at 0900 we're going flying. Buckner, the Marines left you a pilot, Lieutenant Tony Pagnaro. The colonel told me that the guy's really hot on the Corsair. He should be a lot of help. You and your guys need to get used to the Corsairs, and fast. Get with him. Put him to work. Let's find out what he knows, and what he can teach us."

"I'll get right on it, Mike."

Then looking over at Skip, Hollands said, "So how 'bout it Corporal? Can you get these birds checked out in time?"

"I'll check with Captain Murray and Sergeant Browne," Skip said. "We'll get a crew on it right away, sir."

"The initial check flights went really well," Marine Major Hanks began jokingly. "No one crashed! You know, Mike, it was good that my men got to practice in your bird over the past two weeks."

"I'm glad to hear that, Jeff. Tell the men we might be going on a trip soon," Hollands said. "Sessions and I will be talking later today."

Hollands had to contain his enthusiasm as he went into HQ to meet with Sessions.

Nobody on base doubted that the commander would like nothing better than to take advantage of the Corsairs and go after the Japanese for a change.

Hollands had been working on a plan and hoped to sell Sessions on it. However, the meeting was not going well.

"But Commander," Hollands said, "from what your Navy weathermen tell me, we have a front moving in that already has the Japanese grounded. If we hit that base 400 miles south of here, we could destroy their aircraft on the ground, get a shot at their fuel depot, and drop some five hundred pounders on their airstrip. It could be weeks—perhaps months—before they could recover and be operational again, sir."

Sessions was quiet for a moment. "I like your plan, Hollands. It's a damned good idea. It's just too dangerous. You've got a weather front coming in, plus you haven't flown with these men, and they hadn't flown these planes before this morning."

"Yes, sir, that's true, alright," agreed Hollands. "But Major Hanks would be going too, and he says that flying my Jug has helped the men to be ready for the Corsairs. War is dangerous, but *waiting* for a little more training or a little better weather is the real danger, sir. You know the Japs could take a chance and send us some airmail first. They might just be a little pissed off right about now. With all due respect, sir, we do need to act first."

Hollands paused for a moment. "If we can cut their capabilities on that small base, they'll have to draw strength elsewhere for a long time, sir. It might even slow down the new base they're building east of here."

Sessions countered, "If the enemy's planes are grounded because of weather, what makes you think you can do this?"

"Simple, sir! Our heavier Corsairs and the big Thunderbolt can fly in these windy conditions where the lighter Zeros can't. Besides, we're not going to be there long. We'll just surprise the hell out of them and mess up their airfield a little. If we can catch the enemy still in the sack, we'll do okay."

"Do you have any idea how lonely Leavenworth Prison can be if you're wrong?" Session asked solemnly. "Command will nail our collective hides to the bulkhead, son."

"Sir, you can tell the brass hats that I disobeyed your direct orders to stand down," Hollands said. "If I get back, and I'm confident that I will, I'll take the heat."

"You really feel that strongly about it, Hollands?"

"Yes, sir! I do."

The next morning found the weather around Pateroa improved though it was unchanged over the Japanese base 400 miles to the south. At 0300, the winds had calmed to twenty knots and it was still raining lightly. The six American pilots crowded into the tiny makeshift ready room at the base of the tower for their briefing with Captain Michael Hollands. Commander Sessions stood off to the side as Hollands summarized the plan.

"Okay, one more time," Hollands began again. "Because of the weather, it is going to be extremely important to *stay with your wingman*, and in visual contact with the others at all times. Watch your clocks and stay in a tight formation to the target and back. You all have the compass headings. The Navy's weather chart has cleared us for an altitude of twenty-five thousand. At seventy-five miles out from target, we'll drop down on the deck to 300 feet above the waves. We'll probably have some severe wind gusts as we approach the target, so we'll have to play with the flaps, trim, and power."

Hollands looked around. "Any questions?"

There was no response.

Hollands turned to Hanks. "Major, do you have anything you wish to add?"

"Only this." Hanks turned to the other pilots, "We are flying as a group.

It's not an Army, a Marine, or a Navy operation. We are six excellently trained US military fliers on a mission to hit the enemy. Don't second-guess anything! You follow the instructions Captain Hollands has laid out, and we'll all be back for lunch telling lies."

He nodded toward Hollands. "That's all I have, Captain."

Hollands returned the nod. "Okay, Gentlemen, it's 0320. Chow in fifteen minutes; flight line in forty minutes. And, for anyone who wishes, I have asked the chaplain to say a few words. That's all. You're dismissed."

The mood was good, the spirits high. Skip and his men had the six fighters waiting on the flight line. As the pilots climbed into their birds, the ground crew assisted with buckling each man's harness. Then Hollands gave the signal to start engines.

It was 0405 when Hollands radioed, "Pateroa Tower, this is Deputy One. Posse is ready to taxi. Over."

Although the Marine major outranked Hollands, Hanks was happy to be second in command. This was Hollands' mission; he had planned it and had argued and fought hard for this flight. And Hanks knew as well as anyone just how important this flight was.

The tower had the group taxi in preparation for takeoff. Each of the pilots ran his engine up checking clocks and controls.

"Deputy One. This is Tower Control. You and your posse are cleared for takeoff. Wind gusts from south to north across runway, twelve knots. Use runways two and four, with one-minute intervals. Over."

"Roger, Deputy One, out."

The war was finally on. The pilots, ground crew, and others on the base were no longer waiting for the enemy; they were going calling. All aircraft were heavy with ordnance and fuel, making the controls sluggish and slow. Commander Sessions watched from the front door of HQ. As the last aircraft lifted into the murky dawn he whispered, "Godspeed, boys!"

"Deputy One to Posse. We are over rendezvous, Point Zebra. Close up tight. Assigned altitude. Up we go!" Hollands radioed. Because of their loads, the fighters took extra time to reach twenty-five thousand feet. But everyone was relieved to find the weather much improved at that altitude.

The formation was shaped like an arrowhead: Hollands' Thunderbolt at the point, two Corsairs each on the left and on the right, and the last Corsair centered directly behind the lead plane.

Flying south, Hollands adjusted his compass heading. "Okay, radio silence from here on. Use hand signals, or your signal lights. Check your instruments. If anyone has a malfunction, signal, drop out, and head back to base. Out!"

The group's cruising speed was 240 miles per hour. Pateroa Tower continued to issue weather updates pertaining to the target area but using different island names to throw off Japanese radiomen if they were monitoring.

Seventy-five miles from target, Hollands rocked his bird, and using hand signals to the others, pointed downward. He throttled back and, adjusting the flaps, he put the Thunderbolt's nose down. Descending through heavy clouds, the Posse leveled off at three hundred feet above the water and flew right into pounding rain and gusting winds. Hollands smiled as he increased power and adjusted the flaps and trim. How glad he was for the heavier fighters. This weather would ensure that the Japanese aircraft would stay on the ground. The enemy just might be caught off guard.

At two miles out from the island, Hollands could barely see the coastline. The group climbed to their bombing altitude of two thousand feet. He glanced at his watch. It was 0643. He pressed his mike button and said, "Deputy One to Posse, arm your bombs. I say again: arm your bombs and drop fuel tanks."

Reports from an Aussie coast watcher had placed the Jap airfield two miles inland. One minute after Hollands' group leveled out, the airfield became visible.

"Captain," crackled a voice in everyone's headphones. "Look at all those planes parked! Zeros! Bettys! We caught 'em in the sack!"

"All right," Hollands said. "This is what we came for. Fan out and form two rows of three for a bomb run."

The planes lined up with only seconds to spare. Hollands was relieved that the anti-aircraft guns were silent. It was always possible that someone could have spotted the Posse on radar, but he had contended from the start that—because of their lighter-weight aircraft—the Japanese could not fly in this kind of soup. He hoped they would assume that the Americans could not fly either.

"Bombs away!" sang a chorus of six.

The bombs did their jobs, blasting large craters in the dirt and concrete runways, destroying or damaging nearly all of the parked aircraft.

Hollands knew that their time over the target would be short. They had just enough time and fuel to make one strafing pass and head for home.

Crossing the width of the island, the planes—three left and three right—banked hard into 180 degree turns.

"Good bombing, men! Now proceed two-by-two, on the deck. Concentrate on the remaining planes and hangars."

Swooping down, they flew back toward the airfield just above the palm trees, and a half-mile out, commenced firing long bursts from their machine guns. Lieutenant Buckner was flying far right in the formation and spotted a huge mound of dirt a few yards to the right of his flight path. He quickly pushed the right rudder pedal, banked slightly, and opened fire. Instantly, huge balls of flame erupted rising several hundred feet into the early morning, rain-soaked sky. Surprised, Buckner reacted quickly, turning hard left and pulling up sharply, barely avoiding the fiery debris.

"Sonofabitch, Mike, I must've hit their main fuel supply!" Buckner radioed excitedly.

The surprise attack had been quick and deadly. Most of the enemy planes were burning. Others had been engulfed by flames when one of the pilots clobbered a fuel truck. With the exception of a few rifle rounds, the flight had encountered no resistance.

Flying north out over the ocean and still on the deck, Hollands radioed, "Does anyone have damage to report?"

"None here, sir."

"I'm okay, Captain."

"Me too," came the reports.

"I think everyone's alright, Hollands," announced Major Hanks. "Man, what a flight! I wouldn't have missed this for all the rice in Japan."

"Roger that, Major. Good job, men!" Hollands called. "Okay, Posse, we are not out of danger yet. Slow climb to angels two-zero. And keep your eyes open for bogies."

On the return flight, the group fought a slight headwind. And by the time the six fighters had Pateroa in sight, their fuel reserves had become critical, especially for Hollands' big Jug. Hollands requested and received permission for a straight-in approach for all the planes. With merely a mile separation, all aircraft landed safely, Hollands touching down last.

Three hours later, after a quick debriefing, Commander Sessions assembled all base personnel for a short meeting in one of the hangars. "The film from the raid," began Sessions, "shows decisive damage inflicted on the Japanese Naval Airbase. I congratulate all of the pilots, ground crews, and mechanics for your fine efforts. This has been a team endeavor and has resulted in a single, but important, victory."

CHAPTER 4

Mixed Bag of Nuts to the Rescue

The Japanese had reported Hollands' raid as a "large strike force of over twenty aircraft."

Now Commander Sessions was truly enjoying his talks with the Navy's upper echelons, while trying to explain to them that—in truth—he had no such number of aircraft and pilots. But this explanation was not going well. No one at high command had authorized any such mission. CinCPac was not pleased that Sessions had failed to go through channels.

"Good afternoon, Seaman. This is Commander Sessions on Pateroa Island. No, we're not in South America, son. We're located in the Solomon Island chain. Oh, you're there too. How interesting. Would you connect me with Admiral Johnston?"

While he waited, Sessions lit a fresh cigar.

The admiral's aide came on the line. "Oh, good afternoon Captain Stoner. This is Commander Sessions on Pateroa. No, no, sir, Fleet Command does not understand. We have only six fighters. Last week we lost our only bomber. ... Oh, no, sir, it wasn't shot down. We just had to give it back to the Army. ... That's correct, sir. We've never had that many planes. Three weeks ago, we had just one fighter on this base, an Army P-47 that a squadron had left for dead."

Sessions shifted the cigar to the other side of his mouth. "No, Captain, an Army Air Corps pilot by the name of Hollands found it. And—with help from Army Air and Navy maintenance—they resurrected it. ... That's correct, sir, just one plane. Well, two days ago your command ferried in five Corsairs. ... Yes, that is correct, just six planes went on that raid, sir. ... That's right, sir. All planes returned safely. ... Yes, sir, I did authorize the mission. I know I should have checked with your office first, but it was a matter of opportunity and priority, sir. We wanted to quit diving into foxholes and bomb shelters. And, frankly sir, we're all getting tired of filling in bomb craters. ... We have had no fighter protection for two months, sir. No, sir, the Army's 9th fighter squadron moved closer to the Russell Islands, sir, to assist the Marines with ground action in that sector."

Sessions and the rest of his officer corps found it unbelievable as well as amusing that the U.S. Military, not to mention Washington, D. C., had once again bought into a Japanese report.

It was an unusually warm day in the South Pacific region on 17 April 1943. It was even hotter inside the hangar where Hollands, Buckner, and the other pilots were assisting mechanics with maintenance on their six aircraft. Captain Murray and Major Hanks were at the far end of the building. The *Beep-beep* of a jeep's horn echoed throughout the cavernous interior of the hangar. Everyone immediately looked up to see Commander Sessions at the wheel of the jeep. Someone hollered, *"Atten-hut!"*

Sessions gestured to Hollands, Buckner, Murray, and Hanks, "You four officers, if you please. The rest of you men, as you were."

The four men quickly stopped what they were working on and hurried over to where Sessions waited.

"Gentlemen, something big is in the wind. I don't know what, but for several hours this morning, radio traffic between our ships and the Marine and Army airbases has been unusually heavy. Then an hour ago the radio traffic abruptly stopped. I understand that the Nip's radios were also hot for a while. But for the past three hours, not so much as a radio squawk or the click of a key. I've never experienced anything like this."

Pausing for a moment, he looked into a mostly clear blue sky before continuing, "Until someone can tell me what the hell's going on, I'm putting the base on full alert."

Then with guarded candor, he said, "Let's get patrol planes up. Tell your pilots to be extra alert and careful up there. When I know more, I'll let you know. That's all. You all know what to do. Carry on."

As the commander drove off, Hanks said, "Something serious has got a hold of Sessions, that's for sure."

"Does anybody have a clue?" Murray asked.

"Gee, I bet it has something to do with the Japanese, or perhaps, the war," Buckner joked.

The four stood there for a moment, digesting what they had been told.

Murray said, "I think we need to extend our air patrol range, but not in pairs. And let's do a hundred-miles-out-circuit, with the exception of east towards Munda Island. Fifty miles that direction is known enemy territory and a large airbase. But let's brush up against their boundary lines."

Within minutes, the four had gone over their maps twice. Major Hanks got on the phone to the Tower. "Chief, Hanks here. As you know we'll be going on alert. I'm sending a new flight plan. Over."

The patrols were uneventful; shortly after eleven-hundred hours the next day, Sessions called off the alert and convened a base-wide briefing with all available personnel gathering in front of the hangar.

"Gentlemen, may I have your attention? I asked all of you here because the information truly affects us all."

When everyone had quieted down, he finally said, "Thirty minutes ago I received this communiqué from Fleet. I'll read most of it: '...at approximately 0830, 18 April 1943, a squadron of Army P-38 Lightnings shot down and killed Admiral Isoroku Yamamoto as he was flying in his twin-engine Betty en route from Rabaul to inspect troops. Two squadrons, one Marine, flying Corsairs, and the other Army, flying P-51 Mustangs, flew together in support of the P-38s. They engaged and shot down several enemy fighters. We had no losses.'"

Sessions took a deep breath and folded up the slip of paper. "I've heard scuttlebutt which suggests that the encounter with Yamamoto's plane was *not* a coincidence. I've also heard speculation that our Navy has broken the primary Japanese military code, and that our radio operators intercepted and decrypted Yamamoto's planned itinerary."

Sessions scanned the faces of the assembled personnel. "Frankly, I don't know whether we've broken the Japanese codes or not. I'm not cleared for that information, and neither is anyone else on this base. I don't want to hear any of you repeating rumors about what we may—or may *not*—know about the enemy's plans. If such rumors are *false*, then spreading them is a waste of time and energy. If the rumors happen to be *true*, then every time we repeat them, we jeopardize classified information that is vital to the war effort."

"So, enough with the rumors," he said. "Let's concentrate on facts. And we now know for a fact that Admiral Yamamoto is dead."

A loud cheer went up from all in attendance as Sessions stood quietly. The cheers quickly faded when he raised his hand for silence.

"This was an unusual, necessary act. We've all heard the reports that Yamamoto was the architect of the attack on Pearl Harbor and on other U.S. installations following 7 December 1941. Hopefully, his death will shake the morale not only of every Japanese soldier and sailor, but also of every government official and civilian. That's all I have, gentleman. As you were."

For several days following the news of Yamamoto's death, predictions of an early end to the Pacific war circulated throughout the base. The enemy action had all but stopped.

While on patrol a few days later, Buckner and his wingman

encountered their first Japanese recon plane in many days, a twin-engine Betty, heading for the Pateroa Island Airbase.

Fifty miles out, Buckner radioed, "Pateroa Control, this is Blue Fox Leader. Over."

"Blue Fox Leader, this is Pateroa Control. Over."

"We are shadowing a Betty fifty miles southeast of base. There is no escort. Shall we splash it?"

Hollands was in the tower that afternoon and, overhearing Buckner's call, he took the microphone. "Buckner, this is Hollands. Buzz him a few times. If he runs leave him alone. If he won't disengage, splash him. Over."

"Roger, Blue Fox out."

The two Corsairs buzzed the enemy bomber close in. "Pateroa Control, this is Blue Fox Leader. Over."

"Go ahead, Buckner."

"Well Hollands... as it turns out, this Nip pilot either can't swim or he's a family man, because he turned his bird around and is heading for home."

"Roger, Blue Fox. Pateroa out."

An uneasy quiet lasted for over a week with little or no enemy action. Finally, on a Sunday morning around 0900, Hollands and Buckner were returning from chapel services when the clerk chased them down. "Captain Hollands, Lieutenant Buckner, sirs, the commander would like to see you in his office on the double."

The two pilots headed for HQ on the run. Arriving at Sessions' office, Hollands and Buckner saw the commander talking on the phone. He looked up as the two entered and said, "No, never mind. They just walked in. Are the others there now? Good! Let's get the birds ready."

"What's up, Commander?" Hollands asked. "You wanted to see us?"

Sessions slowly rose from his chair. "You won't believe this, but CinCPac and most of the top admirals still think we have a whole fighter squadron here."

Walking over to his large wall map, he continued, "Boys, I am told there are twelve B-17s that will soon be in serious trouble. Their escort— your 9th, Hollands—couldn't rendezvous with them. They got bushwhacked on the way."

He pointed to an area on the map. "Right here, northwest of the Russells. The Nips fared poorly, but were able to keep the 9th from their mission. In less than thirty minutes the bombers will be 200 miles away from any other help. That puts them over these three small islands: Topoa, Gantara, and this smaller no-name dot."

"What's our job, sir?" asked Buckner.

"Two of these dots have enemy fighter aircraft on them. I want some cover for these bombers. The Japs are just waiting for them; our guys won't have much of a chance. Once you're airborne, it will take about twenty minutes to rendezvous over these islands. You'll probably be outnumbered three to one. But the Japanese command is convinced that *we* are unable to send help, so you might be able to surprise them."

Sessions turned from the map back to the two fliers. "You two intercept 'em before our guys get there. Do whatever you can to give our bomber-guys a fighting chance!"

Hollands nudged Buckner. "Come on. It's a nice day for flying."

He headed for the front door.

"I'm right behind ya, Army."

At the base of the steps, Sessions' jeep was parked with the clerk already at the wheel. As the seaman drove hard across the tarmac, Hollands and Buckner could see their six planes lined up, engines idling.

Within a few minutes, all of the aircraft were airborne. As the six fighters slowly gained altitude, the tower called, "Pateroa Control, calling Badger One. Over."

"Badger One. Over," answered Hollands.

"Pateroa Control. Bandits no longer on screen; last radar contact had them moving east of rendezvous Tango Charlie. Over."

"This is Badger One, roger your message. Any further instructions? Over."

"Stand by, Badger One, while we check.

Sessions' voice came over the headset, "All decisions are up to you, Captain."

"Well, sir, what we know for sure is, there is still a flock of B-17s in the sky that has no escort. We'll go and say Hi! Over."

"Roger, and good hunting."

Hollands took the group up to thirty thousand feet to get better visibility. The sky was partly clouded with only a few white billows.

The bombers, flying at twenty thousand feet, came into view at the rendezvous point. Flying between the two distinct layers of billowy vapors, they were easy to spot even though they were still some distance away. Hollands contacted the bombers to let them know he and his friends would be around for awhile. Minutes later, he received a transmission from the aircraft carrier Enterprise that had been monitoring all radio traffic and happened to be in the sector.

"Badger One, this is Enterprise Control; be advised you have ten bogies coming up from the deck directly below your location. Over."

"Enterprise Control; Badger One. Roger and thanks!"

"The Enterprise must be close by," Buckner acknowledged. "Nice to have an extra set of eyes."

"Bomber Command, this is Badger One," Hollands radioed to the bomber group leader. "Grab as much sky as you can. Bogies are on their way up. Over."

"That's a roger. Thanks, Badger One."

"Badger One to group: company's coming. Let's be good hosts."

Hollands was about to give the order to start down the ladder to intercept the Nips when the Navy radioed again, "Badger One. This is Enterprise. Be advised, second group of five bogies two miles north. Wish we could help."

"You've done just fine, Navy. Thanks again."

The bombers had reached their ceiling limit, and Hollands gave the order for his six fighters to descend. A few miles ahead, they could see a mixed group of Zeros and Oscars slowly gaining altitude to emerge from the broken clouds.

"Buckner, after our first pass, I want you and your wingman, to get down below and cut off that second group."

Lieutenant Cameron, a new replacement pilot for the Marines, was Buckner's wingman. He had been introduced to this hodge-podge flying club just a few days earlier.

"Roger, Hollands."

The enemy pilots saw the bombers fifteen thousand feet above and several miles ahead of them, not at all where they had expected to find them. But while concentrating on the B-17s the Japanese had failed to see the six American fighters. With surprise firmly in hand, Hollands' small group quickly closed in.

The Corsairs and Hollands' Thunderbolt formed two layers of three planes each and descended at a near 45-degree angle, with 500 feet separating the two groups of American fighters. Closing in on the enemy, Hollands began his slow spiral. Seeing this maneuver, couple of the other pilots did the same and began firing on their unsuspecting adversaries.

Diving at over 475 miles per hour, the attacking U.S. force flew beyond the enemy formation, rolling under before quickly regaining altitude.

"Hey, Captain, where did you learn that roll and shoot trick? It really works," Cameron radioed to Hollands.

As the Americans peeled off, Buckner said, "He just makes this stuff up as he goes."

"Okay, quiet and listen up," radioed Hollands. "Good shooting! Several enemy planes have been hit, are smoking, and most will probably not make it to their base. Let's keep the pressure on and go after the others."

Lieutenants Buckner and Cameron banked away from Hollands and the others and descended through the broken clouds to find the second group of enemy planes that were reportedly on their way up. Cautiously, the two lone Corsairs began to weave a flight path around the clouds.

Back at Pateroa, Commander Sessions, Major Hanks, and Captain Murray were in the tower huddled around the radio as if they were listening to a prizefight. They could envision the blow-by-blow descriptions of what was going on.

"Lieutenant Buckner, the second Jap group is behind us, about nine o'clock, and climbing fast."

"Roger, Cam. I see 'em."

But the party was about to get interesting.

"Okay, Cam. They see us. Our job is to take some heat off the four guys above. Stay close; do exactly what I do. This is just like flight school."

As the two pilots rolled the Corsairs on their backs, Buckner yelled, "Take a deep breath, and pull back hard on the stick. Add a little left pedal, and let your breath out slowly."

In nothing flat and at near full throttle, the two birds came out of their half loop heading up towards the five Zeros. Lighting off their machine guns again, Cameron raked the Japanese planes, sending two down in flames, and the other three back down through the clouds. The two Corsairs followed closely behind them and fired, leaving the three Zekes smoking badly and heading for the sea.

Seeing a hole in the clouds two miles away, Buckner and Cameron shot through and gained more sky. The bombers were now safe and all but out of sight. As the two Marines continued to climb, Cam saw one of the other Corsairs with a Zero on his tail.

"Pagnaro, open up your throttle, you've got a Zeke a half mile back and closing."

"Okay! Thanks, Cam."

When the enemy pilot saw Cameron heading for him, the lone Nip flipped his Zero over and headed down through the clouds.

"Badger one, this is Bomber Command. Thanks again. I hope you boys are okay. Over."

"Roger, Bomber Command. We're fine," answered Hollands. "Don't forget to put your gear down."

With a chuckle the group leader replied, "Roger. So that's what that little yellow handle is for. And all this time I thought it was the parking brake. Bomber Command out."

The group had been in the air for just over an hour when Captain Hollands turned them for home. The skirmish had lasted a long ten minutes and had taken the group an additional twenty minutes from their base. Looking around his formation, Hollands came up one bird short. Panic suddenly gripped him, as he radioed, "Sound off; who's missing? Over."

Everyone except Lieutenant Morgan checked in. "Badger One to Badger Six. Over," Hollands radioed.

"This is Badger Six, sir. I'm below you at angels eight, and a mile north. Losing power. Over."

"Were you hit? Over," Hollands asked.

"I think so, sir."

"How's your speed?"

"I'm holding at 2-5-0. Cylinder head and manifold temperatures are going up; oil pressure reads low. Running rough; hard to maintain RPMs. Controls are mushy. Over."

"Hold on, Lieutenant, we'll get ya home. Lean out your fuel mixture some and throttle back. Bring your air speed down to 2-0-0. Over."

"Roger. Hey, she's smoothed out some, sir. And temperatures have begun to drop, too."

Waving at Buckner, Hollands signaled him to switch to their alternate radio frequency.

"What do you think, Mike?" asked Buckner.

They could see Lieutenant Morgan's plane trailing dark smoke. "I'd estimate a distance of nearly a hundred and twenty miles or so back to Pateroa," Hollands said.

Switching his radio back to command, Hollands called in. "Pateroa control, this is Badger One. Over."

"Go ahead, Badger One. Over."

"What is your radar fix on our position? Over."

"Badger one, this is Pateroa Tower. You are one hundred-forty miles northeast. Adjust course 15 degrees north. Over."

"Roger. Badger One out."

Hollands called Buckner again, "Take the rest of the group to angels ten and fly high cover for us for fifteen minutes. Then take the group home. I'll stay with little brother from there."

"Roger. All Badger units, this is Badger Two," radioed Buckner. "I want Three, Four, and Five to form up on me."

As he joined Morgan, Hollands said, "Lieutenant, I'm going to take a look at your aircraft. Keep her nice and level. Coming up behind on your port wing and a few feet below."

"Roger, Captain. I see you."

Performing a cursory look at the ailing Corsair, Hollands found where the tail section and undercarriage near the engine had been hit by enemy fire.

"Pateroa Tower, this is Badger One; we have a wounded eagle. Engine running rough and hot; losing oil pressure. There's structural damage to the tail section. Put some help on the line. Over."

"Roger, help standing by. Pateroa out."

"Pateroa Tower; Badger One. Are any of our boats close by to assist if necessary? Over."

"Badger one, we read you. Stand by."

Air-sea rescue was a pretty unlikely prospect for the Pateroa sector. And with all that water down below, Hollands really wanted to get Morgan closer to some dirt if at all possible.

"Badger One, this is Pateroa Tower. Closest ships are heading north, two hours away. Over."

Hollands knew that was too much time in the water if Morgan should have to ditch or bail out. "Roger, Pateroa. What's your reading on us? Over."

"Badger One, you are about twelve minutes to runway. Over."

Coming up on his left side, Hollands said, "Lieutenant, you're doing fine. Looks like your ship has some new ventilation holes in it. But you'll be on the ground in a few minutes."

Hollands looked directly overhead where Buckner and the others were flying cover and radioed, "Badger One to Badger Two. Take 'em on home. Over."

"Roger, Badger One. See you two on the ground."

Morgan radioed to Hollands and said, "Thanks for sticking around, Captain."

"Hey, you'd do it for any of us," Hollands said. "Watch your speed. You're down to 1-7-5. Try adjusting your trim and bring her back to 2-0-0."

A few seconds later, he said, "You did it, Lieutenant. Good job!"

Hollands knew full well what was going on in Lieutenant Morgan's mind. Each passing minute would seem like an hour. Then the tower called. "Badger One and Six. This is Pateroa Tower. Angle your descent ten degrees; adjust compass north 3 degrees."

"Badger One. Roger. Almost home, Lieutenant."

"Yes, sir, but she's still hot and oil pressure almost gone."

"Don't worry about it; Corporal Lynch will fix her up."

"Oh, you mean Skip?"

"That's right. Say, what's your first name, Lieutenant?"

"Billy, sir.

"I'm, Mike."

"Sir, ah, Mike... I can't see very well. There's oil all over the front and sides of my canopy. A lot of smoke inside."

"That's all right, Billy, stay calm. Open your canopy. Let's get some fresh air in there. I always preferred a convertible, myself. Never had one; but I sure like 'em."

Billy slid open his cockpit.

"Tower Control to Badger One and Six. No need to respond. Come down to angels three. Adjust heading to your right two degrees. You are twelve miles out."

"On three, Billy, adjust your heading. One-two-three! Good! You're lined up just right. Trust your instruments, Billy. Can you see anything through the windscreen?"

"Yes, yes! I have a little line of clean. Oh! Thank God, there's the base, sir."

Both pilots lowered their landing gear and prepared to meet the runway.

"Say, Mike... Are you sure this is our base?"

"Funny man! Now you're a comic. Billy, as soon as your gear touches the ground, kill the engine. Just let her roll to a stop."

"Okay, Mike; and thanks!"

The tower took over from there, and Hollands touched down simultaneously with Morgan's ship, one runway to the left.

Hollands taxied over to the maintenance area, parking fifth in line with the four Corsairs. Getting his gear together, he climbed out of the cockpit, stepped down to the wing, and jumped onto the grass. Then he walked around to the rear of the plane where he met Captain Murray.

"Hi, Ben, how are the other boys?"

"They're fine, Mike. Giddy and wired," Murray answered. "The six of you must have gotten into one hell of a fight. All your planes have holes in them."

"Japanese termites," Hollands said smiling. "It's their new weapon. But there will be about a dozen fewer Zeros and Oscars flying tomorrow."

Still smiling and looking at his plane and the Corsairs, he added, "I sure do like these big planes."

The two officers saw a jeep coming towards them. Major Hanks was at the wheel and Lieutenant Morgan, wearing a huge grin, sat in the right front seat.

"Lynch is at Morgan's plane now, doing a preliminary inspection. He'll tow it over here later," commented Murray. "His left tire was flat when he touched down."

"Billy did good. We need that plane. I hope it can be saved."

The jeep came to a stop in front of the two Army officers, and Hanks offered his right hand to Hollands as he said, "Thanks, Mike, for taking care of my pilot."

"Captain Hollands," began Morgan, "I want to thank you again, sir, for sticking with me."

Then the young Marine pilot blurted out, "I was scared shitless!"

Hollands studied him for a brief moment. He looked so very young. He reminded Hollands of his own kid brother back home.

"You did well today, Billy," Hollands told him. "I was scared too. But just too busy to notice it at first."

After shaking hands with Lieutenant Morgan, Hollands turned to Hanks. "Lieutenant Morgan will be credited with two splashed, and two damaged."

CHAPTER 5

Although June was usually one of the driest months, 1943 saw a late tropical storm move through the region. The unseasonable weather brought days of high winds and heavy rain, which grounded all aircraft. However, the lull in air combat allowed for some much needed servicing of the aircraft and for the pilots' respite. Unfortunately, this break was of equal benefit to the Japanese.

For several days the rains were relentless. The runways were covered with nearly a foot of mud and water. Cabin fever was setting in and everyone grew restless and a bit testy. Ground crews had done everything possible to protect the fighters, most of them parked outside. But even tarpaulins tied over the cowling and oil sprayed directly on the more sensitive external engine parts, could not keep the humidity and salt air out. Rusty-red rapidly began to appear on almost everything metal. The mechanics cleaned and re-cleaned constantly.

A platoon of Mud Marines had finally arrived, including one anti-aircraft battery. They were a comfort, but didn't offer much firepower. As the weather slowly moderated, Sessions wanted to get some patrol planes back into the air as soon as possible. With a bit of squabbling, the Marines were drafted to clear the mud off the runway, but the only two planes ready for duty were Hollands' Thunderbolt and Buckner's Corsair.

Hollands was now in his fourth month at the Pateroa Naval Air Station, his reliability and leadership proven. Sessions knew that he could count on the young airman, but on June 24, 1943, Commander Sessions received a communiqué that would test the mettle of any man.

"Captain Hollands, Captain Hollands, sir; it's me, Skip, and Lieutenant Buckner. You've got to wake up, sir."

Hollands finally opened one eye and looking at Buckner through the dim light in the hallway, he said in a gravelly, sleepy voice, "Don't you guys ever sleep? What time is it?"

"Mike, c'mon," Buckner announced, "you and me gotta get over to operations, like five minutes ago; Sessions' orders. It's 3:15, and our birds have been gassed up and sitting on the tarmac."

"Where are we going?"

"Don't know for sure, Mike. But when an oak-leaf speaks, I listen," answered Buckner.

Lynch groused, "Oak leaves seldom ask a corporal or private their opinions."

Partially sitting up, Hollands looked at Lynch who had moved nearer to the door, and joked in a half whisper, "Do corporals or privates ever have an opinion?"

He placed his feet on the floor and his head in his hands.

Taking a deep breath he reached for his travel case of toiletries.

Buckner grabbed his wrist, "You don't have time, Mike. Rinse your face, and let's go."

This was an uncharacteristic gesture by the Marine. Hollands sensed that this was more than a local emergency. "Okay, guys, what's up? Tell it straight and tell it now."

"Mike, this is only scuttlebutt," began the young Marine, "but your brother joined the Army back in late March and he could be part of the Kamberra Bay assault. There is a naval battle going on there right now."

"He can't be out here; he's just graduated from high school this month. If he'd joined up I would have heard."

"Hell, Mike, we've hardly had any mail in weeks," Buckner said. "And most of that's months old. Point is, the Navy is requesting air support from any group who can get into the air. The Marine 288th piled up four planes yesterday trying to get off the deck in this soup. The Black Sheep 214th can't get up either; their field is under more than two feet of mud. The Army 9th lost two. The sea is too rough for the damn carriers to launch any planes and, besides, they're all too far out."

Buckner lit a cigarette. "We're it, buddy! I just hope we can get off the ground."

The meeting in the ready room was short, but not sweet. Sessions had confirmed that Hollands' younger brother Steven was indeed part of the joint Army and Marine amphibious group. Naval and Army Intelligence had badly underestimated the enemy's strength on the ground as well as on the water, and the GIs were heavily out-numbered and taking a licking.

During their briefing, Hollands and Buckner hurriedly downed coffee and doughnuts. A few minutes later, they were standing in the rain and in ten inches of thick muddy water. They inspected the condition of the runways and looked at one another glumly. Buckner said, "Mike, I have to be honest, I would not try this if you weren't the one asking and those poor troops, your brother and my Marines, needing help."

"Well, with that load we'll be carrying, I give us a 60 percent chance of *not* leaving the runway," said Hollands. "This doesn't look encouraging."

Once buckled into their cockpits, before releasing their brakes, the pilots slowly pushed their throttles forward. The two birds vibrated violently as if with a sense of intense eagerness. Simultaneously, the pilots released the brakes and both aircraft lurched forward. Rolling side-by-side down two runways, the tails came up quickly and the planes sloshed through the standing muddy water. With auxiliary fuel tanks and two five-hundred pound bombs each, the planes were loaded to the limits. The controls were sluggish and the two pilots used nearly the entire available runway to get airborne.

Buckner's Corsair lifted off first, then Hollands' Thunderbolt a couple of seconds later. Immediately, they banked left for their compass heading and began to climb. The only bright spot in this whole mess was that there would be no enemy aircraft in the vicinity, because the Japanese fighters were grounded.

The two American fighters labored hard as they slowly gained altitude. During their two-hour flight, the tower radioed that the naval battle had concluded, but that there had been no report on the outcome. Dawn was breaking when Hollands and Buckner arrived over the Kamberra Bay area. The heavy rain had changed to a drizzle and there was intermittent thick ground fog.

"What do ya think, Mike? I can't see a damn thing down there. None of the landmarks are visible," Buckner radioed. "With all the fire and smoke down below, I sure hope we came out on top."

"I know. Me too!" Hollands responded. "Look, if we fly too low, our guys on the ground just might open up on us. Buckner, circle the area and stay at angels-five. Try contacting our guys on the ground. I'm going inland a few miles for a look-see."

"Roger, changing frequency now."

Hollands dropped down through the soupy clouds and fog to what he hoped would still put him above the vegetation and low hills. Although the sky was turning a brighter shade of gray, the visibility was still poor.

Hollands couldn't help getting a sick feeling in his gut when he thought about Steve being somewhere down below, and he wondered if he and Buckner had arrived in time to be of any help.

"Mike, coming up on your starboard wing," radioed Buckner.

"Were you able to contact anyone back there?"

"Roger, one rather excited Army buck-sergeant who told me that the Japs have moved their dump-sites. Follow me in."

Buckner read off the new heading, and the two planes turned north for a short distance. Five miles north of the bay they turned west. As daylight improved, Hollands and Buckner spotted the two sites, about two-hundred yards apart without much camouflage, making them unbelievably easy to see.

"Hey, Hollands, I've got an idea."

"Well, let's have it."

"My wing tanks are nearly empty. How's yours?"

"About the same, a few gallons, I guess!"

"What say we drop these first over the target," Buckner proposed. "With the few gallons they have left they should explode on contact. Just might be enough. But on our second pass, if needed, we can deliver the two eggs."

"Sounds good to me. You take the dump on your left and I'll take the right."

Flying about a thousand feet above the terrain, Hollands and Buckner lined up on their respective targets and released their wing tanks as they approached the two Japanese depots of fuel and ammo. The tanks exploded on impact and flames soon covered much of the ground. Moments later, secondary explosions began lighting up the gray-dawn sky.

"Sonofabitch, will you look at that," Buckner radioed.

Hollands keyed his mike. "That was good thinking, Bruce."

Each pilot made a 180-degree turn to take another look at the damage.

Then Hollands said, "Buckner, do not drop your bombs. I repeat; do not drop your bombs. Climb to angels five. Tight counter-clock-circle."

"Roger. Right behind ya, Army."

As the two airmen watched the additional fireworks, one huge ball of fire came up from Buckner's target, and Hollands exclaimed, "That must have been their main fuel depot."

Other than some light arms fire, the two fliers went about their business unopposed.

Hollands contacted the sergeant back on the ground for close-by enemy positions. The Marines and Army fired a few mortar rounds of red and white smoke into the jungle to indicate suspected enemy locations, and the two pilots began strafing those areas resulting in a few minor explosions. More small-arms fire erupted from beneath the canopy. After about ten passes, Hollands said, "Okay, let's break off and head for base. Fuel is beginning to be a factor."

After notifying the ground, Hollands asked them to tell his brother hello for him. Then with one more strafing pass over the jungle, the two airmen headed out over the bay. Seconds later Hollands and Buckner spotted a Japanese troop-cargo ship about five miles from shore. Accompanying her were two damaged escort-cruisers that were listing seriously. Because of the damage, the three ships were making dead slow headway.

"Hey, Mike, these must be what's left over from the naval engagement."

"That would be my guess. Since we still have our bombs, this could be as good a spot as any to leave them."

"My thought exactly. We have to drop these eggs somewhere, so let's concentrate on the troop-cargo ship," said Buckner.

The two planes dropped down to 2,500 feet. This brought sporadic antiaircraft fire from the few working guns on the three enemy ships. With Buckner flying directly behind Hollands, they lined up on their target, bow to stern, and released their bombs. At first, it seemed that they had missed. But as they climbed beyond range of the escorts' guns, the fliers saw that the troop ship was on fire and going down fast at the stern.

"Let's head for home."

The weather had closed off their original route, so Hollands altered their flight plan. "Let's make a leisurely climb to angels two-zero. See if we can escape these clouds."

"Roger, Hollands, two-zero. This plane sure seems lighter with the bomb and tanks gone."

"Yeah, mine too!"

It seemed impossible that clouds could be so thick, but these were. The rain and winds had picked up, buffeting the two war birds and slowing their progress. As the planes continued to gain altitude, the surrounding sky of clouds seemed to get darker. Passing fifteen thousand feet, relying only on their instruments, both men let out a sigh of relief when they saw clear sky again.

"HAL-LE-LU-JA!" exclaimed Buckner.

"This is high enough. Let's level off," Hollands directed.

At sixteen thousand, it was as clear as a bell. From early training, every combat pilot knew as soon as he found clear, open skies, to take a serious look around for other aircraft, enemy, or friendly. Several minutes into the return flight, Buckner broke the silence as he called, "Hollands... behind us, eleven o'clock high. I make 'em at about angels three-zero. A formation of twelve, no, *fifteen* bogies."

"Yeah, I see 'em."

"I can't make out who they are, Mike. Can you?"

After a few seconds, Hollands answered, "Well, they look like Hellcats; carrier planes."

"Where the hell did they come from?" Buckner called. "I thought the Navy had been grounded, and our carriers were too far out."

It was obvious that Hollands and Buckner had not as yet been spotted. Hollands got on the horn to base, "Pateroa control, this is Deputy One. Over."

"Deputy One, this is Pateroa. Over."

Hollands gave a quick ten second report on the mission. Then said, "We have encountered a carrier squadron of Hellcats at about angels three-zero on our heading. Do you have their frequency? Over."

"Stand by, Deputy One."

A few seconds of radio silence can seem like an eternity. "Deputy One, this is Pateroa. Hollands, this is Sessions. We're still looking. You're still too far out for radar. Are you sure they're ours?"

"Yes, sir; Hellcats. But at briefing we were told our carriers were out of the area. Any idea what ship they may be from, sir? Over."

"Sorry, Hollands. Not a clue. That was the information we were given. Over."

Finally, the tower came up with a radio setting. Hollands waved to Buckner and they both changed their radio frequencies.

"This is U.S. Army P-47 Thunderbolt, and Marine F4U Corsair, Deputy One and Two, calling U.S. Navy flight at angels three-zero on heading one-niner-five. We are the two dark dots below you at angels one-six; one-hundred-sixty nautical miles northeast of Pateroa. Over."

"Someone heard ya," Buckner announced. "We have three dropping in for tea."

After exchanging a short introduction with the flight leader, Hollands and Buckner learned that these Navy-jocks had been lost for some time, but had finally made contact with their ship.

"Lieutenant Briggs. What is your fuel situation?"

"Captain, we have less than thirty minutes before we become gliders and a hundred-fifty miles, plus or minus, to our carrier, the Enterprise. They will begin steaming toward us as soon as they turn around. Hell, it will take thirty minutes just to do that."

"You sound a bit short on helpful arithmetic, Lieutenant," Hollands said, then read off the headings for Pateroa and radioed ahead that guests were on the way.

"Lieutenant, lean out your fuel as much as possible and drop the nose ten degrees. You are ten minutes from a long runway and a gas station."

"Thanks, Captain. I hope to buy you and your wingman a cold beer sometime soon."

"Sounds good," Hollands said. "Happy landing."

"Pateroa Tower to Enterprise and Pateroa aircraft. Recommend you stay on this frequency till you are on the ground. Pateroa out."

The group flew along quietly for several minutes. Buckner suddenly radioed, "Mike, this is Buckner. Over."

"Yeah, what's up?"

"You have smoke coming out of the bottom of the engine cowling. Check your clocks; might be serious."

Hollands quickly swept his gauges and reported, "The fuel reading is a little on the low side, but doable, and everything else seems to be okay."

"Hollands, smoke is getting heavier and darker."

"Yeah... Shit! I can smell it now. There's smoke in the cockpit," Hollands growled. "Think I took a hit back there at the bay... maybe in the oil cooler."

"I'll take a look, Army. Hold her level."

Buckner maneuvered his gull-winged Corsair a few feet below Hollands' Jug for a closer inspection. "Couple of holes in your tail, Hollands, but nothing up front that I can see. Must be something mechanical."

"Thanks, Buckner. I still have good oil pressure and no heat problems."

The radio speaker then crackled, "Deputy One and Two, this is Lieutenant Briggs; bandits, bandits. Oscars coming up eight o'clock off port wing. I count ten."

Three additional Navy planes left their formation and came down to engage the enemy. Normally the Japanese Oscars were no match for the newer U.S. fighters. But the Navy didn't have fuel to waste on a dogfight, and the Thunderbolt was no longer in any condition to engage.

Hollands swept the dials again and frantically radioed, "Buckner, I'm going to have to take her down. Engine is getting hot and she's losing oil pressure and power. Starting to surge. RPMs are dropping and she's running rough."

While Hollands tried to keep the Thunderbolt in the air, Buckner flew cover for him. It appeared the enemy hadn't expected anyone. Perhaps they were just taking advantage of the break in the weather. The Hellcat pilots really knew their stuff and had surprised the Japanese, immediately dropping three Oscars.

Buckner rolled off to take on two enemy fighters, pulling them away from Hollands' crippled aircraft. "Hey, Army, bank hard right turn," radioed Buckner.

"Roger!" Hollands replied, and rolled his ship into a starboard turn.

Hollands' radio picked up a volley of rapid fire commands from the Navy and from Buckner. After several minutes of zigzagging, Hollands heard an unfamiliar voice in his headphones. "Captain, you have a Zeke on your tail. Roll tight left. I'm right behind him."

Hollands assumed it was one of the Navy pilots as he made his turn. Then he heard Buckner yell, "HOLLANDS, TWO ZEKES, ON YOUR TAIL, PORT SIDE."

Several rounds from one of the Jap fighters tore through the Jug's undercarriage behind the cockpit and exited through the canopy, barely missing Hollands. He rolled the canopy open with the idea of bailing out. But he wasn't too keen on floating helplessly through the thick gray clouds or swimming around in an ocean owned jointly by sharks and the Japanese.

Hollands worked hard with trim and flaps to control the gallant lady, but it was becoming increasingly evident that he could not save her. Slowly, they entered the dark billowy clouds as he continued his descent. One of the Japanese fighters, clearly damaged, suddenly emerged from the clouds, the pilot fighting the controls. The enemy plane flew past Hollands' own ailing ship. He pulled back slightly on the stick and sent a short burst of fire in the general direction of the enemy plane. At first he thought he had missed, but the Oscar slowly rolled over and went straight down, splashing into the water.

The other Zeke had followed Hollands down through the clouds. He was quickly made aware of its presence when a dozen or so tracers flew past, only inches away from his open cockpit. Then a strange thing happened. Looking over his right shoulder, Hollands saw the Jap plane suddenly explode into flames, instantly filling the sky with spare parts. But most curious, it appeared that a third Japanese fighter was responsible for doing the shooting!

Slowly this plane closed in on Hollands' right wing, and then that same unfamiliar voice came over the radio. "Are you alright, Captain?"

Hollands couldn't believe what he had just witnessed, or what he was now hearing. He found himself nodding his head, in answer to his adversary's question.

"Check your compass and turn left eighteen degrees to a heading of one-six-niner. There's a small island atoll about three miles ahead. It's safe there! Oh, don't bail if you can help it. It's shark season. Gotta go now. Bye!"

The Japanese pilot opened up the throttle on his Oscar and disappeared back into the clouds.

Hollands adjusted his glide to that heading and added what little power was left from the Thunderbolt's ailing engine. Checking over both shoulders and down below, he could see neither plane nor boat. Then, looking straight ahead, he saw a small island and said to himself, "That must be the island the Ja..."

It was hard enough to finish the thought in his head, but impossible to say it out loud. *Who the hell was that guy?* Hollands wondered. *And why did he want to help me?*

It certainly hadn't been the normal Japanese gibberish Hollands was used to hearing. It was perfect American lingo. Had he *really* seen one Japanese pilot shoot down another Japanese pilot?

When a person's life is running like an express train before his eyes it's amazing how words form in his thoughts. With all that was going on, Hollands figured his brain was operating like a cracked phonograph record. Then, with some frightening humor, he chuckled as this thought floated through his head along with the smoke and gas fumes. *Oh great! A new experience; you don't get to crash a plane every day, do ya!*

"Hollands, this is Buckner, where are you?"

"Buckner, I'm barely flying at one-six-niner degrees; fifteen hundred feet altitude, air speed is 150. There's a small island... Damn. The lady just died. I'm gonna get my ass wet."

"I'll fly cover for you just as soon as I can find you."

Hollands pushed the stick forward trying to increase his air speed. Most fighters when the engine quits have the aerodynamics of a falling brick, and a P-47 was among the worst. The water was coming up pretty fast, as was the island coastline. *I'd prefer the water to crashing on land,* Hollands said to himself. At about a hundred feet above the water and a hundred yards from the shore, Hollands pulled back hard on the yoke. Seconds later the Lady hit the water tail first. Then the belly of the fuselage slammed down and bounced twice before coming to rest in the shallows near the shore. Except for the hissing steam that displaced the dark smoke from the engine, there was sudden silence. A few seconds later, Hollands looked out of the front of the canopy and beyond the bent propeller blades, to see just a few yards away a sandy beach backed by boulders and palm trees.

Hollands took a deep breath and slowly let out a big sigh of relief; he was safe. He unbuckled, climbed out of the cockpit, and sat on top of the windscreen. Looking his plane over he said, "Well, ol' girl, that wasn't exactly a graceful landing. But all things considered, not bad I guess."

Then he heard two engines overhead and slightly behind him. The first plane, an Oscar, came into view rocking its wings. *Who the hell is that guy?*

Hollands waved. Then the familiar whistling-sound of a Corsair filled his ears; it was Buckner and he was obviously gunning for the Japanese plane, a natural reaction. Hollands tried to wave him off, but it was no use. Jumping back into the pilot seat and hoping the radio still worked, he keyed the microphone, "This is Deputy One calling Deputy Two. Buckner, do you read me. Over?"

The radio crackled with static, "Roger, Mike! I've just about got this yellow bastard in my sights!"

"Buckner, break off, break off! That's an order! Get back upstairs now! Get those Navy jocks to Pateroa or there will be a lot of Navy pilots practicing their breaststroke or feeding the sharks."

Buckner didn't answer and both planes disappeared through the clouds, followed a few seconds later by what Hollands recognized as the Corsair's six .50 caliber machines guns taking care of business.

"Damn!" Hollands exclaimed.

"Mike, I got the sonofabitch that shot you down."

"Thanks!" Hollands answered. "But I wasn't shot down, remember?"

"Oh, ah... right! Heading for home. Air sea rescue should be by soon to pick you up. Out."

Perched again on his shot-up canopy, Hollands anxiously watched as the Japanese aircraft, engulfed in flames, came pin wheeling slowly down through the clouds accompanied by bits of debris. Then, much to his surprise a parachute appeared close by and at about three thousand feet altitude. The Japanese pilot was on course for a hard dirt landing a hundred yards inland, if he didn't hug a palm tree first.

Hollands grabbed his survival gear and slid off the port wing. He jumped into the water and began wading the few yards to shore.

As soon as he reached land, he fell against a large rock to catch his breath. "That landing must have taken more out of me than I thought," he muttered.

Glancing up at the sky he saw the chute as it gently floated past, still on course. Clutching his gear, Hollands forced himself into an easy run, following the direction of the parachute. After a good distance, he came to a halt, huffing and puffing.

"I know he's close by," Hollands said aloud. The area was heavy with palms and smaller nut trees.

With pistol drawn, Hollands continued his search. He checked a small clearing but found nothing. It was as if the pilot had just evaporated. Leaning against a palm tree, Hollands dropped his bag and was holstering his weapon when he heard a voice on high.

"Reach for the sky, partner; I've got you covered... literally. This is a big parachute ya know."

Startled and looking directly overhead Hollands could see his quarry dangling from his chute sixty feet up.

"Of course, if you prefer; hey Joe, you got Amelican ciggalet? But if not, I'll just surrender anyway."

Startled, Hollands quickly looked up in puzzlement at the Japanese pilot. Assaying the man's predicament, he said, "Reach down, release the crotch and waist latches, and let yourself down on the tether."

"Hey, thanks! I can't see 'em, but I know they're there."

Landing in the palm tree had resulted in some minor cuts on the enemy pilot's arms and face.

Unclasping the two latches, the young Japanese pilot lowered himself to eight feet above the ground and fell the rest of the way, landing in a ball at Hollands' feet.

Taking a deep breath he moved into a sitting position, getting an eyeball full of the business end of Hollands' re-drawn .45 automatic.

"Put your hands on your head," Hollands ordered. But to his amazement, the young Japanese officer just smiled broadly and stared back.

"What the hell's wrong with you?" Hollands demanded.

"Captain," began the Japanese pilot, "it has been a long time, nearly two years, since I've had so much of my native tongue spoken to me."

He chuckled. "It sounds great; you speak good *American* English!"

"Put your hands on top of your head anyway, NOW!" Hollands insisted.

But instead of complying, his adversary took a quick look skyward and slowly stood up. Then he suddenly pushed the gun to one side and shoved Hollands backwards. Hollands landed hard on his butt, rolling back and ending up some ten feet away, against a short palm tree.

The Japanese pilot fell flat on his face in a crumpled position on open ground, looking quite dead.

"Captain," the young pilot said sharply, "If you wish to keep breathing, don't move. Stay out of sight."

Two enemy planes immediately flew overhead, slow and low.

"If we're lucky they'll think we're both dead and not send anyone here to check," the Japanese pilot said. "Stay there; they may do this several times."

Hollands was beside himself with curiosity and disbelief. Leaning against the trunk of the palm and still holding his sidearm, he listened as the Japanese planes made three passes.

"What's your name?" Hollands finally asked his captive.

"Ron Yoshida."

Looking at him still sprawled out on the ground, Hollands said, "Ya know, you look really uncomfortable lying there."

"I am. I landed on a damn rock with horns, I think. Just hope my bastard comrades buy this act. One of those pilots is probably taking pictures of me and of your plane."

Blowing some sand away from around his mouth, Yoshida continued, "However, I do believe they would be more interested in you right now, unless they knew that I had shot two of the Emperor's aircraft."

After the enemy planes' third pass and some target shooting at the dead Thunderbolt, they left, the drone of the engines fading in the distance.

"I'm Captain Hollands," he finally said. "I've never heard of a Japanese national with an English first name before, and I've never heard one speak the English language so well. How did you come by both?"

"Well," Yoshida said, and began stripping out of his flight suit, "I've found names similar to mine are quite common in my homeland."

Breaking into a sly smile, Ron added, "I was born in May, 1923 near Patterson, New Jersey. In '27 my father moved us to California. He's Nisei, an American born Japanese. We—my dad—inherited a small farm from my grandfather in the San Joaquin Valley."

Using the indentations his body had left in the wet sand and clay, the Japanese pilot began laying out his flight suit on the ground. "Hey, give me a hand. We need to place a few large rocks inside the pant legs and sleeves to weight this down."

Hollands helped collect some coconuts and rocks, and Yoshida placed a larger coconut where his head had been lying and fastened his leather helmet, goggles, and scarf to it. Then, after laying a few palm leaves across it, the two pilots walked away.

"Eventually, command will have a pilot fly over just to see if I'm still lying here," Ron explained.

After several minutes of walking and listening, Ron took out a newspaper clipping from his wallet and handed it to Hollands. "I'm Sansei, third generation Japanese-American, Captain. My father was born and raised in New York and served with the U.S. Navy in the last war."

Hollands carefully unfolded the weathered piece of newspaper and asked, "Why, then, did you join the Japanese military?"

"I didn't! I was conscripted. Forced into it. I was part of a cultural student exchange program to Japan; a lot of us were, including some Caucasians. My parents still have family in the old country and wanted me to visit them, to experience and to know a little of the traditions and culture. So I applied and was accepted into the program. After my freshman classes were finished at UCLA, I went to Japan, where I expected to stay for only a year, meet the relatives, and attend school. Hell, I could barely speak the language. I do pretty well now; I can even write it a little."

"So what happened?"

"Pearl Harbor is what happened. I arrived at my relatives' home in Osaka the middle of June of '41. After two weeks of visiting and getting settled, I checked in at the small university UCLA had contracted with and began attending classes starting the first week in July. No one, by that I mean the common citizen, had any idea that the government was planning to attack the United States. I sure wouldn't have gone over there if I had known."

A light rain shower had started. Taking a breather, the men took refuge under a large palm tree. The quiet was deafening as the two sat silently for a few minutes and listened to the light wind, the rain, and the distant surf.

After a few moments, Ron sighed and said, "I had been living with my mom's cousin's family going on five months and attending classes. Then around four o'clock one morning in mid-November, the Army and police showed up. I think they're one and the same. They just walked into the house and began searching. When they found me, I was arrested and taken away. I barely had time to put my trousers on. Humiliating. I went straight to jail. No trial, no lawyer, no charges."

Standing to stretch his muscles, Ron went on, "About three weeks later, the news came out that the Imperial Japanese Navy had successfully attacked Pearl Harbor plus several other U.S. bases in the Pacific. I went numb! A week after that, I was given a choice: join their military, or be shot for treason. I chose the military and managed to fool a lot of brass somehow, as I got into flight school. The others, Americans and Brits, were brutalized, especially the girls. I know some died. I was able to help two others escape out of Japan. Not a nice place to live if you're white; unless, of course, you happen to be German or Italian."

Looking grim, Hollands held up the newspaper clipping and asked, "Where did you find this?"

"I was given that clipping several months after the war broke out. News items like that were used to coerce other Nisei into joining the military. This one," Ron pointed at the clipping Hollands held, "is from the *New York Times*. I figure it was just some dreamed-up propaganda. Was it?"

The article and photographs told how the U.S. and Canadian Governments had rounded up Japanese in the Western regions and Hawaii, and sent them to internment camps.

Hollands wondered how he could answer.

CHAPTER 6

The rain had let up on Pateroa as Buckner led the squadron of U.S. Navy fighters in. "Pateroa Tower, this is Bandit Two. Navy planes to land first. My fuel okay. Over."

"Roger, Bandit Two. Helen Leader, this is Pateroa control. Your group is cleared for a straight-in approach. Spread your chicks out: two-minute intervals, three abreast on runways one, three and four. Do you copy? Over."

"Pateroa Tower, this is Helen Leader; roger we copy, and thank you!"

"Bandit Two, this is Pateroa Tower; what is the status of Bandit One? Over."

"Pateroa Tower, this is Bandit Two; Captain Hollands is down. He had to ditch off an island fifty miles east by northeast. I notified air-sea rescue."

"Roger, Bandit Two. Stand by. Over."

The Navy planes landed safely, although three of them ran dry of fuel upon touch down and had to be towed off the runway. The base quickly refueled the squadron and soon they were headed for the sky and on to their carrier.

Buckner entered the commander's office where Sessions was at his desk. The Marine marched across the room and came to attention. "Lieutenant Buckner reporting, sir."

"Stand at ease, Lieutenant. I've just received this message from our Air-Sea Rescue boys, 'Please be advised, Captain Hollands too far inside enemy territory to send help at this time. Will advise when conditions improve'."

Sessions put the message aside, stood up, and said, "Okay, Lieutenant. Go ahead."

"Sir, the mission was a success. But, Commander, there has to be some way to get a plane or boat to that island."

Buckner pointed to a flyspeck of a dot on the commander's wall map.

"Sir, I'm sure this is the island right here. A PBY or a Duck could land near the beach. Or an R4D could at least air drop some supplies. If we can get either one, sir, I'll volunteer to go, either as pilot or crew."

"Son, there isn't a man on this rock who doesn't want to see Captain Hollands back here safe, any more than I do."

Re-lighting a well-chewed cigar, Sessions continued, "Understand, Lieutenant, that island is over fifty miles inside Japanese-held territory. Hell, Pateroa is on that line. With our meager force, God help us if the Japs ever wanted this piece of dirt back."

Pausing and looking at the map once more, Sessions shook his head, "You take any slow-flying aircraft, PBY, or Duck in there, the Nips would chop 'em up faster than you could open a can of beans. And if the rescue failed, you could get Hollands and the crew killed."

"Gee, sir, I hadn't thought of it like that," Buckner replied.

Taking a few puffs from his cigar, Sessions went on, "However, we might be able to drop him some supplies, perhaps from a couple of Corsairs."

"I'll fly it, sir."

"Yes, I know you would, Lieutenant. Look, I'll get a hold of our coast watcher and see if his group has any ideas. Maybe we could sneak a sub in there at night and pick him up. I just don't know enough about those waters."

"But in the meantime," Sessions paused as he took a thin, small box from his desk drawer, "you'll pin these railroad tracks on your collar as acting Captain. You'll be Major Hanks' XO for the time being. These were my old Navy Lieutenant's bars from many years ago. I didn't pick up my oak leaf until I was recalled to active duty shortly after the attack on Pearl Harbor. The acting part will be between you, Hanks, and me. The Major requested you, and I'm sure we can get the rank approved through fleet in a few weeks. Congratulations, Captain!"

Buckner was so surprised he could only say, "Yes, sir, and thank you. I'll do my best."

"By the way, Buckner, was it air combat that brought down Hollands?"

"No, sir. We figured it was a busted oil line."

With a grin on his face, Sessions nodded and said, "Now get out of here and report to Major Hanks and see to your men and planes. There are big things brewin' on the horizon, son. Remember, I want Hollands back, too. Dismissed!"

With that, Captain Buckner came to attention and snapped off a salute. As he left the base CO's office, Sessions said to himself, "I knew they didn't shoot him down."

Once outside, Buckner changed his collar grade insignia and, looking up into the dark clouds, he whispered, "Army, you gotta be all right. God, I've never been big on praying, but you got to make him all right."

Captain Buckner hitched a ride to the area near the hangars. The Marine headquarters and operations buildings were adjacent to the Army Air maintenance. Major Hanks was leaving headquarters just as Buckner's vehicle arrived at the front steps. Buckner quickly exited the vehicle and thanked the driver.

"Major," Buckner began as he came to attention, "Major, I want to thank you for requesting me as your XO. I'll do my best, sir."

"No need to thank me, Captain. You've earned it—and," Hanks was smiling, "I'm going to work your ass off. The paperwork's a killer. How's your typing?"

Both men laughed and shook hands. Then, more seriously, the major said, "Now Buckner, tell me what happened up there. How is it that Hollands was knocked down?"

"Well, sir..."

"Knock off the, sir! Name's Jeff."

"Yes... *Jeff*! Thank you."

Buckner composed himself. "Well, as I was telling Sessions, Hollands and I figure it was a broken oil line or maybe a plugged oil cooler. There was no sign of damage up front."

Hanks walked a few steps in a circle as he listened. "I think we need to go have a talk with Murray and Corporal Lynch."

"My thoughts as well."

As the two Marines began walking to the hangars, Hanks said, "If Hollands *did* go down because of mechanical failure, it's important to make sure that our other pilots won't have a similar problem."

Back on the small atoll, Hollands worked to get his bearings. He was absolutely exhausted, and he was hungry. The mission he and Buckner had flown had begun at 0315. They had gotten almost no sleep, and—except for coffee and doughnuts—Hollands hadn't eaten anything since the previous night's chow.

The bumpy, wet landing that had ended his flight had taken its toll on him. He was sure his younger brother Steve was, for the moment, safe. There was nothing further Hollands could do under the present circumstances anyway. Right then, Hollands really wanted to find a hole somewhere out of the rain where he could get a few hours rest. But what to do about Lieutenant Yoshida? And what about his fantastic story? Could

Hollands put his pistol in the holster, close his eyes, and feel safe enough to sleep?

As the two men continued to walk slowly, Ron asked Hollands about the validity of the newspaper article and the Japanese relocation camps back home in the States.

"Couldn't we talk about this a little later, Lieutenant?" asked Hollands with a sigh, hoping to buy some time.

"No, Captain, we can't!" Yoshida said firmly. "I've got to know."

The palm trees were thick and dense, so when the two men found a boulder large enough for both of them to sit on, they stopped to rest for a few moments, sheltered from the light rain, and out of sight from the air.

Ron took a nearly empty cigarette pack out of his pocket and gesturing to Hollands asked, "You want a smoke? They're American."

"No thanks, Lieutenant. I don't smoke."

"I've had to hide these last ones for months. I used to swipe 'em from the stolen Red Cross packages. The Japanese make terrible cigarettes."

Taking one out of the package, the young man grunted, "Well, it looks like I'll have to quit anyway. After this one, I'll have just two left."

"It's true," Hollands said softly as he watched the flame from Ron's lighter ignite the end of the cigarette.

As a small cloud of smoke billowed from Ron's mouth and nostrils he looked around the area and asked, "I'm sorry, what was that Captain? What's true?"

Holding up the newspaper clipping, Hollands said again, "It's true. Nearly all people of Japanese ancestry living on the West Coast of North America including Canada, or in the Hawaiian Islands, have been interned. Sent to relocation camps."

The pain on Ron's face said it all. "That's my country," he sighed, "my native land. Why is this happening to my family, to my friends? It's unbelievable! My God, what my parents must be going through. The humiliation! What a mess."

The sincerity in his voice and the expression on his face convinced Captain Hollands of the honesty of Yoshida's story. Hollands carefully lowered the hammer on his .45 and holstered it.

"Try to understand something, Lieutenant," began Hollands. "Suppose you were the head of the Japanese government, and I and hundreds of other Americans were living in Tokyo; suppose hundreds of bombers and fighters sneaked in under a flag of peace, bombed the hell out of your Navy and Army, strafing and bombing cities, killing thousands of military personnel and civilians. What do you think you, the Japanese government, would have done with me and others like me who, perhaps, had had homes and businesses in Japan for decades? Even if we had been born there."

Ron blinked a few times. "Was the attack on Pearl Harbor that severe? We heard that the Japs had pulled off a successful raid, but that's about all we were told."

"Two Japanese Ambassadors and two aides were in Washington, D. C.," explained Hollands, "to meet with the Secretary of State, Mr. Hull, and others in our government to negotiate a treaty. However, they arrived two hours late for their appointment. Pearl had already been attacked. The Philippines were hit the next day."

Hollands took a deep breath, and fell quiet for a moment. As he glanced up through the canopy of palm trees, he said. "The Arizona went down at her moorage with over fifteen-hundred sailors below decks. Nearly eighty percent of the U.S. Pacific Fleet was put out of commission. Most of the aircraft based on or around the main island were destroyed or damaged. Fewer than a dozen of our fighters were able to respond. It was just another sleepy Sunday morning in Paradise."

Yoshida was quiet for several moments. Then he said softly, "The Japanese people were never told the truth and no wonder. The government, the Emperor, said that there had been a one-hour advance declaration of war given in Washington. Talk about losing face."

Solemnly and slowly Hollands said, "There isn't anything fair about this war. But we didn't start it with either Japan or Germany."

After a few more minutes, Ron jumped to his feet and said, "Hey Captain, am I your prisoner?"

"Hell no. Why?"

"Cause I'm hungry and tired. If I were your prisoner, according to the Geneva Convention, it would be your responsibility to feed me."

"Or just shoot ya," Hollands quipped.

"Hmm... I hadn't thought of that possibility!"

"What would you have said if I had answered yes, you are my prisoner?"

Yoshida smiled. "The same thing; tired and hungry, and according to the Geneva Convention, it would be your responsibility to feed me and let me rest."

"Well, I'm tired and hungry too!" Hollands admitted. "Actually, I wasn't aware that Japan signed the Geneva Convention."

"Well, I don't know that for sure either," he said smiling. "It was just a thought."

In Hollands' survival gear were several boxes of K-rations. Although not fine dining, at least they were a buffer between hunger and starvation. As they made their way through a small area of dense jungle, Hollands shared his food with Ron and wisecracked, "I've always thought of the 'K' in K-rations as some sort of an algebraic symbol. An unknown variable of dubious origin."

Ron laughed and said, "Well, it's nice to eat real food, even if it is field rations." Taking a couple of bites, he added, "The Japanese Army has similar little packages. Cans of rice and fish or cans of rice and pork. But the smell... I could barely stand to open any of it, let alone eat it. Boy, what I wouldn't do right now for a loaded hamburger and a Coke!"

"What, no rice balls?" Hollands joked.

"I hate that stuff. We rarely ate it at home, except when we had relatives over for dinner. We had American food, you know, like spaghetti and chop suey."

Looking wistfully into the cloudy sky, Yoshida sighed, "How 'bout a baked potato lying alongside a nice, thick, juicy steak, smothered in onions and mushrooms."

"Oh, knock it off. These rations are bad enough as it is," Hollands groaned.

A short distance farther, Hollands suddenly spotted what appeared to be a well-used path through some heavy grass. Stuffing his empty ration can inside his tote bag, he led Ron over to the path and they cautiously continued their trek, keeping a wary lookout as they strained to hear anything besides their own breathing, heartbeats, and the rain.

Drawing his pistol once more, Hollands turned to his new companion and was surprised to see Ron also had a pistol, a revolver. Seeing a stunned look on Hollands' face, Ron softly mimicked the voice of what Hollywood many times had portrayed as a Japanese officer, and in a strained, high pitched voice he said, "Japanese velly smaat. Amelican velly stupid, but make good house pets. We must be velly caaful and velly sneaky."

Hollands smiled slightly as both men crouched down. "*Velly* funny, Lieutenant. Now tell me, did the Nips... Ah, the *Japanese*, have anyone stationed here?"

"If they did, or do, I hadn't heard of it," Ron answered. "This has always been one of the islands where loose bombs get jettisoned. Not a good place for peace and quiet. This rock is on a flight path from base. It was not unusual for us, especially the new pilots, to practice strafing and bombing when not on a mission."

Crouching and watching for possible booby-traps, the men slowly moved along the path. Every twenty to thirty yards, they stopped to listen, and after a few moments they moved forward. The path meandered through differing terrain, even crossing a small creek. After several minutes, they finally came to a small clearing. To the north, they spotted two small huts.

Stopping dead in their tracks, they dropped to the ground. After a few seconds, they moved to a kneeling position.

"What do you think, Captain?"

"Someone's been around here. This trail is well used. See? Old boot prints," observed Hollands.

Looking cautiously around, Ron said, "Who do think you are, The Lone Ranger?"

"Yes, in my previous life! C'mon, let's move up."

The light rain that had fallen since early morning had gradually increased to a steady downpour. The two would-be enemy pilots split up, and, with their sidearms still in hand, approached the first hut from opposite sides, meeting up at the doorway.

"No one's home," Ron said softly.

Stepping inside and looking around, Hollands added, "Maybe not now. But it sure appears that someone has been here off and on. What's that odor?"

"Something's rotten," responded Ron. "Smells like fish heads."

They backed out of the doorway and went to check out the second hut. Cautiously they stepped in the entrance. It was definitely cleaner and more lived in and didn't smell as bad as the other hut. A worn canvas cot leaned against a wall, and two others lay folded in a corner.

Hollands' curiosity and energy were waning fast. There were signs that both the Allies and the Japanese may have used these facilities at some time.

"This place is creepy. Do you think anyone's around, Captain?" Ron asked.

Hollands stripped off his wet flight suit. "It may not be smart to stay here, but I would guess if these huts were used, it was many months ago."

He hung the flight suit on a wooden post hook to dry. Both men gathered up some dried palm boughs to make bedding for their cots.

"Maybe coast watchers or local fishermen take shelter here sometimes," Hollands guessed.

Ron kicked a large, rusty tin can out from under some rubbish in a corner.

Hollands stood still for a moment and suggested, "Hey, let's make a little stove. Gather up some bits and pieces of dried wood and fronds. We'll heat up some more chow. The rain and mist should cover any smoke."

It was late afternoon when they finished eating. Hollands checked his flight suit and found it was nearly dry. Throwing it over the fragments of palm-bough bedding, he sighed, "I need some rest."

As Ron finished getting his cot ready, he said, "I'll take first watch and wake you in a few hours. Okay with you?"

"Fine with me," Hollands agreed, adding with a touch of mockery, "You know, Lieutenant, if there are any Americans or Aussies on this rock and they see you, they're apt to shoot first and ask... no questions at all."

The Japanese nodded thoughtfully. "That's not funny."

"Look, if there are Nips on this rock and they find us together they'll probably assume I'm your prisoner, question me, offer a bit of torture, then shoot me regardless. On the other hand, if the Yanks stop by, I'll just tell them you're *my* prisoner, at least until we can explain your situation. That should keep you safe."

"That sounds workable. Just don't forget whose side I'm really on."

"Ah, and just what side might *that* be, Lieutenant?" Hollands joked.

"I don't think that's funny, either!" snapped Yoshida.

Hollands settled onto the makeshift bedding on the cot, and was quickly sound asleep.

Lieutenant Yoshida stood guard.

Hollands awoke slowly. The rain had stopped. With his eyes still closed, he could feel sunshine warming his face. Then a thought occurred... *He didn't wake me for guard.*

Sensing the presence of others in the hut, he slowly reached down under the cot for his 45, but grabbed only his empty holster. Lying on his belly and opening his eyes, he muttered, "Yoshida, you bastard, you're quite the con artist."

Then he pushed himself up and turned to a sitting position on the cot, half expecting a hut full of Japanese. Instead, he found himself looking into the barrels of two M-1 rifles and his own pistol. Three extremely dirty, tattered, and threadbare Caucasians, two men and a woman, were at the opposite ends. Looking quickly around the room, he saw that Ron was not there.

"Okay, what the hell's going on here," Hollands demanded.

"Shut up," a gravelly voice ordered. "Move it outside."

Hollands repeated his question, but was harshly nudged in the ribs by a rifle barrel. He pulled on his boots, laced them part way up, grabbed his shirt, and stepped outside of the shack into a gloriously, hot, humid South Pacific morning. Glancing at his watch, he saw that it was 6:30. He mumbled to himself, "Damn! I've slept for almost thirteen hours."

In the daylight, Hollands could clearly identify what was left of U.S. Military uniforms on his captors. All rank and related insignias were faded or had long been missing.

Looking back toward the hut, Hollands saw that the woman was carrying his pistol and survival bag, along with the two wallets which held his and Ron's identification.

Hollands surveyed the immediate area and soon located Yoshida on the other side of the clearing. Tied and gagged, he was being guarded by a third man, who also carried an M-1.

"Don't hurt him, he's an American," Hollands hollered frantically, "We both are!"

The three initial captors huddled together, keeping a wary eye on Hollands as they talked things over. Then the older man, the one with gravel in his voice, finally asked, "Were you the pilot of the U.S. Army fighter that went down in the lagoon yesterday?"

Hollands figured this man for a non-commissioned officer. "Yes! I'm Captain Michael Hollands, Army Air Corps, presently attached to the Navy Command on Pateroa Island."

Gesturing towards Ron, the second man asked, "If he's American why is he wearing a Jap uniform?"

"He was in Japan as an exchange student prior to the war, and was forced into their service. His other option was to be executed. So he joined. At twenty years old what would you have done under the same circumstances? He saved my life yesterday. Twice, I think."

The woman held both men's wallets and began looking through them.

Hollands hoped there wasn't anything incriminating in his new friend's effects. "You have both our ID's," he said. "What do you think?"

Finally, the woman said, "The Jap has a California driver's license with a San Francisco address, and there's also a U.C.L.A. student body card. This second man's ID seems okay, too, Sarge. His driver's license says he's from Seattle. And here's his Army Identification card, too. It reads just what he said."

The process had taken over ten minutes, and Hollands still had his hands raised high. Irritated, he slowly lowered his hands.

"Okay, this has gone far enough!" he snapped in his best early morning Army Captain's bark. "You all know who we are. Now identify yourselves."

The older, grizzled man studied Hollands for a few moments before he answered, "Sorry, Captain, but we have to be careful, especially after seeing the Nip. I'm Beckett, sir, Gunnery Sergeant Elmore Beckett, U.S. Marines Corps. Roberts and me, sir, well we've been stranded on this gawd-awful rock passing five months now, ever since late one night last February when our troopship got torpedoed. I loaded as many men as possible into an LCVP, sir, before the ship went down. But when the LCVP, that's a landing craft, sir, became a bathtub we had to make a swim for it. I think we were the only survivors out of over two thousand men on board that ship."

"And I'm Boatswain's Mate Third Class Timothy Roberts, sir" the other man said. "U.S. Coast Guard. I was coxswain of the Higgins boat—the landing craft, sir."

Hollands glanced at the young soldier who was guarding Yoshida, and at the woman and turned back to Beckett. "What about those two?"

"They were here when we came ashore, Captain."

The young man who had been guarding Ron exclaimed angrily, "We didn't desert! No one would come for us. We've been waiting for a long time."

"At ease, Private," snapped the old Marine. "Tell the captain who you are." Then with the speck of military humor left in his soul, the old gunny said, "He's Army, sir. No offense!"

"None taken, Sergeant."

Making an effort to come to attention, the young soldier said, "I'm Private First Class Carl Minetti, U.S. Army, sir."

"We were the ones who've been deserted, Captain," the woman added. "Our units have known our location for months."

She was about five feet, three inches tall with medium brown hair, now somewhat matted.

Hollands figured that she had to be about twenty, but her eyes looked to be those of a much older woman, and her face showed the effects of fear and exhaustion.

Then with a deep sigh, she said, "I'm Sergeant Janet Gilbress, sir. Hospital laboratory technician, Women's Army Auxiliary Corps."

Hollands walked over to the woman and retrieved his pistol, survival kit, and his and Ron's identification papers and wallets.

Looking the Marine in the eye, Hollands softly but firmly ordered, "Sergeant, release Lieutenant Yoshida."

After a slight hesitation, the well-worn Marine nodded, and the young man who had been guarding Ron untied his captive. Then he and Yoshida joined the others.

Hearing some movement from behind, Hollands turned and was surprised to see a fifth person, another woman—a little taller than the first—approaching through the wet, tall grass and shrubs. Her torn and dirty uniform appearance was similar to that of the others, but there was an air of survival and strength about her.

Hollands looked at the Marine. "Just how many are you?"

"I'm the last one, Captain," answered the woman as she approached the group.

Stopping in front of Hollands, she made an effort to come to attention. As she began to raise her hand to salute, Hollands gently caught her wrist.

"We'll forego military formalities for now," he said. "All of you, at ease. Rest."

"Thank you, Captain. I'm Army Nurse Second Lieutenant Gail Elliott. And as Sergeant Beckett has stated, he and Petty Officer Roberts have been here on this nameless pile-of-rocks for five months now. Janet, Carl and I, have been here for most of six months... or seven."

She paused for a second. "What month is it, Captain?"

"Unbelievable!" Hollands whispered. "It's June, Lieutenant, the twenty-fifth."

"Seven months!" the two women said in unison.

Leaning lightly on his weapon, the old leatherneck said, "We haven't seen any of our ships close enough to flash a signal. The damn Nips like to jettison their loose bombs on and around this island, and practice their strafing."

Slowly he knelt down on one knee, resting more heavily on his rifle. "Sorry, Captain, I've got a bum hip. I got knocked around pretty bad when we were torpedoed."

"That's quite all right, Sergeant. Please continue."

"Thank you, sir." Seating himself on a large rock, the sergeant gave a big sigh.

"The two of us only had five days of rations. After meeting up with the others, we pooled what we had. Later, we started catching some fish. A turtle once in a while. And we collected what fruit and rainwater we could. But we're constantly watching for Jap ships, or listening for their planes."

"Or praying for a PBY," Sergeant Gilbress said. "*Anything* to get us out of here."

"But the fishing isn't much," the old gunny said. "Sea turtles are good, but they're also scarce."

Looking around at their gaunt, hungry faces, Hollands raised his survival kit high into the air. "It's not gourmet, but it is food. How about some K-rations? There are several boxes here to pick from; enough for everyone for a day or so."

The older man looked longingly at the bag. "I never thought I'd live to say it, but I've missed K-rations."

Hollands leaned down to the old gunnery sergeant and said wryly, "No offense, Sarge; it's Army, not Marine rations."

With a slight grin, the old Marine answered, "No offense taken, Captain."

As everyone ate, the group took turns explaining to Hollands how the island had been a base for amphibian aircraft for both sides at different times.

Lieutenant Elliott said, "For a time, we ran a four-bed hospital. Two tents laced together. And well camouflaged."

Pointing southeasterly, she said, "It's a short walk from here. You two nearly walked into it yesterday. It's up a slight rise, a few hundred yards from the lagoon."

"When the Allies decided they no longer could hold on here, their pilot promised to return for the rest of us," Sergeant Gilbress said.

Private Roberts said, "The next day, sir, the Navy sent in a PBY, but as it approached the lagoon, an enemy fighter swooped in behind it and shot it down, killing the three crewmen. The crippled ship passed the beach area and crashed into the ocean a couple miles off the point."

"They tried again a few days later, but that plane was chased off and we think it escaped," said Nurse Elliott. "That was the last time any rescue was attempted, Captain. We had the two remaining Navy pilots in our med-tent. They would have lived if we could have gotten them to a real hospital. We buried them about five months ago."

Within an hour, it was clear to Captain Hollands that the only way anyone would get off the island was to have everyone working together. He didn't have a clue as to how, but he knew time and weather were not on their side. These people were tired, malnourished, and demoralized. The little food Hollands had wasn't a cure; perhaps it was only a postponement of the inevitable. If anything positive were to happen, it would have to be soon.

"Let's not waste any more time or energy," Hollands said as he firmly took command. "As of right now, we are an American military unit."

Seizing the moment, he established a chain of command by turning to Beckett, and staring in the old Marine's eyes. "Sergeant, tell one of your men to fetch Lieutenant Yoshida's and my gear out of the hut."

As Beckett studied Hollands' face, he slowly answered, "Yes, sir. Right away."

Then turning to Roberts, he gave him a nod and the lad slowly headed into the hut.

Looking around the group, Hollands said, "I will need to take complete stock of what food, medicines, weapons, and ammo you have here."

"We ain't got much, Captain," Minetti said.

"That's not quite so. Everyone listen up! We do have some equipment. From out of my fighter, we can pull the radio, batteries, compass, and anything else we can use that hasn't been broken or that can be repaired. We should be able to get the radio operational again if the Nips haven't shot it up, or the salt water hasn't gotten into it."

As it turned out, both of the young men were good mechanics.

"I'm good with radios, sir. I can pull that," said Minetti.

"I'll give you a hand, Carl," Roberts volunteered returning from the hut.

He placed Yoshida's and Hollands' belongings on the ground at Hollands' feet. "How about the fighter's machine guns, sir? Shall we pull some of them, too?"

"Now you're thinking," Hollands said. "They were working just before I hit the water. Should be a little ammo left, too."

Looking around, he added, "I won't lie to you. It's a miracle of God's Grace that all of you are still alive. But pulling together, we will eventually get off this rock. It's *all* of us, or *none* of us."

Hollands turned to the old Marine and asked, "How's your hip, Sarge?"

"Doing much better, sir, thanks."

"Good, you're in charge of this detail. Stay on the beach and keep a keen ear to the sky and an eye on the horizon."

Sergeant Beckett gave an enthusiastic, "Yes, sir!"

"Now, before anyone leaves," Hollands announced, "Let me officially introduce to you Ron Yoshida of San Francisco, California. He will give you a brief rundown concerning his past two-and-a-half years. I think you'll find what he has to say pretty interesting."

Ron gave his audience a shortened version of how he became involved in the Japanese military. When he finished, Hollands explained how Ron had saved his life the day before.

"Now, let's get started on the plane. Remember, if the Japs fly over, you might have to dive underneath a wing, so everyone, keep alert."

Looking at the two young men, Hollands guessed they were maybe eighteen, going on forty. "Can you men handle this?"

"Can do, sir," they answered in unison.

"We also have a few basic tools, sir," Minetti said.

As the three men started off toward the lagoon, Hollands turned to Ron and said, "I'd like to know just how big this island is, Lieutenant, so take a hike."

"It takes under two hours to walk its shoreline, sir," Sergeant Gilbress said.

"Thank you," Hollands acknowledged.

He turned back to Yoshida. "That's your job, Ron. Take a defensive look around. Check under rocks, shrubs, in and around trees. I want to know what's here, and what's not, and from what direction we might expect trouble. Since you were part of their air arm on that island nearby, you figure out where they may come ashore. Sooner or later, they will come, even if only for a little practice."

"On my way, Captain."

"Wait a second. When you get down near the lagoon, call out to Sergeant Beckett. Otherwise, he's liable to clean your ears out with a round from his M-1."

"You know, Hollands, you've got a real sick sense of humor," the Japanese pilot stated. "But thanks for the warning. That had occurred to me."

"Seriously, Lieutenant, stay loose and keep close to the trees."

"Will do. See ya soon."

Pausing for a moment before starting on his hike, Ron tossed back over his shoulder, "Boy, you all sure sound good to me."

As Yoshida started his walk, Hollands turned to the women and asked, "Would you ladies give me a tour of the camp and med-tent?"

"Yes, sir. It's right this way. We'll write an inventory of all the food and medical supplies we have on hand and make a short list of basic needs."

Somehow Hollands had to get a message to Pateroa. He had no desire to stay on the island any longer than necessary. With the war so close by, he preferred doing more than throwing rocks or coconuts at enemy planes.

"If only that radio still works," he whispered to himself. He was convinced it could be the key to getting help and their eventual rescue.

Hollands and the women slowly walked to the area the five marooned Americans had been using as an encampment. As they hiked along, he could see craters where the enemy had been practicing bombing and jettisoning their ordnance. The area looked like a war zone. He casually, filled the women in on all the news and events he could remember from the states and that he thought would be of interest to them.

From a few yards away, Hollands saw the camp. It was an open area dotted with huge palms that concealed it from the air. Two small lean-tos and a larger tent were the only structures. Debris from the trees covered nearly every inch of ground.

Suddenly, Hollands stopped and threw up his hands for quiet. "I hear something!" he whispered.

"I don't hear a thing, Captain," Lieutenant Elliott whispered back. "Oh! Now I do."

Concentrating hard, Hollands said softly, "Two engines, non-radials, running slowly."

As the sound grew closer he asked, "Is there a quick way back to the lagoon?"

"Yes, sir," answered Gilbress. "See that break in the brush? There's a path beyond. The lagoon will be about two hundred yards."

"Thanks, Sergeant."

Hollands nodded to the two women. "I know I don't have to remind you to stay out of sight. So I won't!"

"We'll be fine, sir," Elliott said.

Hollands took off on a run. Cutting through the high grass, he crossed over where Yoshida's flight suit was still in place. In less than a minute, he reached the small berm a few yards from the water's edge. With lots of tall grass and palm trees, as cover, he dropped to the ground to listen and observe.

A few seconds later, he heard Sergeant Beckett call out, "Over here, Captain."

The three men were in position, their rifles ready.

A small twin-engine Japanese floatplane was on approach, still about two miles out. A large amount of smoke was pouring out of the starboard engine. Once inside the breakwater of the lagoon, the craft, still a mile or so from shore, gently settled onto the water and the pilot shut down the smoking engine.

The tall grass and tree line concealed the four men well.

"Their engine trouble may just be minor," Hollands said. "Hopefully, they'll be able to fix it quickly and leave."

As they continued to watch, Hollands said, "Okay, listen up. You are to fire only on my orders. Keep quiet; stay out of sight."

"Sir, why not just kill the pilots and anyone else on board and steal the plane. You could fly us all out of here," suggested Beckett.

"I wish we could," said Hollands. "But they've probably radioed their position. We can't take that chance, Sergeant."

He studied the aircraft. "I wish Yoshida were here right now."

"I'm over here, second palm on the right. What's the matter, Captain? You miss me already?"

Turning to the right, the four could see Yoshida flat on the ground, breathing hard, and with his face in the grass.

"Damn, Hollands, that was about a four-hundred yard dash I just ran. I haven't done that since high school."

"Okay, Ron—get your face out of the salad, and get over here."

Although the lagoon was large, it had a rock spit that connected with the inland part of the two beach areas. Another spit hid the corpse of Hollands' Thunderbolt from ground level. Directly in front of Hollands and the others was a well-worn dock with a shack-like structure at the far end.

Ron crawled over to the others. At their position several yards from the water, they could look straight down the old dock. The Japanese plane was still some distance out, and the smoke from the one engine had lessened considerably.

Hollands asked, "Sarge, who's the best marksman here?"

"I'd have to say Minetti, sir."

"How about it Minetti? How's your shooting?" Hollands asked.

"I'm pretty good, sir," the young soldier answered confidently. "And I've kept my rifle clean, sir. We all have."

"Sergeant, I want you and Roberts to stay here and cover us if needed."

"Yes, sir."

"All right men, I have a plan. Minetti, Yoshida, and I are going wading. We'll be out of sight because we will be beneath the dock. We'll work our way out to the hut at the end, hiding beneath it. We need to be in position before the Japanese pilot reaches the dock."

"I just hope the water isn't too deep," Ron muttered.

"Captain, sir," Minetti began, "in this area of the lagoon, the bottom is pretty uneven. It's full of loose rock and some coral. The water is deepest at the end of the dock. We're at low tide now, so the water will be about waist high and warm, sir."

"Thanks, Private. That's good information. Now, let's go."

The three men cautiously crept to the right, staying in the tree line. Then, to the right of the dock where they were out of sight of the approaching small seaplane, they went down on their bellies and crawled toward the water. Moving to a crouch, they waded a few yards into the water, and ducked beneath the boardwalk. The dock was less than a hundred feet long, but it seemed like miles as they moved slowly so as not to disturb the water. They made their way just out to the hut, but not under it. The dock proved to be excellent cover.

After all three were in place, Hollands said, "Ron, I want you to get as close as you can and listen to their conversation. What you hear will determine whether or not we have to kill them."

The Japanese pilot shut down the second engine and the plane gently drifted toward the dock. There were only two men on board. One of them, probably the co-pilot, was trying to open the small side door but it was stuck fast.

Hollands whispered to his two companions, "If they can repair the engine and leave, fine. But if they try to call for help, we'll have to take 'em out before they can get to the radio."

He made eye contact with both Minetti and Yoshida. "Is that understood?"

The two nodded.

The side door finally opened to what Hollands figured was a flurry of Japanese expletives. Once the plane was secured to the dock, the pilot climbed out the top hatch carrying a small toolbox. The other man joined him atop the wing.

Quietly and slowly, Yoshida moved from under the wharf and reached a spot beneath the tail section of the plane. Then he continued moving along the starboard side of the fuselage. As he had hoped, the two fliers quickly became engrossed in their work. Their backs were to him as he slowly made his way forward, stopping under the wing near the pontoon strut. There he waited and listened, his revolver in hand.

Yoshida had moved out of Hollands' sight to the opposite side of the aircraft; Hollands hadn't expected him to move in so close. But other than occasional bits of laughter and the clanking of tools, no one could clearly hear the voices of the two Japanese as they worked. After several minutes, Ron waded back to where Hollands and Minetti were waiting.

"Well, what did you find out?"

"They will probably have the plane ready to go in ten to fifteen minutes," Yoshida whispered. "It's just a short piece of oil line that needs to be repaired. But Mike, I got a good look inside; it's a damn flying radio-command center. It's crammed full of radio gear the likes of which I've never seen, along with what looks like volumes of code books."

Shaking his head he repeated, "I've never seen anything like it. We can't let this plane go! We've gotta stop 'em from leaving. We have to destroy that equipment."

If Hollands had held any lingering reservations about Lieutenant Yoshida's loyalties, this certainly settled the question. But what kind of danger would Hollands be getting everyone into if he agreed with Ron? He and Yoshida were pretty fresh and physically fit. The others were worn beyond endurance. Then there were the two women to consider. This plane's radio-gear would be a prize, and there was no doubt that they had to either destroy everything or salvage what they could and maybe use it to the Allies' advantage.

Carl had overheard Ron's report. He moved closer and kept his voice low. "Captain, you asked me a while back what kind of a shot I was."

"I'm listening," Hollands said. "Make your point, Private, we're a little short on time."

"Well, sir, I agree with the lieutenant. And the way those two are sitting on the wing, I can kill them both with one round or no more than two. Neither of them will reach the radio."

Hollands and Yoshida looked at each other and were quiet for a few seconds as they considered their next move.

"Don't let my age fool ya, sir," the young private said. "We need that equipment, and we've got to keep that plane from leaving. Even a private knows that, sir."

Hollands was surprised and reassured by Minetti's obvious maturity. He nodded to the young soldier. "Okay, I pray to God we're correct. If we're wrong, we could have their buddies here within an hour."

Thinking hard for a moment, then with a quick look at Yoshida, Hollands nodded at the young Army private and said, "Okay, do it!"

Minetti slowly and quietly waded back through the water to the airplane side of the dock. Two minutes later, his M-1 rifle rang out the moment of truth. With his one shot both enemy fliers fell into the water. At eighteen, Carl Minetti finally killed two of the enemy in this war. Hollands observed the young soldier who had been absolutely convinced that it was the correct thing to do.

Minetti slowly waded to the opposite side of the dock and sloshed up out of the water onto the nearby bank where he quietly puked. Hollands quietly followed him and, putting a hand on Carl's shoulder, said, "I hope killing never becomes easy for you. It still isn't for me. I get sick every time."

With a voice of relief, the young soldier said quietly, "Thank you, sir!"

Hollands and Minetti returned to where Ron was waiting. The three quickly climbed onto the dock to inspect the aircraft.

"That's a Grumman Widgeon," Hollands said. "Hey, Ron, how did the Japanese come to have an American aircraft?"

"Don't know for sure, Captain. Perhaps confiscated from a British civilian in Shanghai or Hong Kong," guessed Yoshida.

As they looked over the aircraft, Hollands said, "Jeez, look at all that gear!"

Then he had a sudden inspiration. Hollering for Beckett and Roberts to join them, he turned back to Yoshida, "You're sure about what you heard and saw?"

"Absolutely! From what they said, no one knows where they are. But you can bet your fortune cookies that some admiral in the Imperial Japanese Navy will want this plane and all this equipment back. And *soon*."

Beckett and Roberts hurried down the dock toward the aircraft. Hollands briefed them, explaining what equipment had been discovered in the plane that led to his decision.

"Couldn't do anything less, Captain," advised the old Marine, who quietly placed his arm around Minetti's shoulders.

"Nice going, son," the leatherneck said quietly. "Okay, get into the water, men, and move those two bodies out of sight."

"Right away, Sarge!" Roberts answered.

"A slight change of plans," Hollands said. "Gentlemen, we could have minutes, an hour, or most of a day. We just don't know. Lieutenant Yoshida can read a little Japanese, so he will be in charge of dismantling the large radio. Sergeant Beckett will be our eyes and ears while we work inside the plane. Should enemy fighters appear, only the Lieutenant will be visible. The rest of us must stay out of sight. Any questions?"

All were quiet.

"Okay, let's get some tools down here and get started; on the double."

Dividing the work, the five planned to concentrate first on stripping the floatplane while being careful of the wiring and any attached radio batteries.

Minetti suddenly remembered, "Hey, the Japs had a tool box on top."

Removing the radio gear was going much faster than expected and was nearing completion. The women had hurried down to help, and began carrying some of the radio gear off the dock to the cover of the trees. Hollands sent Sergeant Beckett and his two young men over to begin stripping the downed Thunderbolt.

"Hey, Mike," Yoshida called out.

"What's up?"

"Look what I've found! Give me a hand with these," he said as they off-loaded three large wooden crates and a half a dozen smaller boxes.

Seeing the Japanese writing on the crates and boxes Nurse Elliott asked, "What is all this, Lieutenant?"

Looking up at Hollands and at the women with a huge grin on his face, Ron explained, "Now, I really don't much care for Japanese food. However, I dislike being hungry even more. This is a hell of a lot of food!"

Seeing his listeners' blank expressions, Yoshida said, "So, how about it, will you trust me and eat enemy food?"

Picking up little emotion from his audience, he said, "Hey, there must be over two hundred pounds of canned food here; meats, vegetables and—

I think bamboo shoots. Oh, and a large bag of rice and a few small bottles of sake."

Under his breath, he muttered, "I hate bamboo shoots!"

Pointing to the smaller boxes, he added, "This is all part of an extremely complete medical kit. This is what would usually accompany high ranking officers, like admirals or generals."

The two women glanced uneasily from Yoshida to Hollands.

Lieutenant Elliott fidgeted for a moment and looked uncertainly at the crates. "This is great," she half-heartedly admitted.

There was enough food for the seven of them to eat well for a long time. Food to help rebuild their strength, and to help heal minds and bodies. Food to last, perhaps, until help could come. But, as Yoshida had said, it was *enemy* food.

The second part of Captain Hollands' plans seemed, at least on the surface, not only gruesome, but impossible. It was nearing the noon hour. With everything off-loaded and out of sight, Hollands and Ron returned to the plane.

As they walked the length of the dock, Ron asked, "What can we do with the plane, Mike? We certainly can't sink it or hide it under the trees."

"First, we're going to turn her around, Lieutenant," Hollands said calmly. "Then your two cousins are going to fly her out of here,"

"Whoa!" exclaimed Ron, putting his hand on Hollands arm to stop him. "You want to run that by me again, Hollands?"

"Look, Ron," Hollands answered. "Here's a list of can'ts; part of which you just covered. We *can't* leave the plane here, we *can't* hide it, we *can't* dismantle it, and we sure as hell *can't* burn it. That would be like sending your relatives an engraved invitation."

Pausing, and looking up into the bright blue sky, Hollands added, "Actually, I had a brief idea of trying to fly us all out of here, but I think there are too many of us."

"Sorry, Hollands. I'm still not following you," Ron admitted.

"You will. But first you need to finish what the pilots started and fix that oil line."

The two Japanese bodies had been tied to the dock out of sight.

As Hollands and Ron approached the front of the plane, Hollands jumped into the water. "First, help me turn the plane around. Then, we have to get the pilots buckled into their seats and tie the controls, and..."

"Okay, okay, now I get it. You sure you didn't bump your head when you crashed yesterday?"

Hollands shrugged. "Crash? What crash? I thought that was a pretty good landing, considering I wasn't flying a seaplane."

He looked up from the water at his new comrade. "Okay, let's get to work. Untie the rope."

Turning the small seaplane around and reattaching the line to the wharf was a cinch. Untying the two Japanese, pulling them out of the water, loading them into the plane and lashing them into their seats was more difficult.

Ron had climbed onto the starboard wing, so he could finish the work on that engine. When he was sure the repair was complete, he slid into the cockpit to restart both motors.

Then they heard the warning; two M-1 rifle reports from the shore. A few seconds later, they heard the sound of two single-engine aircraft approaching from the northeast.

"They can't be ours," said Ron.

"Which 'ours' are you referring to?" Hollands asked.

Through the window of the plane, he saw two Zeros approaching the lagoon, just above the trees.

"Damn! Step out and wave," he said. "But don't look up at them."

Ron scrambled through the overhead hatch and waved to the Zeros. "I sure hope they don't recognize me, or that they're not close personal friends of their departed comrades."

As the Zeros flew overhead, he remarked, "Personally, I'd prefer a flock of Corsairs or Hellcats right about now."

"Amen to that," Hollands said.

As the Japanese fighters prepared to make their 180 degree turns for a second pass, Ron dropped back into the cockpit, frantically flipping switches. "Why won't they turn over? Hope those kids didn't cut the main power cable."

He took a fast look at the gauges. "Cross your fingers, Captain. We're just about out of chances."

Then he hit the primer and starter at the same time. The port engine roared instantly to life.

"They're circling back; coming in much slower and lower," Hollands announced.

"Sonofabitch!" Ron gasped. "They've probably been trying to call their dead buddies on the radio."

"What's wrong?"

"Starboard's still not responding," said Yoshida. "No juice."

He climbed back through the overhead hatch and crawled to the silent engine. The cowling was not totally fastened down and offered some flex-room.

"I found the problem! The lead cable was not connected. Why the hell didn't I see that before?"

He pried up the cowling with his left hand, reached in with his right hand, and hastily secured the cable.

He dropped back through the hatch and hit the starter switch again. The propeller began to turn slowly, just as the Zeros made their second pass, not more than fifty feet above them.

"Come-on, come-on. Fire off, you bastard!" Ron yelled again.

With a cloud of bluish-white smoke, the engine finally rumbled to life.

Looking out the front they saw the two Zeros fly past, rocking their wings, signaling their good-bye or good-luck, or both.

"Whew! That was close," Hollands said hoarsely.

He exited the aircraft and stepped onto the dock. "Okay, Ron, set the controls for takeoff. When I give the word, open the throttles and jump clear."

"Gotcha!" Ron answered.

Cutting a length of strap off a parachute, Yoshida tied the controls back to what he hoped would be a good takeoff position, and blocked the foot controls with loose pieces of radio cabinetry. He adjusted the trim tabs and flaps, and ran the engines up to near full power. Then he turned a butterfly adjustment screw to the fuel flow valve.

Two ropes tethered the aircraft to the dock. Hollands untied the front rope from the fuselage and then rushed to the rear of the plane to wait for Yoshida's signal.

When he got the thumbs-up, Hollands tugged on the rope, pointing the plane away from the dock and heading the craft toward the open sea.

With one more yoke adjustment, Ron leaped through the open side-hatch into the water as the seaplane surged forward.

Hollands quickly helped Ron onto the dock.

From the hut at the end, they watched the small enemy aircraft as it raced, fish-tailing across the calm water of the lagoon.

For over three hours, the two men had worked on this. The whole exercise could still end in disaster.

Finally, leaving the water, the plane began lifting into the air, flying almost straight and true. It listed slightly to port.

"How far do you think she'll fly, Mike?" Ron asked.

"Damned if I know," Hollands said. "I wouldn't have bet on her getting off the water."

The plane gained speed and continued to climb slowly. A commotion on the dock caught the attention of the two pilots. Stepping out from the cover of the hut they saw the old leatherneck limping hurriedly towards them, followed by the two women.

"Everybody, inside the hut, out of sight," Hollands ordered.

Sergeant Gilbress had tears streaming down her face. "I thought you had left us, sir. I thought you had gone."

In a gesture of comfort, Hollands put his arm around her. "I just got here, Janet! Why would I leave?"

He looked at the old Marine and the Nurse Lieutenant. "You haven't quit, and I won't quit either. There's no quitting by any of us. As I explained earlier, we'll get through this together or not at all."

From the cover of the hut, they all turned back to watch the seaplane again.

The old Marine handed his binoculars to Hollands.

Hollands took a quick look. "The Zeros have just flown past her, and that right engine is smoking again."

Before he could say another word, the plane—now perhaps five or six miles out—exploded into a large ball of fire, sending flaming debris tumbling into the ocean. After a few seconds, even at that distance they heard the explosion.

"Damn, imagine that!" Ron said coolly.

Everyone suddenly looked quite inquisitively and earnestly at Yoshida.

At long last Hollands asked what the others really wanted to know, "What the hell did you do, Lieutenant?"

"Oh, I guess that fuel valve leak just got a bit worse, that's all."

"What fuel valve leak?"

Yoshida shrugged. "Oh, just a fuel valve leak. At least there isn't anything for the Japanese military to tie *that* accident to this island. Right, Captain?"

Looking at Ron in disbelief, Hollands nodded. "Right, Lieutenant."

As the group made their way off the dock, Hollands stopped Beckett. "Sergeant, how's the stripping of my old plane coming along?"

"Those kids are a wonder, sir. Another half hour or so and it will be completed. If we don't get any more Zeros."

"That's fine. Remember, Beckett, it still has to look the same from the air."

"Yes, sir," agreed the Marine. "Roberts has trimmed some small palm fronds and stuck the stalks in the three empty gun ports."

Beckett hesitated for a moment. "Ya know, those boys are all right, Captain. But I just can't understand it."

"What can't you understand, Sergeant?" Hollands asked.

"Well, sir, it's just... Ah, well, they're not Marines."

"Perhaps they've been learning from you, Sergeant."

He rubbed the stubble on his weatherworn face and smiled "Yeah, that makes sense, Captain. I guess I am a good teacher at that. Maybe I should start working on you, sir."

"Maybe so, Sarge. Maybe so."

Hollands was pleased to have the Japanese seaplane away from the island. He was also glad to see the will to survive in Sergeant Beckett, as well as in the others. It was a good beginning. And for now, there would be plenty of food and medical supplies, compliments of the Imperial Japanese Navy.

Yoshida tackled the job of getting the Japanese radio and the one from Hollands' fighter functioning. Late on the third afternoon, he, Carl and Tim were testing the radios, when part of a coded message from the Japanese base on Munda came through. Quickly checking the captured enemy codebooks, Ron roughly decoded the message and casually stuck the slip of paper into a shirt pocket. During dinner that evening, he remembered the note. Taking it out of his shirt, he handed it to Hollands and said, "What do you make of this, Captain?"

Hollands slowly read the information, and scratching his head, he asked "Do you believe this message? Is the Akai leading a large flotilla, heading towards the Russells?"

"I don't know, Mike. Maybe so."

CHAPTER 7

It had been a couple of weeks since Hollands had been forced to ditch. Marine Captain Buckner hadn't given up on somehow being able to help his friend. But with the island located so far inside enemy-held territory there didn't seem to be much anyone could do.

During this two-week period, Commander Sessions had been able to procure ten additional fighter aircraft and pilots with TDY (Temporary Duty) status, giving Pateroa fifteen aircraft altogether. Although they were not a designated squadron, the pilots were effectively defending Pateroa, and Fleet Operations had ceased to ask questions.

One morning, Buckner and four other pilots took off on a recon mission to film an area around the Russell Islands, a distance of about 250 miles. They were still climbing to their assigned altitude when Pateroa Tower called, "Red Ball leader, this is First Base. Over."

"First Base, this is Red Ball Leader. Over."

"Red Ball Leader, Red Ball Two will take over the flight. You are to return to base. Over."

"This is Red Ball Leader. Roger."

Keying his microphone, he called, "Lieutenant Horne, you're in command. Looks like you've just been awarded the golden bullet, Clint. Bring 'em home safe."

"Roger. What's going on, Captain?"

"Don't know," Buckner responded. "But it must be important."

"Hey," one of the other pilots broke in, "Maybe the brass wants you to map out the end of the war for them."

"Can the chatter!" Horne growled angrily in the microphone.

"You just concentrate on the mission," Buckner said. "I'll see you back on the ground in a few hours."

Within ten minutes of takeoff, Buckner's Corsair touched down on the runway.

Sessions and a second naval officer waited in a jeep near the hangars. Buckner jumped off the starboard wing onto the ground and made his way to the waiting officers.

He came to attention and saluted. "Sir, may I ask why I was relieved?"

"You weren't relieved, Captain," said the other officer.

He shook hands with Buckner. "I'm Captain Gordon Flowers, Naval Intelligence. You have an enviable record, son."

This man was a *Bird* Captain, the same as a colonel in either the Army or the Marines.

"You're slated for a briefing in my office," announced Sessions. "Climb in."

Buckner handed his gear to the waiting ground crewman, and climbed into the rear seat.

Beyond a few comments by the intelligence officer about the hot, sticky weather and a desire for a cold beer, there was little said during the short ride to HQ.

The three men seated themselves at a small, round table in the commander's office.

Sessions was the first to speak. "Captain Buckner, we're going back to two days after Hollands went down. That was when Naval Intelligence monitored an enemy radio transmission between two of the Jap fighter pilots. Apparently, they spotted one of their small seaplanes that had failed to return to base. The Navy thinks they have figured out what the fuss was all about."

Sessions turned to Flowers. "Captain, this is your party. You tell him."

"Thanks, Commander. The plane in question was a seaplane all right. A small twin engine Grumman G-44 Widgeon that we believe may have been commandeered out of Singapore. We think it was probably used by a Nip admiral, and it may have carried sensitive radio gear."

"I don't see what this has to do with me, sir."

"You *will*," Flowers said. "Earlier two Zeros reported sighting the seaplane on an island lagoon and then a few hours later they saw it again, several miles away, in the air—just before it exploded. We believe that the atoll where they first spotted the plane is about thirty miles southwest of Munda, and is probably uninhabited."

Buckner still had that *so-what* look written all over his face. "Sounds like an accident. Things like that *do* happen."

Sessions picked up a slip of paper. "Buckner, listen to this. Over the past couple of weeks, there has been strange, but helpful radio traffic coming from that area. Maybe from that very island."

Holding up the sheet of paper he read, "Message received 28 June, 2100 hours: Enemy ship, *Akai* leading convoy up through the Slot. Result: two Jap troop ships, one supply ship, and one tanker, sunk; and three cruisers damaged. Message received 27 June, 0451 hours: Allied battlewagons, a tanker, one aircraft carrier, in convoy. Naval trap set by the Japanese. Result: we were able to intercept and attack the enemy instead, resulting in the sinking and or damaging of several Japanese cruisers and one of their subs."

Sessions set the slip of paper aside. "Apparently, during this same time period, many of our units on station have received similar messages. All containing speed, coordinates, and destinations. These little bulletins have proved accurate nearly every time."

"Someone is definitely sending decoded enemy information, right from the Nips' own playbook," said Flowers. "CinCPac has also intercepted top-level messages from Tokyo. The Japs figure they may have a spy in their midst."

Sessions added, "Our own tower has reported receiving several weak transmissions from the vicinity of that atoll."

Buckner slowly stood up and lit a cigarette. "So, if I understand you correctly, you think that Hollands somehow had something to do with all this. Blowing up a seaplane, learning Japanese, sending these messages—all in a couple of weeks." He shook his head and exhaled a small cloud of smoke. "Absolutely unbelievable. Impossible!"

He took a deep breath, and crushed out his cigarette. "It sounds like Hollands, that's for sure."

"Yes," agreed Sessions, "I'd bet my oak-leaf that Hollands is still at work."

All were quiet for a few seconds. The three men moved to a large wall map of the region.

After they studied it for a few moments, Sessions turned abruptly. "Buckner, you and a volunteer—pick one—fly over that island. I want you to fly low and slow, down on the deck, staying out of radar contact. See if there is any life there."

He paused for a moment. "I'll have supply fix up a couple bundles of necessities that can be easily dropped from the cockpit if you spot Hollands. If he's there, you high-tail your butts back here, and we'll fly the Duck with two or three Corsairs for cover and pick him up."

With an ear-to-ear grin, Buckner exclaimed, "Yes, sir! Right away, sir."

Seaman Pruitt, the clerk, waited in the jeep to give Buckner a ride back to the Marine compound.

As the jeep neared the hangars, Buckner spotted Skip. "Stop right here, Pruitt, and thanks!"

"Good luck!" Pruitt said. "I hope you find him, sir."

Buckner nodded to the clerk, turned and hollered, *"CORPORAL LYNCH!"*

Skip held his salute as he ran up to Buckner and responded, "Yes, sir!"

"An on-the-run salute again, huh, Skip?" Then more seriously but with a huge smile, he added, "I've got good news; Naval Intelligence believes Hollands is alive."

"I knew it! I knew it!" Lynch yelled.

His face took on a menacing expression, and he raised a fist. "Captain, SIR. If you're joking about this, I'm going to forget you're an officer and..."

With a hand on Skip's shoulder, Buckner said, "It's no joke, Skip. I'm sure it's him."

He straightened up and laughed. "No one else could have the Japs so pissed off and our own military this confused! Now, is my bird up to a fast, flat-out, wave-height flight of around a hundred and fifty miles?"

"Well, yeah. I mean you hardly used any fuel this morning, sir. Why?"

"How about Lieutenant Morgan's ship?"

"Well, Billy—I mean the Lieutenant, said it was overheating a little when he pushed it. But we adjusted the intercooler, and it's fine now."

"Have you seen Billy?"

Skip pointed over to a group of guys playing baseball a hundred yards away. "He was over there last I saw of him, sir."

"Thanks! Get his bird ready and top off my tanks."

"Yes, sir! I'll get right on it."

Sessions had already briefed the Marine pilots' CO, Major Hanks, by phone, and Buckner headed for the Marine's ready room to confer with him. As he hurried along he saw one of the other pilots heading out to play some ball. Buckner hollered to him, "Hey, Larry, if you see Morgan over there, send him to the ready room on the double."

During the next fifteen minutes, Buckner and Hanks mapped out a flight plan. It was slow going, as Buckner seemed a bit preoccupied. Finally, the major looked over at him and snapped, "Buckner! You with the program?"

"Sorry, sir. I just keep thinking about Hollands."

"Okay, Captain, but this is your escapade. So how will you keep away from the Nips' radar?"

Buckner pointed to the map and said, "There's a ridge of mountains on this large island. The Nips have a main tower on one of the peaks. Flying at five hundred feet above the water, we'll be well below their beam."

"Very good, Captain! Hopefully they will think this is just a routine patrol if they do see you."

Lieutenant Morgan arrived at Marine HQ and walked in, sweaty and somewhat winded. Coming to attention, he saluted and said, "Sir, Lieutenant Morgan reporting as ordered, sir."

"Billy, at ease," said Major Hanks. "Captain Buckner wants to talk to you."

Buckner said in a composed voice, "Your country appreciates your willingness to volunteer for this hazardous mission, Lieutenant. We're all proud of you. You'll probably get your picture on the front page of your hometown newspaper, too."

Nervously, Morgan cleared his throat and said, "Are you alright, sir? I haven't volunteered for anything since boot camp."

At that Major Hanks broke out laughing.

Buckner looked Morgan in the eye, smiled broadly, and said, "We think Hollands is alive. In a few minutes, you and I are flying out to that little flyspeck of an island to check it out. Go get your gear."

"Yes, sir!"

The scuttlebutt concerning Captain Hollands quickly spread across Pateroa. Everyone eagerly offered to assist.

Fifteen minutes later, Captain Buckner and Lieutenant Morgan were walking toward their two aircraft. Buckner had their flight plans in his hand and continued to brief Morgan, having the young lieutenant repeat the instructions back to him.

"Let me see if I got this right, sir; we take off on a heading southeast and climb to fifteen thousand feet." Looking again at the orders he added, "...and at a cruising speed of one-ninety, we stay on that heading for twenty-five minutes or about seventy-five miles. Then we drop down to five-hundred feet above the deck, change to our new course as written here, and fly due north, increasing our speed to two-five-zero. We rendezvous with some small reef of an island about eighteen minutes later."

"That's it. Simple, ain't it?" Buckner assured Billy. "This way we will start out on the enemy's radar screen. But on the deck, we will be under it and so it should take them hours trying to figure out where we might be."

When they reached the aircraft, each pilot was handed a small package of emergency rations. Billy hollered over to Buckner, "What do we do if we come across some Zekes?"

"It will depend on how many and if we're spotted. If just two or three attack us, we'll knock 'em down. If there are more, we'll try our best to elude or outrun them. But I would rather not engage any Nips on this mission. Oh, and once we make our turn north, remember—radio silence to the island."

The tower cleared the Corsairs and the two fighters lifted off into the heavy, hot, humid air of a clear blue sky. "Pateroa Tower, this is Badger One and Two; climbing to angels one-five, on a heading of two-five-niner.

Over."

"Roger, Badger One and Two. Climbing to angels one-five; heading two-five-niner. Good luck! Pateroa out."

On the small island reef, Hollands and his troops had managed to keep themselves busy improving their base. The camp area had been a dung hole, but soon after his arrival, Hollands had gotten the group busy with some much needed clean up. Digging two separate latrines was first: one for the men, west of the camp, and the second for the women, northeast of the med-tent. Next, the men hastily built a small shack to house the two radios, one from Hollands' fighter and a larger one from the Japanese seaplane.

Thirty yards north of the med-tent was a small fresh-water pool, fed by an underground spring. It was not deep enough for swimming, but it was adequate to allow everyone to rinse off from time to time. Hollands insisted that the men wash their tattered uniforms using scraps of bar soap the women had managed to save. It was a small thing, but one that would help to reestablish morale.

Months before Hollands and Yoshida had arrived, Sergeant Beckett and the two young men had been able to utilize some leftover ten-gallon lard buckets to fashion a cistern that they used to catch rainwater for drinking and cooking.

Hollands worked with the men to strengthen the lean-to they used as their sleeping quarters. The ladies generally slept in the med-tent. Only on unbearably warm nights would they take their cots out and set them up close to the lean-to. The crew also built a covered area for a mess hall and cooking space. They managed to create a rough-hewn table with two benches and even a couple of stools.

Ron Yoshida had been invaluable in getting both the Japanese and the American radios operational, and Hollands put him in charge of the com-shack. Ron taught the group the basic code of dots and dashes with which the enemy usually began its transmissions; this made it possible for the others to take turns monitoring the radios. Early on they learned that the Japanese command had become convinced their small seaplane had gone down because of mechanical failure. So, other than their usual fly-overs and occasional strafing, the Japanese didn't show any real interest in the island.

The boxes of Japanese food had come in handy. Hollands had hoped it would have lasted much longer, but the food was now nearly gone. Just the same, it had done the trick. Some decent meals, along with a little fresh-caught fish, had significantly improved the health of the long-marooned group of five, as well as their mental outlook. Beckett's hip had improved, too. Overall, spirits were high. Getting to know Yoshida had also changed their hatred of a race of people to a hatred of dictatorial governments, both Tojo's and Hitler's.

It was early evening and Boatswain Tim Roberts was on guard duty down at the lagoon. Cautiously, he walked the length of the dock. The sun was low on the horizon, casting long, dark shadows to the east, over the sandy bank of the lagoon. Near the small hut at the end of the wharf, he knelt down to survey the beach. Suddenly he heard a series of light splashes near the shore. He hastily brought his rifle up to the ready and strained to identify the source. At first he saw nothing. Then he spotted the intruder, partially submerged and heading out to sea paralleling the dock.

"Oh, there you are," Roberts said quietly to himself. "Wow, you're a big one!"

He fired two rounds into the air and leaned his weapon against the hut. As fast as he could, he picked up a loose length of rope from the hut and jumped into the water.

Hearing the rifle rounds, the other men came running, half expecting to find an enemy incursion. Instead they found Roberts, dripping wet, standing on the dock.

"What is it, Roberts?" called out Beckett.

"One huge turtle, Sarge."

"Hold on, Tim, I'm on my way," Minetti hollered, and handed his rifle to Hollands.

"No need to hurry, she's quite docile," Carl replied as he held up the drooping rope wound about his wrist. The other end was secured around the out-stretched neck of the outward-bound sea turtle. "I think she came ashore to lay her eggs. She was heading back to open water when I spotted her."

Suddenly there was a loud splashing noise and Roberts let out a "WHOA!" as he cart-wheeled through the air, diving headfirst into the water.

Carl sprinted to where his friend had been standing and jumped into the water, grabbing the tail end of the rope.

"I've got the line, too!" Minetti yelled. "Let's turn her around and bring her to shore."

Yoshida turned to Beckett and Hollands, "That's good eatin', Captain. A little bit like salty chicken."

Later that evening, Hollands had to agree with Yoshida's assessment, as the whole crew enjoyed fresh turtle soup.

On the morning of Buckner and Morgan's mission, Hollands was on duty in the radio shack.

As Ron entered, he asked, "Have you heard anything?"

"No! It's been pretty quiet. How about you? What's been going on behind my back?" asked Hollands with a chuckle.

"You won't believe this, Mike, but you gotta come see it."

"Gotta see what?"

"That crafty old Marine has set up two machine guns high up in some palm trees!"

With a look of disbelief, Hollands asked, "He did *what?*"

The two men hurried to the spot where they first met and looked up. They couldn't believe their eyes. Gunnery Sergeant Beckett and his men had installed and camouflaged two guns at the top of a tall palm tree.

"Hi, Captain," Beckett said as Hollands and Yoshida approached.

"I'm seeing it, but I don't believe it," Hollands said as he looked up into the tree. "What gave you this idea, Sergeant?"

"Well, sir, I'm real tired of getting strafed with no real way to express my displeasure. Whattaya think?"

"Well, Sarge, this is fine," began Hollands. "But why here? And how do you aim them? Explain it to me."

"Okay. You see, sir, the Nips almost always fly directly above these two long rows of trees."

Taking a breath and moving the two officers along, he explained, "These trees average about twenty feet apart and the center pathway here, sir, is nearly sixty feet wide. I've figured out why the Nips use these trees. It's because these two rows are nearly straight and they run for maybe a hundred yards. Why is this group of palms so straight? I reckon the Lord had a plan."

Hollands noted that a long rope hung down from the guns, and he scratched his head in disbelief. "What are these ropes for?"

"Well, I call them my triggers, sir. As you can see, the two are tied into one lead. They end up behind this large boulder. The guns are pointed up at maybe forty-five degrees, in kind of a crossfire."

Beckett pointed to the base of one of the trees. "I've rigged the lines through an eyelet guide, so both guns will fire at the same time."

"Ingenious, Sergeant," Hollands said. "Have you tested them yet?"

"Only dry, until we checked with you, sir. But I think they'll work."

Beckett looked up at the trees and held the line in his right hand. "Would you do the honors, sir? They're loaded now and ready."

Hollands nodded. "I'd be pleased to, Sergeant."

The old Marine ushered the two officers over toward the boulder. Beckett held up the already tightened rope. "Here you go, sir. Just a smooth, hard pull should do it."

Taking the rope in his hand, Hollands looked into the face and eyes of this grand old warrior and saw the hint of the young Marine he had been some thirty years earlier.

He handed the line back to Beckett. "This is your show, Elmore; you test it."

The Marine reached out a leathered hand and took the rope from Hollands. "Thank you, sir."

Then, as he turned back to face the trees, he said under his breath, "I'll never make fun of Army officers again."

Sarge pulled slowly and steadily on the rope. There was a sudden reverberation from the two machine guns as each belched out a short five-round burst of fire.

With a surprised but pleased expression, Petty Officer Roberts blurted out, "This really works!"

"Of course it does," snapped the sergeant, but with a bit of his own disbelief still mirrored on his face. "Did you doubt me, son?"

"Oh no, Sarge, I didn't doubt you at all. I just didn't think it would work."

Hollands turned back to Beckett, "You and your men did a fantastic job! Are the guns removable?"

Minetti, who had been standing nearby, piped up, "Yes, sir. In less than five minutes."

"Good, 'cause we just sent about five or six bright red tracers into the air,"

Hollands told the group. "Take a thirty minute watch for any enemy activity."

Twenty-two minutes into their flight, Buckner checked his watch and figured that another two or three minutes would put the two pilots at their rendezvous point. They were right on schedule. The weather was perfect. The winds had been non-existent and precise timing was assured. Everything was going according to plan.

"Badger Two, this is Badger One," Buckner radioed. "Execute rendezvous on three. ONE... TWO... THREE."

The two planes began their descent, leveled off at five-hundred feet above the ocean, and immediately made their turn north. Buckner adjusted his compass to the new course. Throttles in hand, the pilots settled their aircraft into their new cruising speed of 250 miles per hour.

"Billy, I've gotta break radio silence. I doubt anyone can hear us down here on the deck. Just gotta say, for a nineteen-year-old kid you are one hell of a flier."

Billy didn't respond for several seconds. "Captain, watch my canopy," he radioed. Using his signal light, Billy sent Buckner a quick response that was unbelievable.

As the two Corsairs cruised along, Buckner, now deep in thought, couldn't even hear the purr of the engine. What he *should* do about Billy's confidential message had nothing to do with what he truly *wanted* to do.

Billy was every bit a man. Every bit a Marine, and a pilot. He was a big, fun-loving, and good-hearted kid. The outfit teased him a lot, but there wasn't a pilot in the group who didn't respect him as a flier, and as an officer. Everyone wanted him as their wingman.

A couple of times, he had led patrols. Several of the pilots owed their lives to Lieutenant Morgan's flying abilities. He knew his job and did it well. He had been credited with three kills and many more aircraft damaged, plus the sinking of a Japanese Navy cruiser.

Thinking about this was beginning to hurt Buckner's head and he was glad to hear Billy's voice on the radio again. "Captain, bandits. One o'clock, heading east at plus-angels twenty."

Looking overhead, the two men counted ten Japanese fighters. Buckner was sure the two Corsairs had not been spotted, but both pilots breathed a sigh of relief as the enemy planes flew out of sight.

Buckner keyed his radio. "If my navigation is correct, we should be over that island in a few more minutes. Keep your eyes peeled for more Zekes; we're in their front yard."

Billy gave a wave.

Each pilot got his bundle ready. Parachutes had been attached to the small packages and if the fliers could confirm Captain Hollands' presence on the ground, they were to drop the parcels.

It was nearly noon when most of the group returned to camp after testing the palm tree-mounted guns. Because of the heat, Hollands encouraged everyone to take a rest break each day, and Minetti and Roberts sat against a palm trunk as they rested in the shade and chewed chunks of fresh coconut.

The day was one of the worst for heat, humidity, and insects. Even in the shade everyone was hot, sweaty, and exhausted.

"Hey, Carl, let's go dip in the pond," Tim suggested.

"Good idea, Tim. Wake me in an hour," Carl answered listlessly.

Yoshida left the radio shack to get some water from the med-tent. Hollands and Sergeant Beckett had been checking on the machine gun emplacements along the east side and were returning to camp with the thought of a siesta.

All seemed peaceful and quiet except for the cries of distant birds. Carl and Tim were nearly asleep, but Minetti abruptly opened his eyes. His eyes darted back and forth and up and down as if searching for something. Then, leaning forward, he softly asked, "Hey, Tim, do you hear something?"

"Other than your yammering and those damn birds, I don't hear a thing."

Moving to his knees Minetti whispered, "There it is again. Long way off; two radials."

Roberts began to stir and cocked his head to listen. "Your brain must be sunburned, 'cause I still don't hear a thing."

But he had no more gotten the last word out of his mouth when his expression abruptly changed. "Shit! I hear it now!"

At the entrance of the lean-to hung an old hand-crank siren that they had found and repaired. It worked well and could make an awful wail to warn everyone of approaching aircraft. Scrambling to their feet, both men dashed to the siren. One held the base steady while the other turned the handle and the message went out loud and clear for all to hear.

Within seconds, Ron came flying out of the med-tent followed by the women. As he ran past the siren toward the radios, he yelled, "What's up?"

"Two radials," began Carl. "Coming in low from the south."

Ron ran to the com-shack. Carl and Tim left the siren and followed to help with the radios. The noise of the motors was growing louder, more intense. They could tell the planes were flying close to the water, but the tree cover made it nearly impossible to see any aircraft approaching from the south. No one wanted to take the chance of moving into the open. Quickly the roar became deafening, and above the canopy of palms, two forms suddenly passed overhead in a blur of dark blue. Carl yelled excitedly, "They're ours, they're ours! Two Corsairs! Look at those beautiful stars on their wings!"

Hollands and Beckett had stopped by the fresh-water pool, but when they heard the siren they broke into a hard run for camp. Winded and dripping with perspiration, Hollands reached the compound first and stopped at the com-shack.

Panting hard, Hollands asked Yoshida, "Has anyone—tried—to call us?"

"No. Not yet."

Hollands picked up the microphone and keyed it, still breathing hard. "Buckner, this is Hollands. Over."

He looked at Ron and the others, who were now standing around.

Hollands keyed the mike again. "Buckner, this is Hollands. Over."

After many agonizing seconds, a scratchy voice came over the small speaker, "Hey, Army, is that really *you*?"

And a cheer went up from everyone.

"Roger! It's nice of you to stop by! Can you send us help? Over."

"We have two small packages for you. Where would you like them dropped? Can't stay too long; you're in a rough neighborhood. Over."

"Fly from south to north over the lagoon where my plane rests, try and drop them just past the tree line. It's a bit more open. We'll meet you there."

"Roger. On our way."

Vastly relieved to hear Hollands' voice, Buckner radioed Morgan. "Okay, Billy, you heard the man. Let's turn 180, fly south 2 miles, and repeat approach. On the north run move flaps to full, bring airspeed to 130, and deliver the mail."

"Roger, Captain," Billy said. "You know we will be close to stall speed in this heavy air."

"That's correct. Just keep your hand ready for the throttle."

While Buckner was relieved to have heard the voice of his friend, something Hollands had said did not make sense. What was it?

Lining up on Hollands' downed fighter, Buckner and Morgan tossed the packages. The small parachutes opened, gracefully floating the two bundles to the ground.

Ron sat next to Hollands monitoring the Japanese radio. "Hey, Hollands, some of my cousins are getting curious. The Corsairs must have hit their radar. Five Zekes are on their way. Get your friends out of here; they've got less than five minutes."

Hollands keyed the microphone. "Okay, hero, tell everyone 'Hi' for me. Now, get out of here. Five Zekes on their way; less than five minutes. Over."

"Roger, Mike. See you soon."

Buckner made a turn to the west. As he flew, he repeated Hollands'

earlier radio transmission to himself, mumbling aloud, "Can you help us? Can you help *us*? *Us!*" Hollands had said "us!"

"Mike, is there someone down there with you? Over."

"Affirmative. There are seven here. Five men, and two women—a WAAC hospital tech and an Army nurse. Over."

Buckner keyed his radio. "Roger! I'll get help to you, somehow. Hang in there, Army. See you soon! Out."

The two Corsairs quickly gained altitude and speed, and leveled off at five thousand feet. The two Marine pilots were several minutes ahead of the Nips and there was no danger of being overtaken.

Back on Pateroa, Buckner was answering a lot of questions.

"That's right, sir. He said two women and five men. There are seven people stuck on that island."

Before Sessions could respond, Buckner spoke again. "Sir, I'd like permission to sneak a Duck in there. Using the lagoon, I could go in at night. As slow as the Duck is, it'd be a cinch."

Sessions relit his well-chewed cigar. "Yeah, a *sitting* duck. I know we talked about this, son. But *seven* people! I didn't expect that. I'll have to brief Captain Flowers and Admiral Johnston on your mission, and advise you later."

Sessions looked Buckner in the eye. "You and your wingman flew a good mission and brought back some vital information, Captain. Thank you. You're dismissed."

Anytime a superior officer says, "dismissed," it means that the conversation is over. And so it was, for the moment.

Billy had waited outside HQ for Buckner. "Well, how did it go, sir?"

"Damn it, Billy; quit calling me 'Sir' all the time!" Buckner snapped.

He lit a cigarette and spoke softly. "Sorry, Billy. It was a bit tense in there. The ol' man has to take this upstairs. We'll see."

"Sir—I mean Buckner—I'd like to fly cover again."

"I don't know right now. It could be a day or so."

"How about the message I flashed to you earlier?"

Buckner raised an eyebrow and looked directly at Lieutenant Morgan. "You're really just seventeen?" he asked.

"I'll be eighteen in three months, sir."

"How old were you when you joined?"

"I'd just turned sixteen."

Buckner shook his head. "How the hell did you pull it off?"

"My parents were killed in a car crash when I was a little kid, and my aunt and uncle raised me. They faked all my papers—even my high school diploma. I wanted to fly—and since we didn't get along too good, they helped me pack."

Buckner mulled over the implications of what he had learned about Billy. Then, he raised an eyebrow. "You were flashing a message to me up there? Hell, I thought you were just playing with your flashlight."

He rested a hand on Billy's shoulder. "Just the same, I wouldn't practice that code on anyone else around here. At least not 'til after your eighteenth birthday."

"Thanks, Captain," Billy said. "I won't."

CHAPTER 8

Minetti and Roberts dashed off and quickly found the two bundles that Buckner and Billy had dropped. They collected the containers and parachutes and hurriedly carried them back to the cover of the palms just minutes before the five Zeros passed overhead in their effort to overtake the two Corsairs. As the droning of the Japanese aircraft faded in the distance, the two young Americans headed back to camp.

Everyone was more than a little curious about the contents of the packages. Yoshida and Hollands watched while Roberts and Minetti carefully opened up the canvas containers.

"Hey, more field rations," Janet announced. "Oh, and there's a small tin of coffee, too."

Minetti looked over at Beckett. "Look, Sarge, some of these rations are from the Marines."

Roberts found a bottle opener and, held it up. "Why would anyone send us *this* thing?"

The bundles also yielded several Hershey bars, some bath soap, and canned food items—a few days' worth for one man. A steel container held two one-quart cans marked *Potable Water.*

Gail pulled out a narrow wooden box, which was about the size to hold a thermos bottle. It had been carefully wrapped.

Hollands' curiosity got the better of him, "Let me have that one, please."

The seven sat cross-legged on the ground in a small circle. All eyes focused on the wooden box. Using his pocketknife, Hollands slowly pried the lid off and carefully removed the packaging of cotton batting and paper. Hollands pulled out the single item and lifted it high over his head: a dark-glass bottle.

"Here's the answer to the bottle opener question, Tim," Hollands said.

Everyone instantly recognized the label. Soft sighs and whispers went around the circle: "*R o y a l C r o w n C o l a.*"

A piece of paper was rubber-banded to the bottle. Hollands slipped it off, unfolded it and read it out loud, "*I have an extra on ice in my water bag, Captain. I'll save it for you."*

There was no signature but Hollands knew. "Thanks, Skip!" he whispered.

Hollands quickly got to his feet and retrieved the bottle opener from Tim. As he slowly popped off the cap, the fizzy foam dribbled down the side of the bottle, and every mouth began to water.

"Anyone who wants a drink of this better get a cup—and fast," Hollands said. "Before I drink it all myself! Hey, it's still cold, too!"

Of course, it wasn't actually cold, but even the idea of a cold RC seemed to spark everyone's imagination.

The group quickly scurried around for cups, and soon Hollands was pouring small amounts into a variety of containers. And with no more than a mouthful apiece, they drank a toast to themselves.

"Here's to our friendship and safety," said Hollands.

For a brief time, spirits were brightened as they savored the moment.

As Hollands looked around at his friends, it dawned on him that if their radio transmissions were an asset to the allies, it would probably mean that there would be no real hurry to get the seven off the island. The real danger was that the Japanese might discover that their radio messages were being compromised and start investigating. If that happened, it would certainly warrant a swift visit to the island.

Hollands said softly, "It looks like we may be here for a while longer. Perhaps a real airdrop could be commissioned."

Later Hollands stopped by the med-tent and found the women adding packages of food and cans of beans and vegetables to the scant store. Two large tins had the word **SPAM** stenciled in bold black lettering.

Hollands picked up one of the cans, studied it, and finally asked, "Ladies, I know what beef is, and I know what pork is, but just what is *this?*"

Both women laughed, and Lieutenant Elliott answered, "It's a precooked, processed meat of some kind. Pork, I think. It's not bad!"

"We had it aboard ship several times," Gilbress added. "It can really cover up the taste of powdered eggs."

"Other than what the ship's mess cook named it," Elliott said, "we're not sure what it is. In civilian life I saw it on the grocer's shelf a few times. Perhaps we'll try some tonight."

Then with a giggle, Sergeant Gilbress remarked, "Maybe it's better than K-rations."

"Bite your tongue," Hollands chuckled. "Sarge will boil you in oil for speaking such blasphemies against the holy ration of K—the mysterious unknown."

For several days, Japanese radio transmissions had been nearly non-existent. This made Hollands curious.

"Do you think something is in the wind, Ron?" he asked one evening as the two sat by the radios. "Could your cousins be monitoring us somehow?"

"It's possible," Ron acknowledged. "Look, we put ourselves on the hook every time we click the key. I suggest that unless we hear something that seems plausible and important, we stay off the air and just listen for a day or so."

"Sounds reasonable," agreed Hollands. "Let's do it."

Beckett had set up specific locations around the island for nightly guard duty. The men rotated from post to post every few hours. As long as supplies allowed, the two women would take coffee and food out to the various guard emplacements, and sometimes relieve a man so he could get an hour or so of rest.

It was nearly dawn when Sergeant Gilbress hurried down the path to the camp and the lean-to. She paused for a moment to catch her breath, and then moved around the five cots to the sleeping Michael Hollands.

"Captain Hollands," she whispered tensely.

The captain didn't budge. "Captain," she whispered again.

Still meeting no response, she yelled, "Captain Hollands!"

Hollands immediately sat bolt upright on his cot. Groggily he responded, "Yes, who is it?"

"Sorry, sir. It's me, Janet. Carl is asking for you and Sergeant Beckett, sir."

"Where is Carl?" Hollands asked, as he slowly got to his feet.

"At the north point, sir. I had taken him some food and coffee. He's holding someone at gunpoint," Janet said. "Carl told me to come and get you and Sergeant Beckett, fast."

"He's doing *what*?" Hollands inquired anxiously. "Is it a Japanese?"

"No, sir, I think it's a native."

Hollands took the canteen of water that hung on the pole near his cot and doused his head in an effort to wake up more quickly. As the cold water ran down his face, he knelt down and tied his boots.

Beckett and Roberts had returned an hour earlier from guard and awakened, by Sergeant Gilbress' loud report to Hollands, they scrambled off their cots. With weapons in hand they all followed Janet. From inside the med-tent, Lieutenant Elliott had also heard the commotion and ran to catch up.

As the five began their trek, Yoshida—who was returning from the latrine—called out, "What's going on? Where's everyone going?"

"Carl may have captured someone," Hollands called back.

"Well, hey," Yoshida said. "Wait for me!"

The trail had taken the group to a small meadow of tall grass encircled by indigenous trees and open to the sky. On the far side, they could see Minetti. A gentle slope rose behind him for several yards, forming a hundred-foot high bluff above the ocean.

Under the light of a bright moon, they were able to cut across the meadow at a quick pace. Within a few minutes, the five arrived where Carl was waiting. His rifle was cradled in his left arm as he talked with a native of the Solomons. Both sat on a large rock, casually sharing coffee.

Seeing Hollands and the others, Minetti stood up and said, "Oh, good morning, Captain. Sir, this is Mr. Toullii. Mr. Toullii, this is our CO, Captain Hollands, U.S. Army Air Corps."

"Good morning, Captain," the islander said in nearly perfect British English. "I think it will be a lovely day."

"What gives, Carl?" asked Hollands. "Who is this man?"

Minetti explained, "He works with an Australian coast watcher who'll be back in a few minutes. He needed something out of their rubber raft. He says they were dropped off ten miles out."

Moments later, through the moonlit darkness and early hints of dawn, Hollands saw the form of a man walking toward them down the gentle slope from the bluff.

Still some distance away the man shouted, "Oh, hello chaps. Sorry to have wakened you."

The Australian accent immediately gave him away. As he came closer, Hollands could see that the man was older and Caucasian. The old man continued toward them. As he carefully made his way through the overgrown path, his walking stick made a clicking sound on the rocky surface.

Instinctively picking out the group's leader, the Aussie marched up to Hollands and thrust out his big right hand. "Good! I see you've all met Mr. Toullii," he said as he and Hollands shook hands. "He's actually from up north, you know, a small island off Bougainville. But the past few days we've been doing a bit of snooping nearby, thanks, in part, to your Navy."

The old gent was quite tall, well over six feet with a full head of wavy silver-gray hair. Nodding to everyone, he apologized, "Sorry to have kept you waiting. I've been rather rude. My name is Philoe P. Quigby. Originally from Darwin, you know."

Hollands started to introduce himself, but Quigby held up his hand and said, "Yes, my dear boy, you'd be Michael Hollands, captain, Army flier. Nice to finally meet you, lad. I've been hearing a lot about you. Your name, sir, has been bandied about amongst us coast watchers, for... Well, it must be close to a month now. It appears that your Commander Sessions has been a might concerned and has put the word out on you. In fact, you are why Toullii and I are here."

Looking around at the others, he spotted Lieutenant Elliott, as she joined the group.

Quigby added wryly, "We didn't expect quite so many in your party. Sessions *did* say he thought your pilot friend had misunderstood a garbled message about that. But I must assume that Buckner didn't misunderstand you after all."

Taking a breather, Quigby seated himself next to Toullii. Each of them carried a large rucksack. Quigby patted his. "We've brought along a few items of food from your Navy."

Carefully lighting his pipe, he looked around at the group. "My, my, both Sergeant Beckett and Petty Officer Roberts are considered dead. Lost at sea, you know. The rest of you, except for the captain here, are reported as missing in action."

He looked directly at Yoshida for a moment. "But *you*, sir... You are not on my list. However, I know you quite well. Yes, quite well indeed. You would be Mr. Yoshida, *leftenant* late of the Japanese Army Air Force."

His eyes looked to where Toullii sat. "Toullii and his family, like most of the islanders, truly hate the Japanese."

Ron Yoshida suddenly looked tense and nervous. It was widely known that the Australians also hated the Japanese, and for good reason. Earlier in the war, the Japanese had bombed parts of the Australian northern coast and taken over half of New Guinea.

Sensing Yoshida's uneasiness, Quigby walked over to him and placed a reassuring hand on Ron's shoulder. Then he turned back to the group. "I can tell all here that they have one hell of a partner in you. That, ol' chap, is meant as a compliment."

Relighting his pipe, he continued. "First off, let me clarify. The Nips have reported Leftenant Yoshida as killed in action by the American Naval Air Forces here in the Solomons. However, and unbeknownst to his former mates, he has been responsible for the downing of several enemy... *harrumph*... Japanese aircraft, if you please. Fighters, bombers and such. At extreme peril to himself, he has protected many Allied pilots and ground troops. This includes some of my own Aussie countrymen."

Studying Ron's face, Quigby added, "He has been shot down twice before by Allied fighters; this makes the third time, I believe. But he took his war to the true enemy."

Looking intently at Yoshida once more, he concluded, "I offer my hand to one so young and so brave."

Then Mr. Quigby and Mr. Toullii both shook hands with Yoshida.

Hollands moved a bit closer to Ron and whispered, "Hey, your mouth's open! Why didn't you tell me you had been shot down before?"

Ron quietly said, "I guess when we first met, I wasn't sure of you, and you sure as hell didn't trust me. Later on, it just didn't seem all that important."

The dawn was getting brighter and illuminated the path of flattened grass the group had made as they crossed the meadow. Quigby gave a quick nod to his dark-skinned island friend who immediately went to work on the grass.

"From the air," the coast watcher explained, "that matted grass would be an open invitation for some of our little yellow adversaries to come calling."

He gestured toward Yoshida. "Harrumph. Sorry ol' chap."

"That's okay, Mr. Quigby. I didn't give it a thought."

Hollands looked at the grass and said, "Thank you, Mr. Quigby, for bringing this to our attention. We'll certainly be more careful from now on."

Suddenly Ron put up his hand. "Aircraft approaching. They're probably on their way to fly a mission. I bet they'll swing near the lagoon to test their guns on your old plane."

"Okay, let's all get back to camp," Hollands ordered. "Everyone stay close to the trees. Mr. Quigby, would you and your friend care to stay for breakfast?"

Smiling, the Aussie nodded. "We would be delighted, Captain. Besides, we need to empty our rucksacks of the food we brought."

Minetti and Roberts dashed off ahead of the group. The rest, including Mr. Quigby, returned to camp at a slower pace.

Ron and Toullii hurried to get to the radios.

"May I be of some assistance, *Leftenant*?" asked the native.

"Yes, Mr. Toullii, you may. And thank you."

The two reached the radios and Toullii began to pedal the generator.

Hollands and the others had taken a few extra minutes to reach camp, where congregating, they anxiously waited for any enemy transmissions. After the radios had warmed up, Ron monitored for only a few moments.

"Hollands, it's a practice run, and we're their target."

Shaking his head as he let out a big sigh, Ron added quietly, "You know, they could be overhead for quite a while. Might be safer if we all moved about a hundred yards to the north to wait it out."

"Too much danger of being spotted if we're moving around," Hollands countered. "No. We'll take cover and stay put."

The sun was coming up over the horizon as the enemy aircraft began their strafing and bombing practice. Minetti and Roberts had gone directly to the lagoon and nearly got caught in the open as the first wave of planes appeared. Running for cover, they ended up near the palm trees that concealed the machine guns.

The skies were full of Japanese aircraft: fighters and light bombers. For nearly two hours, planes strafed and bombed the Thunderbolt's motionless hulk. This practice was more intense than others had been. Some planes came in so low that they nearly clipped the treetops.

Back in the compound, Sergeant Beckett looked around and asked, "Has anyone seen Minetti and Roberts?"

Sergeant Gilbress answered, "I think they headed straight for the lagoon, Sarge."

"The fifties, the fifties!" Beckett growled, and took off to find the two young men, with Yoshida and Hollands following close behind.

"Would the boys actually fire those guns, Sarge?" Hollands asked panting.

"No, Captain, I don't think so, sir, because I've told them not to," Beckett puffed. Coming to where the trees made two natural rows, Beckett and the others stopped.

Crouching low and staying out of sight of the enemy airmen, the three men watched as two Zekes rolled in from the east, for another strafing run. Ron commented, "That lead plane is too low. *Way* too low."

As the two planes continued to close in, both enemy pilots commenced firing their guns. Moments later the unmistakable sound of two American .50 caliber machine guns echoed their response around the lagoon. They belched out a short burst of fire, hitting the lead plane full force, nearly severing the starboard wing. Immediately exploding into flames, the fighter began to cartwheel through the air and crashed onto the rocks a few hundred yards offshore, resulting in a huge secondary explosion. The pilot of the second aircraft quickly pulled up, banked hard left and headed out over the lagoon.

"Sergeant, get those guys off those guns," Ron said. He scrambled to his feet. "I've gotta get back to the radios, Mike." And he sprinted off to camp.

"I'm right behind you!" yelled Hollands.

Arriving at the com-shack Hollands and Yoshida joined the women, who had been hiding behind a large boulder. As the two men approached, Nurse Elliott called out, "What happened down there, Ron? We heard an explosion!"

Yoshida answered angrily, "Roberts and Minetti shot down one of the planes."

Toullii came out of his hiding place and resumed pedaling the radio's generator. Ron turned on the speaker and adjusted the dial. Then the gibberish began, hot and heavy, lasting for several minutes. Two additional planes from the group flew over the crash scene, but there was nothing left of the plane other than burning pieces of wreckage and an oil slick. And there was no sign of the pilot.

With a big sigh of relief, Yoshida looked up at Hollands. "Man, I believe in God more each day I'm here on this island!"

Hollands stared at him. "What did they say?"

Ron motioned for the native to quit pedaling. "Between what the pilot in the second plane reported to the flight leader, and what the flight leader reported to base, it sounds like they think it was an accident. The second pilot claims he shot his comrade down."

"Any chance they may come to investigate?" Hollands asked.

Yoshida stood up to stretch. "I tell ya, guys, there must be an angel or two watching over us, because the flight leader has radioed his base that there was nothing left. But, if they *do* investigate, it'll be curtains for us. Because one look at the undercarriage of that wreckage, and they'll see that the rounds came up from beneath, not from above. And here's a really swell addition... Our .50 caliber round makes much bigger holes than the smaller caliber they use. Two really big reasons to pray they don't get curious."

Hollands whistled through his teeth. "Damn..."

He lifted one shoulder in a half-shrug. "Well, okay. Keep a close ear for any changes. I don't know what we'll do if they show up and come ashore."

"I know," Yoshida said. "I know."

As the sights and sounds of the enemy aircraft faded off into the morning sky, Quigby came out of his hiding place. "That's what you Yanks call a 'close shave' I think."

A short time later, Beckett came up to Hollands and asked quietly,

"Captain, can I have a word with you, sir, alone?"

"Sure," Hollands responded. The two walked a few yards away from the others. He looked around. "Is this okay, Sarge?"

"This is fine, sir," Beckett said.

Beckett took a deep breath. "About Minetti and Roberts, sir. Well, I really started to chew their asses out..." He hesitated.

"Go ahead, Sergeant. What is it?"

"I... would, ah... Well, sir, I think you should hear it from them."

"Okay. Where are they?"

"They're right over here, sir."

He took a couple steps backward and called to the two young men. "Get your tails over here, and tell the captain exactly what you told me."

Both men were visibly shaking and began talking excitedly at the same time.

Beckett interrupted with a growl. "At ease! One at a time."

Minetti went first. "Tim was certain we'd been spotted, sir."

In a trembling voice, Tim blurted, "I tell ya, Captain, he looked right into my eyes. I had to pull the cord."

"Who? Who looked into your eyes?" demanded Hollands.

"The Jap pilot, sir, in the lead plane."

Menitti added quickly, "I was face down on the ground when I heard Tim say, 'Oh—shit!' And then he pulled the rope to fire the guns. After the plane went down, I asked him why he did it, and he told me just what he told you, sir."

Hollands looked at the two men. "I believe you, Tim. But do you both realize you may have jeopardized our position?"

"Yes, sir. We do," the two answered almost in unison.

Hollands walked back to the radios and stood next to Yoshida. "Did you hear that?"

Ron nodded.

"Have you picked up any other radio traffic that might indicate that we've been sighted?" Hollands asked.

Yoshida shook his head. "No. Nothing. But like any military, the Japs will have a board of inquiry. Probably won't know for several days."

He sighed heavily. "You know, Captain, any one of us could have been spotted. The kid did the only thing he could."

"I know," Hollands said. "I wouldn't trade either of them. They're good soldiers."

Shortly afterward, Hollands gathered everyone together. "Okay, listen up. As you've all heard, we may have been spotted. But it will be awhile till we know for sure. So until we do, we are going to have our own alert.

For the next day or two, Lieutenant Yoshida will closely monitor the Japanese frequencies."

He paused for a moment, and looked at Beckett and the two young men. "Minetti and Roberts will take turns on the generator, and assist the lieutenant. They will also rotate between the radios and gun emplacements."

"Yes, sir!" answered Beckett.

"I want everyone to understand," Hollands said. "This is not punishment. It's war. We'll all be pulling double duty. This situation is not of Carl's or Tim's making. At 2100 hours, we will proceed to the gun positions, Lieutenant Elliott and Sergeant Gilbress included. We need all eyes and ears. After breakfast there will be no cooking during the day. And be extra careful of any light at night. There will be a moon again tonight. That should help us as we move around. That's all I have."

A short time later, Gail announced, "Okay, everybody, breakfast is ready."

Hollands noticed that the two young men were still standing apart from the group. "Tim and Carl, that includes you two. Come on, let's eat."

While they ate, everyone including Yoshida, wrote letters home, to be sent back to Pateroa with Quigby.

When Minetti and Roberts finished with their breakfast, they prepared for the day's duties.

Minetti said, "You know, Tim, I think the captain is really pissed off at us. What do you think?"

"Well, maybe a little," Roberts answered. "But the CO's okay. Besides, I screwed up royally. We both did, by getting caught out in the open like that."

Carl nodded in agreement and headed to the radios. Tim got ready to clean the weapons.

Calling Beckett to the side, Hollands said, "As soon as their gear is in order have the boys take down the machine guns and place them here in camp for now. Hopefully, we won't need them."

"Yes, sir, right away. I'll work out a camp perimeter."

"Oh, and Sergeant, when you find the right moment, tell the boys they are still all right in my book. They're good soldiers. None better. Under the circumstances, they did the right thing."

"Yes, sir, I will," Beckett answered. "Is there anything else, Captain?"

"Yes. When... no, *if* we survive this, you can have those guns put back up in the trees. They do work, Sergeant."

"Yes, sir. And thank you, sir."

The coast watcher and his friend stayed in camp all day, and observed how Yoshida collected enemy messages, decoded them, and radioed them on to Pateroa. As it got dark, Mr. Quigby and Mr. Toullii said their good byes and departed the island.

The next two nights and three days were uncomfortably warm, long, and tedious. There was little rest or regular food. However, the Japanese had apparently written off the crash as an accident. Except for one fly-over by a small observation aircraft, the enemy took no further action.

The following week, all radio traffic increased dramatically. It soon became obvious that things were heating up again. The U.S. Marines had taken the Russell and Christmas Islands a few weeks earlier. Guadalcanal was still fresh in everyone's memory from the year before. A lot of blood had been spilled. Allied losses of men killed or wounded were extremely high. The Japanese losses were even higher. The Allies were now planning to take Rabaul and Rendova.

However, the Japanese had plans of their own: the retaking of Guadalcanal was key to their longer-range strategy for taking back all of the Solomon Islands, New Georgia, and New Guinea, thereby pushing the Americans back to Pearl Harbor.

"Hi, Ron. You sent for me?" Hollands asked as he stepped inside the radio shack.

"Yeah, Mike," Yoshida said. "My cousins are off and running. I've been monitoring three different frequencies. They're makin' plans to send a large flotilla up the Slot. Don't know when. But I've sent what little information I *do* have on to Pateroa."

Hollands read the copy. "Any news from our side?"

Yoshida shook his head. "No. Only requests for clarification, and for more enemy intercepts."

Pateroa had become much busier over the past month as more troops had moved through. Two Army Air Corps bomber wings, a B-17 group and a B-25 group, had moved onto the base. In addition, two new Army fighter squadrons of P-51s and P-38s were now on the island, along with a

Navy squadron of F6F Hellcats. Together, these squadrons were making the Japanese take notice of what *Made in America* really meant.

One morning, as Captain Buckner sat in the nearly empty mess hall eating breakfast and going over pilot reports, a visitor came calling. A tall, slender young man entered the building.

The young soldier wore two chevrons on his sleeves. With the use of a cane, he walked boldly to the captain's table.

"Excuse me, sir. I'm told that I could find Captain Buckner in here."

Buckner barely glanced up. "Well, you found him. What is it, Private?"

"Sir, it's *corporal*, not private. And I only have a short layover for refueling. I was told that you could probably tell me something about my brother."

Still looking over a file, the captain asked, "And who might that be, kid?"

The young soldier bristled at the lack of courtesy. "Captain, I'm not a kid. I'm a corporal. A soldier in the United States Army."

Buckner finally looked up.

The young soldier stood resting heavily on a walking cane.

The Marine captain nodded. "Fair enough, Corporal. I may have been out of line. I apologize. Who are you, and what's your brother's name?"

"My name is Steve Hollands, sir. I'm looking for my brother, Captain Michael Hollands."

Buckner extended his hand to be shaken. "Steve Hollands? Wow! It's good to meet you. Have a seat, please. Yeah, I know your brother. We arrived on the same transport last March. Have you had breakfast? Want a cup of coffee?"

"I could eat, sir," the soldier said. "That would be swell, thank you!"

Buckner signaled the mess steward for coffee and a tray of food. As a cup was set before Steve, the steward said, "I'm sorry, Captain, and you too, Corporal. But this mess hall is for officer personnel only."

"Louis," Buckner said, "This is Captain Hollands' younger brother, Steve. I'll take the heat."

"Oh! Yes, sir. Sorry, sir. I'm sure it will be all right, Corporal. Excuse me, Captain! I'll get some chow for the corporal."

"Thank you, Captain," Steve said. "Every person I've met so far on this base seems to know Mike quite well."

Buckner nodded. "I suppose that would be true. And you can include the Japanese in that. They know your brother quite well. Or, they know his work."

He grinned. "Now tell me. What can I do for you, Steve?"

Steve took a sip of coffee. "While I was in the hospital on Guadalcanal, our parents wrote to me saying the War Department had reported Mike as missing-in-action. That letter was weeks old. Can you tell me anything?"

Buckner took a deep breath. "Your brother is safe. He's on an island about fifty miles from here, deep inside Japanese-held territory."

Steve's brow furrowed. "Is he a prisoner?"

Buckner shook his head. "Not at all. The island is small, and there are six other Americans marooned with him. As far as we know, the Nips believe the island is unoccupied."

After Steve had eaten, the two men got up and headed outside.

Buckner continued, "Shortly after Mike's plane went down, one of my men and I flew a look-see mission. A few weeks later, a coast watcher stopped in to see him, and brought back letters from everyone. We've forwarded them to the families, with copies to Washington D.C. Your parents have probably received Mike's note by now."

The two men walked slowly, Steve limping a little. "Would you like a ride?" Buckner offered. "I can whistle up a jeep."

"Oh, no thanks, Captain. I need to keep exercising the leg. Walking is good for it."

Heading toward the hangar area across the busy base, Steve got a thorough briefing on how his brother and Buckner had first met ,and how Hollands had taken on the Japanese, right from the start.

"Mike is stuck on a fly-speck of an island," Buckner said, "but that doesn't keep him from waging war on the enemy."

"Yep," Steve said. "Sounds like my big brother all right. You must have been his wingman that morning over Kamberra Bay. Is that right, sir?"

"Yes I was," Buckner answered. "We were on our way back to base when his plane lost power and went down."

"Boy, did you two ever piss off the Japs that morning. You popped their whole store—ammo, gas, and groceries."

As they continued their hike, Buckner spotted Commander Sessions and his clerk driving toward them.

When the jeep came to a stop, the two men quickly snapped off salutes, and Buckner introduced Steve to the base CO. After a brief exchange of concerns and pleasantries, the commander drove on.

"Thanks, Captain, for filling me in on my brother. Mom and Dad will be pleased to know that we had this talk."

"That's quite all right," Buckner said. "If I see Mike, is there a message?"

Steve nodded. "Tell him the family is praying for him."

"I can do that."

Buckner stuck around and kept Steve company while his transport was being refueled and serviced, introducing him to a few of the other pilots and to Skip.

Twenty minutes later, Corporal Hollands was on the transport, bound first for Pearl Harbor, and then on to the States.

As the plane lifted off, a runner handed Buckner a message alerting him to an immediate officers' briefing at HQ.

"Gentlemen," began Sessions, "recent intercepts from Hollands and CinCPac indicate that a general Jap offensive may be brewing. The Nips have got something up their kimonos, that's for sure. We're doubling our air patrols."

Relighting his cigar, Sessions turned to Major Jeff Hanks, the Marine Air CO. "Hanks, we need six or seven flights for patrol each day. See to it. Let's see if the Army would like to join in with four of their bombers as well. Two Fortresses and two Mitchells."

"Right away, sir. What sectors do we cover?"

"All information will be found in your packets," Sessions said. "I can tell you this much. We will be probing deeper than ever into enemy territory. Even as far as Espritos. Check with my clerk on your way out."

As the meeting broke up, Sessions took Buckner off to the side. "Well, what do you think of Steve Hollands?"

"He's a good kid, sir," Buckner said. "Good soldier."

Sessions raised an eyebrow. "It appears young Hollands is cut from the same wood as his older brother."

"How so, sir?"

"That soldier is on his way to Washington D.C. for ceremonies," explained the commander. "He's to be awarded the Congressional Medal of Honor and two Purple Hearts. The citation states that Steve was twice wounded while he and a medic served up cover fire, saving the lives of over three hundred Army and Marine personnel. Sadly, the medic did not survive his wounds."

"I figured that Steve had been wounded when I saw the cane," said Buckner. "But I had no idea he had earned the CMH. I guess he really is like Mike. He lets his actions do the talking for him."

Sessions switched the cigar to the other side of his mouth, and abruptly changed the subject. "Captain, tell me honestly, what kind of a pilot is Lieutenant Morgan?"

"Billy? Well, sir, he's one of the best I've ever seen, and one of the few I can turn a flight over to. All the guys depend on him. Why? What's up, sir?"

"It appears that our young Mr. Morgan has a birthday coming up soon, and the records show him to be a tad short of legal pilot age at this moment. He won't be eighteen for over two months."

Sessions shook his head. "I'm supposed to send him home for reassignment."

"Sir, how did you come by that information?"

"Well, it was in the usual daily fleet communiqués a day or so ago. Why?"

"Have you discussed this with Major Hanks yet, sir?"

"No, not yet. But he probably got the same message. Why? What's on your mind, Captain?"

"Sir, you know that we have ground Marines, Navy swabbies, and Army soldiers that are fifteen, sixteen, seventeen years old. And they're out here fighting alongside the rest of us."

Buckner looked the commander in the eye. "Sir, I'm going to pull a 'Hollands' and ask that you lose that report, at least for two or three months. I'll ground Billy from flying if needed. But don't send him home, sir. Not for this."

"Is this so important to you, Captain?"

"Yes, sir, it is. But not just to me. Not only would it disrupt morale, I don't want to—I *can't*—lose that good and experienced a pilot. It's even more important to Morgan."

Sessions asked, "Is he really that good?"

"I've never told Mike this, sir, but when Billy's plane was damaged a few months back, he dropped two Zekes that were about to flame Hollands. A third Zero put a few rounds into Hollands' ship. Billy Morgan played dead, then rolled over and blew that one out of the sky when the Nip banked around for another target and lost visual. No, Commander. Morgan isn't just a *good* pilot. Next to Hollands he's the best I've ever seen."

"Okay, Captain. I'll take it under advisement," Sessions said. "Besides, I'm sure I will not be able to find that message for quite some time. Unless it comes down as an order. If that happens, there won't be a discussion. Until then, you can keep him flying or ground him. That decision is between you and Hanks."

"I understand. Thank you, sir!"

As he and Buckner walked toward the main door, Sessions said, "Captain, I want you and one more man to make another flight to the island at daybreak tomorrow."

"Yes, sir. What's the mission?"

CHAPTER 9

To Survive or fight

The deep purple of dawn had begun, but the sunrise was still nearly thirty minutes away. Something, a sound, had awakened Gunnery Sergeant Beckett from his slumber. He moved to a sitting position on his cot, head in hands, still not sure what he had heard. But then, there it was again.

Quickly getting to his feet, he called, "Captain! Captain, sir! Aircraft approaching. Extremely faint. Coming in from the west, sir."

Scarcely awake, Hollands sat up for a moment and listened. "Hmm! Slow turning radials."

He pulled on his boots and followed the Marine the short distance to the radio shack.

Yoshida and Minetti had also heard the droning motors and were already at the radios.

As they waited and listened, Beckett said, "I think two aircraft, Captain."

Hollands asked in a husky, early-morning voice, "Have you picked up anything, Ron?"

"No," Yoshida said. "It'll be a few seconds. The radios are warming up. Do you want me to try to raise the birds?"

"Not yet," Hollands answered. "Let's just listen."

Sergeant Gilbress put the handle of a G.I. tin cup full of hot coffee into Hollands' hand as he leaned against a support pole, and then she passed a second cup to Ron.

Although the planes were still some distance away, the low droning sound of their engines was getting louder. Rotating the dials of the captured Japanese radio and the one from Hollands' downed ship, Yoshida continued to search for any transmission. But the airwaves were silent from both camps.

"Still quiet," Yoshida said in a low voice.

Hollands could feel the tension building.

The Japs might be returning from a night raid. But it was also possible that this group of marooned castaways had somehow been discovered, and the enemy was coming in from a different direction to throw everyone off.

Suddenly, two dark shadowy silhouettes whizzed past, just above the trees. The engines were deafening.

Someone yelled, "They're *ours*, Captain! Corsairs!"

Hollands tapped Yoshida on the shoulder. "Quick, Ron! Say Buckner."

Keyed the radio. "Buckner, Buckner, Buckner."

A crackling answer came over the speaker. "Good-morning, Michael. Sleep well?"

A relieved grin spread across Hollands' face, and the others sighed in relief as he took the handset. "Hi, Bruce. What's up?"

"Messages and care-packages. Usual place," Buckner announced.

Quickly tying his boots, Carl said, "I'm on my way, sir."

"Me, too," announced Janet, and the two headed off for the clearing.

"Who's your wingman this time?" asked Hollands.

"It's me again, sir," answered Lieutenant Morgan.

"Good to hear from you, Billy."

"Mike, stay alert," warned Buckner. "The sun is rising again, and the Slot is full and narrow. Request any air shipments you may have. Over."

"Roger. Will try. Thanks for checking in on us."

"That's all right. Steve says 'Hi.' He's on his way home."

Hollands keyed the handset. "Thanks. We need a new cooker on our end. Anything else from your end?"

The aircraft made one pass and dropped their bundles.

"One more thing," Buckner's voice said. "Dumbo flies at dawn."

Then the Corsairs climbed to two thousand feet, and turned west again with a glint of morning light on their wings.

Nurse Elliott, who had joined the group during the transmissions, stared at Hollands. "What's all that doubletalk mean?"

"It's a highly-sophisticated military code," Hollands said, straight-faced.

The nurse poked him in the arm. "Come on, Captain, what gives?"

Hollands rubbed at his arm, as though her fingertip had somehow injured him. "We need to be doubly careful," he said. "The Japanese are on the move, planning something big. They're sending a lot of supplies and troops through the Slot. CinCPac and Pateroa need information. More intercepts. Oh, and I asked for a new field stove, which we probably won't get."

Hollands scratched his head and turned back to Yoshida. "It's just dawned on me; your kinfolk have been pretty quiet the past few days. With all of the reported movements, have we been monitoring the wrong frequencies?"

The young Japanese-American shrugged. "I honestly don't know.

Maybe. I'll get to work on it right away."

Still confused, Elliott interrupted, "And what is meant by 'Dumbo flies at dawn'?"

"A transport," Hollands said. "It could be an R4D, but more than likely it will be the smaller Duck floatplane. One or the other will unload on us tomorrow morning."

That evening, as they were eating a dinner of rice and Spam, the conversation centered on the packages dropped that day. Mail had finally reached the marooned troops. As the group read and reread the letters each had received, the mood lightened up noticeably. Shared pieces of back-home news interested all.

Ron was the lone exception. Except for a post card from his parents, the government had held up all of his mail.

The packages also contained several stateside newspapers, including issues of the Military's *Stars and Stripes*. But nothing meant more than the letters from home.

After a while, as the others were talking and sharing, Hollands signaled to Beckett and Yoshida to join him and led them about fifty yards out of camp.

"This is fine here," he said, and then began pacing in a circle. "If the Japanese are concentrating their move to retake Bougainville, the Russells, and Guadalcanal, I think that it would be unlikely that they would be busy in this sector for a while. The next few days are crucial. We really need to concentrate on the radios. We must know what the enemy is planning."

"Well," began Ron, "my 'cousins' *had* switched to a lower shortwave band on the dial. It took some searching, but we found them. Actually, Tim discovered it."

Lighting a cigarette, Yoshida added, "You know, Mike, we could try moving the antenna higher in the tree. It's highly unlikely anyone could spot it from the air or sea."

"That's right, Captain," Beckett said. "It could easily be raised another thirty feet. Maybe fifty."

Hollands nodded. "Good idea. Let's do it."

The next morning, a half an hour before sunrise, Buckner made good on his delivery promise. Piloting a Navy single-engine amphibious Grumman JF Duck, he made one pass over the compound before he eased the ship down onto the lagoon. Ron kept an ear to the radio should the enemy's radar spot the Duck. Lieutenant Morgan flew at five hundred feet above the water, orbiting the island.

Buckner killed the motor just as the Duck's portside hull kissed the dock. Carl ran down to tie off the craft. Buckner climbed out of the cockpit and stepped down to the lower wing and onto the dock.

Minetti came to attention and saluted. "Good morning, sir. Welcome to Paradise."

Returning the salute, the pilot asked, "Where's your CO, Private?"

"Right behind you, Jar-Head," Hollands answered, as he hurried down the dock.

Turning around, Buckner smiled as he saw Hollands hurrying toward him, "Hey, Army. How the hell are ya?"

The two men grabbed each other in a bear hug.

"Gee, it's swell to see you," Hollands said. "How did you get this job?"

"Hell, someone had to bring this stuff to you guys. Besides, I have three dozen fresh eggs on board, and didn't want any to get broken."

He looked back at Carl and said, "Open the side storage hatch and we'll unload this turkey of an aircraft."

Hollands helped with the cargo door and said again, "It's good to see you."

With Yoshida pedaling and monitoring the radios, the rest of the company was free to wander down to the dock. Hollands introduced Buckner to the group, and Carl and Tim took charge of unloading the rest of the supplies.

"This is quite a crew you have here, Army," Buckner said, shaking his head.

There was a brief moment of silence and then he asked, "Hollands, is there someplace where we can talk privately?"

"Sure. In a few minutes I'll show you our penthouse—a little something we built. By the way, congratulations on the new hardware on your collar."

"Thanks, I think. But being a first lieutenant was definitely easier. I'm squadron XO now, and it is a lot more work."

The two friends talked excitedly as they made their trek to camp.

"I've got to ask," Buckner suddenly interjected. "Did you have anything to do with a Japanese float plane going down last month?"

"Well, yeah, but it was a team effort," explained Hollands. "I just wanted to get it the hell away from this island. Why do you ask?"

"Well to start with, you had Naval Intelligence all over Sessions and me," Buckner said. "Someday, you and this Nip lieutenant of yours will have to explain to me just how in the hell you pulled that off."

Beckett had been following eagerly behind. As the three men hurried along, he gave Buckner a quick, impromptu tour of that part of the island.

Hollands grinned at him. "Elmore, you're acting as giddy as a new boot."

"Captain Buckner is the first Marine officer I've seen in over half a year, sir. 'Semper Fi!'"

He turned and pointed out two palm trees to Buckner. "This species of palm tree grows its own .50 caliber machine guns, sir."

Buckner seemed to be impressed, but asked, "Will they work?"

Hollands nodded. "There's a Nip Zero pilot resting in the water off to the west. He found out the hard way that our tree guns definitely work."

Lieutenant Elliott caught up to the three men. Holding a small package of freshly-ground coffee and carrying a crate of eggs, she announced "I'll have some coffee and eggs ready in a few minutes, Gentlemen."

"I've been up since 3:30," Buckner announced. "Usually I can't eat much this early, just coffee. But for some reason, I'm almost feeling hungry. Maybe it's nerves."

Beckett immediately excused himself and went back to assist the boys with the supplies, and to help camouflage the floatplane.

After a few minutes, Hollands and Buckner arrived in camp. Stopping at the lean-to sleeping area, Hollands pointed out their com-center a few yards away.

Buckner nodded his recognition. "This reminds me of the story of 'Robinson Crusoe,' Mike."

"Yeah, I guess so. Haven't read that since high school. Come on, I'll show you the penthouse."

The two men walked a short distance north of the camp to the mess hall lean-to, an open-sided structure with a thatched roof.

Buckner stepped inside and looked around. "Hmm. Not bad."

Settling onto one of the handmade stools, he reached into his flight jacket to pull out a sealed envelope. He handed it to Hollands. "This is from Commander Sessions."

Twenty minutes had passed and the odor of fresh coffee began to fill the air. Gail emerged from the med-tent carrying coffee and a tin plate of hot scrambled eggs and Spam for Buckner. "I brought some coffee for you too, Mike."

Looking at the two, she added, "I overheard what you said about being hungry, Captain. This should hold you till you get back to base."

Her graciousness under severe conditions surprised Buckner. "Thank you, Lieutenant," he said quietly. "I can really use this."

"You're quite welcome, sir. Thank you for taking so many chances to bring us supplies. And, Captain, my name is Gail."

With a smile, Buckner said, "Thanks again, Gail. And please call me

Bruce."

Lieutenant Elliott smiled, and headed back to the med-tent's cooking area.

Hollands put the envelope from Sessions down on a small table and took up his coffee. "I'll look at this in a moment. Go ahead and eat."

The sun was now prominent on the eastern horizon. Even at that early hour, it was warming up.

Hollands sipped his coffee, exchanging a bit of chitchat with his friend. Finished, Buckner put his plate aside and sipped his coffee.

Lighting a cigarette, he said, "Back to business, Mike."

"Right." Hollands put down his cup and took up the envelope.

Ron Yoshida had quietly walked over from the radio shack and was standing a few feet to the rear of where Buckner was seated. "Excuse me, Captain Buckner, but could I have a light?"

Buckner stood up and turned. Startled at the presence of a Japanese officer standing so close, Buckner finally nodded. "Sure thing, Lieutenant."

As Buckner handed his lighter to Ron, Hollands apologized to both men, "I'm sorry. My manners must have gotten lost out here in the jungle. Bruce, this is Ron Yoshida, originally an exchange student from San Francisco. He was living near Tokyo, going to the university just prior to Pearl Harbor. He and many other Japanese-Americans were conscripted into the Japanese military."

The two former adversaries shook hands.

Hollands gestured toward Yoshida. "Ron is the pilot who saved my butt. My bird was in trouble, and he shot down the two Oscars who were about to blow me out of the sky."

Then with a grin and a chuckle, Hollands turned his attention back to the envelope in his hand.

Buckner stared at him. "What's so damn funny?"

Hollands looked directly at Yoshida. "Ron, this guy was my wing man. He's the pilot who flamed *your* butt."

For just a few seconds, the silence was almost deafening.

Then Yoshida started laughing. "I thought it was one of the Navy planes that got me. What the hell, we're all on the same side now. Right, Captain?"

Buckner's face was beet red. Embarrassed, unable to speak, he tried to say something—*anything* intelligible.

Finally, he held up his hands as if surrendering. "I'm glad my shooting wasn't any better, Lieutenant. And I'm glad to have finally met you. Your message intercepts have been an enormous help."

Hollands finally tore open the envelope and read the message. His expression changed as his eyes moved down the page.

He handed the slip of paper to Yoshida and looked intently at Buckner. "You do know what this says?"

Buckner nodded. "I haven't read it, but I know the general idea."

"Well," began Hollands grimly, "this island is now designated as an official forward observation post for the U.S. Navy. Volunteer personnel only."

Yoshida turned to both American pilots. "Mike, how are you going to explain this to the others? The women will probably be sent back home, but what about the others? Will they have a choice?"

Gail had been close by. "Excuse me, Mike," she began. "What about us women?"

Hollands sighed. "We are about to become an official observation post. Manned by Navy volunteers only. You and Janet will be leaving soon."

Sergeant Gilbress walked up, having apparently caught the tail-end of the conversation. "Are we going home?"

Gail put an arm around Janet. "We're not sure yet," she said softly.

Hollands took the communiqué back. "Ron, let's get the others in here."

"On my way, Mike."

Within a few minutes, everyone was present and accounted for.

"Everyone take a seat and listen up." Hollands said. "This is from my commander: 'To: Captain Michael Hollands, U.S.A.A.C., From: Commander Delbert P. Sessions, U.S.N.R. Commanding Officer of Pateroa Naval Air Station.'"

Pausing, Hollands smiled. "Now I know why none of us ever knew his first name."

Yoshida smirked. "Does he have a nickname?"

"Of course," Buckner replied, also with a smirk. "It's 'Sir!'"

After a few chuckles from the group, Hollands took control again. "Okay, at ease. Let's continue... Ah, 'This is to inform you and your group, that your position is to be considered a Navy Forward Listening Post. It is to be an entirely volunteer operation. We are making arrangements to transport you off the island, and to insert volunteer personnel to take your places. You have my thanks for a job well done, and my appreciation for the hardships your group has endured for so many months. The information received from your radio monitoring has been vital to the war effort in the Pacific. You have saved countless American lives, and you have given Allied forces a significant tactical advantage in several military engagements. God Bless you! Sincerely, D. P. Sessions,

Commanding Officer, Pateroa.'"

Captain Hollands slowly folded the slip of paper and placed it in his shirt pocket.

Looking at the group he announced, "I, for one, will be staying. At least for a while. As for Lieutenant Yoshida, I will also volunteer his services."

Ron gave him a look of mock surprise.

Hollands smiled ruefully. "The Army wouldn't know what to do with him anyway." Then, he looked intently at Yoshida. "You're needed here, Ron. And your actions here will be felt all the way to Tokyo."

Hollands turned back to the group. "You have all done far more than *any* command could have asked of you. You have my personal thanks. I'm proud to have served with every one of you."

As the meeting broke up, Yoshida and Roberts went back to the radios.

It was nearly 0630, and Buckner was getting a bit antsy. Morgan had been circling the island continuously.

While sitting in the mess hall lean-to, Buckner had told Hollands about running into Steve, and how he had spent an hour or so getting acquainted with the young soldier. He also let Mike know that Commander Sessions had personally written to the Hollands family in Seattle.

As the two men talked, Roberts appeared at the door of the hut. "Excuse me, sirs, but Lieutenant Yoshida was curious as to how long it would take Captain Buckner to get the Duck airborne."

"Depends," Buckner said. "Maybe three or four minutes. Why?"

"Oh, ah... he's not real sure of their final direction yet, but he said to tell you some enemy planes may be in our area in about ten minutes, sir."

Buckner jumped up and raced toward the lagoon, hollering as he ran, "Gotta go now! Bye, Army! Bye, everyone! Yoshida, if this is a joke, I'll get even with you! You take care!"

The camouflage cover had been removed from the Duck, the plane turned around, and the engine re-started. After helping Buckner with his parachute and life jacket, Coast Guardsman Minetti jumped down onto the dock and saluted.

Buckner gave a quick wave of his hand as he gunned the motor, and the Duck headed out for its takeoff.

But it turned out not to be a joke. Buckner had been in the air for no more than a few minutes when his headphones crackled. "Ruptured Duck, this is Hollands. New problem, Captain. Several enemy surface ships eight miles dead ahead of your spinner. Heavy radio traffic. Stay low, bank hard to starboard... head north for five minutes; then turn west. Request that your wingman climb to angels thirty to get an accurate fix on flotilla. Over."

Buckner keyed his radio. "Roger. Turning north now. I'm on the deck, playing with the dolphins."

Buckner then radioed Morgan. "Duck to Escort Two. You heard the message, and what was suggested. Get your oxygen mask on and execute! Over."

"Roger," Lieutenant Morgan answered. "Don't want to leave you defenseless, sir."

"I'll be fine, Billy. Just get that information and radio it in. When Pateroa acknowledges your message, you get your tail feathers back down here and keep me company. Over."

"Bruce, this is Mike. White flame that engine and get out of here! Morgan can get the info, and decoy the Nip's interest in you. Out."

Buckner didn't take time to answer; he just opened the throttle wide. The 190 mile-per-hour top speed of the Duck would certainly not impress any enemy pilots, but it might cause them to die laughing.

"Come on, you Moby Duck!" he growled. "It's embarrassing to be out-planed and unarmed!"

Hollands' Army radio went quiet, but there was a lot of activity on the Nip's set, which indicated heavy naval movements from the south.

With binoculars, Hollands could just make out smoke on the horizon. As far as Buckner's flight went, the Japs either didn't know or just didn't care about the small American seaplane visiting their airspace. But there was some radio chatter concerning the lone American fighter.

Five intense minutes later, Yoshida switched on the small speaker from Hollands' radio. "Mike, Morgan has made contact with Pateroa. Listen. 'Pateroa Control, this is Duck Escort Two. Heavy enemy naval activity in sector Zulu, ten miles South-Southeast of Tango Charlie, speed twenty knots. Coordinates are...'"

Hollands and Yoshida each offered a sigh of relief as they listened to Billy call out the location of the enemy ships. Several minutes later, they monitored plane-to-plane radio from American carrier pilots.

Hollands smiled as he and Yoshida continued to listen to the radio account.

"Why are you smiling like that?" asked Yoshida. "You look like the canary that swallowed the cat."

"Oh, I was just wondering what the Majestic Japanese Navy might think if they knew that they had been spotted and reported by a seventeen-year old kid."

After a three second pause to digest what Hollands had said, Yoshida broke out laughing, "You gotta be kidding! Seventeen? God! Wish I could tell 'em, just to see their faces."

After dinner, Roberts and Minetti were discussing the merits of island life as they readied their gear for guard duty.

"Why do *you* want to stay, Tim?"

"Well, it's like you said earlier—whether onboard ship or on the ground—there are always those sergeants, chiefs, and officer types. 'The shine on those shoes is not good enough, soldier. Do it again.'"

"Yeah," Carl said. "They come in to check our bunks. 'My quarter didn't bounce high enough, sailor. Do it again.'"

"No, I like it here just fine," Tim said. "But a hot shower would sure be nice."

Both men laughed.

They located Captain Hollands and Gunnery Sergeant Beckett a few minutes later. Tim spoke first. "Sir, could we talk to you and Sergeant Beckett for a moment?"

"Sure," Hollands said. "What's up?"

"Well, Captain, Carl and I have been talking it over. We think we're the best to volunteer, because we know this island so well. Some new guy, well... He could get hurt, break a leg. Anyway, we'd like to stay, sir. That is, if you think we can do the job."

Hollands started to say something but was cut off as Beckett grinned and added his two-bits worth. "Well, sir, if these two are staying, I think I should stay, too. You'll need an old gunny around here, ya know. Someone who can maintain some military decorum."

The conversation spilled over and the women overheard Beckett and the two young men. Gail smiled. "Well, we gotta stay as well, if you guys are. Cuz if you get hurt or sick, who's gonna hold your hand?"

"...or tuck you in at night?" laughed Janet.

"Now that that's settled," Beckett said. "Let's get back to work."

Hollands was a little surprised at Janet's request. As Beckett and the boys walked away, and Gail headed back to the med-tent, Hollands looked at Janet. "You've been pretty anxious to get off this island, and rightly so," he said. "Why the change of heart?"

Janet thought for a moment. "Well, sir, I no longer feel forgotten. I am part of a real command. And this is where I belong. Where I'm needed. With you and Gail—I mean, Lieutenant Elliott—and the others."

CHAPTER 10

The Feathers of the Phoenix

Hollands was slow to wake up. He had slept remarkably well, but in the early morning hours, his eyes were still closed. Still more asleep than awake, he lay quietly and listened to the calls and songs of the island birds. But in the back of his foggy brain, he knew something was wrong. It was quiet. *Too* quiet.

Hollands guessed that the sun had been up for some time. But he heard no voices, no sounds of any human activity. With a major effort, he opened his eyes and sat up on his cot. A slight twinge of panic washed over him. He saw his four comrades sleeping. And the women's tent, a mere sixty feet away, was also quiet. The ladies were usually up first.

Hollands glanced at his watch, 0610. Still groggy, he rolled to his feet and stumbled out of the lean-to. His mouth and throat were as dry as cotton.

He tried to call out, but produced only a hoarse, inaudible whisper. "Hey, we're late on the radios." He half coughed, trying to clear his throat.

It was imperative that someone monitor the radios every morning. Trying again to clear his throat, Hollands made another attempt. "Hey Ron, come on, get up. We're late on the radios. Beckett, Roberts, let's go."

His weak voice still brought no response. With a growing fear, he turned and stepped back into the lean-to. He took his pistol out from under his pillow and grabbed his canteen from where it dangled off the lodge pole.

Backing out into the compound once more, he stopped just long enough to gulp some water. Then he cocked his weapon and fired two quick rounds into the air.

"Everyone, get up!"

The two pistol reports startled everyone. Both Tim and Carl fell off their cots. Within seconds, Nurse Lieutenant Elliott came on the run, loose shirttail flying behind, and bootlaces slapping from side to side with each stride.

Sergeant Gilbress was only moments behind. Both women stopped in front of Hollands and Elliott, out of breath and gasping. "What's wrong? Is anyone hurt?"

"No! No one's hurt, Lieutenant. We're all still asleep. *That's* what's wrong!" Hollands said angrily.

The four men had gathered outside. They knew that Hollands was more concerned than angry.

Beckett and Yoshida tried to speak at the same time, but the old Marine took the lead and said, "Captain, this is entirely my fault. It won't happen again, sir."

Hollands looked around at the meager formation and answered, "I'm not looking for blame. Besides, I overslept too. Perhaps I should have Buckner fly alarm clocks in for all of us."

He turned to Ron, "We are well over an hour late getting those damned radios started. Let's get going. All of us."

Ron grabbed hold of Carl's shirtsleeve and the two headed for the radios. The women retreated to the mess hall lean-to. Within a few minutes, the radios were warmed-up and working and by 0630, breakfast and coffee were on their mess table.

Just before noon, Hollands stopped by the med-tent to talk with Gail. Sitting down on a wobbly old chair, he said soberly, "I need an answer to something, Gail."

"What you want to know, Captain," the nurse began coolly, "is why seven human beings screwed up. Why they overslept an hour or so. Seven, mostly-terrified human beings, who just happen to be in a war they can't fight. Who may at any moment become victims—injured, killed, or worse—to be taken prisoner by an enemy who has little or no regard for human life or decency, especially toward women. Seven human beings who have averaged fewer than four hours of sleep during any twenty-four hour period these past weeks, not to mention all the months that five of us have been marooned here..."

Taking a deep breath, she added sarcastically, "Sorry, Captain, I don't have a clue. Do *you*?"

Somewhat stunned, Hollands stared at Gail. "Thank you for this little chat, Lieutenant," he said.

Muttering an expletive to himself, he stepped back outside. His mood had definitely turned darker as Yoshida met up with him.

"Hey, Mike, I was just out to find you."

"Hey, yourself," Hollands growled. "What do you want?"

Ron took a long look at Hollands and asked, "What the hell's wrong with you? You eat something bad?"

"Women," barked Hollands. "I need more practice in how to

understand them."

"Oh, you've been talking to Gail," said Ron.

He gave Hollands a sympathetic look. "Many years ago my great uncle shared a piece of profound wisdom with me on his fiftieth wedding anniversary. 'Lonold,' he said. (He didn't speak very good English.) 'Lonold, there are no ancient proverbs that tell us how to better understand woman.' That's not an exact quote, but it's close enough. I guess we just have to wing it."

"I believe that, all right," Hollands said. "Okay, my woman problem is unsolvable. What's *your* problem?"

"According to the OBC radio; it looks like a full blown tropical storm is brewing; typhoon size. Two or three days' worth."

"What the hell is OBC radio?"

"That's the Oriental Broadcasting Company," explained Ron. "I made it up."

"Oh! Well, when can we expect this big blow?"

"It could be here late tonight. The Nipponese are estimating that sustained winds of over 100 miles per hour will hit the northeastern part of the Russells by late evening. The Imperial Naval Command has recommended that all vessels in the vicinity should immediately seek a safe harbor, and wait out the storm."

"Try raising Pateroa," Hollands said. "See if there is any storm confirmation."

An hour later Ron saw Hollands coming across the compound. "It's confirmed," he said. "It's a monsoon!"

Looking up into a clear blue sky, Hollands said, "Okay, let's get everyone in the med-tent. I'll meet you there in fifteen minutes."

"Roger. On my way!"

Within a few minutes, everyone was gathered in the med-tent and Hollands began his briefing.

"Okay, you've probably all heard by now that a major storm is heading for us, complete with heavy rains and 100 mile-per-hour-plus winds."

He paused for a moment. "The five of you have weathered some pretty rough bouts while stranded here. From what the ladies have told me, it appears this is the best shelter available to us. Is there anything we should do to ensure our safety? Does this structure need anything?"

Gail spoke first. "The fabric has been treated with something like tar, which makes a sort of hard shell covering."

Looking at Sergeant Beckett she asked, "Do you know what that stuff was? And if there is any more?"

Beckett stroked the stubble on his face. "It's a tar-based compound all right. The Navy uses it. I think there is still some out back near the area of the ladies', ah—latrine. Ah, sorry, ma'am. Should be some more line laying around somewhere, too."

Turning to Tim and Carl, the old Marine asked, "Have either of you two seen those gray barrels out there?"

Both nodded in the affirmative.

"How long does it take to apply? And how long will it take to dry?" Hollands asked.

"There are only a couple small areas that could use a touch-up," Gail said, pointing to the ceiling and doorway. "Like here at these center posts and also around the two entrances."

Beckett considered the matter. "It should take less than a half hour to apply, Captain. And about three or four hours to harden. It'll be ready in plenty of time. We'll all have to sleep in here again, so we better bring our cots and any personal items we may want to save, not that we have that much. The lean-tos will be leaning flat after the storm, sir."

"That brings us to the radios," Hollands said. "Elmore, I want you to help Lieutenant Yoshida and me to move them in here and get them set up. We'll have to store all our weapons and ammo in here, too, including the machine guns from the trees."

Then, with a sigh, he looked at Gail and Janet. "Can you think of anything else, ladies?"

Taking a deep breath, Janet smiled feebly. "This is a really difficult, personal subject. But since the storm won't hit until late tonight, there should be plenty of time. Due to these close living quarters, it would really be appreciated if certain members of the group would, ah—well, I mean—take advantage of the soap that Captain Buckner brought, and head out to that small fresh water pool to bathe."

Looking at Hollands, she said, "That's all I have, sir."

Hollands gave a nod to Carl and Tim to get started on the tar. Then he asked the ladies, "How's our food supply?"

"We're in pretty good shape, sir," Janet said. "We won't starve."

Lieutenant Elliott waited while the group exited the tent, then caught Hollands by the sleeve. "Excuse me, Captain," she said quietly, "But could I have a word with you?"

"Certainly! What is it?"

"First, sir, I want to apologize for how I acted, or perhaps *reacted*, this morning. You know, for what I said. I was really out of line. You asked for my help and, well, I blew it."

"Gee, Gail, you don't have to *Sir* me," Hollands began. "However, you were correct with the earlier assessments. I didn't like it, and it's not easy to say so, but thanks. Now, is there something else?"

"Yes there is. You may have noticed how Janet and Carl have been acting around each other of late."

"Well, now that you mention it, I guess I have noticed they seem to spend a lot of their free time together. Is there a problem?"

"Potentially, yes, if it should go too far."

Pausing for a moment as if searching for the right words, Gail said, "This is neither the time nor the place for a courtship. It's hard enough for men and women to work together, and being marooned for so long certainly doesn't help any. This could create a real challenge for these kids, and for the rest of us. Would you have a talk with Carl?"

"These 'kids' as you call them," Hollands said, "are grown-ups. They're shouldering adult responsibilities. There are sixteen, seventeen, and eighteen year-old kids out here. They fight, and work, and sacrifice, and even *die*, right alongside everyone else. They've earned the right to be treated as adults."

Hollands sighed. "Nevertheless, you're right. Kids or not, we don't need that kind of trouble right now. I'm not sure how to approach Carl on the subject, but I *will* have a chat with him. I guess I should have seen this coming."

"Thanks, Mike!" Gail said. "I really appreciate it. And I'll do the same with Janet. They're both good, ah… *kids*. And I agree that they are doing a difficult job, and doing it well."

As the two stepped outside of the med-tent, Gail turned to Hollands. "Perhaps it could work out. Later on."

"Maybe so," Hollands said. "And since we're on the subject..."

He paused and looked around, as if to make sure they were really alone. "After this storm is over, how about you and I sneak down to the lagoon some night for a little moonlight skinny dipping?"

Gail blushed and tried to stammer an answer. Then, she realized that he was teasing. She gave him a gentle shove. "Michael Hollands, you are a bad person!"

Before he could respond, she gave him a quick wink, turned, and walked away.

The storm was more violent than expected. It raged for three days, lashing the little island with vicious winds, and pounding it with torrential rains.

With the group living so closely together, friendships were tested almost to the breaking point. But the storm finally broke, and tempers eased with the end of the bad weather. Things soon returned to normal. Well, *almost* normal. Carl and Janet no longer seemed so close.

The radio shack and the two lean-tos had been flattened, but were quickly rebuilt. Hollands marveled at how well the med-tent had survived.

Later on, Gail caught Hollands alone for a moment. "Hey, thanks for helping out with Carl. What did you say to him the other day?"

"Oh, probably something similar to what you said to Janet."

Gail grimaced. "To tell you the truth, Mike, I never got the chance."

Hollands shrugged and smiled. "Neither did I!"

Standing quietly in the center of their small compound looking at each other in disbelief, they erupted into laughter.

Catching his breath, Hollands said, "It looks like nature and the weather took care of the problem for us."

Still laughing, Gail finally said, "I think you're right, Captain."

It was just a week after the storm when Sergeant Beckett entered the rebuilt radio shack where Yoshida and Hollands were going over recent enemy radio intercepts. "Excuse me, sirs. Captain, could I have a word with you, sir?"

"Sure, Sergeant, just a moment." Hollands quickly finished up with Yoshida, then stood up to meet with Beckett.

Janet was standing a few yards off.

"Sir, Sergeant Gilbress, ah, well... We've just had the strangest conversation, sir," Beckett said. "Don't misunderstand, sir. Janet's a pretty smart girl. But I think she needs to tell you personally."

"That'll be fine, Sarge, but why all the mystery?" Beckett then motioned for Janet to join them.

"Well, Janet, what's on your mind?" asked Hollands.

"Well, sir, night before last I made several trips of taking coffee and sandwiches out to the guys, and I found something. Actually, what happened was that—in the dark—I got lost a couple times because of all the downed trees, and I *tripped* over it."

Sergeant Beckett nodded. "I went to see it myself, sir. And at first I didn't think it was important."

"What are you two yammering about? You're not making sense."

Nurse Elliott had been walking toward the radio shack and overheard part of Janet's comments. "Let's dispense with all the mystery," she said. "Why don't you two show us whatever it is that you're talking about?"

"Excellent idea," Hollands said. "Please lead the way to this mysterious *thing*."

Janet nodded in agreement, "Right this way, sir."

By then, all the members of the group had assembled.

Ron was also interested in the mystery and decided to take a little break from the radios.

As they marched along, the trail took them past the now fallen huts where Hollands and Yoshida had spent their first night on the island. When they came near the spot where they had met Mr. Quigby a couple of weeks earlier, they left the trail and turned west.

Everywhere they looked was evidence of the havoc wreaked by the monsoon: huge palm trees felled, mounds of dirt partially eroded, and areas that nature had carved out anew.

Then Hollands spotted something glistening several yards ahead. "Is that metal I see?"

"Yes, Captain, it is," responded Beckett. "That's what Janet found, or tripped over the other night, sir."

Shafts of light streamed in from the sun, making a small reflective glare. The ground was still quite muddy from the rains, and it slowed everyone's progress as they made their way through the debris and downed trees.

"Easy, everyone," Hollands cautioned. "This is no place to break a leg."

Tim piped up, "It would sure be hard to pack a litter out of here. Right Captain?"

Yoshida grinned. "Knowing our good captain, he'd probably treat you like a horse, and simply shoot ya."

"Funny, Lieutenant," Hollands said. "Possibly true, but still funny. Don't anyone fall. Especially, those of Asian genealogy."

As they got closer, Beckett hollered for Minetti and Roberts to move ahead with him. "We need to uncover this a bit more men, so the CO can get a better look at it."

Maneuvering for a closer look, Hollands asked, "What do you think, Sarge? Any idea what it is? Or *was?*"

Beckett and the two young soldiers dug around in the muck for a few minutes. They pulled away smaller downed palm trees and fronds, and uncovered something sticking up out of the mess.

"I think it used to be an airplane, sir," said Beckett.

As more debris was moved away, he nodded. "This looks like part of a tail section."

"Are there any markings?"

"Just on one spot, sir," the sergeant said. "I'd say she used to be a Beechcraft. You know, the same kind of plane that Amelia Earhart was flying when she went down, what? Five or six years ago?"

Beckett's voice took on a solemn tone. "Sir? Do you think this could be..."

Hollands shook his head. "No. I don't believe we're anywhere close to her route, Sergeant. Besides, she was flying a Lockheed Electra."

Yoshida squinted up through the palms at the clear sky. "Ya know, Mike, since we've got good flying weather again, my 'cousins' will be flying over this rock again. One little glint of sunlight off this wreckage, could invite an investigation."

Hollands looked up too. "You're right, Ron."

He turned to Beckett. "Make sure this thing stays covered. We don't want anything shiny that can be seen from the sky."

Everyone agreed that finding the airplane was interesting, but no one had any illusions that it would ever be of any use. It was simply a wrecked plane. Junk. Another casualty of their island prison.

September signaled the beginning of spring in the South Pacific and radio traffic increased, coming fast and heavy from both sides. September also marked the start of a major push by the Japanese to retake some of their lost real estate.

They had regrouped and brought in fresh ground troops, more aircraft, and more pilots. And, according to information from Pateroa, the Japanese had a newer, faster version of the Zero, too.

A couple of weeks after the storm, Buckner flew in additional supplies, including a larger U.S. military radio to replace Hollands' smaller aircraft version.

As everyone pitched in to unload the Duck, Buckner asked why they had all decided to stay.

Janet explained it best. "Captain Hollands is staying, so we're staying. We're a team."

Although it was part of everyone's responsibility to stay vigilant, many hours were filled with boredom, the worst of enemies.

So, early on—when there was no soldiering to be done—Minetti and Roberts began to work on the wrecked aircraft. Hollands knew of it and figured that it gave them time away from the stress of being stuck on a small island, and from the constant underlying fear of being discovered by the enemy.

It was still early in the month when Beckett excitedly ran through the compound looking for Hollands, going first to the radio shack.

Ron looked up when Sarge walked in. "Sorry, I haven't seen him for a while. Maybe he's in the med-tent."

At the med-tent, Gail said, "No, Sergeant, he left several minutes ago. Try down at the lagoon."

As the old leatherneck headed towards the lagoon, he spotted Hollands walking back to camp. "Captain! Captain!"

"Hi, Sarge. What's up?"

"Sir, you need to come and see something," Beckett said.

"Okay," Hollands answered. "But how 'bout you catch your breath first?"

"Whew! Thank you, sir. I'll be fine, if we could just walk slowly for a few minutes."

Hollands nodded. "What's got you so riled?"

"Oh, you wouldn't believe me if I told you, sir" Beckett said. "Hell, I saw it myself, and I'm still not sure I believe it."

Bypassing the compound, they headed off through the jungle.

When they reached the spot where the wrecked plane had been buried in several feet of sand and mud, Hollands caught sight of the aircraft. He couldn't believe what he was seeing.

"How did you do this, Sarge?" he asked softly.

"Oh, not me, sir," the sergeant said. "It's those two boys who did it. They've been working on it every day. I hadn't been out here since the morning Janet brought us all out."

Looking admiringly at the aircraft, Beckett said, "Roberts and Minetti came to me this morning. They asked me to come and see it. Ain't she beautiful, sir?"

"She sure is!"

Roberts and Minetti proudly stood at the front of the Beechcraft. She was out of the mud and stood on her own two, albeit flat, tires. There was hardly a speck of dirt on her exterior.

Beckett broke the silence. "Sir, it must have been used as a cargo plane before the war. Maybe locally between the islands and around New Guinea, or even to Darwin. The boys found a whole lot of old equipment stored inside. Oh, and they've found an underground bunker close by, too."

"Sergeant," Tim called out, "can we show the captain the engines we found?"

"Yeah, that's a good idea." Beckett said.

He turned to the still-speechless Captain Hollands. "This way, sir." And he led him toward the bunker. "I figure this was once an active foreword observation post, prior to the war."

Pointing to some downed trees they were about to climb over, Beckett said, "Watch your step here, sir. The footing is a bit rough."

Stumbling along, they walked the length of the plane. Hollands found it difficult to keep his eyes off of the airship. "She's sure beautiful," he said.

A few yards beyond the plane, Hollands saw a kind of door in the earth, that stood propped open by two long struts as if it were standing guard over the yawning, dark cavern that led into the side of the hill. Approaching it quietly he studied the entranceway cover and was surprised by its enormous size. It was six feet wide and twelve feet long. Cut with the dirt and foliage completely intact, it was camouflaged so well, that when closed, it would effectively disappear into the surrounding terrain.

"What was this, Sergeant, a guard bunker?"

"No, sir," answered Beckett. "It's a storage bunker."

Hollands knelt down and inspected the underside of the hatch and saw its rotting wood-frame. From where he was positioned, he could also make out two huge rusty-hinges that attached to an interior framed header. Although well-weathered, it appeared to be quite sturdy. Eight wide steps were cut into the earth. They obviously led to the underground storage area.

Cautiously, Hollands stepped inside, the others following close behind. Coming out of the bright sunlight, it took them several seconds to adjust to the dark interior.

Carl, last in line, lit two large kerosene lanterns the young men had left at the entryway. He handed one to Sergeant Beckett, who led the group down the steps. Ten feet below the surface, they came to a framed doorway five feet wide by eight feet high and to a level floor of moist sand.

Hollands guessed that the room measured twenty feet square. Neatly framed heavy-wood beams supported the walls and roof. Although displaying some rot, the structure appeared to be in good condition.

As his eyes slowly got used to the darkened interior, Captain Hollands was able to see crate upon crate of engines and spare parts. Barrels of oil were neatly stacked and stenciled, *United States Navy*. Along a wall were stored machine guns, mortars, and cases of ammunition. The smell of engine oil, cleaning solvents, and packing grease mixed with the musty, damp, salt sea odors of the island.

"What do you make of this Sergeant?" Hollands asked.

"Well, sir, it's like I said. I think this island was some sort of a naval observation post prior to the war. The girls, I mean Lieutenant Elliott and Sergeant Gilbress, said they were part of something like that."

Beckett stepped over a row of engines and continued, "My real question is about these engines, sir."

"Why's that, Sergeant?"

"The boys tell me that these motors couldn't have been here for more than twenty-four months. Some are fairly new designs, sir. From Pratt and Whitney and Curtiss-Wright."

Carefully reading the engine designations Hollands agreed. "These engines are used in a variety of our newer aircraft."

Hollands walked around, looking at everything. "But what is all this doing here?"

Beckett stroked the stubble on his jaw. "My guess, sir, is someone panicked. Maybe the Japs got too close. The Beech hasn't been here any longer than the rest of this stuff, if we can believe the logbook the boys found. It only reports five hundred hours flying time. In the cockpit the boys found the manufacturers plaque and I/D number. The plane was built in 1939, sir."

Slowly, Hollands and the others climbed out of the bunker and back into bright sunlight.

"This is quite a find, Sarge. We'll have to notify Pateroa and see if they can make some sense of this."

As he walked past the airplane again, Hollands could barely believe what the two young men had accomplished. Using crude tools and a homemade block and tackle, the two had worked a miracle to get this ship to stand.

As he moved around her, thoughts filled his mind. Would she—*could* she—fly again? He glanced at her undercarriage and silently tallied her shortcomings: "*The landing gear looks weak; the tires are flat... How's the tail section?*"

Taking a deep breath he sighed. "There's no way. No way!"

Standing at the nose of the Beech, Hollands looked at her longingly, just as he had as a kid, years before, at air shows around Seattle.

Suddenly, the siren in the compound sounded its mournful wail. Tim and Carl grabbed their rifles and took off, followed by Hollands and Beckett.

"I don't hear any planes, sir," Sarge said as he tried to keep up with Hollands.

"I don't either, Sergeant," Hollands called back. "But something's got

Yoshida's attention, that's for sure."

Yoshida met them at the door of the radio shack. "Damn, Mike. They've dispatched a boat with troops. They're coming here."

Beckett was still trying to catch his breath. "Do you know when the boat left?"

"Within the past hour," Yoshida said.

"How do you know this? And why are they coming here?" Hollands asked.

"I picked it up off their maritime frequency, directly from the boat itself. And then a minute later from their aircraft. I haven't heard anything about why they're coming. It could be just a routine exercise."

Pacing a bit Hollands asked, "What's their ETA Ron?"

"I'm not sure. I think the craft is similar to your, ah... *our* LST landing craft. Perhaps a little larger."

Petty Officer Roberts added, "If it's the boat I think it is, the top speed would be ten to twelve knots, sir. They could be here in about four hours. And, they can carry upwards of fifty men."

Hollands stood quietly as he leaned against a pole at the shack entrance. He looked at Yoshida. "Let's see if any of our birds are flying today."

"You got it."

Carl hustled to the generator and started to pedal as Ron keyed the handset. "Pateroa Outpost to any Pateroa chicks. Over."

Everybody knew that if the enemy should pick up the broadcast, they could triangulate the location of the radio. It was reassuring that it took just three quick calls to raise a response. And it surprised even Yoshida.

"Pateroa Outpost, this is Jigsaw Five. Identify yourself. Over."

Looking up at the Captain, Yoshida asked, "Well, Hollands, what do I say? *Help?*"

Hollands wrote out a quick message he hoped the Japanese wouldn't be able to understand or decipher in a short time. "Make it short and sweet."

"Jigsaw Five, this is Pateroa Outpost." Yoshida read off the longitudes and latitudes of where the small troop craft should be. "Jigsaw Five, this is Pateroa Outpost. Can you cancel our dinner guests? Over."

"Roger, Pateroa Outpost. Coming from Russell, to rendezvous with big mamma. Should meet your party in fifteen minutes. Out."

A very nervous group of seven Americans stood by the radio waiting for that horrible scratchy sound to come through the speakers.

Eleven minutes later, the confirmation came. "Pateroa Outpost, this is Jigsaw Five. Your guests have made other plans. Over."

"Thank you Jigsaw Five. Safe landing. Pateroa Outpost, out."

Yoshida switched his attention to the enemy's radio and put on his headphones to listen intently. Slowly holding up his left hand for everyone to stay quiet, he finally smiled. "The landing craft has been sunk. A cruiser has been dispatched to pick up survivors."

Everyone offered up a huge, collective sigh of relief.

Although pleased at the news, Hollands was still troubled. He was deep in thought as he walked away from the com-center.

Yoshida turned the radios over to Tim and Carl and hurried to catch up to Hollands.

The two men walked away from camp. Pulling a cigarette from a shirt pocket, Yoshida lit up. "What's bothering you, Mike? We've just dodged another bullet."

"You know as well as I do, they'll be here eventually," countered Hollands. "But first they may just wonder *how* our Navy just happened to spot their boat and sink it. Especially so far inside their own territory. It's too damn much of a coincidence, even for your cousins to buy."

A large, freshly-downed tree lay across the path ahead, and Hollands gestured for them to sit down.

"I'm glad we came out here, Mike," Yoshida said. "I can tell you that there are a couple things bothering me. First, there's the fact that the enemy has a higher amount of shipping going on."

He crushed out his cigarette with the toe of one boot. "Second, we haven't heard from Buckner or been able to raise Pateroa now for two days. My guess is they've been attacked and hit pretty hard. Their communications may have been knocked out."

"That's a real possibility," Hollands said soberly. "I have an awful itch on the back of my neck that's making me think we may be cut-off, and for a long time."

The ex-Japanese pilot nodded in silent agreement.

Suddenly, Hollands and Yoshida heard men's voices calling for them from the direction of the camp.

They made a quick dash back to the compound.

Sergeant Beckett intercepted them, "There's a hell of a lot of radio traffic, sirs! On all bands, from both sides."

Yoshida went back to work on the radios, listening first to the Japanese for a few seconds then turning to the Allied military set. "We were right! Pateroa is being hit hard! So are Henderson Field and the Russells! The Navy seems a bit busy as... oops, wait a minute."

Yoshida held up a hand. "Okay, this makes sense, Mike. Did you have anything to do with a raid flown against a small Japanese naval air installation about four hundred miles south of Pateroa? Let me think. That would have been around the first of April."

"Yeah," Hollands said. "In April. Why?"

"Well, it's payback time, buddy," Yoshida said. "I was at that base when you pulled that off. That was one day I'll never forget."

"Why's that?"

"We—I mean the Japanese flights—had been grounded that day. The weather was so bad, no one expected to see even a seagull flying."

Smiling his approval of the raid, Yoshida continued, "Everyone was shocked when we heard the sounds of approaching aircraft. Boy, did you ever take care of business! Two minutes and you were gone. Oh, it was beautiful!"

Yoshida took a sip of water from his canteen. "Did you know you destroyed *all* of their fuel? They had to wait two whole months for new ground tanks to be installed, and for a tanker to sneak in to fill them. It was magnificent. That's when they transferred me, along with several others, to Munda."

Hollands wondered about Pateroa, the possible damage, and how all the guys were faring. He felt helpless. Sidelined. Benched. There *had* to be a way to get back into this fight, to do his part.

"Any word from Pateroa?" he asked.

"Nothing," Yoshida said. "But I'll let you know if I hear anything."

It had been a sobering day. The islanders were mostly quiet during chow and into the evening. Conversation was limited to an as-needed basis.

At 2100 hours, Hollands headed to his cot. He had a prayer on his lips for his comrades back at Pateroa and for the rest of the Americans in the Pacific Theater.

He was tired but restless and couldn't sleep for a while. By 0200, he was wide awake again. He laced up his boots and walked out of the lean-to. As he buckled on his pistol belt Ron Yoshida joined him.

"Can't sleep. Mind if I keep you company?"

"Not at all. Come on!"

With flashlights in hand, they headed to the med-tent for coffee.

Gail was on duty, and had just filled a large thermos she had intended to take to Sergeant Beckett, Tim, and Carl who were standing guard duty, rotating hourly among the four gun emplacements.

As Hollands and Yoshida drank their coffee they volunteered to make the coffee run.

"Thanks," Gail said. "Here's the coffee, and three sandwiches." She spoke softly, so as not to disturb Janet who was asleep in the adjoining area. "I appreciate you two taking them out for me."

"That's all right," Hollands said. "Glad to do it."

As they started outside, the nurse abruptly asked, "Say, do you mind if I walk out with you guys?"

"Of course not," Hollands said.

In the dim light of the quarter moon, they took a few minutes to visit with each man.

As an afterthought, Hollands led Ron and Gail over to where the Beechcraft sat. The boys had made camouflage netting out of palm fronds and seaweed that covered most of the plane. Hollands shone his light on the aircraft.

She had sustained a few obvious wounds from sitting so long on the ground. As they looked up at her, no one uttered a word. Then Hollands and his two companions climbed aboard. The interior was still covered with silt and plant life. Vines crawled up the inside of the fuselage.

They worked their way forward to the cockpit, and the two men used their lights to survey the instrument panel. Most of the gauges were either broken or missing. The windshield had been broken out, as had the rest of the ship's glass. The two cockpit seats were badly weathered, torn and covered in dried, caked mud, but the two pilots sat down in them without hesitation.

Then like two kids on an amusement ride, they began flipping switches. Of course, there were no batteries and no response. After testing the yoke and the rudder pedals, satisfied with what they had seen, they got up and exited the plane.

Yoshida was first to break the silence. "Think we can we do this?"

"Do what, Lieutenant?" Hollands responded.

"You know damn well what I mean, Mike. We're both on the same course here. Do you think she can *fly*?"

As they exited the aircraft, Hollands said, "I don't know, Ron. Interesting idea, though."

Gail stared at them in astonishment. "You guys must be nuts! Did you both get hit in the head with the same coconut? If you were kids back in the States, I'd think you had been reading too many Buck Rogers comic books."

She took a breath and looked up at the nose of the plane. "What are you thinking? What kind of craziness are you considering?"

At first the two didn't say a word. Hollands just shone his light on the path and he and Yoshida began the trek back to camp. "Hey Ron, do you have any comic books in your stuff?"

"No, I loaned all of mine to Buckner when he was here. There was a new Superman, too. Oh, and two or three older Buck Rogers."

"Damn!" Hollands said. "I would've liked to have read them."

"You guys are truly nuts!" Gail yelled after them.

As the two men disappeared into the darkness, she realized she was being left behind. She called out, "Hey, guys wait for me!" And she began to trot after them.

At 0530, Janet started her rounds to wake everyone up. Beckett had returned to his cot in the lean-to a few hours earlier.

After rousing him, Janet turned to wake Yoshida and Hollands. Their cots were empty.

"Hey, Sarge," she called over her shoulder. "Have you seen the lieutenant and the captain?"

Beckett shook his head. "No, missy, not since last night..."

Tim and Carl were dragging their butts in from guard duty, ready for some serious sack time.

As they approached, Janet asked, "Have either of you seen the lieutenant or the captain?"

Tim responded with a sleepy nod. "Yeah. They've been working around our airplane since 0400."

Ron checked his watch. "Shit! It's after five-thirty. I've gotta get to the radios."

He gave Hollands a sideways-look. "If Buckner gets a break in the fighting, maybe he could bring us a couple of batteries for the radios. A small welding torch would be good too."

Hollands grinned. "Not a bad idea. I'll have him throw in a swimming pool, too."

Yoshida scratched his head. "Well, I wasn't exactly thinking of a pool. How 'bout a bath tub instead? The welding torch, though... Now *that's* still a good idea."

He checked his watch again. "I've got to get back to camp. You coming?"

"No," Hollands said. "Not right away. But have one of the girls bring out some food and coffee."

"Will do!" Then Ron disappeared into the grass and palms as he headed to camp.

Hollands held several scraps of paper and a worn pencil stub and he continued to make notes and diagrams.

It was an hour later when he heard something moving in the brush and grass near the path.

He pulled out his .45. "Who goes there? Identify yourself."

A woman's voice rang out. "It's me. Gail."

Hollands holstered his weapon. "Oh, Hi. Thought you'd still be asleep. Isn't Janet up?"

"She's up. But for some reason, I couldn't sleep. Here's some coffee and some hot food. Or at least it was hot twenty minutes ago. I ran into Ron and got your message."

Hollands smiled. "Wow, thanks! I'm so hungry I could eat a palm tree. And that coffee smells fantastic!"

CHAPTER 11

The Erector set!

Two days later the radio crackled, "Pateroa Outpost, this is Pateroa Control. Over."

The radios were not quite warmed up, so Yoshida could hear, but he couldn't broadcast.

Tim began to pedal the generator to save the battery and Ron fumbled for the microphone.

"Pateroa Outpost, this is Pateroa Control. Do you read? Over."

The fighting had let up and Hollands had requested that the group be evacuated from the island. Even if the Japanese didn't yet suspect the presence of Americans sitting in their front yard, it was only going to be a matter of time.

"Pateroa Control, this is Pateroa Outpost, go ahead. Over."

"Pateroa Outpost, this is Pateroa Control; ruptured Duck in route; ETA your pond one-five minutes. Over."

"Roger, Pateroa. Thank you. Pateroa Outpost, out."

Ron put the handset down and nodded to Tim. "Go find the Captain, fast. Have him meet me at the wharf. I'll monitor the calls for a few more minutes. Oh, and find Carl and have him get the camouflage cover ready for the Duck."

"Yes, sir!"

A few minutes later, Yoshida headed out to meet the incoming flight. With binoculars in hand, he scanned the horizon for the Navy floatplane. After fifteen minutes, he still was unable to detect any sign of the Duck.

"Hi, Ron. Is he late?"

Yoshida continued to stare through the binoculars. "He will be, in about half a minute."

He passed the glasses to Hollands. "What do you think he's bringing us this time?"

Hollands squinted through the binoculars. "Candy bars. Nylon stockings. A generator. Maybe a small welding torch. Nothing important."

He grinned at his friend's raised eyebrows.

The Duck finally came into view, hugging the waves, then suddenly executing a hard turn to port.

"*Evasive action?*" both asked at the same time.

Yoshida scanned the dawning sky. "Why? I don't see or hear a thing."

Hollands hollered over to Tim, "Off the dock! Now!"

And they all quickly ran for cover of the palm trees along the sandy edge of the lagoon.

From out of nowhere, two Zeros streaked by, closing in fast on the Duck.

"Shit," Hollands muttered. "He's defenseless in that plane!"

The whistling high-pitched whine of a fourth plane reached their ears.

"Maybe so," Yoshida said. "But there's a Corsair! 'Whistling death' my cousins called them. See? Circling in from the north. Man, look at him go..."

The roar of the engine and reverberations of the big bird's six machine guns cut off the rest of Yoshida's remarks.

"Yeah! Splash two Zekes," yelled Hollands.

"That was pretty neat!" Yoshida said excitedly. "He got both on a single pass. They never saw him coming in from that angle."

A few minutes later, the Duck settled onto the smooth water of the lagoon while the lone Corsair continued to fly cover, slowly orbiting the island at about 500 feet. Within seconds of the Duck's hull kissing the lagoon, the plane was tied off at the dock, and Buckner was out of the cockpit.

Sunrise was fast gaining now and Buckner yelled, "Hey, don't just stand there. Get your butts down here and help get this unloaded; I want to get the hell out of here. Flying a Duck is *one* thing. But being a *sitting* duck for the Nips is not my idea of fun."

"For a Marine you're a bit testy this morning, aren't you?" Hollands asked as the three men hurried down the wharf.

"Shit, Hollands, if this thing was any faster I could quit paddling."

Yoshida motioned to the light gray sky of dawn. "Who's your guardian angel?"

"Two guesses," answered Buckner hastily.

He looked back at Hollands. "It's Billy. Do you know he just turned 18 years a few days ago?"

"I've never seen anyone fly like that," Yoshida said. "Two down with one pass. Wow!"

He whistled. "I'm going to the radios, Mike. To see if the neighbors are missing two Zeros."

"Good idea, Ron!" Hollands acknowledged.

They quickly hauled the cargo towards camp.

Hollands asked, "How's everything back on Pateroa? Did the base get it bad?"

"Yeah, we got hurt some" Buckner answered. "But it could have been devastating. The Nips didn't do their homework! We had two squadrons visiting, an Army Air Corps unit still flying P-40s, and a group of Navy Hellcats. Those two squadrons, along with our twelve Corsairs, really surprised the Japanese. They sent nearly sixty planes, and lost over twenty-five."

"We've been concerned," Hollands said. "Not hearing from Pateroa. Any major damage? Anyone hurt?"

"No, and no! Out of twenty-five Nip bombers, only three got through, but they missed the airfield completely. We lost a total of six fighters. No one killed, but a dozen or so wounded. Mostly minor injuries."

With a sigh of relief, Hollands said, "You look like you're in pretty good shape. So tell me, how long does it take a Marine captain to run a quarter of a mile?"

"Why, want to race? What's going on?"

"I want to show you something before you go, and it's about half the length of this rock. You won't have to stay very long, but you've got to see this."

Hollands motioned toward camp. "Ron's monitoring the radios. If any Zekes are coming, you'll get about fifteen minutes warning. So, whattahya say?"

"I think you've been on this damn island too long," Buckner said. "Okay, I'll bite."

After all of the boxes and crates had been placed in the med-tent, Hollands took Buckner over to the radios. "Did you catch any kind of transmission after the Zeros went down?"

"No. Not a chirp! And I left the radio tuned to their air traffic channels."

"Bruce is going with me to see what Janet and the boys found."

Yoshida said, "That's fine, Mike. You two take off. Tim and I will continue here. If I hear so much as a whisper, Tim will fire two rounds."

He adjusted a dial. "If my cousins are coming from their base east of here, you and your buddy in the Corsair will have enough time to get out of here. I'll personally see to it that Sergeant Beckett runs down to the dock to get her turned around and fired up."

"Fair enough," Buckner said.

Before Buckner could say another word, Hollands grabbed his arm. "C'mon, let's go!"

They took off, running easily through the jungle, staying out of the open grassy area and hugging the tree line.

A they leapt across the small stream, Hollands grinned. "We call this Trickle Creek. The huts, or what's left of them after the storm, are the Hotel Astoria. Ron and I camped there, our first night on the island."

Hollands could see that Buckner was breathing hard, so he slowed to a walk. "It's just another hundred yards or so."

They reached the area where the trail split off to the Beechcraft. Buckner fell to his knees, panting, nearly soaked through with perspiration. He looked up at Hollands. "What-am-I-supposed-to-see-here?"

In a serious tone, Hollands said, "You'd better work on some boot camp conditioning, buddy, and cut down on the smokes, or you won't make it to the next bomb shelter."

After helping the young Marine up, Hollands pointed to an open area beneath the heavy palm canopy.

Buckner took a healthy drink of water from his canteen, then used his sleeve to wipe away the perspiration dripping into his eyes and down his face.

He could just make out the outline of an airplane. His breath was still coming hard. "It must be a mirage. My eyes are playing tricks on me."

Slowly getting his wobbly legs working again, he ventured closer for a better look. "Is that a Beechcraft?"

"That it is! One of the ladies tripped over it after that heavy storm three weeks back. I think someone had buried it on purpose. I have no idea *why*. But the severity of the weather has compounded any damage. The Coast Guardsman and the Army private basically got her out of the mud and standing on her own. Come on. I'll give you a quick peek at our supply depot."

Above them, Lieutenant Morgan continued orbiting the island as the two men trekked back toward camp.

Buckner shook his head. "You've got enough parts back there to build two or three planes."

"Yeah, I know. But I want to fix just one. And to do that I need a few things—like an engine hoist and stand, a block and tackle, chain and cable, some basic tools along with welding equipment. Oh, and some fuel might be nice."

Buckner snorted. "Hell, Mike I'll just borrow the Queen Mary and load her up. I couldn't carry a load like that in the Duck. With its fuel tanks full and your normal load and me, it's all I can do to get it off the water."

"Humor me!" Hollands said. "Check with Skip and some of your buddies in the Seabees."

His voice grew more serious. "On your next trip out here, I think I'd like to send the girls back with you. Jap activity has moved closer again."

He pulled several slips of paper from his shirt pocket and handed them to Buckner. "Give this stuff to Skip for me. It's my shopping list."

"Right! I'll look it over with the Skip and the crew."

They were only a few hundred yards from camp when two rifle reports rang through the trees.

"That's my signal, Army! Gotta go now!"

And they ran the rest of the way to the lagoon, where Beckett had the Duck turned around with the engine idling.

"What's up, Sarge?" Hollands asked.

"Yoshida said to tell you and Captain Buckner, that there is nothing imminent; but there seems to be a lot of radio traffic interested in this area. He doesn't know of any planes headed our way yet, but apparently, the two Nips had reported this island as their last position. The lieutenant thought it safer to have you leave now, sir."

Buckner put a foot on the pontoon, and prepared to climb into the pilot's seat. "Are you two absolutely sure about Lieutenant Yoshida? I mean about his loyalty to our side?"

Beckett nodded gravely. "Other than his eyes, he's as American as apple pie, hotdogs, and baseball."

"Do you agree with that assessment, Army?"

"I have from that first day," Hollands said. "He saved my life twice, and he has saved a lot more American lives since then—probably yours as well."

Buckner heaved himself into the cockpit and began to buckle in. "Fair enough," he said. "Have Ron unwrap the brown paper bundles."

He threw Hollands a quick wave. "Gotta go now. But I'll be back soon."

A minute or so later, the Duck was airborne, with Lieutenant Morgan's Corsair flying cover.

Yoshida walked up to stand next to Hollands. Both men watched the two aircraft head out towards the horizon.

Yoshida cleared his throat. "I was wrong, Captain."

"Say that again?"

"My relatives are on their way here. But I think I misinterpreted part of their message. It's an air-sea rescue mission. They'll be looking for those two Zeros, and we are right at the center of their search area."

Hollands began walking up the beach toward camp. "How much time do you think we have?"

Yoshida fell into step beside him. "They could have a few planes overhead within twenty minutes or so. Maybe an hour. The main effort will probably consist of small, shallow draft ships."

He rubbed the back of his neck. "I'm only guessing, but I'd bet they'll send a couple small cruisers to patrol and search farther out. And I wouldn't rule out the possibility of a ground search."

Sergeant Beckett caught up with them. "Excuse me Captain, but may I ask a question?"

"Of course, Sergeant. What's on your mind?"

"It's the Beechcraft, sir. If the Japs come ashore and find that aircraft, they'll stay until they find all of us, sir. But if we can somehow settle her gently back to the ground, I think we could cover her with enough fronds to keep her well out of sight. Then, we could hole up in the underground supply bunker, sir."

All three men stopped walking.

Yoshida nodded. "I agree."

Beckett said, "I'll get the others to the radio shack on the double, Captain."

"Thanks, Sarge!"

A short time later, the crew gathered and Hollands explained the bad news to them.

"We have a possible hiding place, that being the storage bunker. We have two important jobs to do first. We must assume the worst, that the enemy *will* come ashore. So this island and camp have to look and smell like no one has been here since Noah's Ark. We also need to camouflage the plane, and make the area around it look uninhabited."

"When do you think the Japanese will come ashore?" Gail asked, struggling to hold her voice steady.

"That's a good question. Unfortunately, we can only guess. They might not set foot on the island at all, but we must assume that they will. A lot will depend on their search, and whether the two pilots they are looking for are still in or around their downed aircraft. If the two planes are easily accessible, and in shallow water, they may just simply recover the bodies and leave."

He looked around the group. "Okay, we've often talked of this possibility. Sergeant Beckett will be in charge of collecting the machine guns. Lieutenant Elliott and Sergeant Gilbress will start making the camp area look as unlived-in as possible. So the first thing is to take down the lean-to, mess hall, radio shack and latrines. The cots and what bedding we have we'll take with us to the underground. This whole island has to look as natural as if a storm had passed through."

Hollands turned to Lieutenant Elliott. "Gail, as soon as I can, I'll send someone back to help you and Janet."

Then addressing everyone again, he concluded, "This isn't going to be easy. The ball is in the Japs' court now. But you all know what has to be done, so let's get started."

It took the rest of the day to get things ready for company that might not come. The island-rock did indeed, look untouched, as if it had been years since anyone had set foot on it. Only the med-tent was left standing, but the two women threw several buckets of muddy seawater and seaweed over the top and covered it with fronds from toppled palm trees. By the time the hot afternoon sun hit the camp, all the dry vegetation had turned sufficiently smelly, and the air was heavy with rotting vegetation.

All of the food had been removed from the med-tent and taken to the bunker, and the ladies brought their medical kits and the cook stove. This was the first time the girls had been inside the bunker. The air inside was pungent with salt water, foul seaweed, and engine oil.

Earlier Yoshida had set up the radios in the back of the bunker. He hid the antennas outside in a nearby tree. The men worked to reorganize some of the smaller boxes of engine parts to make room for the boxes of rations.

Hollands was aware that Carl had become quiet and increasingly anxious. He walked over to the young private. "So tell me, Minetti, how do you like our new quarters?"

Carl mumbled something unintelligible under his breath.

Hollands got right in the young man's face and spoke firmly but softly. "Carl, whatever is bothering you, get rid of it. Shake it off, and fast. You are a good man, and I—and all of the others—are depending on you to help get us through this mess."

Caught a little off guard, Carl said, "Sir, it's just I feel like I've been buried alive. Like the walls are closing in, and it's hard to breathe."

"I don't much like it either," Hollands said in low tones. "But after shooting *us*, what do you think the Japs would do to these two women?"

As the meaning sank in, Hollands said, "I hate being down in this hole, too. I feel like a goddamn mole! But, soldier, we just don't have a choice right now. I know your training didn't prepare you for this, but I need you strong; And I need to know that you're still part of the team. Don't quit on us now."

Minetti appeared to be reaching deep within himself to grab some composure. Coming to attention, he sputtered, "Sorry, sir."

"Being sorry won't save our hides or help these women. Being strong and doing our jobs *will*."

"Yes, sir. I'll be all right, sir," Carl answered.

"Okay! Let's go see what's for chow. It might be my favorite. Cold K-Rations."

"Yes, sir. And Captain?"

"Yes, Carl?"

"Thanks!" The young man added with a bit of a smile.

Late afternoon gave way to evening, and it was nearly dark outside. The women had gotten their stove working and were busy with food preparations. Janet and Gail had warmed up a little coffee and some of the packaged rations. As they passed the thermos and ration boxes around, their situation didn't feel quite so grim. No one complained about how the odor of the bunker mingled with the taste of the food.

"Captain, may I make an announcement, sir?" Beckett said.

Hollands gave a wave of his hand.

Sarge nodded. "Thank you, sir."

He turned to the others. "Like all of you, I don't much like it down here. But eventually I hope I'll be able to fight the enemy as I've been trained—like a Marine."

Pausing for a moment, he continued. "With the help of Roberts here and Lieutenant Yoshida, we have found, cleaned, and enlarged three air vents that were built into this bunker. They run horizontal, opening out at the cliff, but they're well concealed. We checked. No one has to worry about breathing, and it will be safe to use the cook stove with the hatch closed. Unfortunately, we can't do much about the smell. That's all I have, sir."

Hollands smiled. "Thanks, Sergeant. That's reassuring information." He took a seat on a large crate, turned up the two kerosene lanterns, and gestured for everyone to come in closer.

As each found a crate or box to sit on, he held up the brown paper bundle that had been included in the things Buckner had delivered earlier that day. "Now I have a package I want to present to someone, along with a special proclamation from the President. Our thanks are all wrapped up in these packages, and in this communiqué."

Holding the package under his arm, Hollands took a folded sheet of paper from his shirt pocket and ceremoniously unfolded it. "'By special appointment, Ronald Yoshida is hereby commissioned into the U.S. Army Air Corps as a First Lieutenant.'"

The small group erupted in applause and cheers.

"Hold on, there's more." Hollands looked directly into Yoshida's eyes, and held out the bundle. "These packages are for you, compliments of Captain Buckner. Everyone here has written his or her own personal note vouching for you. Copies of the notes have been forwarded to President

Roosevelt."

Overwhelmed, Ron studied the communiqué. Then, he began ripping open the paper bundle. He stopped abruptly when he caught sight of the contents. Tears began to trickle down his face.

Everyone craned their necks to see what the brown paper had concealed.

Yoshida held up a new U.S. Army airman's uniform, complete with insignia, wings and the silver bars of a first lieutenant.

His voice was husky with emotion. "I don't know what to say, except... Thank you. Thank you *all*, very much."

Hollands was still eating his warmed-up K-rations when Ron walked over, resplendent in his new uniform.

Yoshida grinned. "How do I look?"

Hollands looked him over in the dim light. "I like your new uniform a hell of a lot better than your old one."

"Yeah, feels better, too. It smells clean, even down here."

Yoshida sat on a nearby crate. "Something bothering you, Mike?"

Hollands shrugged. "You know, I'd almost kill for a decent cup of coffee, or an R.C. Cola right about now."

He took a bite and chewed thoughtfully. "Ron, if we get through this, I want to get serious about that plane. No more kidding around. We've got about all the parts we need. I think we should make the old gal airworthy again."

Yoshida rubbed the back of his neck. "I know we've played around with it and teased the hell out of Gail, but do you really think it can be done? Can we pull it off?"

"We have to try," Hollands said. "This latest crisis is the icing on the cake, as far as I'm concerned."

"What do you mean?" Yoshida asked.

Hollands sighed. "Sooner or later, we're going to have to evacuate this island. Our luck won't hold out forever. One of these days—maybe even today—your cousins are going to come looking for us in earnest. When that happens, we'll have to be ready to leave at a moment's notice."

He shook his head. "If the Nips come after us... No... *When* the Nips come after us, there won't be enough time for Buckner to ferry us off the island in twos or threes. We'll all have to go at once."

Yoshida nodded. "And for *that*, we need a plane that can carry us all."

"That's exactly right," Hollands said. 'The Beech is our ace-in-the-hole. Our emergency evacuation plan."

He fished in his shirt pocket and pulled out some folded scraps of paper. "I've asked for some things to help us. Here, look these over. They're my notes and drawings on the plane."

Yoshida accepted the hand-drawn diagrams and began to examine them with the critical eye of a pilot.

Throughout that first day in the bunker, only an occasional enemy aircraft overhead could be heard. No major force showed up until the next morning, just before dawn. Faint, strange sounds could be heard, interspersed with the deafening quiet.

After the kerosene lanterns and stove had been extinguished, the grassy door was opened a few feet to allow fresh air to move through the bunker. Tim and Carl took turns standing guard outside.

Providence was with the seven. Evidently, the Japanese had simply recovered the bodies of their two fallen comrades. By late afternoon of the third day, it appeared that the enemy search party had gone.

To be certain, Hollands sent Beckett, Menitti, and Roberts on a quick recon. While waiting for the small patrol to return, Hollands and Yoshida worked on drawings and sketches for the Beechcraft.

A strategy was slowly brewing in Yoshida's brain. "The propellers we've found in this cache, are the three-and four-bladed types," he said.

"Both kinds are too long, and will need to be trimmed. Or we could make the cockpit narrower," he joked.

"The original propellers had two blades," he said. "I think the three-bladed props will work best. But we'll have to take several inches off."

Two hours later, the patrol returned. Beckett reported their findings to Hollands and the others.

"Captain, I don't think the Nips ever came ashore," he said. "They had two motor launches that may have come close to the beach, but that's all. There's nary a footprint, sir."

Roberts stood up. "Sarge, Captain, can I say something please?"

Beckett nodded.

"This may mean something to Lieutenant Yoshida," said Roberts. "I had positioned myself at the tree line and tall grass and watched several Japanese in a small launch approach our dock. They tied off the boat and four of the ten men climbed on the dock to inspect the hut. One man looked through the rubble while the other three walked the length of the dock. The one man was a bit taller and it seemed like he was in charge. Anyway, he reached down and picked up something. I couldn't see for sure what it was. From my distance it looked like a piece of rope or radio cable. But then he reached inside his pocket and took out something shiny. He put it on the windowsill. Then he looked around—and I swear he looked right at me, sir, Sarge."

Roberts shuddered. "But I know he couldn't see me. Then he called the men back. They got back into their boat and left. That's all, sir."

"You never told me this, son," said a surprised Beckett. "Did you go to look see what the shiny thing was?"

"No. There was too much activity going on right then. When it looked clear, I rejoined you and Carl."

"What do you make of that, Ron?" asked Hollands.

"It's a mystery to me. I'll take a little hike down there later, though," Yoshida said.

Pensive for a few moments, Hollands said, "Are all their ships gone, Sergeant?"

"Yes, sir. Nearly out of sight as we started back here," Beckett said. "Minetti kept well hidden in the trees and bushes, and followed and observed the launches as they made their way around the island's perimeter. I didn't see the one at the dock. But the others never stopped; just looked. When all the launches reached the northeast point, they shifted into high gear and took off, joining up with the two larger ships which hoisted them aboard."

"That's good news," Hollands said. "We still have a few hours of daylight, so let's get out of this damn, damp hole and get camp set up again."

By early evening's dusk, both the com-shack and men's lean-to were up. The women had cleaned the med-tent and rolled up the sides so it could air out, and odors of real food wafted across the compound. Only the mess hall was left to be raised and would have to wait till the next day.

After Ron had reestablished the com-shack, and all other structures were again standing, he stopped by the lean-to where Hollands had stretched out for a few minute's rest.

"Hey, Mike, want to take a short hike on a long dock?"

"Tim's story's got your curiosity up, right?"

"I guess you could say that. Come on, get your lazy butt up."

"Man, give you a new uniform and you get downright rude," Hollands joked as he tied his boots.

A few minutes later, the two were walking down the dock heading for the remains of the hut. As they reached it, Yoshida bent down and picked up a piece of radio cable that had been found on the Nip seaplane.

He walked to the window opening and stared at the shiny object. "Hey, Mike, take a look here."

"What did you find?" Hollands asked as he came around the corner.

Ron held up the length of cable. But lying flat on the windowsill was a bright coin, an American half dollar.

Two days later Beckett, Roberts, and Minetti were trying to decide how to go about installing the new, larger, and more powerful engines in the Beech. Roberts said, "Sarge, we should have a talk with the captain and the lieutenant. They'll have some ideas."

Beckett looked thoughtfully at his two young charges. "Okay! You two go ahead. I'll wait here."

Hollands and Yoshida were in the med-tent drinking coffee when Tim and Carl walked in.

"Sirs," Tim began, "may we have a word with you?"

"Sure, what is it?"

"We need help with swapping out the motors, sir."

"Well, we're both here, so let's have it!" Hollands said.

"Sir," began Carl, "the new motors are physically a little bigger in diameter and heavier than the originals. Sarge says they have twice the power. Would you two come and take a look? We need a plan for installing them."

"Of course," Hollands said. "We'll meet you at the plane in a few minutes. In the meantime, on your way to the plane, I want you to check our east coast."

"Yes, sir, right away."

Carl and Tim headed out toward the east side of the island, and delayed long enough to get the binoculars.

Yoshida got up from his stool and stretched his lower back. "Sounds like those two have brains enough to know what they're doing."

"I think so, too, Ron. Come on, let's go take a look."

As they walked, they talked. "You know," Yoshida said, "even if the rebuild of the plane turns out okay, we still need to figure out the fuel issue. Those engines need high-test aviation fuel."

Hollands nodded thoughtfully. "Ron, I'm convinced this is the only game in town. It's our only chance to get everyone off this rock in a hurry. Buckner told me months ago that the water around the island is too shallow for a sub."

"My cousins across the way know that, too," Yoshida said. "But where are we going to get two or three hundred gallons of fuel? Even if Buckner can squeeze a barrel or two inside the Duck, he can't bring more than fifty or a hundred gallons at a time."

"I've been thinking about that," said Hollands. "The Duck doesn't use much fuel on this short of a trip. The next time Buckner comes, I'd like to siphon out some of his gas. Just a few gallons. With that, and with whatever fuel he can carry inside, we can at least test the engines. Providing we can install them."

"It would probably take fifty gallons just to tune and balance those motors, along with the re-worked propellers," Ron said, "And another fifty or more to practice taxiing, and to check the airframe for stress."

Both men were quiet for a few moments before Hollands said, "Hell, Ron, I'll probably crash the damn thing the first time I try to taxi, let alone when I try to get her off the ground."

They reached the aircraft where Beckett was waiting. Hollands said, "Tim and Carl will be along shortly. I put them on a coastal walk."

The three quickly got down to the business of inspecting the engine mountings and nacelles.

An hour later, the young men showed up and reported no sign of ships.

After working the rest of the afternoon together, Carl and Tim had rigged a makeshift block and tackle. The five figured out a plan on how to install the two motors.

A few days later, Roberts reported to Hollands and Yoshida at the radio shack. "Captain, Lieutenant, Sarge wanted me to report that we've installed the engines and propellers. They have spark plugs and oil. We've even rotated motors to force some oil through them, and we checked the propellers for clearance at the same time. We just need fuel."

Hollands and Ron grinned and echoed, "Great news. Good job."

"About gasoline," Hollands said. "Buckner and the Duck are the answer. Do you still have that transmit-key to send messages in code?"

"Yeah," Ron said. He held it up. "Right here behind the radio. Why?"

Hollands stepped back inside the shack and pulled out the Allied codebook from off the shelf.

Hollands took a small scrap of paper and a well-worn pencil and began to write a message. Finished, he slid the paper to Yoshida. "Okay, here's what I want sent, but in code. After you convert it, practice it with the key until you can send it in under thirty seconds so your Asian cousins won't be able triangulate our position. I know they'll hear it, but they won't understand it. And even if they can decode it, it would take another month for them to figure out what the hell it means. By that time..."

Yoshida picked up the slip of paper and read. "This is for Buckner, right?"

Hollands nodded.

Yoshida looked at the message again. "Will he pick up on it?"

"I sure hope so," Hollands said. "I'm running low on ideas and courage."

He took a deep breath and exhaled slowly. "The enemy won't figure it out, but I think Buckner will."

CHAPTER 12

The Riddle Solved!

Darkness hung in the early predawn as Commander Sessions pulled his bathrobe on and rushed from his billets. He jumped behind the wheel of his jeep and drove alone across the airbase.

He skidded to a halt in front of the Marine pilots' Quonset hut. He walked directly to the bunk nearest the front door.

He shook the bunk vigorously. "Captain, wake up!"

The slumbering Marine pilot didn't' stir.

Sessions shook the bunk even harder. "Buckner, wake up."

Buckner groaned from under his pillow. "Who the hell's rockin' my bunk? We'd better be under serious attack, or I'll tear you a new..."

"You'll do what?" Sessions snapped. "I don't think so, Captain."

Buckner sat up, struggling to identify the vague form in the near darkness. He squinted through half-open eyelids and finally made out Sessions' face. "Oh, sorry, sir. I couldn't tell who you were. Late card game. What time is it anyway?"

"Hey, keep it down over there," a voice grumbled from the far end of the structure. "I'm trying to sleep, you dumb shit."

"Never mind that," Sessions growled, trying not to disturb the other men.

He handed Buckner a slip of paper. "The com-center got me up for this a half-hour ago, son. It's some kind of a goddamn riddle. Now it's your turn to lose a little sleep, Captain. What the hell do you make of this?"

Buckner rubbed his eyes with one hand and reached with the other to turn on the small lamp that sat on a makeshift nightstand next to his cot.

He glanced at his clock. "Three o'clock, sir?"

But the stern look on the commander's face quickly forced Buckner's eyes to the note. He read it aloud haltingly. "'Jarhead. Need two Indian tom-toms, full-100 proof fire-water, bird's feathers—dried. Ready to leave nest.'"

Buckner scratching his head while he re-read the message.

Sessions pointed toward the note. "That's from Hollands, isn't it? And

it's meant for you—right, Captain? Is this some kind of a joke you two
have cooked up? The decoding room has been going nuts, working on it
most of the night. They can't make heads or tails out of it."

Buckner yawned. "Sorry, sir. Yes, ah, give me a minute."

He read the message two more times before he jumped to his feet. "Hot
damn! They've got that old bird ready to test; maybe fly. I never thought it
would be possible! Shit! Could it be *possible*?"

Sessions pulled up a chair and barked, "Plain English, Captain. What
are you talking about?"

"Flying, sir," Buckner said. "Remember when I told you about that
plane they found? One of the ladies tripped over it about ten weeks back?
Anyway, Mike, Ron Yoshida, and the three other men have been
rebuilding it, sir."

Buckner sat back down on the edge of his bunk. "Evidently, the Navy,
or someone, had off-loaded several crates of machine guns, ammo and
aircraft engines, along with cases of parts, barrels of engine oil. A regular
supply cache! I saw all of it, sir. The plane, the parts. Remember? It was in
my report."

Buckner shook his head. "Sonofabitch! They really did it."

"Okay. So, he's rebuilt this plane. Explain this message."

"Oh, that's simple, sir," Buckner said.

Sessions rolled his eyes. "Not according to my intelligence officers."

"Here's the scoop, sir. The 'two tom-toms' means two drums."

The Marine looked over at the commander, who seemed even more
perturbed. "*Drums*, sir. You know, as in fifty-five gallon barrels. The '100
proof firewater' is *avgas*. They must be ready to test the engines."

Sessions stood up and began to pace. Buckner started to say something
else, but was abruptly waived off. The commander unwrapped a fresh
cigar from his robe pocket and stuck it in his mouth.

Buckner picked up his lighter and a cigarette, and Sessions leaned
down to share the flame.

Sessions slowly puffed on the cigar, then turned to walk towards the
door. "The answer, is no!"

"Hell, sir, I haven't asked the question yet," Buckner protested.

"You're forgetting yourself, Captain."

Buckner quickly apologized. "Sorry, sir."

Sessions stroked his chin thoughtfully. "However, I understand that
Corporal Lynch will be doing a fresh tune-up on the Duck later this
morning. When he's finished, I think you should flight test it for him.
Shouldn't take you more than an hour or two, eh, Captain?"

He took several puffs on his cigar. "Should be a nice day for flying.

Perhaps one of your new pilots could fly cover for you..."

He yawned. "Good night, Captain. Or rather, good morning. I'm going back to bed."

By 0700 Buckner had located, filled, and sealed two fifty-five gallon drums with aviation gas, and left them on an ordinance cart. Getting them loaded into the Duck was another matter.

As he headed for the hangar area, he spotted Skip leaving the mess hall. He made a beeline for the young mechanic. "Hold up a minute, Skip. I understand you're going to tune-up the Duck this morning. When might that be?"

"Not for a while, Captain" he said sleepily. "I was on guard duty all night. My corporal stripes said I was sergeant of the guard. I'm headin' for the rack for a few hours."

He frowned. "Hey, wait a minute! It was just tuned just a few days ago; couldn't have more than ten or twelve hours on her. Are you trying to fool me, sir?"

Buckner smiled to himself. "Why, that cagey ol' fox!"

"What's that Captain?"

"Nothing, Skip."

Buckner pointed to the ordinance cart with the two barrels loaded on it. "Skip, I want you to get two or three other guys over to the Duck, and put those two drums on board."

"Are they fifty-fives, sir?"

"Yeah! Why?"

"They won't fit through the hatch. What's in them? Maybe I could figure out something else."

Buckner looked around to make sure no one was within earshot. "Avgas."

"I'm sorry, sir," Skip said. "I must be more tired than I thought. It sounded like you said, avgas."

"SHHH! That's exactly what I said, Corporal, but keep it down. One-hundred-ten gallons worth."

Skip motioned the Marine captain away from the front door of the mess hall. "Shit, sir, you can't haul fuel like that in a Duck. Those caps hardly ever seal tight. You'd probably blow yourself to hell, or at least back to Pearl. Come on, sir! What gives? What's going on?"

Buckner showed Skip the note. "I've gotta get Hollands that fuel, so he can fly himself and the others off that rock before the Japs discover them."

Skip suddenly straightened up as he spotted three of his mechanics exiting the dining hall. "Hey, fellas! Wait up a minute!"

He hurried over and gathered them into a huddle. Then he sent them on their way.

Returning to where Buckner waited, he grinned widely. "In an hour, Captain, we'll have the only Duck in any Navy with two-wing tanks."

Skip gave Buckner a crooked grin. "Knowing you. I'm sure you'll get her airborne. But that damn thing's gonna fly like a ruptured goat!"

"Thanks, Skip!"

Ordinarily the Duck would have taken off from the water, but not with the wing tanks in place. Skip and the mechanics had moved the heavily-laden seaplane to the taxiway, where Buckner carefully surveyed their work.

The Marine CO, Major Hanks, had suggested that Lieutenant Alan "Frog" Freeman fly escort.

Hailing from Louisiana's Bijou country, Freeman had picked up the nickname of 'Frog' because of his low drawling voice, and his reputed talent for hunting bullfrogs.

After a short briefing, both pilots headed out to the flight line. Buckner eyed the lieutenant. "You were picked for this mission, because you have excellent scores throughout your flight school. Especially in marksmanship."

Then with a touch of irony, Buckner added, "And, you're the only pilot available. But I *would* like you to get more hours on Corsairs."

"Thank you, sir," Lieutenant Freeman said. "I appreciate the care with which I was selected for this *hazardous* mission, whatever it is."

"I was looking at your training records. Why is it you have so few hours in Corsairs?"

"Didn't have any, sir. In San Diego I logged several hours in Hellcats, before being transferred to New York and advanced flight training. There was a squadron Navy commander who must have had some strong pull in high places, because he somehow requisitioned nearly all of our Hellcats and the Corsairs. The Navy had a training group there too. Hell, we all had to share the same planes. None of us could log enough hours in any aircraft."

Freeman searched his memory. "Let me think... Five Corsairs, I think. Six Buffalos, a couple of incredibly tired Wildcats, and half a dozen A-T6 trainers. We were told that the Buffalos would be similar to flying Hellcats or Corsairs. What a joke. The Buffalo couldn't have fanned a fart in church, let alone stood up to a Zeke."

"What a way for a flier to have to train," Buckner said. "Keep in mind, on the F4Us you don't want to jam on the throttle too quickly or you'll likely flip. Lock your brakes and slowly run your power up to about..."

"Yes, sir, I know," Freeman said. "One of the guys back at training wholesaled one of the Corsairs. He didn't walk away from it."

Tim and Carl were at the radios, spelling Lieutenant Yoshida for what was to be a short nature call, when they began hearing faint radio signals.

"I can't make that out, Tim. Can you?"

"It's in English, I think," responded Tim. "That's all I can tell ya. Plane-to-plane, maybe."

He listened for a few more moments. "We need the lieutenant here," he said. "I'll be right back." And with that he was gone.

About thirty yards beyond the camp, Tim came to a halt in front of the roughed-out three-foot-square shelter that had been constructed around a pit toilet for the men. "Lieutenant, sir, are you in there?"

"No, I'm not!" was the feeble response from within. "God, I feel awful. That fish I ate last night must have been bad."

"Really sorry to bother you, sir, but the radio traffic has picked up. They're all in English, we think, but it's garbled and we can't make anything out."

"Okay, Tim," Yoshida answered weakly. "I'm on my way."

An unpleasantly wet sound came from the latrine enclosure, followed by a painful groan. "Never mind," Yoshida moaned. "I'm not going anywhere for a while."

"What should I *do*, sir?"

"Go get the CO," Yoshida said. "If you don't find him quickly, fire two rounds from your M-1. That will bring him."

"Yes, sir."

"And then send Lieutenant Elliott out this way. Tell her to bring her little black bag."

"On my way, sir," Tim called over his shoulder.

As he approached the compound, Tim spotted Hollands on the far side of the med-tent. "Captain, need you in the com-shack, sir!"

Hollands immediately ran the short distance to the radio shack, and Tim continued to the med-tent.

As he entered, Janet looked up. "Hi, Tim, what's all the excitement about?"

"Not sure yet," Tim said. We're receiving some faint messages, but we can't make them out."

He glanced around. "Is the lieutenant here?"

Gail stepped through the flap-opening on the other side of the med-tent. "I'm right here, Tim. What's up?"

"It's Ron, ma'am. I mean, Lieutenant Yoshida. He's sick, and he asked me to get you."

"Where is he?"

"He's in the can."

Nurse Elliott grabbed her bag and ran out the door, with Sergeant Gilbress close behind.

Tim followed them as far as the radio shack, where he rejoined Carl and the captain.

"Where's Yoshida?" Hollands asked.

"He's in the latrine, sir. Sicker than a dog. I fetched the nurse for him."

"Carl," Hollands began, "go take a look at the antenna."

"Yes, sir."

Tim and Hollands turned their attention back to the radios, and the young sailor asked, "Captain, can you understand any of it?"

"It's not very clear. Coming from the Pateroa area, I think. But not from the tower."

Listening more intently, Hollands nodded. "I'm pretty sure it's two planes. Probably flying low and a ways out, but it's so garbled."

He re-adjusted a few of the dials, and flipped on the broadcast switch. "Traffic on two-niner point three-three megahertz, this is Pateroa Outpost. Over."

Tim checked the wires, and then began to pedal the radio's generator. "Think it might be a Jap decoy message?"

"It's possible," Holland said. "But I don't think so."

The radio had been quiet for two or three minutes when Beckett stuck his head in the door. "Hi, Captain. What's going on, sir?"

"Ron's sick; still in the can," Hollands told the Marine. "The ladies are looking after him. We're getting some kind of signal, but it's too garbled to read. I sent Carl to check the antenna and lead wire."

Just then, Carl returned. "Captain, the antenna was down. I shinnied up the tree a ways and reattached it. Try it now, sir."

"Hi Ron, it's Gail. Is it all right if Janet and I come in?"

"Thanks for coming," Ron groaned. "But this is so embarrassing. My stomach hasn't been this torn up since I won a pie-eating contest in the fourth grade."

"Don't give it another thought, Ron," Gail said. She stepped into the small enclosure. Janet came in right behind her, making the tiny latrine cubicle even more crowded.

"Are you in pain?" Janet asked.

Yoshida gave a feeble nod. "In my abdomen, and my stomach. They're on fire."

"Let's see if we can get you over to the med-tent," Gail said.

It took several minutes, but the two women managed to half-lead/half-carry the ailing pilot to a cot in their tent.

While Janet concentrated on making Yoshida as comfortable as possible, Gail left the tent to find Hollands.

"Thanks, Carl. Good job," Hollands said and Beckett nodded his approval.

Hollands was seated in front of the two radios, half turned away from the entrance.

Gail quietly entered the com-shack. "Mike, got a second?"

"Sure Gail, go ahead, but I can't leave the radios just now."

"Can I speak to you alone?"

Looking at Gail's troubled face, he turned to Sarge and the boys. "Okay men, take a break. Just don't go into town."

When the men were gone, Hollands gestured for Gail to speak. "Okay, what's up? How's Ron?"

"He's dangerously dehydrated," the nurse said. "And he's in a lot of pain. I think it's either food poisoning, or appendicitis. Maybe both."

Hollands shook his head. "This sounds serious."

"He has a fever of nearly a hundred and four," Gail said. "We've cleaned him up and have him resting in our tent."

She let out an exasperated sigh. "Cuts and bruises we can handle. Maybe a broken arm or a leg. But not this! We've given him the last of the aspirin, but that's only going to take the edge off the pain. If it *is* his appendix, Ron is going to need surgery. We have to get him to a field hospital, and fast."

At that moment, the radio crackled loudly. "Pateroa Outpost, this is Ruptured Duck One. Over."

Tim and Carl had been standing a few yards away, and on hearing the squawk from the radio bolted back to their posts.

Hollands grabbed the microphone. "This is Pateroa Outpost. Over."

"Hey, rice ball, is that you? Where've you been? Tried calling several times. Over."

"Ruptured Duck One, this is Pateroa Outpost. Our antenna was down.

Ron is ill. I want you to drop your load as quickly as possible, and get him back to Pateroa."

After several seconds of static, Buckner's voice came out of the speakers again. "Roger, Pateroa Outpost. I copy! Have firewater, need drums. I'm using wing tanks. My ETA is one-five minutes your pond. Over."

"Sounds like Skip has been busy" Hollands said. "One-five minutes. Roger. Pateroa Outpost out."

He looked up at the nurse. "Get him ready to travel, Gail."

Nodding, she hurried out of the com-shack.

Hollands motioned for Tim to stop pedaling. "Go help the ladies. We'll meet ya at the lagoon."

"Yes, sir."

Hollands walked out the door of the shack. "Sergeant?"

"Right here, Captain," Beckett said.

"You and Carl locate some empty fifty-five gallon barrels, and get them down to the dock on the double. We've got to make fast work of this."

Everyone could hear two approaching aircraft. A few minutes later, the Duck settled heavily onto the lagoon and soon the little seaplane was tied up to the dock.

Tim and the two women started carrying their patient to the plane, using a cot for a stretcher.

As they neared the com-shack, Ron suddenly called out weakly, "Stop! Please, put me down. Fast!"

At first, they thought he was just painfully uncomfortable. They slowly lowered him to the ground.

Ron, out of breath and soaked in perspiration, looked up at Tim. "Quick! Go turn up the speaker volume!"

Tim jumped over the litter and dashed to the radios to raise the volume. He looked over his shoulder. "What's all that gibberish, sir?"

"Quiet, please," Yoshida whispered.

Scarcely conscious, he listened intently. "Okay, now get on the pedals, Tim. Janet, see if the microphone will reach out here. Turn the dial to nine point six five, and flip up the green switch."

With the microphone stretched out the door of the shack, Gail knelt behind Yoshida and held the microphone in front of his lips.

Ron keyed the mike and rattled off something in Japanese with as much strength as he could muster.

Finally, he sank back down on the stretcher. "Best I could do," he whispered. "I think I may have bought us some time, maybe fifteen, twenty minutes."

While Ron had been busy with his radio messages, Buckner and company had been working to transfer the fuel to the drums. Skip had used two one hundred gallon-wing tanks, and Beckett had been able to locate four empty barrels instead of just two. The three litter-carriers hurried through the tree-lined berm above the dock and yelled for Hollands as they scrambled down the sandy slope to the dock.

"What's wrong?" Hollands called back.

Too weak to speak over that distance, Ron asked his helpers to set him down again. Gail waved Hollands to come to them.

Sensing the urgency of the request, both Hollands and Buckner hurriedly ran to their friend.

Yoshida swallowed several times before speaking. "There was a force of fifteen planes—Bettys and Oscars—heading for us. For this island."

He stopped for a moment to catch his breath. "I called back on one of the Imperial pilot frequencies, and identified myself as a recon plane. I reported a column of U.S. ships fifty miles south of here."

His face tensed as a spasm of pain wracked his body. When he spoke again, his voice was little more than a croak. "Their control acknowledged my message and diverted the flight. I didn't think they would do it. But once they get to that spot and they see nothing but ocean, they'll be coming back here."

Ron fell silent, and Tim spoke up. "The lieutenant says he may have bought us an additional fifteen to twenty minutes, sir."

Turning back to where the Duck was tied, Hollands called out, "Sergeant, how's the fuel transfer going?"

"Nearly finished, Captain. Filling the fourth drum now."

"Hollands," Buckner began, "I need to drop these tanks. They'll just slow me down. Can your guys push them out of sight?"

"Sure! Go ahead," Hollands agreed.

He looked at Tim. "Go with Captain Buckner. We've got to get that plane turned around, so these two can leave fast. I'll help with the litter."

Running quickly to the Duck, Buckner climbed up to the cockpit and reached in for the microphone. "Freeman, DO NOT ANSWER. Climb to angels three-zero. Formation of enemy bombers and fighters, south-by-southwest. No exact heading available. They were headed here, but we've temporarily redirected them fifty miles south. Find them. Stay out of sight. Do *not* engage! Report their position only."

Frog had been flying a pattern of a five-mile perimeter and was a few miles north of the island when he received the message. Making a hundred-and-eighty degree turn to the south, he moved the throttle of his fighter to its full position. The Double Wasp engine screamed its eagerness as the Corsair clicked off over 390 miles per hour. Passing over the lagoon, he rocked the wings and put his bird into a steep climb.

Buckner set the microphone on its hook. He reached down and restarted the engine.

Ron protested softly, "Mike, I can't go now."

Perspiration had soaked his clothes and was streaming off his face. "I should get back to the radios."

Janet had been kneeling at Ron's side and gently offered him some water from the canteen she was carrying. "Please, Lieutenant, drink some more water."

Then she and Gail hurried ahead to board the plane, so they would be able to assist in lifting Ron in.

Hollands patted Yoshida on the shoulder. "You're leaving, Buddy. And that's final."

At that point, Beckett returned and made his report. "Sir, the tanks are secured."

Then he and Hollands carefully carried the litter to the plane, where the two women worked to get it properly secured for flight.

Seizing the moment, Hollands took Buckner aside. "The ladies are going back with you. Our Asian neighbors are getting a bit too nosey of late."

Buckner gave him a doubtful expression. "Have you told the ladies about this?"

Hollands shook his head. "No. I've just decided. This may be our only opportunity to get them safely off this rock."

Buckner grimaced. "They're not going to like this, Mike!"

"I know! But I want them safe, and rank does have its privilege. Besides if the Beech flies, we'll see you at Pateroa in a few days."

He took a deep breath and gestured toward the women. "They're good soldiers, Bruce. As good as any man."

He moved to the side hatch of the plane and spoke loudly enough to be heard over the idling engine. "You ladies are going back now. We'll follow as soon as we can. I'll see the three of you on Pateroa."

And before either of the women could respond, Hollands and Buckner swung the side hatch cover into place and latched it.

From the far side of Ron's cot in the cargo hold, Gail struggled to move to the hatch cover's Plexiglas window to call out to Hollands. But her voice was lost in the noise of the engine.

Tears filled her eyes and began streaming down her face as she realized that she was leaving the outpost island. Leaving Hollands and the others.

Buckner climbed up into the open cockpit. Looking back at his friend, he yelled, "You know that Gail's in love with you."

The expression on Hollands' face said it all.

Hollands tried to stammer out a reply, but his voice didn't seem to be working. Gail in love with him? That wasn't possible! *Was* it?

Buckner grinned. "At a loss for words, Army? Well, buddy, the next time the two of you meet, she's gonna be pissed! And you'd best be ready to duck."

Beckett freed the rope. Buckner throttled the engine up to full, and the plane began to move away from the wharf, out into the lagoon.

Hollands and the others waved to their friends as the plane roared across the smooth water to takeoff.

"Come on, men," shouted Hollands. "Let's get these barrels up to the tree line and out of sight."

CHAPTER 13

Once he cleared the dock, Buckner opened up the Duck's throttle and raced for takeoff. Just feet off the water, he contacted Lieutenant Freeman and checked on his location, and that of the Japanese squadron.

"Sir, enemy planes still on their heading southeast, now at angels two-five-zero. Speed: one-niner-zero. I'm three miles behind their formation. Over."

"Roger, Frog. Now get your butt back here. I'm airborne, and I'm lonesome. Over."

"On my way, sir. Should see you in three or four minutes."

Lieutenant Freeman was as good as his word, and whizzed back over the island in pursuit of the Duck.

Hollands and the three other men stood on shore and anxiously watched as the Duck gained its five hundred-foot altitude.

Hollands watched the two planes merge with the horizon. "Tell me, Sergeant... Do you really think our *Phoenix* will fly?"

Beckett thought for a moment before he spoke. "Interesting name, sir. I know the phoenix is some sort of bird, but I can't rightly remember what kind. But to answer your question, I would say, yes. I believe she *will* fly, Captain. I believe she will."

Hollands nodded. "The Nips may come back. Let's get these fuel drums safely out of sight."

The amphibious plane was painfully slow. The Duck had an official top speed of 190 miles per hour, but no one took that seriously. Most pilots were satisfied when the plane managed 165 at nearly full throttle. But even 165 seemed fast when the seaplane was skimming the white caps of the ocean.

Janet looked at Gail and could still see tears streaming down her friend's face. Both women continued to work at making Lieutenant Yoshida as comfortable as they could.

Janet shouted to be heard over the noise of the aircraft. "What's wrong,

Gail? Are you okay?"

Gail glanced at Janet, shook her head and mouthed, "Not now."

"I think your emotions are pulling double duty," Janet said. "Is there anything I can do to help?"

Without looking at her friend, Gail bit her lip and gave another quick shake of her head.

Freeman made repeated circular sweeps at varying altitudes, keeping a wary eye out for enemy aircraft. But as the two planes flew closer to Pateroa, he became concerned when Buckner didn't radio the tower for landing instructions.

Slowing his Corsair, Freeman cruised up on Buckner's port wing and pointed to his throat microphone.

Buckner waved, and dangled the hand held microphone by its cord, indicating that his radio was out of order.

Freeman signaled that he understood, and keyed his own radio. "Pateroa Tower, this is Marine Corsair Five Niner. Do you read me? Over."

"Five Niner, this is Pateroa. Read you five-by-five. How's the flight test? Over."

"This is Corsair Five Niner. Test flight okay. Duck's radio is out. Need landing instructions and medics. Have sick man on board Duck. Over."

The tower gave the necessary clearance, then notified the base hospital of the emergency.

Freeman relayed the landing instructions to Buckner using hand signals, and the two pilots adjusted their heading.

Ten miles out from Pateroa, the tower called. "Marine Corsair Five Niner, you have five bogies, four miles astern at five o'clock, angels twelve. Definite bandits. Speed, two-five-zero. You copy? Over."

"Five niner, roger. Could use some backup. Any friendly eagles in this sector? Over."

"Roger, Five Niner," announced the tower. "There are six Army P-40s. Don't shoot them down. Scuttlebutt says those guys are on our side."

Freeman gave the danger signal to Buckner and with full throttle, pointed his bird's nose towards the heavens and turned 180 degrees to intercept the enemy.

"Marine Five Niner, this is Army Red Fox leader. I heard that comment from the tower, but my little red fox-kits are willing to help just the same. We have you in sight. Two miles ahead, and closing on your starboard side. Are we after Zeros or Oscars? Over."

"Red Fox leader, this is Marine Five Niner. Don't know. Could be Zeros. Maybe they're lost, or just out sightseeing. Let's go find out if they would like to go swimming. Over."

"My sentiments exactly, Marine. Over."

Frog quickly located the enemy planes, which were now slightly below him by two thousand feet.

He keyed his mike. "They are Zeros."

Diving behind the Zeros, Freeman came out of the sun, as he banked right and maneuvered the bandits into his gun sights. A mile from the enemy planes, he began firing long bursts from the Corsair's six guns.

Closing at over 400 miles per hour, Frog was a mere blur as he streaked past the Jap formation.

While the Japanese pilots' concentration was on the lone Corsair, the six Army fighters who had followed Frog out of the sun caught the Zeros completely unaware and in the midst of their turns. The enemy never saw them.

It was over in seconds, the enemy planes cut to ribbons and sent smoking to the ocean.

"Thanks, Red Fox leader. Good shooting. Will confirm your group's five kills."

"Negative, Marine Five Niner. You dropped two on your pass. Glad you're on our side. See you later on the ground for a cold beer. You're buying."

Buckner landed the Duck without a hitch and, using the HQ taxi lane, came to a halt near the headquarters building and the waiting ambulance. He climbed down quickly and began to assist the women. "How is he, Gail?"

Janet answered for Gail. "He's unconscious."

The corpsmen assisted in moving Yoshida from the Duck to the ambulance.

As everyone worked, one of the medics leaned close to his buddy. "I never thought I'd ever have to help one of these yellow bastards."

As soon as Yoshida had been safely loaded into the ambulance, Captain Buckner shucked his goggles and leather helmet and tossed them to the ground. He grabbed the corpsman, slammed him hard against the side of the vehicle.

"Listen up, you sonofabitch. That man is an officer in the United States Army Air Corps. And he's a friend of mine. He's also the man who saved Captain Hollands' life and mine."

"Sir, I'm sorry for..."

"Shut-the-hell-up!" Buckner growled. "If I *ever* hear of you saying anything like that about Lieutenant Yoshida again, you'll be eating oatmeal through a straw for at least six months. Do you get my meaning?"

The corpsman's voice was loud, but shaky. "Yes, sir!"

Buckner released him. "Now, move out."

With a quick salute, the two corpsmen jumped into the ambulance and sped off.

Still seething, Buckner turned and knelt down to retrieve his headgear.

Skip and another mechanic had arrived to tow the Duck to the hangar. Skip turned to the second mechanic. "You didn't see a thing. Got it?"

The mechanic smiled and shrugged. "I'm just a lowly private. I didn't hear or see a thing."

Then the young man went to work hooking up the Duck to the tractor. A few minutes later, he nudged his coworker. "Hey, Skip, you comin'?"

And with Duck in tow, both men headed off across the runway.

Commander Sessions had come out to wait in front of HQ as soon as he heard the Duck taxiing near the building. He motioned Buckner over. "Captain, did I hear you correctly? Did you threaten that enlisted man with bodily harm?"

"I sure as hell *did*..." he began angrily. Then, he caught himself. "My apologies, Commander. I think I'll just stop now, before I stuff both feet in my mouth."

"That's all right, son," Sessions said. "I would probably have said or done worse."

He took a few seconds to relight the remnants of a well-chewed cigar. "However, I..."

"Yes, sir, I know. I'll apologize as soon as I calm down. I'm guessing that will be sometime around 1961."

Sessions chuckled. "So, Captain, how was your, ah, test flight? And how's the lieutenant?"

"It went fine, sir. Not sure about Yoshida."

Buckner turned to watch the Duck being towed away. "The radio in the Duck is on the fritz."

Sessions puffed mightily on his stogie, and nodded. "The tower notified us of the problem. Now, tell me about your wingman. What the hell do they call him? Froggy something?"

"Second Lieutenant Alan *Bull Frog* Freeman, sir. Gawd, I think I'll adopt that kid. When those Zekes came up, I figured I'd 'bout bought the farm. But Frog dropped two on his one pass. The Army took care of the rest. I was sure glad he was along. And I was glad to see the Army, too."

Standing a few yards away, Janet and Gail followed the ambulance with their eyes as it sped away.

Janet took her friend's hand. "It's about the Captain, isn't it, Gail?"

She gave the other woman's hand a gentle squeeze. "You've probably been able to hide your feelings from the captain, but you can't fool me. I feel the same way about leaving Carl behind."

Gail looked into the eyes of her friend. "Thank you, Janet. I've been quite selfish. Can you ever forgive me? I wasn't aware that you and Carl were..."

"I wasn't sure myself, until the hatch was locked," Janet said. "Then I *knew*. I love Carl. No escaping it. For a moment as Captain Buckner taxied for takeoff, I felt panic-stricken. Then I saw the expression on *your* face."

"I had no clue that he was going to send us away," Gail said. "Now I'm ashamed, as I think about those four men alone on that island."

Janet wrapped her fingers around the small cross that hung on the chain with her dog-tags. "They're not alone, Gail," she said softly. "They're not alone."

Gail clutched at her own tags where a similar cross hung, and she smiled. Then the two hugged.

Sessions glanced over at them and asked, "Who are the two women, Captain?"

"Oh, shit! I forgot all about them," Buckner said. He executed a brisk military about-face, and called to Gail and Janet. "Ladies, would you please join us?"

Gail and Janet looked a bit lost and bewildered. They were in need of a good bath, hot food, lots of sleep, and new uniforms. The two walked the short distance over to the two officers.

"Commander Sessions, I'd like to introduce Lieutenant Gail Elliott and Sergeant Janet Gilbress, hospital lab technician. These are the two female personnel who were marooned on the island when Hollands and Lieutenant Yoshida showed up."

The women came to attention and saluted.

"Good morning, Commander," Gail said. "Excuse our appearance, sir. But we haven't had a real bath in nearly a year."

"Well, we can certainly take care of that," said Sessions.

The commander looked over to Seaman Pruitt who was standing in the doorway. "Find these ladies some quarters immediately. I don't care if you have to move someone into a tent. Get the cook to warm up something substantial for them. And while he's busy with that, show these ladies to the shower area."

Addressing the women again he said, "I'm sorry, Lieutenant... Sergeant. But we have only two other ladies on this rock—both nurses— and, well, on this side of the base, we all share the one shower area. With appropriate scheduling, of course."

Then in a tongue-in-cheek order to his clerk he added, "Strap on your .45 son. You are now a temporary bodyguard, and if anybody comes sniffing around the chicken coop, shoot 'em. If you don't kill 'em, bring what's left of 'em to me."

"Aye-aye, sir," the clerk said. "Commander, should I take the ladies by the quartermasters first for clothing and toiletries?"

"Good thinking, Pruitt. See to it immediately. Let Doc know they're here as well."

Sessions smiled at the two women. "It's not home, ladies, but we do have hot showers, hot food, and clean bedding."

"Thank you for all your kindness, sir," Gail responded.

Both women gave Buckner a highly unmilitary hug before they joined the clerk.

Buckner had delivered two hundred gallons of aviation gas. Once all of it had been transferred to the four 55 gallon drums, Minetti and Roberts waded into the lagoon to refill the two wing tanks with seawater in order to sink them enough to be concealed beneath the dock.

When they had finished, they scrambled up the beach to move the fuel drums.

Carl glanced behind him and spotted a loose tank.

The two men immediately ran to the end of the dock and plunged into the water to re-secure the bobbing tank. Left alone it would have been in plain sight from the air, a sure invitation for the Japanese to drop in for a visit.

For the remainder of that day and into the night, Hollands, Beckett, Roberts, and Minetti took turns standing guard. But the enemy planes never returned.

Shortly after midnight, Hollands called off the watch. "Okay men, pick up your gear. Let's head for camp and get some sleep." .

As the small band made their way in the dark, they could see a faint orange glow on the night's southern horizon.

"What do you make of that, Captain?" Sergeant Beckett asked. "Us going after them, or them going after us?"

Hollands shrugged. "I don't know. Probably both. But whoever it is, it will keep the war away from us for the time being. I think we're probably okay for a few days. Right now I want us to get a little hot food and some rest."

There were two things that indicated morning to Hollands: warm sunshine on his face, and the smell of coffee.

Slowly he sat up on his bunk. Realizing the hour, he yelled, "Damn it, Beckett, we've overslept again."

Next to his cot on a stool sat a tin cup with nearly imperceptible wisps of steam rising from the contents. It was coffee. A piece of stale bread had been placed next to it.

Hollands got to his feet and reached for the cup. The other cots were empty. His three companions were not in the hut. Wherever they were, apparently they had *not* slept in.

His eyes were drawn to Yoshida's cot. Empty, like the rest. He wondered how his friend was doing. Had Buckner and the ladies gotten Ron to the field hospital in time?

He took a sip of the coffee. It tasted strange. Maybe it was that powdered stuff.

He set the cup down next to the bread, laced up his boots, and buckled on his pistol belt. Taking his canteen of water off the lodge pole peg, he poured some water over his head, rubbing his face with his hands.

With the cup in one hand and the bread in the other, he left the hut in search of the others.

His thoughts went back to his first morning on the island, and the rude awakening that he and Yoshida had received from Sergeant Beckett and his crew. Eventually, the enemy would visit the island. Hollands didn't want to be around when that happened.

He stopped briefly by the radio shack and heard the faint crackle of static from the speaker. He picked up the microphone and keyed it. "Pateroa Outpost, calling Pateroa Control. Over."

Within a few moments, Hollands learned that his comrades had arrived safely, Yoshida was in the hospital. Relieved, he switched off the radios to save the battery.

He shoved the last bite of bread into his mouth, followed with a final sip of now-cold coffee, and placed the tin cup on the bench holding the radios.

After a couple of yawns and some stretching, he began his trek to the Beechcraft.

As he walked, he noticed four sets of wide, deep grooves that appeared along the way. They ran four feet apart on either side of the trail and through flattened grass and shrubs.

Some distance beyond Trickle Creek he heard murmurs of speech and laughter, mingled with the pings and clanks of tools at-work. He hadn't heard the men laugh very often. The sound was both odd, and comforting.

The deep grooves in the ground lead directly to the aircraft. The fuel drums, of *course*... But how had they managed to roll them this far?

He was close enough to hear Beckett's voice now. "Okay men. I found some kerosene in the storage. We need to open the fuel tanks and rinse them out with it before we and add the gas."

"The left tank is ready for the kerosene, Sarge," Tim said.

For a few moments, Hollands watched from a few yards out. The three worked as though they were a team of nine. In no time, the other tank was also ready and Beckett was inspecting it.

As Hollands approached the group, he could see all that had been accomplished.

He patted one of the wings. "These new engines sure give the Beechcraft a different look. This is terrific work!"

Beckett looked up. "Sir, I think we can test the engines in a few hours."

"That's great news, Sarge."

"I'm glad you're here, sir," the sergeant said. "I want these two monkeys to show you what else they've been working on."

He thumped his fist on the fuselage. "Come down from there and show the captain what you've rigged up."

With huge grins, both men slid down off the right wing.

Tim made a flourish of invitation with one hand. "Would you come inside to the cockpit, please?"

Hollands entered the aircraft. It had been several days since he'd looked inside. "Wow," he said. "You guys have cleaned this up really nice."

"Thank you, sir," they said in unison.

At the cockpit entrance, Carl pointed to a newly-installed crank handle. "Ta-dah!"

He patted the handle. "Sir, the hydraulics for the landing gear are gone. But the gear drive is all right. We've cleaned and greased the mechanism. To raise and lower the wheels, we use this hand-crank."

Carl nodded. "We also fixed several control cables to the tail section, but we couldn't get the flaps to adjust evenly. So we decided to leave them in the up position, because up seemed to make sense. But the ailerons work okay."

"They've also made a place for your Army radio," Beckett said. "The one we took from your fighter."

Outside and on the ground again, Carl pointed to the wheels. "Sir, we found new tires, tubes and an air pump in the supply cache."

The four men walked a few yards forward of the plane, and Tim examined the ground. "There was once a short taxi way here, sir. Probably for a small seaplane like the Duck. Definitely not a PBY: The wingspan wouldn't clear the trees."

Beckett sketched a route in the air with one finger. "From where the plane is sitting, you taxi about fifty yards, making a hard right turn here. As you can see, there's a clear runway on hard sand under cover of these trees. It's about fifty yards to the beach, then you can add another hundred to two hundred yards for takeoff room—depending whether the tide is in or out. It might be a bit dicey, but it looks workable, sir."

Hollands nodded without speaking.

"It's the engines that I'm worried about," the sergeant said. "They've got more than twice the power of the originals. We don't really know the structural strength of the airframe, so we can't be sure how well it will stand up to all that extra power."

The old Marine shook his head. "We've gone over your and Lieutenant Yoshida's notes and tightened where we could. But frankly, we just don't know what will happen when the throttles are opened. The motors could pull right out of the wings and cut us to pieces. Or they might yank the wings right off the fuselage, and *then* cut us to pieces."

Hollands patted him on the back. "Don't sell your work short, Sarge. You three have done one hell of a job!"

He surveyed the wings. "Could you manually lower the flaps ten degrees?"

Tim nodded. "Absolutely, sir."

The sergeant and Carl gave Tim a skeptical look. Then Beckett shrugged "If he says it can be done, then I guess it *can* be."

Hollands looked around, marveling at all that had been accomplished. "Men, this is unbelievable. Carry on. I'm going back to camp to monitor the radios for a while. I'll check back with you in two or three hours. Oh! And thanks for the coffee."

With a big smile, Gunny said, "Right Captain."

As Hollands turned to leave, he spotted the drums of fuel off to the side. "I've got to know," he said. "How in the world did you move these barrels a quarter of a mile over that bumpy trail? Did you push 'em?"

Tim and Carl both snickered and Beckett began to scratch his head. "We sort of *pulled* them, sir."

The look on Hollands' face told the Marine that his answer was not going to fly.

"Well, sir, you see," began Sarge, "Minetti and Roberts put together a rope pull system. They took two double lengths of rope and wrapped each barrel around once at both ends. Then they turned the drums over on their sides. They looped the ropes into a continuous belt. We pulled and the drums rolled, sir."

He shrugged. "Frankly, sir, I didn't think it would work, but it *did*. I just don't understand it. They ain't even Marines, sir."

Hollands smiled. "Let's keep that fact to ourselves, Sergeant. And not let the Japanese in on it."

"Yes, sir," Beckett said with a grin.

Hollands monitored the radios for about three hours, before he disconnected them. Loading them and the battery onto a makeshift skid, he pulled the load and headed out again for the plane.

He was anxious to test-run the engines. To taxi a little, and to check for stress. If metal fatigue was going to be part of the equation, he wanted to find out about it while they were still on the ground.

When he reached the plane, he could see that the three men were busy pumping fuel into the craft's fuel tanks. The sight gave him a thrill of excitement.

He wanted to fly. He wanted to get off this damned rock, and back into the war.

"Good afternoon, sir," Tim shouted from atop the starboard wing. "Me and Carl will hand crank to start the engines."

Hollands' memory slipped back to his second day at Pateroa—Skip and Buckner balanced on top of the Thunderbolt's engine and firewall.

"That's fine, Tim. You two be careful. I don't want you to get a mouth full of propeller."

"Yes, sir!"

Carl took the radios from off the skid, and placed them inside the airplane. The two men had discovered a way to connect the starboard engine's generator to a service board they had partially repaired. It would offer limited electrical power to the radio and the cockpit, once the engine was running.

As the three continued their work, Hollands walked several yards towards the water and sat down on a knoll overlooking the ocean to enjoy the quiet. Suddenly it dawned on him how beautiful the little island actually was.

In that flicker of time and with the sound of the surf rushing in and out, there seemed to be no war. No anger. No killing. Only peace.

He was flooded by a deep sense of serenity, as if he were seated in a huge cathedral; the organ was the sound of the ocean, and the wind was the bells.

Soon he found himself praying. Not for *his* safety, but for that of his crew. The prayer brought him strength, and encouragement.

A far off voice slowly broke through the tranquility, *"Sir, we're ready."* Each time it repeated, it seemed closer. Looking behind him he didn't see a soldier, but in his mind's eye he saw himself as a small child calling. That was the voice Hollands acknowledged deep within his soul. *"Sir, we're ready to try the engines."*

Illusion evaporated into clarity. It was Roberts calling.

"Okay," Hollands finally answered. "Let's go give 'em a try."

With a pang of regret, he walked away from his sanctuary of peace, and back toward the chaos of war.

Hollands settled into the pilot's seat and regarded his meager instrument panel. There were a few gauges, but this whole affair was going to be a seat of the pants experience.

A partial Plexiglas windscreen had been installed. If they actually got this beast off the ground, they would be in for noisy ride, with more than enough breeze for comfort.

Roberts and Minetti worked together, and rotated the propellers by hand in an effort to help lubricate the two silent motors. Usually the pitch of the blades would be changed from takeoff, to climb, to cruise. But they had neither the equipment nor the expertise to install hydromatic pitch control for the propellers. On this flight, it would be a fixed pitch only.

"Ready on the starboard engine, Captain," yelled Beckett.

"Ready to prime and turn," Hollands called back.

Tim and Carl stood on top of a large wooden crate from the bunker, and inserted the crank in the side of the engine. They both took strong grips on the handle, and began to turn it.

The whine from the starter generator slowly increased from a low to a medium-pitch grinding whine. Hollands primed the engine as it turned five or six revolutions before falling quiet. So far, so good.

He leaned over to the right side of the cockpit and hollered through the glassless opening, "Shall we try it for real, boys?"

The young Army soldier and Coastguardsman started cranking again.

The whine grew louder, and the tone went audibly higher. Finally, Beckett called out, "Clear!"

"Clear!" came the answer from within the cockpit.

"Switch on. Contact!" The Marine yelled.

Hollands nodded. "Roger. Switch on. Contact."

He flipped on the magneto-ignition.

The two men pulled the crank out, and backed away from the engine and spinning propeller.

The new engine sputtered, and bellows of blue smoke exploded through the exhaust port. The engine was firing, but not on all nine cylinders.

Feverishly, Hollands worked the throttle mixture. Not too rich. Not too lean. Find the happy medium.

He figured that about six of the cylinders were firing. Where were the others?

He patted the top of the instrument panel. Come on, old girl. *Come on..."*

Then, he seemed to find the magic spot in the fuel mixture. The engine smoothed out, and the belching rumble gave way to a steady roar.

"Hot damn!," he whispered. "They're all firing!"

Throttling back the Wasp engine, Hollands left it at idle.

Tim and Carl carefully moved to the port side engine and prepared to replay their effort on number two.

"We're ready, Captain," one of them yelled from beneath the left wing.

Slowly the crank began to turn and Hollands hit the primer.

He leaned out his window. "Let's go for a long start."

"Captain," the sergeant protested, "it would be better to follow procedures."

"A long start," Hollands said again. And his captain's bars won the argument.

As the big engine was turning, he shouted, "Clear! Switch on! Contact!"

The two men removed the crank and ran towards the rear of the plane.

The port engine responded with a deep-throated backfire that erupted into a huge ball of bluish-black smoke.

The propeller slowed to a stop, leaving all parties to choke and wheeze from the acrid engine fumes.

After a few moments, Hollands stuck his head out the side window and said awkwardly, "Let's go back to the procedures, Sergeant."

The Marine simply nodded, while he fanned the smoke away from his face.

"Captain," he yelled, "how about all this smoke? It will rise above the trees."

Hollands was already feeling humiliated. "Tim, you've picked up on some of the Japanese lingo, haven't you?"

"A little, sir. Lieutenant Yoshida was teaching me and Carl some of it."

"Good! Come on in here and hook up the Jap radio. You'll monitor and I'll come down and help with the cranking on number two."

It took Tim less than two minutes to splice some power to the radio and connect the aircraft's antenna.

Hollands and the sergeant were concerned about just sitting there now, because with the starboard engine idling, they wouldn't be able to hear much of anything else.

"Captain, shall we try it again, sir?" Beckett asked.

Hollands hollered up at Tim. "Have you heard anything from the Nips?"

"No, sir, not a peep,"

"Good!" Hollands said. "All right, Tim, you know the drill on starting. I'll be on the crank with Carl."

Tim plopped into the pilot's seat. "Will do, sir. Switch off; ready to prime."

Hollands and Carl commenced cranking, and the engine slowly began to rotate. Tim primed the motor a few times. Carl and the captain released the crank handle, and the engine fell silent.

Hollands bent over with his hands on his knees. "Sonofabitch! I had forgotten just how hard it was to turn one of these things."

He took a deep breath. "Now I know where the military term 'grunt' came from."

Beckett stepped up closer to the left side of the cockpit and hollered, "Tim, are you ready?"

Tim responded with, "Clear!"

Sergeant Beckett looked at Hollands' face, dripping with perspiration. "Are you two gonna turn that damn thing or not, *sir*?"

Hollands gave him a mock glare. "We're on it, Sarge!" He and Carl started cranking again.

As the propeller began to turn, Beckett called out, "Contact. Switch on,"

"Roger. Contact. Switch on."

There were hints of exhaust smoke. Then with a sudden rush, the engine jumped to life as all cylinders lit off.

Hollands scrambled back into the cockpit and took the pilot's seat. Tim moved aft, to monitor the Japanese radio.

Hollands throttled the engine back to a fast idle. Beckett had fixed both tachometers, which allowed him to monitor engine speed.

Carl removed the wheel blocks, and Beckett motioned for Hollands to edge the aircraft forward. Carl was now a lookout, making sure the plane would clear trees, rocks and foliage.

Hollands placed his right hand on the two throttle handles and slowly moved them forward. The engines obeyed without hesitation.

Hollands released the brakes. With a sense of wonder and trepidation, he felt the plane begin to move. He followed Beckett and Minetti for about a hundred feet, until Sarge lifted his palm in the 'stop' sign.

Hollands idled back the engines and locked the brakes. Beckett held up two fingers of his right hand, while making a circling motion over his head with his left.

Hollands understood, and took the RPMs of both engines up. The Wasps were running as smooth as glass, and the Beech barely offered so much as a shiver.

The old Marine had Hollands hold the engines at that speed for a minute or so, before signaling for him to shut them down.

Hollands idled back for a moment then switched off the magnetos and the giant motors coasted into silence.

"How was it, Captain?" Beckett asked.

Hollands gave him a thumbs-up. "Sergeant, if I hadn't experienced it myself, I wouldn't have believed how smooth these engines are. Not a single vibration in the ship."

Sarge looked at Tim who was also smiling. "How about it, son? What do *you* think?"

"Sounded perfect to me, Sarge."

"Okay, sir," Beckett said. "I suggest we move the plane back, and we all go get some chow. We need to let the engines cool off for a while before we can check them and the airframe for any problems."

The four men, two on each side, grabbed the tail section and pushed the plane back to its original parking place.

"Secure the area, Sergeant," Hollands said. "And let's go back to camp."

"Excuse me, sir," said Tim, "but shouldn't we take the radios with us?"

"Good idea, Tim. Thanks! Leave the old fighter radio hooked up. But pull the Jap's and we'll monitor it and our big Army radio for the next day or so."

On the way back to camp, Hollands fell in next to Becket. "What's your gut feeling, Sarge? How much time before we can fly?"

"Minimum, two days, sir."

Hollands grimaced. "I've got a feelin' that we're on a really short leash. I can't really explain why."

The old sergeant nodded. "I know what you mean, sir. I'm feeling it too."

They were out of regular coffee grounds, so Sarge warmed up some of the new instant coffee from the K-ration boxes.

Hollands approached the Marine. "What's that you're drinkin' Sarge? I thought we were out of coffee."

Beckett took another swallow, and made a face. "We are," he said. "This is more of that powdered stuff. It's better than nothing. Maybe."

He handed the tin cup to Hollands. "How do you suppose they make this crud?"

Hollands took a sip of the dark liquid and made a face of his own. "I have no idea," he said. "But something tells me that the process doesn't involve anything that resembles a coffee bean."

"The aftertaste ain't too bad," the old sergeant rasped. "If you wait long enough."

Hollands took another swallow, and suppressed a grimace. "Cheer up," he said. "In two or three days you'll be drinking real Marine coffee in the mess on Pateroa."

The sergeant scowled. "Sir, that's cruel. Marines make the worst coffee in the world, and Navy coffee ain't any better. But damn if being on Pateroa don't sound good, Captain."

Hollands could see some new hope in the sergeant's eyes, and could hear it in his voice. Hope was something that had been in short supply. Spirits were improving as the four Americans imagined leaving their small island continent.

Sergeant Beckett reported to Hollands early the next morning, as the four sat around eating. "Sir, late yesterday we found an engine mount problem. But it was too dark to see well enough to fix it. We'll have it repaired and ready to go shortly after breakfast this morning."

"Fine, Sarge. Keep me posted."

"Yes, sir."

They finished their meal of powdered eggs and the last of some stale bread. No one had gotten much sleep the night before. There had been too much excitement as they took turns talking about the repairs and checks, and how good it would feel to get back to a real military base.

At 0730, everyone but Hollands headed off to work on the plane. He stayed in camp to monitor the radios.

The morning was already oppressively hot and humid. The sticky air seemed to make time drag slowly.

Hollands settled onto a rickety stool in the radio-shack and leaned back against a support pole. He lifted both hands, trying to shade his eyes from the glare of the sun reflecting off the lagoon. An empty canvas canteen carrier hung loosely on a nail above the table. It made a soft, rhythmic rubbing sound as it swayed gently from the occasional warm breeze. All was calm. Even the island birds were unusually quiet. Hollands' eyes began to close and he struggled to stay alert. He and the others were exhausted, from head to toe.

Three mind-and-butt-numbing hours later, Hollands looked at his watch. It was nearly ten-thirty.

He got up and walked and did a few deep knee bends. In the back of his mind, he thought it strange that there hadn't been any radio traffic.

His canteen sat on the table, half full of weather-warmed water. He doused his head with the water, allowing it to run down his face. Taking a big sip, he settled once again on his stool and leaned against the support pole. And the heat and humidity continued to take their toll.

Half-awake, Hollands thought about the Beechcraft, and the prospect of flying again. He had hoped the plane would have been ready sooner, but that didn't seem to be in the cards.

Struggling to keep his mind alert, he began to mentally rehearse the takeoff and the flight. How he would maneuver the plane, and the triumphant moment when he radioed Pateroa Tower to request landing instructions.

Something about the idea of the radio tugged at his subconscious mind. Some half-formed thought, as though he had overlooked an important detail.

It took several seconds for the realization to hit him. He wasn't hearing static anymore. He wasn't hearing *anything*. The radio was completely silent.

He picked up the handset and keyed the mike button. The transmit light did not go on. The batteries had died.

He climbed sluggishly onto the generator and began to pedal. After a minute or so, a voice crackled out of the speaker, using the group's latest call sign. "Phoenix One. This is Pateroa Control. Emergency. Come in. Over."

The person calling was clearly excited.

Hollands keyed the microphone. "Pateroa Control, Phoenix One here. Go ahead with your message. Over."

"Hollands, this is Ben Murray. Damn! We thought you guys were dead!"

Hollands stifled a yawn. "We're still alive and kicking. Over."

"We've been trying to raise you for hours," Murray's voice said. "You gotta get the hell off that island. If that pelican of yours has a feather's chance of flying, you better find out now. Your friend Quigby says 'the outlaws are moving in.' Hell, you can probably see them from your vantage point. We can't send any help. We've got problems of our own. Over."

Hollands stood up and looked south through the trees. No sign of danger.

He keyed the radio. "It looks all clear here, Ben. Oops! Wait a second!"

Out beyond the breakwater, he saw what looked like three Japanese cruisers.

He yelled into his microphone, "Guests have arrived! They are approximately four miles out. Cross your fingers! We're on our way. Out."

His hands trembling from the sudden excitement, Hollands yanked the cables free from the Japanese radio and stuffed the two codebooks into his right hip pocket.

He drew his .45 and fired four rounds through the large U.S. Army radio, sending it off the table to the ground. He grabbed the mortally-wounded device and ran the twenty yards to the latrine, where he deposited it in the hole. If the Nips wanted it, they could swim for it.

He rushed back to the com-shack and grabbed the Japanese radio. When it was tucked under his arm, he took another look at the ocean. Beyond the trees, three Japanese troop carriers were coming into view, advancing steadily toward the lagoon.

Sonofabitch! Landing crafts. Where the hell had *they* come from?

The ships were still some distance off shore, but there was no time to waste. With a last-second look around the camp, Hollands took off on a dead run, heading for the airplane.

As he made his way along the path, his feet seemed as heavy as lead. He remembered what his high school track coach had always advised the boys. "Pace yourselves. Someday it may mean winning a race." Hollands finished the thought by adding, *or saving your life.*

Heeding his coach's admonition, he slowed his pace. He frowned as he recalled the ribbing he had given Captain Buckner for being out of shape.

He frequently checked to his left, peering through the heavy ground foliage and trees to the water. He could see only bright specks of ocean. So far, so good. No sign of enemy ships up this way. *Yet.*

As he raced along, he mentally kicked himself. How could he have been so stupid? His only job had been to monitor the radios, and he had let the damned batteries go dead. He hoped like hell that his men weren't going to pay for his screw-up with their lives.

Then fear set in. Did he remember how to start the engines? It was pretty similar to the Thunderbolt... No, it *wasn't.* The boys had to crank the engines, and then...

His brain leapt ahead to the takeoff. Was their enough room to build up speed? Maybe. If the tide was out. But what if it *wasn't*? He had no idea where the tide was right now.

How could he have been such an idiot? After all of his attempts to maintain discipline, how had he become so lax?"

With each pounding stride, he wondered if his head was going to explode.

He reached the little stream, and vaulted it without pausing. Just a bit farther to the cutoff...

As Hollands made the sharp turn to the left, his foot slipped out from under him and he went down, clutching the enemy's radio tight to his chest. He was back on his feet in a second, running toward the plane, oblivious to his scrapes and scratches—focused only on the importance of the mission.

A hundred yards out, he snatched the .45 out of its holster and fired two quick rounds into the air, to alert the others.

When he reached the plane, he was winded and drenched in perspiration.

Beckett took one look at him. "The Japs?"

Hollands could only nod as he fought for breath. "They're in the lagoon! On one engine or two, Sarge, we're leaving—*NOW*!"

"We've just finished pre-flight, sir," the Marine said. "Both engines should fire off on first try."

"Good!" Hollands gasped. "Because we may not get a second try."

He swung the Japanese radio in through the side hatch of the plane, and then climbed into the cockpit.

He motioned for Beckett's attention. "Sarge, we gotta blow the supply bunker."

Roberts stuck his head in through the side door. "Already set, sir. It'll blow in about ten minutes. And Captain, we really *don't* want to be here when it goes."

Hollands settled himself into the pilot seat. He could hear the whine of the starter. The boys had already begun turning the crank on the port engine.

The shortened three-bladed fan was turning slowly. After a few revolutions, the boys quit cranking and the propeller slowly came to a stop.

Hitting the fuel primer twice, Hollands yelled back, "Contact. Switch on," and leaned toward the right side window.

"Contact. Switch on," came the reply from one of the young men.

Once again, the big Single-Wasp engine began to turn over. Hollands switched on the magneto and, true to Beckett's prediction, the nine holes instantly lit off.

Quickly the two men moved to the second engine and repeated the procedure. Soon, both engines were running strong. The two men pulled the crank, Beckett removed the wheel chocks and the three climbed into the aircraft.

Hollands released the brakes and slowly inched the throttles forward. The aircraft began to roll.

Making a right turn at the designated start for takeoff, Hollands locked the brakes and pushed the throttles to half power. The tail began to dance, trying to come up. He eased the yoke back to keep the tail wheel on the ground.

The main gear shuddered and the aircraft anxiously skidded forward.

With two long belts of .50 caliber machine gun ammo draped around his shoulders and across his chest, his weapon loaded and ready, Beckett had taken a temporary seat at the cockpit entrance. He shouted over the rumble of the motors. "We've got a problem, Captain."

"What's that, Sarge?"

"We have a light wind, sir, but it's blowing the wrong direction! It's coming from behind us."

Hollands snorted. "This old girl is *way* overpowered. She doesn't *care* which way the wind is blowing!"

The sergeant grinned. "Sounds good to me, sir! Open up those faucets and let's get the hell out of here."

Hollands took a quick look over his shoulder. Back in the cargo area, Tim and Carl were laying out ammo belts.

"Welcome to Phoenix Island Airlines!" Hollands yelled.

He released the brakes and shoved the throttles to full. The plane rocketed down the improvised runway, like Buck Rogers' ship.

The sudden power of the thrust tumbled Beckett over backwards, and sent him rolling the length of the cargo bay.

The plane didn't have working, adjustable flaps, and Hollands hoped the ten percent the boys had set them to would be sufficient. He wasn't too sure just what kind of a takeoff it might be for the old bird, but the tail came up immediately.

At the end of the palm trees and over the sandy beach, just a dozen or so yards short of getting her toes wet, the Beechcraft lifted off. The airspeed indicator read nearly one hundred miles per hour. With her nose angled up still gaining speed, she climbed.

Tim quickly made his way forward to crank up the landing gear. "Wheels up and locked, Captain."

"Thanks," Hollands hollered, as the coastguardsman crawled back to take up his weapon and position again.

"Hey Captain," Tim yelled. "We've got company. Starboard—fifteen Jap fighters, about two o'clock! I make them at twenty-five thousand feet, sir."

"Have they seen us?" Hollands shouted.

"I don't think so, sir. They haven't changed course. Still heading west."

Hollands made a slow turn to port and throttled back. Below, he could see a few small ships and a host of larger ones, with a larger formation a few miles off the coast. But what really caught his eye was a small enemy aircraft carrier.

He motioned for Beckett to come up front. Pointing to the carrier, Hollands yelled over the wind and engine noise, "Hey, Sarge, look! The Japanese aren't shooting at us, and the deck of that carrier is covered with aircraft."

Beckett nodded. "Yes, sir. Looks like they're refueling planes topside."

Hollands adjusted the throttles back a little farther. "We can play it safe, and head for Pateroa," he said. "Or, we can strafe that flat top. We might get ourselves killed, but maybe we can cause a bit of damage and confusion. What do you think, Sarge?"

The old Marine stroked the stubble on his chin. "Well, Captain... We wouldn't be very good hosts if we didn't give 'em some kind of a welcome."

Hollands nodded. "Right! Get the boys ready. I'll swing wide astern of her, and come in low and off her port side. We'll have just the one pass."

Beckett stepped back to get ready for battle.

Hollands couldn't understand why the Japanese weren't shooting at them. The Beechcraft didn't have any markings, and the Nips were famous for commandeering local transport planes. Maybe they thought the Beech was one of theirs.

Flying over the small enemy armada, Hollands rocked the wings. The Japanese sailors below waved back.

Steering well clear of the carrier, he flew the plane about two miles beyond before making a hundred and eighty-degree turn. Beckett's squad was set up on the starboard side of their aircraft and had their three guns lined up and ready to fire.

"Listen up, men," Beckett explained, yelling over the roar of the aircraft. "There will be a lot of men on deck, but concentrate your fire on the planes and fuel carts."

Carl and Tim nodded, and each man released his breach bolt, chambering a round. They were ready.

Straightening out the plane, Hollands brought the Phoenix even with the port side of the aircraft carrier's flight deck.

A couple of hundred yards out and still at a thousand feet astern of the Japanese carrier, Beckett hollered, "Open fire."

The three machine guns reverberated throughout the plane as tracers guided the projectiles to their targets.

The fuel drums that dotted the deck began to burn and explode. Aircraft were soon engulfed in flames, and those equipped with extra fuel tanks were also exploding. Liquefied flames roared across the deck, spreading to the lower hangar decks.

The Beechcraft reached the end of her firing pass, and—with a synchronicity that could not have possibly been planned—the cache bunker on the island erupted in an explosion that surpassed anything that Hollands and the others had ever witnessed.

Hollands shoved the throttles to their full position and banked the Phoenix hard to port, angling west towards Pateroa. As they sped away, the four observed several more explosions aboard the carrier.

Beckett moved up to the cockpit. "What did you think of the show, sir?"

"That was some damned fine shooting," Hollands said.

"Thank you, sir," the sergeant said. "We couldn't sink her, but I think we sure as hell made a mess of her."

"Yes, you did," Hollands said. "You and the boys did a top-notch job on this plane, too. When we get to Pateroa, we'll have to send a nice thank you letter to Walter Beech. Give the boys a 'well done' for me!"

The sergeant nodded. "Will do, Captain."

His next words were interrupted by a burst of anti-aircraft flak off the starboard wing. It was followed by a half-dozen more bursts, in rapid succession. The Japanese sailors had recovered from the shock and begun to fire on the Beech.

It was too little, too late. Hollands stayed close to the water, and within a few seconds they were well out of range.

When he was sure they were clear of enemy fire, Hollands throttled back the engines and tried the radio. "Pateroa Tower, this is Phoenix One. Over."

An excited voice responded. "Phoenix One, this is Pateroa Tower. Over."

"Pateroa, this is Captain Hollands. I'm flying a modified twin-engine Beechcraft, that doesn't look much like a Beech. Will need landing instructions in about five minutes. Over."

"Phoenix One—sorry, Captain. The area is closed to all traffic. We are under air attack. Out."

Hollands leaned over to relay the message to Beckett.

The old Marine grunted. "First, we have to fight our way off the ground. Then, we have to fight to get back down."

"Maybe so," Hollands said. "But we don't have enough fuel to play games."

"Could be worse, sir," Beckett said. He jerked a thumb over his shoulder, in the direction of the Japanese carrier they had strafed. "There are about sixty enemy planes back there that won't be getting into this fight."

"Good point," Hollands said. "Let's see if Buckner is in the air."

As he prepared to make the radio call, the outline of Pateroa Island came into view on the horizon. He pointed it out to Beckett. In the far distance, they could see specks darting about the sky. Aircraft—Japanese and American.

"How's the ammo holding out?" asked Hollands.

"I'd guess we have about two hundred rounds each," Sarge said. "He laid a hand on Hollands' shoulder. "You give us a target, Mike. We'll knock it down."

Hollands nodded and smiled.

He was flying so close to the ocean's surface that he was practically sucking sea spray into the engines. He tuned the radio to a frequency that he and Buckner favored when they were flying missions together.

He keyed the microphone. "Buckner, this is Hollands. If you're up here, answer. This is no time for protocol, you Jarhead. Over."

Hollands repeated the message several times before his headphones crackled with a response. "Look out your port window, Captain. Ribbit, ribbit!"

Hollands looked left and could see three Corsairs about a mile off his wing. "Freeman is that you?"

"This is Bull Frog, alright. Should ask you the password, Captain. But what the hell. We were just trying to figure out what that strange looking bird was flying towards Pateroa. Thought you might be some kind of Nip secret weapon. Over."

Hollands grinned. "Where's Buckner? Over."

"He and the rest of the squadron are out chasing the remnants of an earlier enemy air attack on the base. Gotta go, now. Fifteen bogies have been reported, five miles north. Over."

"That must be the group we spotted when we left the island," Hollands said. "Good hunting, Lieutenant."

"Thanks! Roger. Out."

Beckett came forward and yelled over the roar of engines and wind. "Tim had headphones wired in, and I heard part of that message. Since we can't land, we'd like to know if we could go help your friends. They're gonna be really outnumbered, sir."

Yelling back, Hollands responded. "When Buckner's men are finished, the Nips won't know what hit 'em. But, no, we can't go help. Not at their altitude. You need oxygen, and we don't have any."

Beckett nodded and began moving towards the rear of the plane.

Tim suddenly hollered. "Sarge! Off the starboard side, about three o'clock!"

Beckett stumbled up to the cockpit again. "Captain! Look out over the starboard wing. There are three Jap fighters chasing one of ours. And they're all heading for the deck!"

Hollands glanced out the side window and quickly assessed the situation. "That P-40 Warhawk is no match for three Zeros. Let's give him a hand! Hold on back there!"

The pilot of the P-40 had become separated from his group, and he was in trouble. Even so, Hollands was impressed as he watched the American fighter give the three enemy pilots a lesson on flying.

He shook his head, "Damn. We've gotta help this guy."

The Japanese pilots must have been green. They were so intent on their quarry that they never saw the Beechcraft, or if they did, they probably wrote it off as an unarmed cargo plane—something they could turn back and kill, after the P-40 was dispatched.

The Zeros and the Warhawk were two miles ahead. The Japanese were having one hell of a time getting a clear shot at the U.S. Army fighter. The pilot of the P-40 was good, but if this went on much longer, he would eventually zig when he needed to zag. One of the Zeros would get a bead on him, and it would all be over.

Hollands was closing the gap, but not fast enough. He thought about pouring on some speed, but he didn't know how much power the old Beechcraft could take.

Then, he got an idea, and reached for the radio.

"Army Beechcraft calling, Army P-40 on the deck. This is Captain Michael Hollands. If you hear me, flash your running lights."

The P-40's lights flared and went out.

"Good! I'm on your six, about two miles back and closing. Stay on this heading. On my mark, climb sharply to angels three, then drop back down to the deck. If you understand, flash your lights again."

The P-40's landing lights flared again.

Hollands gripped the control yoke and keyed the mike. "Three... two...

one... Mark!"

The Army plane went nearly vertical, climbing quickly to three thousand feet. The pilot executed a roll, and dove back down to the deck.

The Japanese were still on his tail, but the maneuver had halved the distance between Hollands and the three enemy planes.

The airspeed indicator in the Beech read three hundred miles per hour, but there was no way to guess how accurate that gauge might be. Gambling that his engines would stay attached to the wings, Hollands poured on a bit more throttle.

He was five hundred feet above, and slightly behind the Zeros. Tim and Carl were stationed at the starboard side cargo door, and Beckett was at the port side door.

When Hollands shouted the order, they opened fire on the two outer planes in the enemy formation. The barrage shredded the propeller of one Zero, but the two Japanese planes caught most of the fifty caliber rounds in their engines and cockpits. Both aircraft caught fire immediately, and nosed over into the ocean.

The third Zero was a half-mile ahead, apparently oblivious to the fact that he had just become the hunted. Still closing on the P-40, the Japanese pilot wove back and forth, firing short bursts at the Warhawk, which danced up and down, and from side to side.

Waving to his men in the rear of the Beech, Hollands motioned for all three to move to the port side. They would have just one chance, one burst of fire at the enemy plane.

Hollands keyed his radio. "Okay, P-40. There's one Zero left on your tail. Quick! Go full flaps! Cut your power and bring your nose up sharply. Right after that, jam on full throttle and get out of there!"

Hollands' short experience with Japanese pilots had taught him that they rarely changed tactics. If this pilot stayed true to form, he would pull up and bank hard to port. Hollands' plan was to meet the Japanese plane just as it began to bank.

The pilot of the American fighter dropped his flaps, chopped his power, and brought the nose of his plane up. The P-40 slowed immediately, and the Japanese pilot had to react quickly to avoid a mid-air collision. He followed his training, and did just what Hollands had expected him to do.

Hollands gently pushed the yoke of the Beech forward, as his three gunners took care of the rest. Firing simultaneously, each sent a short burst through the undercarriage of the turning Zero.

The aircraft never corrected. Trailing black smoke, the crippled plane rolled over and crashed into the sea.

The radio crackled with an incoming message. "Phoenix One, this is

Pateroa Tower. Over."

"Pateroa, this is Phoenix. Over."

"Captain Hollands, this is Commander Sessions. You're cleared to land. Use the north dirt taxiway. Welcome home, son. Welcome home."

"Roger. You may have a wounded P-40 pilot up here, sir. Give him a gold star. He's a keeper!"

"This is Pateroa. He's talking to us now. Says someone flying an old Beechcraft saved his ass."

Hollands grinned. "You better check that boy for blood loss. Sounds like he's seeing things. Out."

He throttled the Beech down to a hundred-and-twenty miles per hour, and called for someone to come forward and crank down the landing gear. The wheels were soon down, and locked into place.

Hollands adjusted his angle of approach, and set the Beechcraft down on the dirt runway as gently as a stolen kiss.

Enemy bombers had indeed visited Pateroa. Bomb craters were scattered all over, and the two hangars were badly damaged. But the Nips had concentrated on the paved runways, and the dirt run was relatively untouched.

Hollands killed the port engine and taxied to the hangars, carefully maneuvering around the many craters. He heaved the tail around with hard right brake and rudder, and brought the Beech to rest. Then, he shut down the starboard engine and the noisy plane fell into a deep silence that was broken only by the ringing in his ears.

Hollands eased out of his seat, and turned to face the rear of the aircraft. He stood there for several seconds, stooped in the cockpit entranceway. The three men were joking and laughing, busily gathering equipment that had become scattered throughout the plane.

Sergeant Beckett looked up and spotted Hollands. "Captain, we wouldn't have survived this long if you and Lieutenant Yoshida hadn't shown up when you did. We sure wouldn't have been able to escape from that island. Thank you, sir, for bringing us through."

No one had been aware of the jeep that had pulled up alongside the plane. Overhearing Beckett's little speech, Commander Sessions had waited, not wanting to interrupt.

Carl was the first to notice him and called everyone to attention.

"At ease, Gentlemen," Sessions said with a smile. "And climb on down from there."

CHAPTER 14

Team Players, Only!

The four exhausted men stood at attention in the commander's office. "Please, stand at ease, Gentlemen." Sessions observed their gaunt appearance and their worn, soiled uniforms as he shook hands with them. But he couldn't stop grinning. He was immensely pleased and relieved that they were now safe.

He turned away briefly to dab his eyes with his handkerchief, and to wipe his nose.

Stuffing the handkerchief into his pocket, he nodded to Hollands. "I've met the two women, and Lieutenant Yoshida, too. They're all doing fine."

Sessions stepped over to his desk and took a seat. "Welcome to Pateroa Naval Base gentlemen, and welcome home, Michael. You have all been through hell, and it's remarkable what you have accomplished."

Lighting a fresh cigar, the commander puffed enthusiastically before he continued. "What your group has achieved these past five months is astounding. You've provided us with information that has not only saved countless American lives, but it has also enabled us to surprise the hell out of the Japanese! You have made all of us very proud."

"Thank you, sir," said Hollands. "Actually, we have a bit of an update for you. Shortly after taking off from the island, we strafed one of the smaller Japanese aircraft carriers. We destroyed a dozen or so planes that were being fueled on deck and—with any luck—the explosions destroyed more aircraft down below. We didn't stick around to watch!"

"My God, that's unbelievable! You may have been the reason that this latest air attack failed. You took out their reserves."

He shook his head again. "Men, I'm not going to hold you any longer. I'm going to send you off with my clerk. The doctors will want to check you over, and we need to give you some good hot food for a change, and a few days rest if possible. Welcome, and God bless you." He stood up and nodded. "You're dismissed."

Everyone came to attention, and Hollands saluted. "Good morning, sir. And thank you."

As the four men filed out of the office, Sessions called out, "Captain Hollands, wait a moment please. Have a seat, son."

"That might not be a good idea, sir," Hollands groaned. "I may not be able to get up again."

Sessions smiled at the half-hearted joke. "I got a look at that aircraft you flew in on. Buckner tells me you rebuilt it. Is that correct?"

Hollands nodded. "In all candor, sir, it was a group effort. But mainly, it was the three men you just met. They really did the work."

The commander tapped the ash off his cigar. "Well done, Hollands. Well done! You can go catch up with the others, now. We'll talk more later."

"Yes, sir, and thank you for your help."

The clerk was waiting at the main entrance with the others. "Captain Hollands, welcome home, sir. Will you all follow me, please? Our first stop will be the supply room for toiletries, new uniforms, and footwear. Then it's on to the showers."

Minetti and Roberts were quiet as they showered off months of dirt, grime, and fear. The shower water coursing down their faces hid the tears of relief in their eyes. It was starting to sink in. They were safe.

As they dried off, Carl asked, "Well, what do you think? Do you want to stay on this base?"

"Haven't really thought much about it," Tim said. "But I'll tell ya one thing. I would go anywhere Sarge and the captain go."

"Yeah, me too! I'd like us all to stay together," Carl replied. "If the others stay here, I think I will too."

As Carl slid his arms through the sleeves of his new shirt, he sniffed the fabric. "What do you suppose this odor is?"

"I think they call it *new* and *clean*," Tim said.

Both men laughed.

After the shower, all four men rendezvoused at the Navy's barbershop for haircuts.

Later, Hollands found his old room just how he had left it. As he was leaving to rejoin the others at the hospital, he saw the orderly bringing in fresh bedding.

"Good afternoon, Captain Hollands, and welcome back, sir. I'll have your room ready in a jiffy."

"Thank you, Otis," Hollands said. "And thanks for keeping it so clean."

"It was a pleasure, sir. No trouble at all. I'll open the window, to air it out."

It was only a short distance to the base hospital. As the four men walked along, they could hear the crinkling of their new crisp uniforms. It was real. They were finally off that island.

When they entered the hospital, the three enlisted men were taken to another area.

Hollands looked around the officers' ward. About half the beds were occupied. He soon located Lieutenant Yoshida in an area near a window, and somewhat removed from the other patients. Mosquito netting curtained his bed.

Ron was asleep. Hollands stood silently by his friend's bed for a few moments. He was vaguely aware of a woman's voice calling softly to him. "Captain Hollands, will you come with me please?"

Hollands didn't move. He stood, watching his friend.

The soft female voice spoke again. "Michael, will you come with me please?"

He finally nodded. "Yes ma'am, right away. Is he going to be all right?"

Easing away from Ron's hospital bed, Hollands turned slowly and came face to face with Lieutenant Gail Elliott.

"Ron will be fine in a few days," she said quietly. "He's doing really well."

Turning again to Ron, Hollands said in a near whisper, "Why is he so far from the others?"

"I put him there so he could get more fresh air and quiet," Gail said. "And frankly, some of the guys feel a little antagonistic having a 'Jap' in the room with them."

"That's ridiculous!" Hollands said softly. "I owe him so much. We *all* do."

He looked at Gail. "And we *owe* you."

The nurse shook her head. "Not me. *Him*. He put it on the line for all of us."

Hollands met Gail's eyes. "Listen... I'm sorry for giving you and Janet the bum's rush. I just wanted you off the island, where you'd be safe."

But the gentle touch of Gail's fingertips upon his lips silenced him. "We'll talk about that later, Captain. Right now, you have a doctor's appointment."

The two walked down a short hallway to an examining room.

"At least you all smell better," Gail said. She closed the door and surreptitiously locked it behind them.

"I had forgotten just how good *clean* could feel," Hollands said.

He glanced around the examining room. "Where's the doctor?"

"He'll be here soon enough," Gail said. "You and I have some unfinished business first."

She placed her arms around his neck. "I shouldn't even be speaking to you, Michael Hollands. You stuffed me into that damn plane without so much as a word."

On tiptoes, she stretched as high as her 5-foot 4-inch height would allow, then pulled him down and tenderly kissed him.

As Gail relaxed her hold, Hollands looked into her eyes and slowly wrapped his arms around her waist to pull her to him more tightly.

He whispered, "I really like that damned island." And he passionately kissed her.

A few seconds into the kiss, the door began to rattle. "Lieutenant Elliott, are you in there?"

The doorknob rattled again. "Nurse Elliott, this is Commander Brooks. Open this door, immediately!"

"Do you suppose we should let the Doc in?" Hollands whispered, his arms still around her waist.

"I suppose it would be the proper thing to do, under the circumstances," Gail whispered.

Hollands released her and cleared his throat. "Hi, Doc. Sorry about the door. I didn't realize it was locked."

As Gail unlocked the door, she glanced back at Hollands and winked. "You fibber!"

The doctor walked in and gave Gail and Mike a stern look. Then, he stretched out his right hand to Hollands. "Good to see you again, Captain. How're you feeling?"

"Just fine, Doc, Hollands said. "A little tired, but otherwise pretty good."

"Glad to hear it," the doctor said. "Now, let's see how well you held up to your little island vacation."

It was just after 1600 when Hollands reached his room, and Gail was still very much on his mind. He had never thought of an Army bunk as something to long for, but the idea of crawling under the sheets seemed positively enticing.

He wouldn't sleep. He knew that. He was still too wound up from the flight, and too excited to be back on Pateroa. But it wouldn't hurt to take the doctor's advice and lay down for an hour or so.

He stripped to his skivvies and climbed into his bunk. His head met the cool cotton of the pillowcase, and he felt his body begin to relax.

He definitely wasn't going to be able to sleep. Too many things were running through his mind, and he had too much to do...

Ten seconds later, he began to snore.

Hollands awoke to the sound of a gentle rain. It was still light outside, so he couldn't have been asleep very long. He looked at his watch. It was six-thirty.

He sat up and rubbed his eyes. "That's *it*? Two and a half lousy hours?"

A familiar voice spoke. "Try fourteen hours, you gold brickin' SOB."

Hollands turned to see Ron Yoshida, dressed in a bathrobe, and sitting backwards on a chair.

"Damn," Yoshida said. "I thought you'd *never* wakeup."

Hollands grinned at his unexpected visitor. "Hi, Ron. It's good to see ya, Buddy."

He yawned. "Fourteen hours?"

"That's right," Yoshida said. "Fourteen hours."

The Japanese-American pilot glanced at his watch. "The mess hall serves morning chow until 0700. So, if you plan to eat this morning, you've got just about thirty minutes to get your GI butt up, and into your shiny new uniform."

Hollands climbed out his bunk and tried to stretch the kinks out of his back. With a couple of deep breaths, he cleared some of the cobwebs from his head.

He yawned again and stuck out his right hand. "So, how are you feeling, Ron? You okay?"

Yoshida shook the offered hand. "Oh, I'm just dandy. I lost my appendix, but I don't think I was really using it."

He made a face. "They still poke me with needles two or three times a day. I'm a walking, talking, oozing, drugstore. Unfortunately, I'm not supposed to eat anything solid for a couple more days. But I'd be happy to have a cup of coffee and watch *you* eat. And you can tell me what real food tastes like."

"Sounds perfect," Hollands said. He reached for his shaving kit. "I'll be ready in a few minutes."

He shook his head. "Fourteen hours?"

His friend nodded. "Yep. As in one hour less than *fifteen*."

"What the hell," Hollands grinned. "I was overdue for some beauty sleep."

A knock came on the jam of Hollands' open door.

Hollands and Yoshida turned to see a young Army Air Corps Second Lieutenant. "Excuse me, sirs. I'm looking for Captain Hollands."

"I'm Hollands, Lieutenant. What can I do for you?"

The airman snapped to rigid attention, and saluted. "Sir, I'm Second Lieutenant Grant Pritchard, sir!"

Still dressed in his skivvies, Hollands waved away the salute. "At ease, Lieutenant, before you hurt yourself."

He gestured toward his friend. "This is Lieutenant Ron Yoshida. He's on our side. Or at least he is *this* week. Aren't you, Ron?"

Yoshida reached out and shook Pritchard's hand. "Still the comic, huh, Mike?"

The effort at humor seemed to go right over Pritchard's head.

Hollands began gathering up his clothes. "I repeat, what can I do for you?"

Pritchard swallowed before speaking. "Sir, I was piloting my P-40 yesterday morning, and I was told that you were the one who helped me out of that jam. I just wanted to thank you personally, sir."

"I had a part in it," Hollands said. "But there were three other men on that plane with me. *They* did the shooting. I'll pass on your thanks to them."

He reached for his towel. "You did one hell of a job yourself, Lieutenant. You took those Nips on quite a ride, and you managed to keep them from flaming your tail."

"Thank you, sir," Pritchard said. "I shot down two and damaged two before my guns quit. That's when they got my wingman. I couldn't help him. He'll be okay though. A Navy ship picked him up."

"That's great news," Hollands said. "Say, have you had breakfast? Ron and I are just about to head over to the mess hall. I just need a quick shower and shave."

The young lieutenant shook his head. "Thanks, sir. But my squadron has been ordered to Guadalcanal. We're wheels-up in about twenty minutes. Nice meetin' both of you."

He looked at Ron intently. "First time I've ever seen a Jap, ah, sorry... I meant a *Japanese*—up close. No offense, Lieutenant."

Ron shrugged. "I've been called worse."

With that, Pritchard turned and left the room.

Hollands draped the towel around his neck, and he and Ron headed for the showers, talking and joking as they walked.

Ron asked, "Was that kid, Pritchard, *really* that good?"

"Looked pretty good to me," Hollands said. "He took three Zeros on the ride of their lives."

After chow, Hollands and Ron were talking over coffee when Major Hanks entered the building. Spotting Hollands, Hanks grinned and hurried over to the table. "Hey, Hollands, it's great having you back. Mind if I join you?"

Hollands motioned to a chair. "Have a seat, Jeff. Have you met Lieutenant Yoshida from San Francisco?"

He turned to Ron. "The major is Buckner's CO."

Hanks shook Yoshida's hand. "Glad to meet you. Nice bathrobe."

He reached for a coffee cup. "We've heard a lot about you, Lieutenant. There are a lot of GIs still breathing because of you. Welcome back to our side of the war."

"Thanks, Major. It's good to be here."

Hollands poured some coffee for Hanks. "Ron and I just spoke to a pilot from the Army P-40 squadron. Says they're moving up to Guadalcanal. Isn't that gonna run us a bit thin on air defenses?"

Hanks took a swallow of coffee. "Yeah, it sure will. They're going to Henderson Field to train on P-51s."

He rested his coffee cup on the table. "Halsey says the Japanese have a new offensive in the works, to retake the Canal, Rabaul, Munda and some of the other territory they've lost. They're gonna be throwing everything they've got at us."

Yoshida fished a fresh pack of smokes out of his robe pocket, and offered one to the major, "What kind of air defenses will that leave us with? Are we going to have any fighters at all?"

Hanks accepted the offered cigarette, and shook his head. "No, Lieutenant. It'll be just about the way it was when Mike showed up here last March. Remember that, Mike?"

"I sure do!" Hollands said. "This place wasn't an airbase. It was a ghost town." He took a healthy swig of coffee. "Hey, wait a minute. What about the Corsairs that were flying around here yesterday?"

"Gone late last night," Hanks said. "Farmed out to other squadrons."

He regarded the contents of his coffee cup. "The brass don't think the Japs will bother with Pateroa for a long time. So we're back to a handful of pilots, and no planes."

"When are we going to get some?"

Hanks shrugged. "Scuttlebutt says we're slated for some planes, but I don't know from where or how soon."

The three sat quietly for a few moments.

Hanks downed the last of his coffee and stood up. "Well, guys, I gotta go earn my milk and cookies."

He reached out to shake Yoshida's hand again. "It was good meeting you. Then, he grinned at Mike. "By the way, that was a nice plane you were flying yesterday. Did you make it yourself?"

He turned and walked away before Hollands could respond.

Ron nodded toward the major's retreating back. "What about Buckner's squadron? Are they leaving too?"

"Beats me," Hollands said. "I've been asleep for fourteen hours, remember? I don't know what's going on yet. But maybe they'll leave Buckner here. They never were a real squadron, anyway. Just a handful of planes that we scrounged up."

Hollands paused for a long moment. "We kept your cousins off balance last time by pulling every sneaky dodge we could think of. I don't think they'll be nearly as easy to fool this time."

Hollands and Yoshida entered the headquarters building, and stopped at the clerk's desk.

Seaman Pruitt immediately stood up. "Good morning, Captain, Lieutenant. It's nice to see you both."

Hollands poked his head into Session's office. "Thank you, Pruitt."

"Sorry, sir, the commander isn't here. He's across the field at a briefing. I'm not sure, but I think there are several high-ranking naval officers, including an admiral or two."

Hollands frowned. "Was Major Hanks notified of the meeting?"

The seaman shook his head. "No, sir, not to my knowledge."

Hollands nodded toward the window. "Is that the commander's jeep out front?"

"Yes it is, sir. But I can't authorize the use of it."

"That's all right, Seaman. I'll take full responsibility. But I'm *going* to that meeting."

Hollands looked at Ron. "Come on. I'll run you back to the hospital. The admiral and his group might not take to you as quickly as the rest of us have."

"Fine by me," Yoshida said. "Besides, my tank of medicines must be running dry. I'm not oozing as much."

Hollands chuckled and headed out the door toward the commander's jeep.

Yoshida fell into step beside him. "Go ahead and laugh," he said. "You're not the one they're using as a human pin cushion. And that reminds me... You'd better stick your head in at the hospital, and say hi to Gail. Because, when she's pissed at you, she takes it out on me with those damn shots."

Hollands dropped into the driver's seat of the jeep and hit the starter button. "All right, you big crybaby. I guess a couple minutes one way or the other won't make much difference."

At the hospital, Hollands couldn't find Gail anywhere. He asked the doctors and nurses. Finally, as he was walking back toward the jeep, he spotted her coming from the direction of the supply room, her arms loaded.

Her face lit up when she saw him. "Hi, Mike! How are you feeling?"

"Ready to wrestle a crocodile," Hollands said. "But real food and fourteen hours of sleep will do that."

Gail smiled. "Janet and I sacked out for over ten hours when we got here. Where're you going now?"

"Seaman Pruitt said some bigwigs from fleet are running a briefing. I'm gonna try to crash the party."

Gail's smile widened. "Good luck! Think we could have lunch later? I'm off duty at noon."

Hollands grinned. "Sure. If we're done in time."

The sky looked like it was thinking about rain again when Hollands arrived at the hangars across the base. He parked the Jeep between the two buildings.

Walking towards the open staircase, he saw two Marine MPs, a lance corporal and a private, standing near the bottom step.

As he approached the stairs, the Marine private brought his M-1 rifle to port arms, and the corporal saluted. "Good morning, Captain."

Hollands returned the salute. "Good morning, Corporal. I'd like to get upstairs to the briefing."

"Sorry, sir. It's off limits."

Hollands was about to argue when he heard a voice from somewhere behind him.

"Hi, Army, how the hell are ya?"

Turning quickly, Hollands saw Ben Murray and Bruce Buckner walking toward him.

"Hi! Am I glad to see you two," Hollands said, and the three shook hands.

"Hey, Bruce, thanks for bringing Yoshida and the girls back with you."

"Hell, that was easy. The hard part was running into Gail everywhere, and having to tell her for the thousandth time that I didn't know when you were coming back. I was just about ready to start hiding out in the men's latrine."

Murray slapped Hollands on the back. "He's not joking. That girl 'bout drove us nuts. But it's sure good to see you, Mike. Glad you're back from your vacation in Paradise."

Hollands' two friends laughed as they shook their heads.

Buckner said, "I stopped by your room yesterday evening, but you were snoring like a lumberjack. Didn't have the heart to wake you."

Turning serious, Hollands gestured back to the two MPs, "What gives here?"

Murray and Buckner laughed again, and started to steer Hollands away from the stairs.

"The MPs are right," Buckner said. "The big dogs are bumping brains up there, and little dogs like us are *definitely* not invited."

"That's a fact," Murray said. "Heavy-hitters only. There are two Navy captains, two Marine colonels and a general, plus a fleet admiral and his aides. And, of course, our own Commander Sessions... Outranked, as usual."

"Damn!" Hollands said. "That's a lot of collar-hardware, fellas!"

"They've been up there since 0600," Buckner said.

As the three strolled away from the hangar staircase, they heard a sudden loud commotion behind them.

Turning, they saw that the heavy upstairs door had swung open, bouncing hard off the steel railing.

At the top of the stairs, a heated exchange was in progress between lower and upper officer ranks, and a furious Commander Sessions was in the thick of it.

"Commander," the Navy captain snapped. "You are about a half an inch from insubordination."

Buckner's eyebrows went up. "Whattaya suppose that's all about?"

Hollands and Murray shrugged. Neither of them had ever seen Sessions this fired-up before.

"Commander," the admiral said, "he's probably all that you claim he is and more. But we are sitting in the front yard of the Imperial Japanese Navy, and we just can't take such a chance on Yoshida."

The admiral shook his head gravely. "I'm sorry, but he'll have to be interned, at least in Hawaii, until we can get his story sorted out. He can keep the rank for now and..."

With the mention of Yoshida's name, Hollands became riveted on the conversation. He was no longer aware of his two companions tugging at his sleeves.

"Sir, with all due respect," Sessions said angrily, "Lieutenant Yoshida is one of the reasons that you *are* in the enemy's front yard. I know I'm just an old retread from the first war. The dregs of the bilge. But I *know* a good man when I see one, and Lieutenant Yoshida is a good, honest, decent *American*. He has placed his life on the line many times for our— no *his*—country and this command. Even shooting down Japanese planes in order to save the lives of American fliers and ground troops. This has been documented by several pilots, and by the native and Australian coast watchers."

Hollands was stunned. These officers were talking about a man whom Hollands judged as a friend, and who had proved it many times over.

Oblivious to everything but the argument in front of him, Hollands moved again toward the stairs. There was another voice speaking, a familiar voice. It was his own.

He realized that he was standing rigidly at attention. "Admiral, may I speak, sir? A word with you, if you please?"

The admiral stared at him. "Commander Sessions, who is this man?"

"Admiral Johnston, this is Army Air Corps Captain Michael Hollands. This is the man who took a single fighter aircraft, and made the Japanese believe that they were up against an entire squadron. This is the man who saved this base from probable annihilation at least three times. And this is the man who stole a Japanese High Command airplane with radios and codebooks, and who is responsible for all of those enemy intercepts that CinCPac has benefited so much from."

Sessions pointed straight at Hollands. "For the past few months, this man and six other forgotten souls operated an unofficial outpost. Marooned on a nameless rock, because the Navy—*our* military—had written them off as expendable, as being too costly and too dangerous to rescue. Five men and two female Army personnel, sir. Captain Hollands monitored the airwaves continuously, under constant threat of being discovered by the enemy. He and the others have just returned, bringing us the code books I shared with you a few minutes ago."

The admiral moved a step or two down. "Well, young man, we've heard a lot about you. You have quite a reputation, and have done immeasurable service for your..."

Hollands heard himself interrupt the admiral. "With all due respect, sir, you're *wrong*."

A hush fell over everyone within earshot. Buckner and Murray stood in silent disbelief, their mouths open. A mere Army captain did *not* speak this way to one of the highest ranking military officers in the Pacific Theater.

The admiral's aide started to reprimand Hollands, but the admiral stopped him. "At ease, Phil. This man's record speaks for itself. He's earned the right to say his piece."

The admiral gazed intently at Hollands. "Captain, I'm Admiral Johnston. Say what's on your mind, but be mindful of the latitude you've been given."

Hollands discovered that his throat was suddenly dry. "Thank you, sir. I'm honored by all of the kind things that Commander Sessions has just said about me, but his words were not quite accurate. It's true that I was involved in all of those actions, but most of the real credit goes to Lieutenant Yoshida."

Hollands took a breath and plunged on. "Admiral, you're concerned about the lieutenant's loyalty to America. Whether he can, in fact, be trusted. That's understandable. But, sir, he is as loyal an American as any of us standing here. Perhaps even more so, as he has had so much more to prove than any of us. He is also my friend."

"I owe my life to Ron Yoshida, and so do many of the men and women on this base. Frankly, sir, if it weren't for his actions, a lot of your ships would be sitting on the bottom of the Pacific right now. I know for a fact that I would be dead."

"After my plane had been disabled by mechanical failure, I couldn't defend myself. Yoshida shot down two Japanese fighters that were gunning for me, and..."

"That's not quite right," a voice said.

Hollands looked over his shoulder to see Ron Yoshida walk past Buckner and Murray to the foot of the stairs. Dressed in his fresh U.S. Army Air Corps uniform, he stood beside his friend, and faced the battery of officers.

"It was one and a half planes," Yoshida said. "You finished off the second plane as it wandered in front of your guns. I only damaged that one. *You* made the kill."

Yoshida glanced back at Buckner, and then turned back toward the admiral. "Shortly after that, Captain Buckner here, flamed my ass."

Hollands cleared his throat. "Admiral, may I introduce to you Lieutenant Ronald Yoshida of San Francisco, California? It is he and he alone who received, translated, and radioed all of the Japanese messages to Pateroa. He was also responsible for transmitting false messages to the enemy, sending them on many a wild goose chase—and into traps he helped our Navy set up."

Hollands looked at Sessions. "If you listen to the commander, sir, he'll make you think I'm some kind of hero."

Hollands rested his right hand on Yoshida's shoulder. "If you're looking for the real hero, Admiral, he's standing right *here*."

The admiral made his way down the rest of the stairs and stopped in front of the two fliers. "Back on board my old ship, I was revered as old 'deck plate,' because of my bull-headed ways of doing business. Well, I might be a stubborn old bastard, but I'm not too crusty to admit it when I'm wrong."

He didn't crack a smile as he offered his right hand first to Hollands, and then to Yoshida. "Thanks for setting me straight, son. You two have bought us precious time."

He nodded soberly. "Captain Hollands, you've sold me on this fine young American. I'm going to send him home for a couple weeks, to visit his family. Then you and Sessions will get him back, in good trim and ready to fight."

The admiral looked at his aide. "Phil, make a note. We need to scare up some aircraft for these gentlemen."

The aide fished out a notebook and jotted down a few quick lines. "Aye-aye, sir."

As the admiral passed through with his entourage, Hollands, Yoshida, Buckner, and Murray, snapped to attention again and saluted.

Sessions shook his head in disbelief as he trailed along behind the departing crowd. A minute later, all of the upper echelon officers were gone.

Hollands sat down on the stairs, and put his face in his hands. "Holy shit... I can't believe I *did* that."

Buckner sat on the step beside him, and lit a cigarette. "You *did* it, alright, Army. That doesn't surprise me. You're always up to some kind of craziness. What amazes me is that you got *away* with it."

He blew a plume of smoke into the air. "Man... You've either got balls like coconuts, or you are the luckiest sonofabitch alive."

The adrenaline had left Hollands' body, and he held out his right hand. It was shaking like a leaf. "Do me a favor," he said. "Don't ever let me do anything like that again!"

Yoshida looked at Hollands. "Thanks for sticking up for me. I think you were nuts to spit in an admiral's eye, but I do appreciate it."

Hollands nodded mutely.

"I hate to break up this little party," Yoshida said "But there's a nurse lieutenant who's going to broil me with the fish cakes if I don't get back to the hospital. I'm probably overdue to be stuck with needles or something."

Buckner gave him a half-grin. "How did you manage to drag your invalid butt over here so fast? Magic wheelchair?"

"I hitched a ride with an ambulance," Yoshida said. "The driver says he knows you."

"Could be," Buckner said. "It's probably the guy I met as we loaded your butt into the ambulance. He didn't understand the situation, and I had to explain a few things to him."

Hollands stood up. His knees were still a little wobbly, but he figured he could walk now. "Come on Ron, I'll give you a ride to the hospital. You too, Bruce and Ben. Wherever you want to go."

As the four climbed into the commander's jeep, Hollands glanced at Yoshida. "So, what made you decide to drop in on the admiral's meeting?"

Yoshida settled into his seat. "I picked up some scuttlebutt from Janet. She overheard one of the admiral's sailors talking about some Jap on the base who was headed for jail." He leaned back and closed his eyes. "I figured it *had* to be me, so I came over to put in my two cents worth. Plus I thought you and Sessions might be in a jam on my account, and I thought I might be able to help. So, there I was!"

CHAPTER 15

New feathers for the old bird

Gunnery Sergeant Elmore Beckett was hospitalized for a while, to allow his injured hip to heal completely. Because his prior outfit had been lost at sea, the old leatherneck had requested reassignment to Pateroa Naval Air Station. Commander Sessions and Major Hanks were quick to approve. The Marines had needed a non-com above the rank of corporal. Roberts' and Minetti's transfers were also approved.

Everyone rated a survival leave back to the States. Hollands turned his down, but cabled his family in Seattle that he was safe and well. All he wanted to do was to get back to flying.

During his few days of walking convalescence, Hollands split his time between base operations and helping with work on the Beechcraft. Not having any fighters on base was a major concern for all.

The cannibalized hulks of two F-4U Corsairs and three P-40 Warhawks stood in the grass behind a hangar, but the Duck and the Beechcraft were the only two operational aircraft on the base.

Several days after Hollands' encounter with Admiral Johnston, Commander Sessions held a breakfast briefing to share vital information with his officers.

"Gentlemen, according to intelligence from the Army and Naval commands, the Japanese are planning a major counter-offensive. They're going to hit back with everything they can muster. Retake Guadalcanal, all of the Solomons and New Guinea. Because of the fight we put up two weeks ago, the enemy may not realize that our base is without fighter protection again, and that we have limited ground forces."

"As you can guess," he said, "all hell's gonna break loose around here if the Japanese figure out that we're defenseless."

His gaze traveled around the assembled faces. "Pateroa is not a strategic island. We're just one rock among many. But this island *does* have a small deep-water port and an airstrip. And we've been a thorn in Japan's side more than once. Despite the assurances of our senior leaders, the enemy may decide to hit us again at any time."

Hollands said, "I can understand moving the major air assets to expected combat areas. But they could have left us at least *some* fighter cover. We've proven that we can keep the Nips busy with a few fighters. I don't see how we can get by with no fighters at all."

Sessions took a sip of coffee and set his cup down. "The Navy moves in mysterious ways, its blunders to perform."

Buckner cleared his throat. "What about Admiral Johnston's promise of replacement aircraft?"

Sessions shrugged. "I don't know, son. Maybe there weren't any to be had."

Hollands leaned back in his chair. "We're right back to my first day here. We've got pilots, but no planes."

As the men ate, everyone offered up suggestions, but without help from the top echelon leaders, there was nothing anyone could do, other than pray that the Japanese would not discover Pateroa's dilemma.

Just before the meeting broke up, a messenger delivered a cable to Sessions. All eyes were on him as he studied it.

When he was finished reading, he laid the paper on the table. "Listen up! We've just received a message from CinCPac that may offer a solution. There's going to be some kind of high-level meeting tomorrow, at 0800 hours, on Papua New Guinea."

He regarded Hollands. "Captain, is your ship good for a fast trip of about 870 miles?"

"I think so, sir." Hollands said. He made eye contact with Murray. "What do you think, Ben? I know that Skip and his crew have been working on the plane."

Ben furrowed his brow. "Let me think... We've replaced one of the fuel tanks, and installed instruments. The flaps and the hydraulics are working. We've rechecked the engines, and repaired the prop-pitch control."

He nodded thoughtfully. "There are still a few systems that could use some work, but I think she's good for a flight that long."

"That's fine, Ben," Sessions said. "Have her on the flight line at 0400."

Murray gave him a thumbs-up. "Will do, sir."

Sessions rose from his seat and looked at Hollands and Buckner. "It's no secret," he said. "I *hate* flying. But if you gentlemen aren't too busy tomorrow morning, I'd like to take a plane ride."

Both fliers piped up immediately. "Yes, *sir!*"

Sessions turned, and exited the mess hall.

When he was gone, Buckner whistled softly. "Damn, I think he's serious. What has that old fox got up his sleeve?"

"Unless I miss my guess," Hollands said, "that ol' fox is going to war with the United States Navy. And that meeting in New Guinea is gonna be ground zero for the fight. I'd bet my bars on it."

Hollands scratched his head and turned to Buckner and Ben. "If I'm right, we'll need a few pilots. Who do we still have on station?"

"Bull Frog Freeman is still here," Buckner said. "And Billy Morgan."

He elbowed Murray in the ribs. "Ben here is a pilot too, or so he keeps telling me."

Murray shook his head. "Bombers. Not fighters. If you've got a B-17 in your pocket, I'm your man."

Buckner elbowed him again. "You've tested fighters, Ben. I've seen you up in them. You could ferry one, if there really *are* some to be had."

Murray shrugged. "Okay. I guess you can count me in."

Hollands, Buckner, and Skip worked on the Beechcraft late into the evening. They checked and rechecked every inch of the hodge-podge aircraft.

When Skip stood up to stretch his back and leg muscles, he glanced out through the hangar door and noticed the darkness. "Hey, sirs, wanna break for chow?"

Buckner straightened up and stretched his own back. "Damn! The chow halls are closed, and I'm hungry."

"The Navy mess is still open," a voice said.

Buckner, Skip, and Hollands all looked around to see who had spoken. A figure stood in the shadows, away from the circle of illumination cast by the service lights.

Hollands strained to make out the man's features in the gloom. "Who's that? Identify yourself!"

Ron Yoshida stepped forward into the light. "Damn! I'm gone a few days, and you guys forget all about me."

He raised a hand and patted the fuselage of the Beechcraft. "I missed your miraculous flight off the island, but I'm definitely going along for the ride tomorrow."

Hollands and Buckner dropped their tools, and scrambled down to the hangar floor to greet their friend. All three men began speaking at the same time.

Skip stuck two fingers into his mouth and whistled loudly. Everyone stopped talking, and burst out laughing.

When the last of the chuckles had died away, Yoshida repeated himself. "The Navy mess is still open. I just came from there, and the cook is saving some chow for you guys."

Buckner slapped Yoshida on the back. "You don't have to tell *me* twice."

Yoshida grinned. "I *did* have to tell you twice. None of you knuckleheads listened the first time I told you that the Navy mess is still open."

"Come on," he said. "I've borrowed a jeep. I'll fill you in on all the news from back home. If you say 'pretty please,' I might decide to tell you who's probably going to be in the Rose Bowl."

The three officers headed toward the door, laughing as they walked.

Skip turned away, and began to pack up the tools.

Hollands halted the group, and turned around. "Well? Are you coming?"

Skip shook his head. "I'm still just a corporal, sir. I can't go into the officer's mess."

"You're with us!" Buckner said. "You're part of the team, and the team eats together tonight. If anybody has a problem with that, Lieutenant Yoshida will use some of that karate stuff on them."

"I don't know any karate," Yoshida said. "But I can bite 'em on the ankle."

"That's just as good," Buckner said. "So, get your butt over here, Skip. Unless you're not hungry..."

"I'm hungry, sir," Skip said. "Give me two minutes to finish packing up the tools."

"Now that's the Skip I remember," Buckner said.

Skip grinned. "So, what do you think, Lieutenant? Who's going to the Rose Bowl?"

Yoshida gave him mock glare. "You forgot to say *'pretty please'*."

An orderly shook Hollands awake at 0300.

Fifteen minutes later, after a quick shower, Hollands walked into the Navy mess hall. The others hadn't arrived yet, but Lieutenant Gail Elliott sat at a table, holding a porcelain U.S. Navy cup full of steaming coffee.

Hollands grabbed a cup for himself, and sat down at her table. "Good morning. What are *you* doing up so early?"

"That's a silly question," Gail said. "I wanted to see you—and the other guys—off on your mission this morning."

She tipped her cup toward Hollands in a mock toast. "Everyone on the base is talking about your flight. Tokyo Rose may be the only person on this planet who doesn't know about it."

"Well, let's try to keep it a secret from Rosie a little while longer," Hollands said with a chuckle. "I don't like it when strange women know too much about what I'm up to."

Gail winked at him. "How do you feel about not-so-strange women?"

Hollands stood up. "That depends on which not-so-strange woman you have in mind."

He walked around the table and took Gail's hands in his.

She slowly rose from her seat, and he pulled her into an embrace. They looked into each other's eyes, and they both whispered the words '*I love you*' at the same time.

He pulled her closer, and their lips met in a gentle lingering kiss.

After several delicious seconds, Gail broke the kiss and stared into his eyes. "Come back to me, Mike. Come home."

"I will," he said. "We've planned our flight path to avoid enemy installations. We're not going to..."

Her finger went to his lips and shushed him.

"I'm not asking you to shirk your duty," she said. "I'm not asking you to be anything but what you are."

She gave him a rueful smile. "You're a fighter pilot, Mike. I knew that the first time I met you. And I knew it when I fell in love with you."

Her arms tightened around him. "All I'm asking is for you to *try* to come home."

"I'll do my best," he whispered. "I promise you that I'll try."

Gail sighed. "Of all the places we could have met, it had to be *there*..."

Hollands smiled. "God bless that damned little island."

Gail nodded. "Yes. God bless our little island."

She started to say something else, but they suddenly heard the voices of approaching men.

Hollands and Gail released their embrace, and returned to their seats on opposite sides of the table. By the time the other men walked into the mess hall, the pilot and nurse were seated and drinking coffee together.

Buckner, Yoshida, and Lynch bumbled sleepily through the routine of grabbing coffee cups and finding chairs.

Buckner clapped Lynch on the back. "I decided to bring Skip along," he said. "Corporals are pretty much expendable, so—if anything goes wrong in flight—we can send him out on the wing to fix it."

Skip poured himself a cup of coffee. "I thought it was *Marines* who were expendable, sir."

Buckner gave him a hard stare. "Hey! What have I told you about thinking? Don't try it. Corporals aren't *built* for that."

If Skip had a retort for Buckner's jibe, he didn't get a chance to use it, because the cooks brought in the hot food at that moment. Everyone took up trays, and loaded them up with chow.

Seaman Pruitt briefly ducked in to fill a couple of trays with food. "Gentlemen," he said, "the CO sends his greetings, and says he'll meet you in the ready-room in fifteen minutes."

He nodded respectfully to the small gathering, and backed out the door of the mess hall with a tray in each hand.

As they ate, the group began to wake up, gradually becoming more upbeat about the mission. The clink of utensils mixed with conversation and occasional laughter.

The conversation reached a brief pause, and Gail selected that moment to take her leave. She stood up from the table, and smiled. "I think this is a good time for me to go," she said.

She turned her face away and walked slowly toward the door.

Every man in the room stood up, observing a courteous and respectful silence as the nurse left the room.

Gail's eyes were glistening as she stepped out into the pre-dawn darkness. She held her body erect as tears of fear, pride, and love rolled down her face.

"Come home," she whispered softly. But her quiet plea was not just meant for Michael Hollands. She was talking to them all.

Hollands took the pilot seat, and Ron sat at the co-pilot's position. Buckner huddled in the cockpit entryway to help with navigation.

Commander Sessions climbed in through the starboard cargo door, followed by Captain Ben Murray, Lieutenant Alan Freeman, Lieutenant Billy Morgan, and one other pilot, newly-arrived and unassigned. Counting Yoshida and Buckner, this made for a total of seven pilots who could ferry aircraft back to Pateroa.

Hollands and Yoshida busied themselves with the preflight checklist.

Through the partially-open pilot's window, Hollands heard someone calling his name. He slid the window the rest of the way open, and stuck his head out. He could barely make out three shadowy forms standing in front of the engine.

He nudged Yoshida. "Ron, flip on the landing lights for a moment."

Yoshida flipped the switch.

The darkened silhouettes instantly became identifiable as Sergeant Beckett, Private Minetti, and Petty Officer Roberts. They stood, shielding their eyes from the sudden glare.

"Captain," the old Marine sergeant said, "we'd like to come along, sir."

Hollands saw that the three men were each carrying a pair of .50 caliber machine guns, two ammo cans, and had several long belts of ammunition draped around their shoulders. It was quite a sight.

No one on the plane had even thought about weapons, let alone machine guns.

Hollands turned to Buckner. "Do we have *any* fire power on board?"

Buckner dashed back to check with Sessions, who was seated in the rear of the plane. The Marine pilot reappeared several seconds later. His voice was heavy with embarrassment. "Ah... Except for our side arms, there are no weapons onboard."

"There are *now*," Hollands said. "Open the door and give those guys a hand."

Buckner unlatched the starboard side door, and the three men boarded the aircraft.

Hollands and Yoshida finished the preflight checklist.

"Ready on number one, Captain."

"Roger. Turning number one. Number one is turning."

What a difference it made to have a working electrical system, complete with batteries and starters. A working compass had also been installed, and Buckner and Yoshida argued a little about the proper procedures for using the new instrument.

As they taxied toward the runway, Hollands intervened. "Listen to yourselves. You're both saying the *same* thing. You're both correct!"

It was 0530, and a deep purple haze of dawn had begun to replace the darkness.

"Phoenix One, this is Pateroa Tower; you are cleared for takeoff. Have a good flight, Captain. Good luck. Over."

As unofficial as this flight was, they might be heading for a planeload of court martial offenses.

"Roger Tower. Phoenix One rolling."

It was a flawless takeoff, the Beech climbing effortlessly through the morning air.

The controls were smooth and responsive in Hollands' hands. He smiled to himself. "Damn, I love those working flaps."

At around five thousand feet, he tapped Yoshida on the shoulder. "It's your plane, Lieutenant. Take her up to angels ten, and bring her around to our assigned heading."

"Roger, Mike. Angels ten."

In addition to mechanical improvements, the maintenance group had also added military decals. The Navy insignia was on the port side of the fuselage, the Army Air Corps insignia on the starboard. Marine and Navy emblems emblazoned the top and bottom of both wings. The tail assembly held U.S. Coast Guard emblems.

Maybe it was overkill, but no one could mistake this ship for a Japanese plane. With a touch of irony, someone had added a large panel full of Japanese flags, signifying downed enemy aircraft.

Commander Sessions appeared at the cockpit door and complimented the pilots on how well the Beechcraft was behaving. "I haven't flown much over the years, but this is great."

Captain Hollands unbuckled his safety belt and climbed out of the seat. "Sit here for a while, Commander."

Sessions took the offered seat. "Thank you, Captain. Thank you very much."

Ron looked over at the commander and smiled. "Next stop: Tokyo, sir."

The actual distance to Papua was 800 miles. At a cruising speed of 225 miles per hour, the flight time was estimated at three and a half hours.

Fifty miles out from the coast of New Guinea, the Phoenix was intercepted by three P-38 Lightnings. It took Buckner a few minutes to establish the correct radio frequency.

"This is High Cap leader calling Beechcraft. Identify yourself. Over."

"High Cap leader, this is Phoenix One. This is Captain Buckner, U.S. Marines Corps. Commanding Officer of Pateroa Naval Air Station is on board, and has urgent business with Admiral Johnston. Over."

"This is High Cap leader. I'm Major Haroldson. You are in restricted airspace. You will turn your aircraft around, and leave this area at once, or we will fire on you. Over."

Hollands slid back into the pilot seat and took the microphone from Buckner's hand. "This is Captain Michael Hollands, U.S. Army Air Corps, pilot of this craft. Say again your message."

"This is High Cap Leader. I say again: you must leave this airspace immediately. Over."

"Sorry, Major, no-can-do! I repeat: the Commanding Officer of Pateroa Naval Air Station is on board. He needs to meet with Admiral Johnston immediately, on urgent Navy business."

He glanced at his gauges. "Also, be advised that we do not have enough fuel to return to our base. Over."

The radio was quiet for a minute, and then three Navy Hellcats showed up. A new voice came over the radio. "High Cap, this is Navy Red Bull. I'll lead this aircraft in on my responsibility. Over."

"Roger, Red Bull. Returning to patrol. High Cap out."

The P-38s peeled away, and the new voice spoke again. "Captain Hollands, this is Lieutenant Briggs. Glad you survived your crash last June. I'll probably be reduced to Swabby First Class, but you sure as hell saved our tails that day. Follow me down."

As they approached the airfield, Briggs radioed the tower. "Red Bull calling Dover Control. Over."

No response.

Briggs tried again. "Red Bull calling Dover Control. Over."

Still no response.

Briggs tried a third time. "Red Bull calling Dover Control, escorting flight Phoenix One. Over."

This time, the tower responded. "Red Bull, this is Dover Control. You are escorting an unauthorized flight. Over."

Without a pause, the tower continued. "Phoenix One, this is Dover Control. You are in a restricted airspace. You are ordered to leave this area at once and return to your base."

Yoshida looked at Hollands. "They don't sound too friendly, Mike."

The voice of Lieutenant Briggs came over the radio again. "Dover Control, this is Red Bull Leader, Lieutenant Briggs. This flight is landing *now*. Is that clear? Over."

There was a pause of perhaps five seconds before the tower responded. "Roger, Lieutenant. Phoenix One, this is Dover Control. You are cleared for runway six-right. No wind. Over."

"Phoenix One to Dover Control. Roger. Phoenix One calling Red Bull Leader. Thanks, Lieutenant. Don't let them take those bars! I'll stand with you."

Stripped of all the niceties, Sessions and his crew were trespassing, and subject to arrest. Violating restricted airspace was serious business, and crashing a flag-level briefing was just about as unhealthy.

Hollands taxied to his designated parking spot and shut down the engines. Before the propellers had spun down to a stop, a jeep and a truck arrived, both carrying Military Police personnel. The MPs deployed quickly, surrounding the aircraft.

Commander Sessions was the first to disembark the plane. The rest of his crew piled out behind him and assembled on the tarmac.

The MPs held their weapons ready. The expressions on their faces were hard and unsympathetic.

An MP sergeant stepped forward and saluted. "Good morning,

Commander. This field is closed. Off limits. No unauthorized personnel allowed."

A lone figure in civilian clothes walked through the circle of MPs and approached the strange looking aircraft. It was Mr. Quigby, the Australian coast watcher.

He stopped a couple of yards away from the sergeant. "Hold on there, mate. This is part of that group I was telling you chaps all about a couple months back. The ones who were marooned on that small atoll east of Pateroa."

Quigby eyed the Beechcraft and turned to Hollands. "Captain Hollands... Still pulling miracles out of your ditty bag, I see. I heard a rumor that your lot had bodged together a plane out of tin cans and coconuts. Is this the lady in question?"

Hollands patted the tip of the Phoenix's starboard wing. "We've cleaned her up a bit since then, but this is *definitely* the lady in question."

Quigby started to speak, but the MP sergeant raised a hand. "Just a second, sir. Did I hear that right? Are you Captain Michael *Hollands*, sir?"

Hollands nodded. "That's right, Sergeant."

The MP broke into an enormous grin. "Sonofabitch!"

He turned to Ron. "And you, sir... You'd be Lieutenant Ronald Yoshida?"

Ron nodded. "Right again, Sarge."

"Holy shit!" the MP said. "You two are famous around the South Pacific. Everybody knows who you are, and what you've done."

His voice grew serious again. "How can I help?"

Hollands nodded toward Commander Sessions. "Our CO here has urgent business with Admiral Johnston. Can you send a note to the admiral that the commander is here? In fact, let him know that all of us are here, and we are in vital need of some fighter aircraft for our base. The Nips could hit us any time, and we have no defensive air cover at all."

The MP sergeant didn't hesitate. "I'll probably get busted for this, but war is hell, sir. And I think I can do better than a note."

The MP turned to Sessions and pointed to his jeep. "Commander? Can I offer you a ride, sir?"

As Sessions took a seat in the jeep, the MP turned to Hollands and the others. "The rest of you gentlemen can wait in our mess hall. Private Jones here will escort you."

He caught the private's eye and winked at him. "Swing by the bone yard on your way, and show them where the old airplanes are parked."

The private looked puzzled. "If you say so, Sarge. But that's the long way around."

The MP sergeant dropped into the driver's seat of the jeep, and started the engine. "Just *do* it, Private."

The young MP private waved toward the truck. "If you gentlemen will hop in, I'll give you a ride to the mess hall, by way of the bone yard."

Hollands nodded, and turned to face Beckett. "Sarge, I want you, Roberts, and Minetti to stay here and guard the Beechcraft."

Beckett saluted. "Will do, Captain!"

Private Jones decided to leave two of his MPs behind as well. "No offense, sir," he told Hollands. "But we *are* supposed to be guarding this plane. If I leave a couple of guards posted here, I'm *technically* following orders."

Hollands walked toward the truck. "Good thinking."

Private Jones strode over to the truck and climbed up into the driver's seat. The rest of the pilots and Skip clambered into the back of the truck, along with the MPs.

Hollands slid into the passenger side, next to Jones. "So, Private, tell me about these aircraft."

The MP started the engine and pointed off into the distance. "They're over there, sir. On the back side of that hangar. Maybe a dozen or so."

He put the truck in gear and it lurched forward. "Most of this base was built by the Aussies, sir. The Japs grabbed it for a while, but lost it for good after the Battle of the Coral Sea, nearly a year and a half ago. I've only been here for five months."

The truck rumbled across the nearly empty tarmac. The driver made a wide turn to the right, going behind two main buildings and continuing on a dirt path a short distance beyond them.

The field behind the hangar looked like an Army-Navy surplus lot. Standing forlornly in the dirt and weeds was a motley collection imaginable of old, outdated aircraft. Hollands could see a trio of F2A Buffalos, a couple of Aerocobras, a few bi-planes, and several hard-used P-40s.

Captain Murray surveyed the derelict planes, and shook his head in disbelief.

Skip had brought a small service toolbox along. When the truck came to a halt, he and Buckner jumped off and made a bee-line toward the rusting hulks.

"Jeez, this isn't a bone yard," Buckner groaned. "It's a junkyard. There's nothing here but scrap."

Skip shrugged. "Maybe, sir. Or maybe not. Let's find out..."

As Skip and Buckner began looking things over, ten men approached riding atop two service tractors, toolboxes in evidence.

Hollands noticed a lone ship, sitting in a clearing some distance from the rest of the group. The MPs had left a pair of binoculars in the truck, so he picked them up to look at the dark form.

The lonely aircraft was covered by a tarp, but the silhouette under the canvas was familiar. "I can't be sure," he said, "but that sure looks like a Jug."

Private Jones nodded. "You're right, Captain. It is a Jug. The pilot landed it four, maybe five weeks back. He taxied to that spot, and threw a tarp over his plane. Then, he lit a cigarette, walked fifty yards or so into the jungle, and blew his brains out."

Hollands winced. "That's nasty. Any idea why he did it?"

The MP shook his head. "I don't think anybody has a clue, sir. Maybe the war got to him. Flipped his cams. I don't know."

Hollands nodded solemnly. "What about the plane?"

"It's a P-47," Jones said. "Other than that, we don't know anything about it. We contacted the squadron. A day or so later, they sent some guys out to claim the body. But they never came back for the plane."

Hollands stared at the man. "So, they just *forgot* about it?"

"I don't know, sir," the MP private said. "Could be."

"Thanks," Hollands said.

He and the MP walked over to the old P-40 that Buckner and Lynch were poking around.

Hollands pointed toward the tarp-covered P-47. "Let's go take a look at *that* one."

The four men jumped into the truck, and Jones drove them cautiously across the rough ground.

As they got closer, Hollands yelled over the noise of the rattling truck. "Does anyone know the pilot's name?"

Jones shouted over his shoulder to one of the MPs in the rear. "Hey, Cooper! You were one of the investigators on the pilot who shot himself, right?"

"Yeah," the other MP said. "I was on that one."

"What was the pilot's name?"

The other MP thought for several seconds before answering. "It was a Lieutenant Colonel, last name started with an 'R'... Rhoades! Yeah, that's it. Colonel Joshua Rhoades."

"Damn," Hollands said. "Damn, damn, *damn*."

Buckner gave him a concerned look. "What's wrong, Mike? Did you know the guy?"

"Yeah," Hollands said. "I knew him."

Private Jones brought the truck to a stop, and the men swung down to the ground.

Hollands opened his door and made the short drop to the dirt. Buckner met him at the side of the truck a couple of seconds later.

"I met Colonel Rhoades in the summer of 1940," Hollands said. "He was a captain back then. I had one more year of college, and I had started flight school as a cadet."

Hollands strode over to the covered aircraft and found the bottom edge of the tarpaulin. "He was my first flight instructor. And a damned good one. I wonder what happened."

He shook his head and lifted a section of the tarp, revealing part of the plane's fuselage. On the medal skin below the canopy were eighteen red circles—one for each enemy aircraft shot down by Lieutenant Colonel Joshua Rhoades.

"Here we are, Commander," the MP sergeant announced. "The meeting is through these front doors and straight down the hall. You'll see one of my men on guard at the door. Tell him Sergeant Cox said to let you in."

"Thank you, Sergeant," Sessions said. "I hope this doesn't get you into trouble."

"Sir, may I say something?" asked Cox.

"Of course," Sessions said.

"I'm not concerned about getting into any trouble, sir. But a few months ago my brother wrote me and told me that his group of Hellcats were lost and low on fuel. Two fliers, one Army and the other Marine, helped them to Pateroa. The leader of that Navy Hellcat squadron was the same officer who escorted your plane down today, sir. Anyway, the Japs jumped the formation and one of the planes—a Thunderbolt—went down. That was Captain Hollands wasn't it, sir?"

Sessions nodded. "I believe it was, Sergeant. I remember that day."

"My brother was part of that squadron, sir," the MP sergeant said. "He's alive because of those two men."

The sergeant fell silent for a moment. Then he cleared his throat. "Go get your planes, Commander."

Sessions climbed four stairs to the doors of the wood-framed building, and continued to where the sentry was standing. At the mention of Sergeant Cox's name, the MP guard waved him through.

Sessions reached the door and laid his hand on the doorknob. He took a deep breath and released it. "In for a penny, in for a pound..."

He pulled the door open and walked in. The room fell instantly quiet.

Sessions counted twelve high-ranking officers from the Navy, Marines, and Army. Except for a few aides, no one had less than an eagle on his collar and most had two or more stars.

Admiral Johnston spotted Sessions and let out a sigh of frustration.

Commander Sessions, intently aware of the mere oak leaf on his collar, strode forward and came to attention a few feet from the admiral. He snapped out a brisk salute. "By your leave, Admiral... I've come for my aircraft, sir."

CHAPTER 16

A Strange Flock of Birds

While Commander Sessions was engaged with the business of military diplomacy and protocol, Hollands, Buckner, and the mechanics were busily going over every aircraft in the bone yard, trying to figure out which—if any—had potential.

After a half-hour or so, Hollands turned to Captain Murray. "Ben, I'm going to check back with Beckett, and see how he's doing."

He glanced around at the old war birds. "Look these over closely, and meet me in the mess hall at 11:30 with your findings. That's about two hours."

"You got it, Mike!"

The MP gave Hollands a ride to the Beechcraft.

As they approached the aircraft, Hollands laughed and pointed. "Look, Private. Who's guarding whom?"

Beckett, Roberts, and Minetti, sat with the two MPs in the shade of a wing, playing cards.

Beckett looked up and saw Hollands approaching in the MP truck. He immediately hustled everyone to their feet.

By the time Hollands walked over, the Marine sergeant had called the men to attention. He snapped out a quick salute. "Hi Captain. Any good airplanes back there?"

Hollands raised his hands in a palms-up gesture. "There might be some hope for two or three of them. Captain Murray and the others are looking them over now. How's everything going here, Sergeant?"

"Everything's shipshape, sir."

Beckett lowered his voice. "These Army MPs are right nice guys, sir, but they can't play poker worth a damn. I'd like two or three more hands, sir, so we can give some of their money back."

Hollands looked at him. "Are you developing a soft spot, Sarge?"

Beckett shook his head. "No, sir. Call it inter-service respect and cooperation, sir. I'm beginning to like some of you Army boys. No disrespect intended."

"None taken. We're going to rendezvous with the inspection team in the maintenance company's mess hall at 11:30. That gives you about an hour and a half before we have to close up the plane and head over to meet the others. Till then, Sergeant, carry on."

"Thank you, sir. An hour and a half should do it."

The mess hall was about a half-mile from where the Beech was parked. At 11:10, Hollands and his three men secured the plane, climbed into the MPs' truck and headed out.

When Hollands entered the hall, he saw his team, plus an additional twenty or so men from the airbase maintenance company.

The cooks had drinks, sandwiches and doughnuts waiting.

When the men were seated, Hollands rapped a table top for attention. "Okay everyone. At ease. Keep eating, but listen up."

He turned to Captain Murray. "What did you find out, Ben?"

Murray nodded in Buckner's direction. "I defer the question to Buckner. He has most of the information."

Buckner stood up and pulled a scrap of paper from his shirt pocket. "Well, we gave everything in the bone yard a good once-over. We've selected eight planes that don't look too bad. That includes the P-47, four P-40s, two F2A Brewster Buffalos, and one Boomerang from the Aussie Air Force. The Jug has very few hours listed in the log. The rest of them have been worked long and hard, but they may still have some life in them."

He folded the paper and returned it to his pocket. "Those miserable old Buffalos... I recommend we leave them here. They're too damn slow, and no match for even a kite in the wind. As for the Boomerang, I just don't know enough about them. There are also two P-39 Aerocobras that look okay, but they can't hold enough gas to get back to base. For that matter, some of the others will need external fuel tanks to make it home."

"Okay, we'll forget the Cobras" Hollands said. "I don't much care for the Buffalos, myself. The P-40s are a better—*much* better—fighter. And the Boomerang is similar to the old P-36 Hawk. Regardless, we need aircraft. We can use the P-40s for air-to-air combat. We'll hang on to the Boomerang and one of the Buffalos for close-in reconnaissance around the island, and for ground support."

Buckner nodded. "Roger. What about the other Buffalo?"

"We've only got seven pilots," Hollands said. "Pick the better of the two Buffalos, and leave the other one. How long will it take to get those old girls flying?"

"Well," Buckner said, "the mechanics here say they have plenty of parts. Unless we run into something unexpected, all of the planes should be ready by 0800 tomorrow."

As Hollands' briefing was winding down, a staff car stopped near the front of the mess hall. Through the window, it appeared to Hollands that Commander Sessions was practically ejected from the rear seat of the vehicle, which sped away at once.

Sessions straightened his uniform, and walked with slow dignity to the entrance of the building.

As the commander walked in the door, Hollands called, "Atten-hut!"

Commander Sessions grabbed a coffee cup and waved a desultory hand. "Carry on. Carry on."

He made his way to Hollands' table. "Captain, dismiss everyone but our group."

"Yes, sir," Hollands said.

Turning to the others, Hollands said, "You men have a job to do. We thank you for your much-needed help. Pateroa group will stay. The rest are dismissed. We'll join you shortly."

Those who remained were eager to hear the news from their CO. When were they going to get some planes? How many? What type?

Sessions set down his coffee and took out a fresh cigar. He shook his head as he unwrapped it.

He lit the cigar, took a few puffs, and settled into a chair. "I thought I was so damn smart."

Hollands whispered to Beckett, "Sarge, you and the boys wait outside with the others."

"Yes, sir. Good idea." The sergeant motioned for Roberts and Minetti to follow him.

Sessions took a long puff, and exhaled a cloud of smoke. "He threw me out of the meeting. Threatened to have me court martialed for insubordination. It looks like we flew down here for nothing."

He lifted his coffee cup, and then set it back down without taking a drink. "Admiral Johnston, in his *infinite generosity*, told me that we could have anything we could scrounge out of their bone yard. That's all the help he's willing to give us."

Hollands said, "Well, sir, that wasn't exactly what we'd hoped for, but we knew things might go that way. But the trip wasn't a complete loss. We've got some things to show you."

Motioning for the little group to move towards the back door, Hollands added, "Sir, let's see if there is a jeep or a truck we can borrow out back."

"Gotcha covered, Captain," a voice called out. "My jeep is a-waitin' your orders, sir."

At the rear entrance, the men saw their favorite MP, Sergeant Cox.

"Commander, I heard what happened," he said. "I'm sorry not to have been at the door when you came out, sir. I was called away for a few minutes."

"That's all right, Sergeant. I appreciate your efforts just the same."

"Hey Sarge," Buckner said, "how about a ride out to your back forty for all of us desperados?"

Sessions still had an air of defeat about him as he climbed into the front of the jeep. "Captain Hollands, would you mind telling me what this is all about?"

"Be patient, sir!" Hollands said. "You'll see in a couple of minutes."

As they approached the area where the so-called derelict planes were parked, Buckner nodded with approval. "Ya know, Hollands, some of these junk heaps are starting to look suspiciously like aircraft."

Alighting from the jeep, Sessions stared at the wrecks in various stages of disrepair. "What is all of this, Captain?"

"Airplanes, sir. And they now belong to you. To Pateroa."

Hollands made eye contact with Skip. "Find some paint and put the CO's insignia on the tail of each plane. Then see if you can rustle up insignias for U.S. Army Air Corps, Navy, Marines, and Coast Guard, and our country's colors."

Skip gave him a thumbs-up. "Will do, sir."

Hollands turned back to Sessions. "Commander, the mechanics tell me—that with some work—the seven aircraft we've selected can be ready to fly by tomorrow morning. They're not exactly shiny and new, but I think we're back in business, sir."

"Well, I have to agree with Buckner," Yoshida said. "They're starting to look like airplanes."

"Here's how I see the line-up," Hollands said. "Yoshida, you'll fly the Beech. Buckner, pick out a P-40 for yourself, and assign the other planes. I'll fly the Jug."

"Sounds good to me," Yoshida said. "Do we need any more pilots?"

"Why" Hollands asked. "Have you got a spare in your pocket?"

"Not exactly," Yoshida said. "But I ran into a guy who's trained on both Lightnings and Mustangs. He got sent out here to meet up with a squadron that got shuffled somewhere else before he arrived. Before he could track 'em down and wrangle a ride to catch up with them, his orders got canceled. He's been at loose ends for a couple of weeks. Typical military paperwork snafu."

"Where is he?" Hollands asked.

Yoshida pointed. "Right over there, working with the mechanics."

Hollands rubbed his chin. "Lightnings and Mustangs, huh? What do you think, Commander? Should we try to hijack this guy? He could come in handy, if we ever get the chance to misappropriate a P-38 or P-51."

"We might as well," Sessions said. "That seems to be the only way we ever get what we need."

Hollands nodded. "Go ahead with it, Ron. Let's see if we can get his orders approved by morning."

"That doesn't leave us a lot of time," Yoshida said. "What if we can't push the paperwork through in time?"

Commander Sessions raised his eyebrows. "Then, we take him anyway, and ask for forgiveness later."

Hollands and the other pilots bedded down at 2200 hours. There was still work to be done on the planes, but the fliers would have to get at least a few hours of sleep before their long flight in the morning.

The mechanics would continue working. Unlike the pilots, they could sleep in the next day.

The men from Pateroa were given the best available quarters—tents. It was the first time Hollands had slept in a tent since leaving North Africa. The sloping canvas walls felt familiar, and comfortable.

He and the others fell asleep quickly.

After what seemed like only a few minutes, someone shook Hollands awake.

"Captain," a quiet voice said. "You have to wake up now."

Hollands tried to roll over, but the intruder shook him again.

"Sir, you have to get up."

Hollands opened one bleary eye. His tormentor held a red-filtered flashlight.

Hollands could see Skip's face in the weak red-tinged glow. He glared at the young enlisted man through his one open eye. "What time is it, Private?"

"It's 0400 hours," Skip whispered. "And I'm a *corporal* now, sir. Remember?"

"Not anymore," Hollands grumbled. "Anybody who wakes me up at 0400 is automatically demoted one pay grade."

He yawned so hard that his ears rang. "What the hell are you up so early for?"

"I've gotta get back to that damn deserted island," he groaned. "I need the peace and quiet."

He waved a dismissive hand in Skip's direction. "The planes won't be ready for three or four more hours. Go back to bed."

Skip shook his head. "Can't, sir. The CO woke me up, and he's waiting for all of us. Something urgent."

Hollands grudgingly sat up and yawned again. "Okay, where am I going this time?"

"The commander said to get everyone to the mess hall, fast."

Skip took two steps toward Yoshida's bunk.

The Japanese-American pilot's eyes were still closed, but he raised an open hand in a choking gesture. "You try to wake me up, and I'll *strangle* you."

"That goes double for me," Buckner growled. "Check the Marine Corps regs. It's perfectly legal to strangle a former-corporal at four in the morning."

Murray draped an arm across his eyes to block out the feeble red glow of the enlisted man's flashlight. "I don't know if it's legal or not, but I'll hold him down while you choke the life out of him."

Skip grinned. "Sounds like everyone is awake. The commander is waiting for you in the mess hall."

He ducked out of the tent, and was gone.

Buckner sat slowly up and groped for his uniform. "You know, I could really learn to hate this war."

Hollands reached for his boots. "Come on. We'll shave and shower back on Pateroa. Let's go find out what the old man has for us."

Ten minutes later, Hollands and his fellow pilots filed into the mess hall. Most of the base mechanics were already there, curious about the emergency announcement.

The cooks had been ordered to prepare an early breakfast. Time was of the essence, and everyone was about to find out why.

Sessions stood up. "We don't have much time, Gentlemen, so grab some chow, and eat while I talk."

Men stood up and began the routine of filling trays and pouring coffee.

"I apologize for the early wakeup call," Sessions said. He held up a sheet of paper. "Admiral Johnston's clerk brought this note to me an hour ago. I won't take the time to read it to you, but here's the meat... Six hours ago, our Navy received information about a large Japanese naval taskforce.

They were spotted four hours ago, about twelve hundred miles north of New Guinea, steaming southeast at 25 knots. Based on last-observed course and speed, Naval Intelligence has narrowed the probable destination to four possible targets: Espritos Marco, the Russell Islands, Bougainville, and Pateroa."

Sessions slipped the message into a pocket. "We've known for several months that the Japanese plan to retake Guadalcanal as a first step to regaining dominance in the region. If they succeed, they could push us back to Hawaii."

Sessions leaned forward and rested his hands on the table. "This taskforce consists of troop carriers, heavies, and as many as three aircraft carriers. Intelligence projects that the taskforce may split into two or more smaller formations en-route, to go against separate targets, but there's no way to be certain until we actually *see* what the enemy does."

The commander's voice grew more grave. "We must be ready for the worst. It's possible that this taskforce will pass us by, but we have to prepare for the very real possibility that the entire flotilla will show up on our doorstep at Pateroa."

"When Admiral Johnson received this report, he sent extra manpower to help with the final repairs to our aircraft. We will be airborne in thirty minutes, Gentlemen. We will return to Pateroa, and make preparations for combat with the enemy taskforce. I thank every one of you for your efforts in getting our planes ready to fly, especially those of you who worked all night. We will do our best to make your hard work pay off. God bless. Be safe. And good luck to us all."

A half-hour later, the strange assortments of aircraft were gassed-up, armed and ready to go, their engines warmed up and idling.

Yoshida was at the controls of the Beechcraft, and Buckner's P-40 would fly rear guard for the ragtag squadron.

Hollands climbed up on the wing of the Thunderbolt, and took a last look at these brave pilots. This might be a one-way flight for some of them. Maybe for *all* of them. But not one of the men had hesitated.

Despite the patchwork nature of their aircraft, this was the finest bunch of fliers he had ever known.

He lowered himself into the cockpit of his P-47, closed the canopy, and belted himself in.

When all was ready, he keyed the radio. "Dover Control, this is Phoenix One. Pateroa Group ready for takeoff. Over!"

"Phoenix One, taxi your chicks to west end of runway six. Your group is cleared for takeoff. Watch for green light. Launch at thirty-second intervals. Safe flight, Pateroa. Dover out."

"Phoenix One to Pateroa Group. Our mission is to get our butts back to base. We will try to avoid any contact with the enemy. Once in the air, keep off the radio unless it's an emergency, and stay in tight. If all goes well, we should be on the ground in about four hours."

As the pilots waited for the green light from the tower, they cycled their controls, checked their oil pressure, manifold pressure, and temperature gauges, and ran up their engine RPMs.

Hollands caught the green lantern. The soft purple of dawn was just beginning to overtake the dark gray remnants of night. He released the brakes and slowly moved the Thunderbolt's throttle forward.

Within a few yards the tail came up and soon after, his bird was airborne.

Hollands circled the field in a wide pattern, watching the rest of his group leave the ground. Because the Beechcraft did not have oxygen, Ron had been instructed not to form up with the rest of the group. He was to maintain an altitude of twelve thousand feet. The others would fly at higher altitudes staggered from fifteen thousand to twenty thousand feet.

When all planes were airborne, the group settled onto their compass heading.

Hollands was pleased to be back in a fighter. He spent the first couple of hours of the flight getting to know his new aircraft—learning her feel, and how she responded to the controls. Like all P-47s, she was a big plane, but she was powerful and nimble.

Gradually, his preoccupation with the new Thunderbolt gave way to other thoughts. He began to replay and analyze what he knew about the Japanese flotilla. There was no way to know how accurate the reports had been. If the enemy ships were steaming at twenty-five knots, they could reach the Solomons within thirty-six hours. If the estimates of either speed or position were off, an attack might occur sooner than that, or later.

The islands around Pateroa all had one characteristic in common: shallow waters for many miles around. Submarines could not approach any of the islands closely, but waters were sufficiently deep for most surface vessels.

Commander Sessions had talked about preparing for the worst. That was a good idea in any combat situation, but Hollands began to mentally apply the concept to Pateroa. What if the Japanese taskforce made a direct run toward Pateroa at maximum speed? How soon could it reach the island?

Hollands started doing some mental arithmetic. When he arrived at an answer, he decided to do the math again. The answer came up the same.

He scaled back his throttle and dropped back to a position off of Buckner's port wing. He signaled for Buckner to take the lead.

As Buckner's P-40 surged forward, Hollands throttled back a bit more, and allowed his altitude to decrease until he was within signaling range of the Beechcraft.

He flashed a message for Commander Sessions. "Convinced enemy could attack Pateroa by tonight."

As Hollands waited for a reply, he did another set of calculations, and decided that they were still about ninety minutes out from Pateroa.

The reply came a minute or so later. "Climb to angels thirty. Establish radio contact with Pateroa. Order base to full alert."

Hollands and Buckner were the last to land. According to the tower, no sign of enemy ships or aircraft had been detected yet.

Hollands and Buckner caught up to Yoshida and the new pilot as they walked away from the Beechcraft.

Yoshida spotted Hollands and grinned at him. "I don't like to toot my own horn, Mike, but that old Beech flies a lot better with me at the controls."

Hollands rolled his eyes. "Your brain is still mushy from all of those needles they poked you with, Ron. I think you're delirious."

Yoshida nudged the new pilot. "Larry, set this numbskull straight, would you? Tell him how I played that Beech like a well-tuned violin."

The new guy raised his hands in mock surrender. "Hey, I just got here. I don't know you guys well enough to get into the middle of a family squabble."

Hollands reached out to shake hands. "I haven't met you officially yet, Lieutenant. I'm Captain Mike Hollands."

The man returned the firm grip with one of his own. "Lieutenant Lawrence McKenna. Glad to meet you."

"Likewise," Hollands said. "Are you checked out on the P-47?"

"I haven't flown one yet," McKenna said, "but I've read all the manuals, and I can fly pretty much anything I get my hands on."

Hollands caught sight of Skip, and beckoned to him.

The young mechanic came over at a trot. "Yes, Captain?"

"Skip, refuel and check over the Thunderbolt. I want her ready to fly, immediately. Then give all the planes the once-over. Get them refueled, check the guns, and have them on the flight line within the hour."

Skip nodded. "Yes, sir." He took off at a near-run, shouting instructions as he went.

Hollands looked at McKenna. "Okay if we call you Mack?"

"That's what I'm called, sir."

"I'm Mike," Hollands said. "You've read the manuals, so you already know the ratings of the P-47. In this case, the book happens to be right. The Thunderbolt can out-fly anything the Japanese have to offer."

"So I've heard," Mack said. "I take it I'm about to find out for myself?"

Hollands nodded. "We need you to do a recon. I want you to cruise at 200 knots for one hour, on a compass heading we will radio to you when you're airborne. Check in with the tower every fifteen minutes. This mission should take you about two and half hours. Stay at twenty thousand feet, and watch for enemy fighters. Avoid them if you can. If you make visual contact with the Nip convoy, radio their position immediately. Then get your tail out of there. We need that plane, and we need *you*. Okay?"

McKenna nodded. "I understand."

"Good," Hollands said. "Keep your eyes open for U.S. ships and air patrols as well. Buckner will brief his CO to contact our naval forces in the area, so they don't shoot you first, and ask questions later."

"Thanks," McKenna said. "I'd rather not be shot down by my own Navy."

"Exactly," Hollands said. "Use your radio for check-ins, location reports for enemy ships, or if you get jumped. Otherwise, stay off it."

McKenna stuck out his hand again. "Thanks, Mike."

Hollands shook it. "Thanks for *what?*"

"I've been out here for eighteen months," McKenna said. "Sitting on the bench, and waiting to get into the game. Thanks for giving me a chance to get into the war."

Yoshida rubbed his palms together. "Speaking of getting into the war, I've got an idea I want to bounce off you guys."

He knelt down and brushed a patch of dirt with his hands to create a smooth area. "This came to me back on the island, but I never got around to telling you about it."

The other three pilots squatted down beside him.

Yoshida picked up an elongated rock, and began to scratch a crude map in the dirt. "There's a Japanese fuel depot on a little island off the southwest tip of Munda. I flew over it a couple of times, back when I was still working for my cousins."

He continued to mark in the dirt. "The fuel depot consists of two very large tanks. They sit side-by-side on a low hill, a couple of hundred yards from the runway. If we can blow those tanks, the burning fuel should envelope most of the airfield, and probably destroy a majority of the aircraft. Any planes that survive will only have whatever gas they're already carrying."

Yoshida jabbed at the center of the map with his rock. "If we knock this place out, we can throw a wrench into the enemy's plans for this whole sector."

Hollands gestured toward the drawing. "Are you sure about these placements of the fuel tanks and aircraft?"

"The scale is probably off," Yoshida said, "but the basic layout is pretty close."

McKenna frowned. "How do you know that the Japs haven't moved everything around since the last time you saw the place?"

"That's not how the Imperial forces operate," Yoshida said.

He tossed his rock aside. "In the American military, we adjust things in the field. We improvise. We change things around. Whatever we have to do to complete the mission. Even a buck private can pass an idea up the chain. If he's smart and has personal initiative, he might tackle a problem himself, without asking for permission."

Yoshida looked around at his comrades. "That's not how my cousins do business. The high command lays out the plan, and the local forces follow it to-the-letter. Anything but strict obedience is treated as a failure in military discipline. They *don't* deviate. Any change has to come from Tokyo. Period."

The other three pilots exchanged glances.

Hollands spoke first. "Okay, so you want to raid the fuel depot. Do you think we can do it?"

"Hell, no!" Yoshida said. "But we specialize in things that can't be done."

He pointed to where the Beechcraft sat in its parking spot. "I would have bet every nickel I own that the old gal over there would never fly. And I sure as *hell* never expected to see an Army captain bust in on a top-echelon briefing, and come away with an apology from the admiral."

His voice grew serious. "It isn't really a question of whether or not we can do this. The real question is what will it *cost* us? Because this is probably a one-way trip."

Hollands examined the map in the dirt. "We use the Beechcraft?"

"I think that's best," Yoshida said. "At night, the Beech will resemble a small Japanese transport."

"At least up until the shooting starts," Buckner said. "After we open up, they're probably going to figure out that we're not friendly."

Hollands rubbed the back of his neck. "This definitely sounds like a one-way trip."

"We've got six .50 caliber machine guns, four .30 cals, and a couple of Browning Automatic Rifles," Yoshida said. "I figure we'll need about a dozen Marines when we're on the ground."

"It sounds plausible," Hollands finally said. "But I just don't know if the old man will go for it."

McKenna got to his feet and dusted off his trouser legs. "I've only known you guys for a few hours," he said. "But I think you're *all* nuttier than my Aunt Hattie's Christmas fruitcake."

Buckner looked up at him. "So, you're *out?*"

"Of course not," McKenna said. "You may be crazy, but you're *my* kind of crazy. I'm in!"

Buckner stood up. "I like you, Mack. You're going to fit right in around here. If you live long enough."

Buckner reached a hand down and pulled Hollands to his feet. "Mike, I think we've gotta run this by Hanks and Murray. If they like it, they may help us to convince Sessions."

"Sounds good," Hollands said. "Let's go drop the bomb on 'em."

As the four pilots walked toward the headquarters building, McKenna offered up an idea that brought the small group to halt.

"Just a minute, Mack," Hollands said. "Run that by us one more time..."

"It's simple," McKenna said. "Yoshida's plan needs a decoy. Something to draw attention away from the real danger."

"Like what?" Buckner asked.

McKenna shrugged. "Like a fighter chasing the Beech. Shooting at it with tracers. Ron could be jabbering to the Nip tower about being all shot up. They won't dare use their searchlights or antiaircraft batteries, for fear of hitting one of their own planes. And Ron will be so close to the deck that he could sneak in, taxi to the location close to the fuel depot, and deliver the surprise packages."

"That's not a bad idea," Hollands said. "Having one of our planes shoot at the Beech will distract the tower, and keep any ground troops focused on the air instead of the ground."

McKenna nodded. "I could continue to strafe both sides of the field, the tower and machine guns, and antiaircraft-gun emplacements, leaving Ron free to do his job. And *maybe*, we'd actually get out of this alive."

"Just a second," Buckner said. "Who said that *you'll* be flying the fighter."

"It was my idea," McKenna said. "Besides, I'm the new guy. Everybody else here is an experienced combat pilot. That makes me the most expendable."

"You think the Thunderbolt is best for that job?" Hollands asked.

McKenna shook his head. "If your air maintenance could beef up the firepower, I'd rather fly the Buffalo. It's slower, but it's got a lower stall speed. I'm going to be flying low and tricky. The Buffalo is good for that."

"Damn!" Buckner said. "I think it sounds like one hell of a good idea."

Hollands thumped McKenna on the back. "I like it, Mack. Go with Buckner and get your recon flight cleared with Major Hanks."

McKenna gave him a surprised look.

Hollands grinned at him. "Yeah, I know you're Army and he's a Marine. But he's also a sharp cookie, and nearly all of our flights go through him."

Hollands nodded. "You and Buckner get going. We need that recon info as soon as possible. It might help me sell this plan."

Before meeting with Hanks and Murray about Ron's plan, Hollands decided to check with Skip about the status of the newly-acquired planes. He and Yoshida made the five-minute hike over to the hangar.

When they arrived, they could see several of the mechanics working on the aircraft. Hollands found Corporal Lynch checking the landing gear of a P-40.

He got the mechanic's attention. "Go over the Buffalo," he said. "Check it out carefully. We may need it tonight."

By the time Hollands and Yoshida made it over to see Murray and Hanks, Mack was well into his flight, and just a few minutes from his rendezvous point.

"Ben and I have discussed your plan," said Hanks. "Are you sure you really want to do this?"

"No!" Hollands said. "But we've got to do something. There are two hundred planes on that base, and over five thousand gallons of aviation gas in the storage tanks. If we're successful, it might just discourage the Japs enough to turn the flotilla around, when they find out that their regional air cover has just gone up in smoke."

"Well, I can't pretend that I'm happy with this scheme," Murray said, "But I can't think of anything better. So, you've got my backing."

He reached for his garrison cap. "I'm going to check in with my crew, to figure out how we can give the Buffalo a little extra bite."

As Murray exited the Marine headquarters, Hanks told Hollands, "I'll give Sessions a call, to see if he'll go along with the plan."

"Thanks," Hollands said. "I—that is *we*—appreciate it."

"This is going to be one hell of a dangerous mission," the Marine major said. "But the potential payoff is worth the risk."

"I just hope Sessions will buy it," Hollands said. "I'm on my way over there now. Ron, I'd like you to stay with the major and go over the layout of the base in detail. Get his opinion on the ground attack phase."

En route to Navy Headquarters, Hollands stopped in at the operations shack to check on McKenna's progress.

As Hollands entered the room, a chief petty officer called out, "Attention on deck!"

That brought all but the two men who were reading the radar to their feet.

"As you were," Hollands answered. He addressed the chief, "Where's your duty officer?"

"He's upstairs in the tower, sir."

Nodding, Hollands stepped outside and hurried up the long staircase.

Entering the tower, he overheard a radio transmission from McKenna. "Pateroa Tower, this is Watchdog. That's affirmative. Main group is splitting up. Smaller force seems to be heading for us; remainder of group on a heading for Rabaul. Cruisers and heavies in second group. Cruisers and tenders in first group. I see no carriers. Over."

As the radioman wrote down the information, McKenna called again. "Pateroa Tower, this is Watch Dog. Have large fighter force wanting to get acquainted. Looks like Zeroes. I'm about to find out just how fast this bird is."

"What's his altitude? "Hollands asked.

The Navy lieutenant in charge looked at his notes. "If he hasn't adjusted since his last report, he should still be at ten thousand."

"Find out the altitude of the Zekes," Hollands suggested.

The lieutenant motioned to the radioman. "Okay, Sparks, you heard the Captain. Get the pilot on the phone."

"Aye, sir." Keying microphone he called, "Watch Dog, Watch Dog, this is Pateroa. Over!"

McKenna's answer came in much clearer than it had a few moments before. "Tower, I'm a bit busy, right now. Over."

"Let me talk to him," Hollands said.

The lieutenant nodded. "Let him in there, Sparks."

Sitting down at the radio, Hollands called, "Mack this is Hollands.

What's your situation? Over."

"I've climbed to angels two-five. The nips are below at ten. I'm in their sun, so they haven't seen me yet. Captain, I can see one of our Navy's PBY's. He's about four miles east, at angels ten, and he is going to be in for one hell of a surprise. Ten of the Jap planes just left, heading southeast and moving fast. They left four planes behind, and those are going after the flying boat. Request permission to engage. Over."

"Roger. Engage the nips. Do what you can. Watch your fuel. And get back here. Over."

Hollands stood up and surrendered the chair to the radio operator. "Is there any radar-contact that far out?"

The lieutenant shook his head. "No. Our unit's pretty old. We can only track air contacts about seventy-five miles out, if the weather is good. The newer designs can go out to 150 miles."

McKenna's voice came over the radio again. "Pateroa Tower, this is Watch Dog. Over."

"Watch Dog, this is Pateroa Tower. Over," Sparks answered.

"Two Zekes splashed. Two damaged and heading to their base. Catalina is slightly damaged, but looks okay and should make it back to base. The smaller enemy force is now steaming south by southeast. I'm on my way home. Over."

"Roger, Watch Dog. Well done."

"That pilot is new here," Hollands advised, "As soon as you have him on your screen make sure he knows the heading."

After leaving the tower, Hollands stopped by HQ. Commander Sessions was out, and wasn't expected back for about an hour.

Hollands glanced at his watch and headed for the hospital to find Gail. As he opened the door, he nearly bumped into Sergeant Gilbress.

Janet came to attention and offered a salute. "Good afternoon, sir."

Hollands returned the salute. "Janet, I've been meaning to ask you something."

"Of course, sir. What is it?"

"Why did you ask to come back here after your leave? You could have requested and received practically any duty in the States."

Janet paused before answering. "I came back because of you, sir."

"Me?"

"Yes, sir," Janet said. "They have all of the lab technicians they need back in the States, but not out here. I admit, I was tempted to stay. But I remembered our first meeting, Captain. You said something about us not quitting, and that you wouldn't either. That was the first time I ever truly felt like part of a team. I like that feeling, sir. And this is where my team is."

Hollands raised an eyebrow. "Did Private Minetti have anything to do with your decision?"

"I guess a little, sir," Janet said. With a grin, she raised her left hand to show off her engagement ring. The stone wasn't large, but she was obviously proud of it.

"Congratulations, Janet!"

"Thank you, sir!" Standing a bit taller than her five-foot three-inches, she said, "We really caused a lot of trouble for the enemy, didn't we, Captain?"

"Yes, Janet, we surely did. And it all started when you found that plane."

Janet blushed. "May I speak un-militarily for a moment, Captain?"

"Yes, of course," Hollands replied.

Janet cleared her throat softly. "Thank you, Mike. For making us a team. *Your* team."

She gave Hollands a quick hug and a kiss on the cheek. Then, she backed up a couple of paces and saluted again. "Good afternoon, sir. You'll find Gail in the next ward."

Returning her salute, Hollands said, "Good afternoon, Sergeant. And thank you!"

Hollands and Gail had visited only a few minutes when an orderly interrupted them to deliver a message. "Excuse me, sir, ma'am. Captain Hollands, you are requested to report back to HQ."

Thanking the messenger, Hollands and Gail stood up. "I may be gone for a while tonight, and might not be able to see you at dinner."

He smiled. "Maybe we could have breakfast tomorrow."

Gail reached out and firmly took Hollands' hand in both of hers. Her eyes reflected a dark foreboding. "You just got back from New Guinea, Michael. You're off on another mission already?"

Hollands tried to smile again. "Save a seat for me at breakfast."

Gail squeezed his hand, and then released it. "You come back to me, Michael," she whispered. Then she turned, and walked briskly away.

Hollands knocked on the doorjamb of Sessions' office, walked inside, and came to attention. "Good afternoon, Commander."

"Don't you 'good afternoon' me!" Sessions snapped. "And get that dumb look off your face. You're not fooling anybody."

"I'm sorry, sir," Hollands said. "I'm not sure I know what you mean."

"You damned well *do* know what I mean," Sessions growled. "I've heard a lot of screwball ideas in my time, but this one takes the blue ribbon."

"You mean the plan to raid the Japanese fuel depot..."

"Of course that's what I mean," Sessions said. "Murray and Hanks have both tried to sell me on this damned-fool idea, and they're both lining up to volunteer."

The commander's teeth clenched so tightly on his cigar that he nearly cut it in half. "Who in blazes is running this base? *You*? Or *me*?"

"Commander, I do owe you an apology for not coming to you directly," Hollands said. "But I thought it was prudent to get the opinions of Major Hanks and Captain Murray before I brought the plan to you, sir. I meant no disrespect, Commander."

"Hell's bells, Mike, I *know* you weren't being disrespectful," Sessions said. "It's your damned suicide mission that I'm worried about. *Not* how it came to my attention."

Still annoyed, he waved at a nearby chair. "Oh, at ease. Have a seat. I'm madder than hell, but I'll listen."

Hollands took the offered seat.

Sessions stubbed out his mangled cigar in the ashtray on his desk. "Before you explain your lunatic scheme for attacking Munda, we have something else to discuss. In a few days, Army General Baldwin and Navy Captain McDonald will be arriving to award the seven of you, medals for your many accomplishments. But this, I can give you now."

He handed Hollands a small olive green box and stuck out his hand. "Congratulations, Major Hollands."

Stunned, Hollands lifted the lid of the box. "Sir, I don't know what to say. I don't deserve this."

From behind him, Hollands could hear people clapping and Buckner's voice rang out. "Well, Army, that's only the second time I've ever seen you speechless."

Hollands turned around to see all six of his comrades from the island, along with Buckner, Skip, and several of the pilots. Everyone applauded and shouted their congratulations.

Sessions raised his right hand. "Okay! At ease. I want Second Lieutenant Elliott, Sergeant Gilbress, and Gunnery Sergeant Beckett, Petty Officer Third Class Roberts; and Private First Class Minetti, front and center!"

As the group in the room shifted, the five named personnel moved forward.

"Capta…" Sessions stopped himself and chuckled. "Harrumph! I forgot already. *Major* Hollands here has been bending my ear ever since you all returned from that island, suggesting I do something for the five of you. I regret we were unable to pull this off before you took your leaves, but… Army Nurse Gail Elliott, you are hereby advanced to first lieutenant. Army Technician Sergeant Janet Gilbress, you are promoted to staff sergeant. Marine Gunnery Sergeant Elmore Beckett, you are promoted to master gunnery sergeant. Boatswain's Mate Third Class Timothy Roberts: you are advanced to petty officer second class. And Army Private First Class Carl Minetti, you are promoted to corporal. These orders have been approved and are retroactive to three months. You all will have some back pay coming. Congratulations!"

When the applause ended, everyone came to attention, saluted, and thanked the commander.

Looking around at the group, Sessions said, "Now, with the exception of Hollands, Buckner, and Yoshida, you're dismissed."

The commander settled back into his chair. "Where's the new man, McKenna?"

Hollands checked his watch. "Sir, Lieutenant McKenna should be landing in a few minutes."

"Fine," Sessions said.

The roar of a Thunderbolt reverberated from overhead.

"I assume that's him, now," Sessions said. He drummed his fingertips on his desk top. "We probably should wait for McKenna, but we can bring him up to speed later."

The commander leaned back in his chair. "Now, who dreamed up this so-called plan?"

"I did, sir," said Yoshida. "Actually, Hollands and I discussed the plausibility of something like this while we were still on the atoll."

"I assume you have good working knowledge of the enemy base."

"Yes, sir. I do."

Sessions drummed his fingers on the desk again. "After Murray and Hanks told me about this scheme, I tried to reach fleet command. Unfortunately—or perhaps *fortunately*—the big dogs all seem to be busy with other matters. So it falls to *me* to make the decision."

He opened a desk drawer and pulled out a fresh cigar. He regarded it, but made no move to reach for a lighter. "It appears, *Major* Hollands, that you and your merry band of lunatics are once again prepared to carry out an act of insanity. If I had a lick of common sense, I'd throw all of you out on your ears right now."

He sighed. "Unfortunately, I've been the beneficiary of your craziness too many times not to appreciate how effective it can be."

The commander unwrapped the unlit cigar, and bit the end off. When he had deposited the unwanted portion in the ashtray, he looked around at the faces of the assembled pilots. "Do you three really believe you can destroy the Japs' fuel supply and get out safely?"

"Commander," Hollands said, "that's really a two-part question. Regarding the first part: I'm confident that we can destroy the fuel tanks, and—with a bit of luck—many of the aircraft on that base. But I'm not as sure about the second part of your question. We certainly *hope* to make it back safely, but I don't have any way to calculate the odds."

Yoshida put his hands behind his back. "Sir, no matter what anyone has said about us, we're not heroes. None of us want to die. But the destruction of that fuel depot and airfield could save thousands of our GIs."

"That's right," Hollands said. "As you know, sir, the Japanese have two large naval groups steaming south to this area. I'm convinced that flattening that base will ruin their plans for recapturing Bougainville, Guadalcanal, and other islands in this sector."

"What time would you take off?"

"With your permission, sir, twenty-four hundred hours."

The commander looked past the eyes and faces of the three aviators, and gazed out the small side window of his office. "Tomorrow is Thanksgiving Day. The cooks tell me they have over thirty turkeys for the two mess halls. Dinner is at fourteen hundred hours. I expect *all* of you to be present. That's an order."

He took a handkerchief from his hip pocket, dabbed at his eyes and blew his nose. "Go get some sleep, and fly your mission. Make sure you're home before the turkey gets cold! You are dismissed."

The three pilots saluted and departed.

When it was quiet again, Sessions walked out of his office and headed toward the main entrance. He nodded to Seaman Pruitt in passing. "I'll be at the chapel, son. I'll be gone for a while."

CHAPTER 17

The Roar of the Phoenix

The Beechcraft had three windows on each side of the fuselage, and one on each of the two cargo doors. But for this mission, all glass except that in the cockpit had been removed.

A tripod was installed at each of the side windows, to accommodate the six .50 caliber machine guns. As the mechanics prepared the plane for the mission, Hollands told the ground crew to remove all U.S. insignias and replace them with the red meatball markings of the Japanese Imperial Navy.

Corporal Lynch and his crew struggled to get the Buffalo serviced and ready in time for its part of the mission. The plane had performed reasonably well on the flight from New Guinea, but the aircraft's four machine guns were questionable. Captain Murray ordered them to be replaced.

The briefing room could comfortably accommodate two-dozen people. As Major Hollands approached, he observed several men waiting outside the entrance.

When he stepped inside, he found another thirty men milling around and talking. Master Gunnery Sergeant Beckett, Corporal Minetti, and Petty Officer Second Class Roberts were among them. The air in the room was oppressively hot, the product of too many sweating bodies in too small a space.

Hollands spotted Beckett as he made his way to the front of the room. "How's the hip, Sarge?"

"It's fine, Captain. I mean *Major*. Congratulations on your oak leaf, sir."

Hollands nodded, "Thanks! And congratulations to *you*, Master Sergeant."

The old Marine squeezed past a couple of other men and lowered his voice. "Major, we'd like to volunteer to go with you."

He nodded over his shoulder at Roberts and Minetti who stood behind him. "We're a team, sir. Thanks to you."

"We *are* a team," Hollands said. "We have others here who also want to come along. I'll need to speak with them as well. But I would never dream of going on a mission without you three. You're my backup."

"Thank you, sir!" Beckett said.

Hollands made his way through the crowd to the front of the room. He was gratified to see so many men wanting to volunteer.

He climbed onto a chair to address the group, but the talking continued, unabated. Standing tall and quiet, Hollands gave a nod to Master Sergeant Beckett.

The Marine sucked a lung-full of air and shouted, "Attention on deck!"

The noise died away, and the men waiting outside crowded into the doorway.

"At ease!" Hollands ordered. "Okay fellas, listen up. For those of you I haven't met, I'm Major Michael Hollands, Army Air Corps. Thanks for coming. I know it's hot in here, but no one sits and no one smokes. This is important and I want you standing and alert."

Looking around the room he said, "Our plan is simple. We will visit the enemy on the small island of Takkia, a few miles off of Munda. We will destroy the fuel depot on the enemy airfield there. We will also destroy as many of the aircraft on the ground as we can manage."

Hollands described the physical layout of the fuel tanks and airfield, then went on to explain the plan to use the Buffalo to draw attention away from the Beechcraft by firing on it.

"Lieutenant McKenna will be flying the Buffalo. I hope he's either a lousy marksman, or a damn good one."

This brought a laugh from nearly everyone present.

"Surprise is really our only weapon," Hollands said. "We intend to be on the ground for no more than ten minutes. If it takes us much longer than that, the odds are that we won't make it back into the air again."

His eyes traveled around the faces in the room. "I'm not going to lie to you, gentlemen. This is not intended as a suicide mission, but it could well turn out to be a one-way trip for some of us, or *all* of us. I can't promise that you will return, but I think I can promise that we will destroy that base and do incalculable damage to the Imperial Navy."

"We will cripple the enemy's ability to operate in this sector. We're not out to bloody the enemy's nose, but to break his back. Tokyo will not be able to rebuild and re-supply this island for many, many months, if at all. And, finally, this could open up the way for Admiral Halsey's fleet to assault the island of Munda."

A spontaneous cheer rippled through the crowded room.

Hollands raised a hand for silence.

"Marine Master Sergeant Beckett is in charge of selecting the assault team. He will also be in charge of defending our aircraft on the ground, and suppressing enemy troops. If you are assigned to his unit, you *will* follow his orders, regardless of your rank or seniority. If you're not prepared to do that, do *not* volunteer for this mission."

"U.S. Army Lieutenant Yoshida and Marine Captain Buckner will lead the ground assault on the fuel tanks."

Hollands paused for a moment. "Regardless of whether or not you are selected, I want to thank you all for being here. It makes me proud just to look at you. That is all. Master Sergeant, take over."

He stepped down off of the chair. The instant his feet hit the floor, the old leatherneck yelled, "A-ten-hut."

The assembled men came to attention.

When Hollands was gone, Beckett called, "At ease!"

He moved to the front of the room. He didn't bother to stand on the chair. "Alright," he said. "Listen up. We need those with .50 and .30 caliber machine gun experience. Each man must be able to shoot, as well as load. We will also have three BARs."

At the rear of the room someone called out, "Hey, Sarge, I'm a Marine. So why is the Army involved in this? And why the goddamn Jap? Who does this Major Hollands think he is anyway? General MacArthur?"

Infuriated, Beckett shoved his way through the crowd of men. "Who said that? Who said that? Show yourself."

When Beckett reached the offender, the young Marine was under a mound of sailors, soldiers, and other Marines.

Roberts and Minetti were at the bottom of the pile. They had been the first to tackle the mouthy jarhead.

The kid was a green replacement. He didn't know anything about Michael Hollands and Ronald Yoshida. He was about to get an education.

A few hours before the mission, Hollands stopped by the hangar to inspect the Beechcraft. He looked at the wings, flaps, wheels, inside the engine nacelles, and at the tail section. Coming around to the front, he noticed something different, and stopped.

On the nose of the plane, written in elaborate script was the word *Phoenix*.

Buckner was just coming into the hangar, but when he saw the look on Hollands' face, the Marine stepped quietly off to the side and into the shadows. It was a reflective moment, and Buckner didn't wish to interrupt. Without a word, he slipped away to find the others.

As Buckner rejoined Beckett and the others, Lynch approached him. "Excuse me, sir. Did Major Hollands see the inscription?"

Buckner nodded. "Yes. He saw it."

"Do you think he liked it, sir?"

Buckner gave the young mechanic a smile. "Yes, Skip. He liked it. He liked it a *lot*."

At twenty hundred hours, Commander Sessions held an informal briefing in the hangar, both for the men going and for the mechanics who had worked on the ground preparation. When he wrapped up his comments, he walked among the entire group, shaking hands with each of them and thanking them.

"The mess cooks have asked me to inform you that they've prepared a late meal for everyone who's been involved in this mission. And the Padre said to tell you that he will be available at the chapel with a short message. That's all. Carry on."

Sessions went directly to the chapel, and was surprised to see the entire group following him.

Hollands stopped at the door and knocked.

Gail's voice came through the door. "Who's there?"

"It's me, Mike."

The door to the women's quarters opened, and Gail was standing there. It was obvious that she'd been crying.

She looked into his eyes. "You didn't come to say 'goodbye,' did you?"

Hollands shook his head. "No. I came to tell you that I'll see you tomorrow. Breakfast. I'll be there."

The tears started down Gail's cheeks again. "You will?"

"I *will*."

At 2330 hours, Hollands, Buckner, Yoshida, and McKenna stood in the operations room, going over the flight plan for about the twentieth time—checking and rechecking maps, compass headings, weather, and coordinates. The deception called for the two planes to fly fifty miles Southeast of Munda, staying low to avoid the enemy's radar. Then—

turning north—the Beech would climb to ten thousand feet and onto the enemy's radar screen, followed closely by McKenna in the Buffalo.

A half-hour later, the two aircraft sat across from each other on parallel runways.

McKenna gave his bird a pre-flight check. Skip and his crew had worked wonders on the old fighter.

Hollands, Yoshida, and Buckner were in the Beechcraft, going over their own pre-flight checklist. Meticulously they checked and rechecked everything. There was no hurry. No need to cut corners, or to take any unnecessary risks.

When both planes had signaled readiness, the tower gave the word to start engines.

The crew of the Beechcraft heard the whine of the Buffalo's engine starting.

Hollands looked over at Yoshida in the co-pilot seat. "You think this is a good idea?"

"It's a lousy idea," Yoshida said. "But let's do it anyway."

Hollands flipped two toggle switches simultaneously and hollered out his window, "Clear the prop. Starting number one."

"Number one is turning, sir," Yoshida answered.

Within seconds the engine was humming, smooth and strong. "Clear on two; starting number two."

"Number two is turning, sir," reported Yoshida.

While the two pilots continued to monitor the gauges and adjust the fuel mixture, the crew in the rear—led by Captain Buckner and Sergeant Beckett—were busily setting up positions with the machine guns and loading the weapons from the huge cans of belt ammo.

Hollands brought the Beechcraft to the flight line and locked the brakes. "Ron, go ahead and run the engines up. I'm stepping to the back for a moment."

Climbing out of his seat, Hollands squeezed past Buckner to the cockpit entrance. He crouched to avoid hitting his head on the low doorway, and called out to his troops. "May I have your attention? Please continue with your work, but I need to say this."

It was difficult to talk over the revving engines, but at that moment, Yoshida brought them to their quieter idle speed.

"Now, don't misunderstand me when I tell you this, but I truly do not want to go on this mission. As a fighter pilot, I've have flown dozens of them. I was scared every time, but not like this. This one scares the hell out of me. I think maybe it scares all of us."

Still seated behind Hollands, Buckner nodded his head in quiet agreement.

"That said, I'm still going. However, if anyone here wishes to stay behind, you may disembark now and with no hard feelings."

Every man looked steadily at the major, and slowly every one gave a thumbs-up sign.

Hollands nodded. "Thank you, Gentlemen. I pray that God will guide us tonight."

Hollands returned to the pilot seat and strapped in.

"Hey, Army," Buckner said. "I've got a question for you... What part of the turkey do you like? Dark meat or white?"

Hollands smiled. "Both!"

He looked to his Japanese-American friend. "Lieutenant Yoshida, get us off the ground."

"Yes, sir!" answered Ron. He flipped the landing lights on and off twice. "There's the green lantern, Major."

"Okay," Hollands said. "Let's go."

As Ron shoved the two throttle-handles forward, Hollands released the brakes. The powerful motors effortlessly moved the Beechcraft down the runway.

At a hundred miles an hour, she lifted off. On the next runway over, the courageous old Buffalo became airborne at the same time.

The moon was a slender crescent, but it gave sufficient light for navigation, and for the pilots of the two aircraft to see each other.

Climbing into the clear midnight sky to an altitude of five hundred feet, they turned onto their southeast heading. As soon as they cleared their coastline, they dropped to a hundred feet above the ocean, and were soon cruising at a hundred and seventy-five miles per hour.

At their designated rendezvous point, they made a hard forty-five degree turn northward and climbed to their assigned altitude of ten thousand feet.

Eighteen minutes later, Yoshida pointed down toward the water. "That dot down there should be our old island, Mike. Take over, and reduce speed to one-two-five. In three minutes, we'll be nearing my cousins' airfield, and I'll start in with the radio distress calls. That will be the signal for McKenna to start shooting at us."

He gritted his teeth. "The next time I get another bright idea like this, somebody hit me in the head with a hammer."

"I can do that," Buckner said.

Hollands adjusted his compass heading. McKenna began to chatter on an open frequency, giving the correct coordinates, and reporting that he was trailing a Japanese cargo plane, preparing to attack it. Pateroa Tower radioed responses to substantiate the bluff.

As the two aircraft approached the now-visible coastline of the target island, Mack began firing on the Beechcraft. He climbed a little above the supposed enemy plane and fired a burst.

Then he flew under and on both sides, firing at differing angles, with tracers flying every which way, like swarms of angry fireflies.

Ron did his part on the radio, jabbering in a panicky voice about being hit.

"Need emergency landing clearance!" he shouted in his best Japanese.

He grinned at Hollands. "I hope they don't catch on to my San Francisco accent."

"You're doing fine, buddy. Keep it up. Use lots of expletives."

"I don't know many," Ron quipped.

He keyed the radio again and shouted in Japanese. "Copilot has been hit! There is a fire onboard, and my port engine is damaged—losing power. Please turn on landing lights."

Flying over the Japanese airstrip, Hollands began altering the speeds of the two engines.

"Don't overshoot the field too much," Yoshida said. "Those mountains are about 1,500 feet high. We don't want to bump one of them."

"Roger that!" Hollands said.

He pulled the plane into a slow 180 degree turn. When he steadied up on the new heading, they could see that a few of the ground lights had come on.

Hollands lined up on the airfield, prepared to land. The planes on the ground were in plain sight—Oscars, Zeros, and a few Kates—in groups of three and four.

McKenna's handling of the old Buffalo was masterful. He stayed close enough to the Beechcraft to keep the gunners on the ground from firing at him, while occasionally cranking out streams of carefully-misaimed tracers.

As Hollands began his approach, Yoshida hollered back to Buckner, "Okay, get those flares lit."

From the outside, it must have really looked as if the plane was burning.

The tower called Ron, and instructed him to land at the far west end of the runway.

Hollands brought the port engine to an idle and added a little more power to the starboard motor.

"Ron," Mike yelled. "I need some help here! Hard left pedal, and drop the landing gear!"

Ron let the wheels down, and seconds later, the Phoenix touched the enemy's runway.

They were nearly at the west end of the Japanese airfield, over a half-mile beyond the tower.

Buckner hollered, "Sarge, drop the explosives satchel."

Five seconds later and many yards to the rear of the plane, the pack exploded. In the dark, the eruption was large enough to (hopefully) be mistaken for a crashed cargo plane.

"Okay, there shouldn't be too many troops in this area," Ron said. "Mostly on guard duty, and a few near the fuel tanks."

He pointed to a small tool shed they were speeding past. "Turn her around here Mike, and taxi back to that shed."

With judicial applications of power and brakes, Hollands managed to park the Beechcraft a short distance from the shed. He locked the wheels, but left the engines idling for a quick getaway.

The clock was running. Everybody scrambled out of the plane's two side doors. Beckett had brought three BARs. Roberts, Minetti, and the young mouthy Marine who had insulted Hollands and Yoshida, were given the responsibility of manning those weapons. Four men set up two .50 calibers—one on each side of the plane—to establish the two perimeter positions.

With submachine guns and satchel charges in hand, the demolition team quickly took off on a run, heading for the fuel tanks with Yoshida in the lead and Buckner and the other four men close behind.

Hollands and Beckett knelt down to discuss the perimeter defenses and to make adjustments. A few seconds later, they heard three reports distinctive of Japanese rifles, coming from the direction of the fuel tanks.

"Damn," Sarge muttered. "Whatcha think, sir?"

But before either Beckett or Hollands could say anything else, those shots were answered by two short bursts of fire from submachine guns.

"I don't think there's a problem, Sarge."

McKenna made repeated strafing sweeps, working both sides of the field, hitting barracks, tents, and as many aircraft on the ground as he could. He destroyed a radio transmitter building and antenna. A fuel truck exploded into a ball of fire.

On one pass, McKenna lined up on the control tower and unleashed the plane's four machine guns.

From his vantage point, Beckett could see that the Japanese machine gunners were now training their fire on Mack's Buffalo.

One enemy gun emplacement was near the perimeter line, just a hundred yards north of their position. Muzzle flashes from two guns were clearly visible there.

"BARs, take out those guns," Sarge ordered.

Immediately, the three men trained their automatic rifles on the target and—within seconds—the enemy guns were silenced.

McKenna's Buffalo continued to make strafing passes.

"Why do you suppose none of the Nips have fired on us, Major?" asked one of the men.

"Well, if our ruse is working, they probably think we're friendly."

With the Japanese guards out of the way, the path was clear. It took just three minutes for Buckner and Yoshida and the four others to reach their objective, a point midway between the two fuel tanks.

"Okay, Ron," Buckner said. "I'll take this one on the right; you take the one on the left. Remember, five minutes on the timer. Check your watch: mark from 01:21."

Ron nodded in agreement as he and two others disappeared into the moonlit darkness. The two tanks were less than fifty yards apart.

The plan allowed only ten minutes on the ground. This gave the raiders only one minute to attach the explosives and set the timers.

The men were quick about their work. There was not going to be much time for the Americans to clear the airfield before all hell broke loose.

The two groups met up at the path and began their two-minute dash back to the plane. As they ran through an area of waist-high grass, everyone suddenly came to an abrupt halt. The six men could plainly hear women's voices calling to them in English.

The group promptly hit the dirt.

"Halt! Identify yourselves," Lieutenant Yoshida demanded.

"Please, don't shoot! We're not Japanese."

Three women wearing Kimonos came into the moonlight. At first, the sight of Yoshida seemed to terrify the young women. But when they saw that the group had Caucasians, too, they moved closer.

Yoshida said, "Don't be frightened. I'm an American."

"I know you," one of the girls said. "I'm an American too. Can you take us with you? Please?"

A second voice quickly added, "Yes! Yes! Please take us with you! I'm Australian."

The third woman was of Japanese ancestry and added, "I am Japanese-Canadian. I want to go home."

"Okay, we can swap family histories later," Buckner said. "Let's *go!* We're running out of time!"

Hollands knelt near the tail of the Beechcraft, and checked his watch again. Yoshida and Buckner were two minutes late. In the distance, he could hear voices shouting in Japanese, and the sound of rifle and machine gun fire.

Was this the part where the plan fell apart? Had he tempted fate one time too many?

The plan called for the Beechcraft to be in the air by now. If there was going to be any hope at all of escape, he couldn't wait any longer. It was time to go. Past time.

He looked at his watch again, and then he made his decision. He would not leave part of his team behind. Just like the island... They all *went*, or they all *stayed*.

He knew instantly that the choice might mean prison camp or death for him and the men guarding the plane. But that was the risk they had all taken, the second they volunteered for this mission. He would not leave Ron, and Bruce, and the others.

Suddenly, there were shapes running through the feeble moonlight.

Hollands reached for his .45, and whispered, "Sarge!"

"I see 'em, sir," the sergeant called back.

Then, the old Marine raised his voice. "Everybody hold your fire! That's our guys!"

And he was right.

Hollands got a better look at the group rushing toward the plane. He saw Yoshida, and Buckner, and... Women?

"Hey, Sarge, are those women?"

"Well, I ain't exactly an expert, sir. But they sure look like women to me!"

"Come on!" Yoshida shouted. "Keep moving!"

Hollands stood up. "Call in your perimeter, Sarge."

The sergeant let out a loud whistle. "Back to the plane! *Now!*"

The perimeter guards picked up their machine guns and began falling back to the Beechcraft. About half of them were on board when the demolition team arrived.

Buckner was at the head of the odd congregation. He was gasping for breath. "Thanks... Thanks for holding the bus..."

Hollands stared at him. "Damn it, Bruce! You've been here ten minutes. Where in the hell did you find *women*?"

"No time to explain," Buckner panted. "We've gotta go!"

The Aussie girl staggered to a halt near Hollands, tears of anticipation and excitement in her eyes. "Sir, we've been 'comfort women' for the

Japanese military for two years."

"She means whores," a second girl clarified. "*Please* take us with you!"

"They were exchange students," the third girl added. "I was taken captive in Singapore,"

And in a burst of tearful emotion, the American girl said, "Please, sir... We want to go home."

Before Hollands could respond, Sergeant Beckett tapped him on the shoulder. "Major! We're about to have company!"

Even in the scant moonlight, it was easy to see several ground vehicles advancing on the Beechcraft with soldiers running alongside.

"Okay, everyone on board, on the double!" Hollands ordered. He sprinted toward the open cockpit door.

Right then McKenna zoomed in low, just feet above the center of the runway, firing long bursts from his machine guns at the advancing enemy. One of the vehicles burst into flames, and the Japanese troops scattered to take cover.

Yoshida lunged into the co-pilot seat just as Hollands was slamming the pilot-side door.

"Get on the horn to Mack, *now*," Hollands said. "Tell him we are leaving, and to get his tail out of here!"

He released the brakes and looked over his shoulder. "Everybody in?"

"Yes, sir!" Beckett shouted.

McKenna made one more pass with the Buffalo, then, in a steep climb, banked hard right and pointed his spinner west.

Hollands pushed the throttles forward. "How much runway do we have to the west, before we get wet?"

"A little over five hundred yards" Yoshida said. "Why?"

"'Cause that's the direction we're going," Hollands answered. "We're out of time, and I'd rather get wet than broiled. Full flaps, full pitch on the props."

The ground troops were dangerously close, but Hollands was more concerned about the explosion and flaming fuel that were coming in about thirty seconds.

The tires squealed as he jerked the plane around to line up with the runway. Hollands locked the brakes and slammed the throttle knobs to their full position. The two Single-Wasps came alive and two feet of blue-white tapered flames shot out from their exhaust ports.

"Never tried full power before," he announced.

"I think you chose an excellent time for it!" Yoshida shouted. He flipped on the ground lights, to illuminate their path down the runway. What little there was of it...

"Release brakes!" Hollands called out.

Instantly, the acceleration pushed the two pilots hard into their seats.

The tail came up almost immediately, and at the end of five hundred yards—still accelerating powerfully—the Phoenix lifted off the end of the runway.

Her wheels were so close to the water that they caught a shower of spray from a cresting wave.

And then, the Phoenix did her magic, lifting herself, and company into the sultry night sky.

Behind them, two enormous roiling balls of flame erupted from the ground below, casting a strange holographic shadow on the heavy humid air in front of the Beechcraft.

The concussions from the exploding fuel tanks rocked the aircraft like a leaf in a windstorm.

Hollands fought the controls until his buffeted craft had slipped beyond the range of the shockwave. Then, the Phoenix settled down into level flight, and he swung her around onto a course for home.

McKenna rendezvoused with them, and took up position off of their port wing.

His voice came over the radio. "That was quite a ride! Hey, did you guys see that strange shadow of your plane? Man! That was weird! It looked like some gigantic bird! A condor—or an eagle or..."

Yoshida lifted the microphone. "Like a phoenix?"

"Yeah..." McKenna's voice said. "Like a *phoenix*..."

The pilots of the Beechcraft looked at each other and smiled.

Hollands glanced back into the rear of the plane. The three extra passengers had found safety and comfort in the strong, gentle arms of Elmore Beckett—a tough, gentle man, and a brave Marine.

Buckner yawned theatrically, and scratched his belly. "Hey! Does anybody know what they're gonna serve for breakfast?"

EPILOGUE

July 1993

By late July, the Puget Sound area had warmed up. Michael Hollands sipped occasionally from a tall glass of iced tea as he relaxed in his backyard hammock. Two girls, sisters—ten and twelve years old—played quietly on the grass nearby.

Seattle newspaper reporter Matt Zimmerman sat in a camp chair, taking notes as Hollands responded to his questions.

Unaware that the children had been listening, both Hollands and Matt were surprised when the older girl, Kayla, looked up from her play. "Well, Grandpa, did you all get back in time for Thanksgiving dinner?"

"You ninny," her sister Caroline said. "They made it back in time for *breakfast*, like Grandpa promised."

Hollands smiled. "We were back in time for breakfast, *and* Thanksgiving dinner. And they were both wonderful. Not as nice as your Grandma's cooking, but *wonderful* just the same!"

A woman stepped out the patio door of the house. "Girls, your mommy and daddy are here. Why don't you go around through the gate and meet them. They're just getting out of the car."

"Yippee!! Okay, Grandma," Kayla said. "Come on, Caroline, I'll race you."

Running and giggling, the girls bounded off to greet their parents.

Gail Hollands sat down in a wicker chair next to the hammock. "Matt, will you stay for the barbeque?"

She turned her eyes to Hollands. "Oh, darling, the Buckners called and said they'll be a little late. Janet and Carl say they will be here on time."

Addressing the young man again, she said, "Perhaps you could interview them as well. I'm sure they'd all love to see you again. Ron called a few minutes ago, and he and his family will be here shortly."

"Yes, Matt, why don't you stay?" Hollands agreed. "After all, your Uncle Elmore had a lot to do with this story. You're like family, too."

Looking off into the blue sky, Hollands mused, "I wish he were still with us. He was quite a guy!"

"Well thanks to the two of you, he lived to be almost 90 years old. I'm just glad that he found someone to marry late in life. He was just about the happiest man I've ever known. Aunt Linda saw to *that*."

Matt looked at his watch, and then turned to Mrs. Hollands. "Thanks for the invitation, ma'am. But I'm going to have to get this written up for the Sunday supplement. They've got me on deadline."

He looked back at his former teacher. "I appreciate your time Professor. Or should I call you, General?"

"Call me 'Mike' please."

"Thank you, sir... Ah... *Mike*. If I understand it correctly, you're retired now. Is that right?"

"Yes," Hollands said. "You were in my last journalism class, Matt. And as I said earlier this afternoon, I retired from active duty from the Air Force in '62, with one star on my collar. I stayed on active reserve till '73, and left then with a second star. It was during my reserve years that I went back to the university for my PhD."

He scratched his head. "Let's see... I was 42 when I started teaching. First at a high school, then at U.W. You know, in all the years I taught, you were the *only* student who ever asked about my military career."

Hollands lifted his glass and took a long swallow of iced tea. "I think we'll slow down a little now, take a bit more leisure time for ourselves. Maybe do some serious writing. Gail and I might head over to Lake Chelan and spend more time in our cabin. There's a little stream not too far from the front porch, and a pool of water that is warmed by the sun and rocks. Gets nearly 65 degrees. Maybe we'll do a little skinny dipping."

Feigning embarrassment, Mrs. Hollands affectionately slapped her husband on the shoulder. "Michael Hollands, you're still that bad person I met on that island fifty years ago!" Then she winked. "I'm up for some skinny dipping. When do we leave?"

As the three laughed, the reporter said, "I want to thank you two again, for your hospitality and for the kindness you've shown me over the years."

Hollands climbed out of the hammock, and Gail got to her feet as well. The young man shook hands with his mentor, and Gail gave him a warm hug. "You take care, Matt. Say Hi to your mom and dad for us, and come to see us again soon."

As the young man headed for the gate, Hollands called after him, "You know, Matt, the Phoenix is on display at Boeing Field. In the Museum of Flight. Go take a look at her, son."

He shoved his hands into his pockets and gazed wistfully up at the sky.

"She still flies, tells lies, and is full of history."

About the Author

Vic Mills was born in Los Angeles in 1942. He has three children, Mike, Lisa, and Jason, and—at last count—seven grandchildren.

In the late 1950s, while attending high school in Felton, California (Santa Cruz), Vic was active in Music— singing, writing, and performing with his younger sister, Diana, and a high school friend. When he relocated to L.A. in 1963, he was asked to submit several of his musical compositions for then-current rock and roll artists.

In 1966, prior to his induction into the Army, Vic moved to Seattle. Upon his return from Vietnam and release from the military, he returned to his job there with the city transit system. In 1984, Vic started his own vehicle consulting firm.

He's currently hard at work on his next novel.

24457792R00171

Made in the USA
Columbia, SC
22 August 2018